A

Laney Krogh is a recent graduate of Texas A&M University. Though she majored in health, her goal has always been to become a published author. She grew up writing stories and loved to create new worlds from her imagination, as she did with 'Fairy Tale' when she started it in high school. Laney lives in Texas with her family and their dog, Daisy. When she isn't writing, Laney loves traveling, playing piano, spending time with her family, and thinking of what to write next.

Fairy Tale

Laney Krogh

Fairy Tale

Vanguard Press

VANGUARD PAPERBACK

© Copyright 2025
Laney Krogh

The right of Laney Krogh to be identified as author of
this work has been asserted by her in accordance with the
Copyright, Designs and Patents Act 1988.

All Rights Reserved

No reproduction, copy or transmission of this publication
may be made without written permission.
No paragraph of this publication may be reproduced,
copied or transmitted save with the written permission of the publisher, or in
accordance with the provisions
of the Copyright Act 1956 (as amended).

Any person who commits any unauthorised act in relation to this publication
may be liable to criminal prosecution and civil claims for damages.

A CIP catalogue record for this title is available from the British Library.

ISBN 978-1-83794-328-9

This is a work of fiction. Names, characters, businesses, places, events and
incidents are either the products of the author's imagination or used in a
fictitious manner. Any resemblance to actual persons, living or dead, or actual
events is purely coincidental.

Vanguard Press is an imprint of
Pegasus Elliot Mackenzie Publishers Ltd.
www.pegasuspublishers.com

First Published in 2025

Vanguard Press
Sheraton House Castle Park
Cambridge England

Printed & Bound in Great Britain

Dedication

For my mom, who always encouraged me to write and to never stop dreaming, and who has given my life its own kind of magic.

Prologue

"David, you know I have this under control! Hurry up, now, or Clara and Summer may just drive off without you!" There was laughter in the other room, and my mom and I looked at each other, rolling our eyes and laughing.

"Dad, Al's right," I called, "Mom and I can easily drive to Vermont without you!"

"All right, hold your horses," Dad said, as he and the woman in jean overalls came out of the storage closet. He handed her the rusty keys and began to run through his last checklist. "The upstairs loft is yours, as it has been these last seventeen years. Since the shop is yours now, as well, I have to make some recommendations."

Al ran a hand through her cropped brown hair as she chuckled. "David, as long as I have lived here, I have also worked here. I know how you like things to be done."

"Yes, of course, but I still need to go over the list with you!" he insisted, holding up the crinkled paper for her to see.

"Now, I know you like that cashier, Theresa, but I think she's trouble…" As he motioned for her to follow him around to the backside of the checkout counter, he muttered about which employees she should fire and why.

As Al turned, I could see the tips of the scars on her that stretched up to the tops of her shoulders, peeking above her overalls—she'd gotten those in the stabbing she'd been a victim of before I could even remember her. That's how my parents found her—bloody and alone. After that, my dad converted the space above his bookstore in Rosemary Beach into a safe place for Al to live. She'd been like an older sister to me as I'd grown up, with her constantly around my dad's place of business. It would be strange to leave her behind.

"David, dear, we need to get on the road if we're going to get to the hotel before nightfall. You know they will cancel our reservation if we don't check in on time," my mom said, walking forward and giving Al a quick hug before picking up her purse and walking to the car.

"Bye, Clara." Al smiled, turning to me then.

Her eyes softened for a moment, and I thought back to all the talks we'd had through the years. We'd practically grown up together—she was only seventeen when she'd moved into the shop, and as she worked her way through her twenties, I went through my awkward teenage years. We'd been there for each other, no matter what.

I stepped forward and hugged her tight. "Don't forget to write," she whispered, kissing me on the cheek quickly before turning to hug my dad and thank him for everything. "All right, you two," she said then, wiping some tears swiftly from her eyes, "get out of my shop!" We all laughed and waved goodbye once more before my dad slung his arm around my shoulder and walked me out the front door of the place.

I looked back once before we left, and Al's cheeks were shiny with tears, but her face was bright with, what seemed to be, hope. I nodded once to her, and turned, for the last time, from the store. "On to the next adventure," Dad said as he started the car's ignition. I sighed, leaning my head against the window, trying not to worry about exactly what adventures lay ahead.

Chapter One
A House with a Fence and an Attic

August 1, 2000
Weston, Vermont

The first thing that I noticed about my new house was the lack of a true front yard. There was a small section of grass leading up to the porch, but no walkway. There wasn't even a driveway to park our car in.

Back in Florida, my house had been settled beneath a patchwork of trees, with a path out back that lead straight to the beach. The entire town was surrounded by light, warmth, and sun. Here, at this new house, in a small, insignificant town in Vermont, I could already tell that this place would be nothing close to the home that I'd left behind.

The second strange thing about the Vermont house was the lighting. Not the coloration of the house, which was somehow a shade between moldy and rotting, strewn with dead leaves and moss that hung low from the rooftops. The peculiar part was that amidst the cover of trees that seemed to swallow up the life of this area, there was a single spotlight, a gap in the trees that allowed the sun to shine right on my house—it was sort of eerie.

Compared to the rest of the houses we'd seen on our drive through town, this house looked bright and shadowless, and its multiple levels of windows made it seem like a mansion. The homes in the central part of Weston had trees that hung almost completely in front of them, giving them a haunted look. I felt this house I stared at now, on the outskirts of Weston and closer to the mountains, was defined not by its light, but by its ghost-like quality.

My mother jumped out of the car from the passenger seat, smiling from ear to ear, stretching her arms out, and then pushing her glasses further up on her nose. "See, Summer? The cul-de-sac is inverted, so the fronts of our neighbors' houses face the street, and the back of ours faces in toward theirs. How interesting!"

"Wow, that's neat, Mom!" I smiled in a very forced way, but my mother wouldn't notice.

She wouldn't mind that at the moment, I couldn't even see the street or the other houses because of the heavy blanket of trees around the edges of the house. She also wouldn't notice that I couldn't care less about which part of our house was the front or the back—I wouldn't even care if it was on Jupiter. I didn't care because it wasn't my home, and my stubbornness told me it never would be. I was glad that my mother wouldn't be bothered by the strain I felt.

I hoped my more-observant father wouldn't notice my tension either, and as he began unloading suitcases from our car, he looked up at the dingy old house and smiled. "Rustic, timeless, chic." He nodded as if pleased with this selection. He looked at me suddenly as I got out of the car, furrowing his eyebrows. "How do you like it, kiddo?" he asked sincerely.

If I were a typical, blunt teenage girl, I would respond with an attitude-laden, "It's disgusting and I hate it and always will," or, "When are we going home?" Or the classic, "I wouldn't wish this house upon my worst enemy!" But, knowing myself as well as I did, I knew that I couldn't—and wouldn't—do that to them.

"It's great, Dad. We'll make it look just as pretty inside as it does outside."

My parents both smiled and nodded at me before turning to the car to unload the rest of the boxes.

"Summer," Mom called, "do you want to grab the key and go unlock the front door?" I smiled tightly and nodded, taking the rusty key from her hand and trudging across the dry, dying grass.

I reached the large wooden door, detailed with all kinds of metal artwork. I placed the key in the rusty lock, turning it against the resistance of time. With a click, the key froze, and I was able to pull the creaky door open in a slow and bothersome fashion.

Dust seemed to be the primary interior design theme of the house. The central chandelier was covered in it, as were the stairs, floorboards, couches, and even the mirrors in the front hallway. The windows were boarded up from the inside as if preventing any light from entering. I was creeped out for sure. Standing in there was stressful, and living there was an idea I simply couldn't fathom.

I jumped as my dad clapped his calloused hand onto my shoulder. "Isn't she beautiful?" He admired the house around us. Filth still seemed to settle as he walked in past me and began hunting for a light switch. Flicking it on, the chandelier illuminated—well, part of it, anyways. The other part seemed to contain light bulbs that were years removed from being usable.

I walked back into the fresh Vermont air to help my mom unpack some of the boxes. The back of the truck was full of everything we brought with us from Florida. Everything from my home was back there in the trunk, except for my heart. That was buried somewhere deep in the sand, cast out to the ocean, blowing in on the morning sea-salt breeze of the beach.

My mom bustled in, arms full of her paint brushes and paints. She was an artist, specifically a painter of natural landscapes. She claimed to have run out of inspiration in Florida, so she and my dad went house hunting right before school got out. I never thought they'd be satisfied, seeing as they both tended to dream unrealistically big when previously thinking about where they wanted to settle themselves. I figured their standards would be far too high based on how we lived in Florida.

Unfortunately, my worst fears came true. They felt a pull to this dump of a town, and this house in particular. Maybe it was because it was the only house for sale in the entire area. Maybe it was because it was in the middle of nowhere, and a definite change from everything I'd ever known. All I knew was that they came home from a little trip to tell me I'd be leaving my beach, my town, the bookstore, and Al before the summer was even over.

"Clara!" I heard my dad call as she joined us inside, "Wait until you see this view of the mountains! It's beautiful!"

My mom quickened her pace. "That's great, David! I'm coming back there now!" I sighed. No matter which way I tried to look at it, I couldn't figure out just what they were thinking when they decided to move us here.

My parents were scatterbrained. They took no responsibility for practically anything aside from paying the bills. While my mom spent her time painting and humming whatever tune was in her head, my dad had spent his days as the owner of the local bookstore near our hometown. Now, he was all lined up to take on the occupation of the local librarian. The job had belonged to a woman who, unfortunately, had died soon before my parents took the trip up to Vermont. When they returned home, they told me to start packing my bags so we could go chase our destiny. If this was my destiny, I didn't want to imagine the next decades of my life.

Part of my parents' desire to live their dreams out was that they were older. They were both over sixty-five, the age of most grandparents, and their parenting skills were only so-so. That was probably because they had been well out of practice by the time I'd come along, and they'd adopted me after never being able to have children. I was one year old at the time. They always told me that I was the reason that they saw hope and light in life, hence the name Summer.

I loved my parents with every fiber of my being. They'd taught me so much about appreciating life and love; they showed me how to treat everything in the world as its work of art. No matter how many times they'd made botched attempts at parenting the right, responsible way, they hadn't failed to make me smile, so I could never resent them for this chaotic uprooting of my life. My main goal in life was to repay them for saving me from growing up in an orphanage by keeping them as happy as they'd kept me.

I grabbed a box of my dad's books from the car and walked back into the entryway I'd stood at moments before. More lights were on in the house now, but I knew something had to be done about those boarded windows to let some natural brightness in. I knew that, at least, would be a start to making the house feel more inhabitable, and figured my dad could help me solve that problem later on.

I followed the soft laughter of my mother around the corner and through a low doorway. Mom and Dad were in the kitchen, which was adjacent to the massive porch window and its ratty curtain. There were piled boxes on and around a dining table, which creaked like it was about to collapse beneath the weight.

My parents, though there was no music except for my dad's soft humming, were slow dancing their way around the room. I had to smile as I watched them, and knew that they'd be satisfied here in this house. Maybe, just maybe, I could be too.

A little while later, all of the boxes had been brought in from the car, and the sun had begun to set on the little town. I had worked with my father and a hammer all afternoon, tearing down board after board that covered the windows. The light had shone into the house for a brief minute, hinting that some beauty may lie beneath the filth.

It was around eight o'clock at night when my mother called me to her new artist loft. It was on the third floor of the house—the top floor. I had been concerned about my parents making the multiple-floored dwelling work for them at their age, but they insisted it would be fine and that the realtor had installed a stair lift for them free of charge. We had one of those stair-chair setups at home in Florida too, so it made the Weston house more comfortable and normal.

When I got up to my mom's room, everything that seemed so common and boring about this house had been suddenly put out of my mind. The window of the loft overlooked the odd front yard of our house, our car, the entire town, and the mountains that were a few miles away. My parents had been right; it was amazing here. The environment was much different from the beach that I'd grown up with, but it was beautiful in a unique way.

"Did you find your room yet, Summer?" she asked as she heard my feet behind her. She was already painting the outline of the mountain range onto a canvas.

"No, not yet. Which floor is it on?" She turned back at me and pointed up, smiling mischievously. I looked up, confused. "I thought you said there were only three floors to this house," I said.

"Oh, there are if you're counting full floors. That doesn't include the attic space, though!"

I shivered at the thought of sleeping in the attic of this creepy old scrapyard. "You're making me sleep in the attic? Does it even have a bathroom or a closet?"

She frowned at these questions. "I'm not making you do anything, and yes, you'll have a bathroom and closet. I promise, you'll understand once you see it. The view is supposed to be even better than this one, and with your young legs, you'll be better able to get up there every day." She turned back to her painting in a dismissive sort of way, and I sighed, walking out of the room.

"Summer," my mom called, as I was about to shut the door.

"Yes, Mom?"

"Give it a chance. You'll probably come to love it here." I nodded in response, though she couldn't see me, and shut the door softly.

I walked cautiously around the creaky third floor, searching for stairs or a door that led to the attic. For fifteen minutes, I searched with no luck of finding my room. Finally, I gave up and decided to look out on the balcony, toward the backyard. I twisted the doorknob, pushing hard to force the balcony door to open.

I immediately gasped as I stepped out into the dusk. The back of the house revealed an entire street of houses beneath a thick canopy of mossy trees. At the end of my yard was a makeshift fence, on which hung several 'WARNING' and 'DO NOT PASS' signs. I saw that there were four houses that lined the eerie and silent street.

I backed up, intending to back myself into the house, but instead, my hand hit something cold and metal. I jumped, still spooked by the street ahead of me, turning to see a narrow staircase leading up to a window I hadn't noticed before. The attic, I realized, carefully putting my weight onto the unstable steps.

Clinging to the railway with my left hand, refusing to look down, I forced my fingertips beneath the window with my right hand, coaxing it upward and open. The whole room seemed to breathe as a puff of cold air escaped the window.

I awkwardly forced my leg through, ducking my head, straddling the ledge, and practically falling inside. I landed on the floor and looked around as I caught my breath.

Looking around, I realized that this was the cleanest room in the house. I flipped a switch to find the light bulb in the lamp on the bedside table was working; there was no dust lying around, and the blankets and pillows had been folded and fluffed. It was like someone had fixed this part of the house up just for me.

My mom was right; there was something almost magical about this room. However, I was confident that she hadn't climbed up here and through the window to observe it at her age. She must've had some artistic intuition about this place.

The walls were a deep green color, and there was a desk close to the window, and a bed on the other side of that. Across from me was a door to the bathroom, and a small boudoir-style closet sat against the wall across from the bed. The dark gray bed spread was contrasted by the vibrant color of the flowers and shrubberies that sat in pots all around the room. There were plants on shelves, sitting on the floor, hanging above the window, even painted onto the wall.

The paint was the most defining decorating tool used in the room. There were stars painted like a night sky on the ceiling. Some swirls and marks appeared to be in a different language or writing style, and these continued on each of the walls, behind the plants, and around the windows. They were exquisite and haunting, leaving me wondering who had been in the attic before me.

I looked behind me and out the window. From this height, the back street looked enchanted. The trees and the houses beneath glistened in the rising moonlight.

"Summer!" I heard my mother's voice calling. I leaned over the windowsill to see her staring up at me from the third-floor balcony. "How do you like the room, dear?" She smiled.

"I like it a lot! Who did you send up here to decorate it?"

She seemed puzzled, and then her eyes narrowed a bit, as if she were irritated. "Well, I don't know if you're giving me attitude about the dust or not, but you can clean up just as well as I did in my loft. Your box of clothes is in the living room." She turned and shut the balcony door behind her.

I stood still for a second. If she was implying that this room was supposed to be dusty like the rest, I didn't understand. I figured she and my dad had paid to get it fixed up while we were moving, or had it redone while they were visiting to purchase the house a few weeks before. But then again, that would still be quite a stretch.

These sheets smelled as if they'd been washed freshly that day, and the plants certainly would've needed daily attention from some sort of caretaker. I truly felt as if the room had been mysteriously made for me.

I padded across the soft carpet to the wall to examine the painted swirls that looked like a script. I raised my hand to the wall and moved the first plant to the side to reveal more symbols. I squinted at them, cocking my head and suddenly hearing a silky voice speak words that echoed through my mind as I scanned the symbols.

"The grand faire enchantress exiled Genesis, Katia, Anastrella, Vivyanna, and all offspring of the four aforementioned faire folk, until the end of time."

Darkness suddenly seemed to fade, and the lamplight illuminating the ceiling above me came back into focus. I was lying on the carpet, which my hands clutched to stop their shaking. How I had gotten here was beyond me. The last thing I knew, I was observing the drawing on the wall, and then, the voice.

The voice that had pounded in my head was that of a young man, who spoke in a sad sort of tone. Faire folk? How had that even come into my mind? It had absolutely nothing to do with the words I'd been reading which, upon looking at them again, didn't seem like words at all. They were just scrolls of paint, and I clearly was already losing my mind in this town. I shook my head, standing unsteadily and leaving the room to go downstairs to get my box of clothes.

I decided, on my way down to the first floor, that I wouldn't tell either of my parents about the room's strange appearance. Its condition was unlikely to cause concern for them, though, seeing as age would deter them from venturing up the rickety stairs and forcing themselves through the cramped window. I assumed, by that point, that it just looked the way it did because of whoever lived there previously.

I did, however, need to keep any of my skepticism about the house to myself. I didn't feel that this would be very difficult, seeing as I'd taken a sudden interest in figuring out the mystery of the house, the back street, my room, and everything else I'd discovered only on this first day. At the very least, the odd circumstances would keep me entertained in this small town.

I swore to myself then that I would do some sleuthing and find out what was so abnormal about the houses on the cul-de-sac, including my own. I needed to know the explanation behind the strange fence that had been so hastily added to the yard, as well as how conditions in my attic room had come to be so put-together compared to the rest of the house.

I also was determined to figure out what happened to me in my room just moments before when the ominous, haunting voice had completely overwhelmed my senses. My first day living in Weston, and already, life seemed to be imploding on itself.

The next several days consisted of cleaning and tidying, followed by more cleaning and more tidying. I didn't mind, though, because it gave me time to think about all the mysteries I'd set out to uncover. For example,

I'd done some more observing on the street behind my house.

Neither light nor noise was emitting from any of the houses, and there were no cars on the street indicating people were inhabiting them. The houses were positioned with two on either side, directly across from each other. The grass had grown tall in each of the front yards, and the back yard of my house. It was as if there was life there once, and then the entire street had died away.

The closest house on the left was made of brick. The roof drooped a bit from age, but the structure beneath seemed sound. The further house on the left was made of wood and painted a pale yellow, and it had a broken-down white porch. It resembled what once was a beautiful house. Across the street from the yellow house was another house of brick. This house was almost entirely shaded by a tree that was planted in the front yard. For a second, I thought I saw smoke oozing out of its' chimney, but I realized a moment later that it was just a shadow and mist that the dusk brought in. The house closest to mine on the right was another of wood; however, this one was not painted. The wood appeared to be decaying on one side, and the front door hung ajar slightly, revealing the darkness within the building. It was as if someone walked out of the dwelling, and had not bothered to shut the door behind them.

Surrounding this mystery street was an endless stretch of forest. It appeared as if there were no other houses near these four, except for mine. I couldn't decide if I should be frightened or intrigued.

As for the fence, it looked as if someone lacking any construction skill had built it; there were holes and entire boards were missing from it. The grassy barrier between my house and fence was dead and parted by a walkway leading to the porch. It appeared as if this backyard had originally been the front yard of this house, which was central to the cul-de-sac of this newfound street. While I didn't have much explanation for why things were the way they were, I felt certain that this street was different from any other I'd ever seen.

The only mystery I'd decided not to look into after my first night was the disturbing voice I'd heard from the wall. I hadn't dared to look back at the painted swirls since I fainted on my first night. My newfound hesitation to do so was caused by a fear that I'd hear a strange voice in my head again. I knew that I should set my curiosity at ease, and look at it directly again to prove that I'd been dizzied simply due to lack of food and water on moving day, but a part of me feared there was some hidden truth there on the wall.

On Sunday evening, my mom called me down to her loft. I walked downstairs into the main part of the house to find her and my father chatting as they surveyed her art from the past few days. She'd painted several canvases of the mountains and town from the view of the front of the house.

"They're beautiful, Mom!" I exclaimed as I entered.

She and my father turned around, smiling. "Thank you, Summer, I'm glad you like them. I hope you're liking it here, in Weston, just as much."

She gave me a questioning gaze as if trying to see if I'd crack and say that I hated it. I remained stoic and smiled even bigger in response. "Of course! I mean, it's no Florida, but there's beauty here." Both of my parents nodded, and my father sighed in a melancholy way.

"What's wrong, Dad?" He looked at me in the eye nervously before looking back to one of my mom's paintings.

"Well, there's the matter of school to be discussed..." his voice trailed off as he looked to my mother for help.

"Oh, it's okay, Dad," I assured him, "we don't have to worry about that until September! It's August sixth today, right?" I smiled and looked back and forth between the two of them. "It's still my season!"

"Well, you see, Summer, things are different in this town. School starts earlier and ends earlier." My smile dropped as I realized that the freedom I'd found in this house was quickly coming to an end. Sooner than I'd thought, I'd have to become engulfed by the town.

"When do I start?" I asked in a hushed voice.

My parents glanced at each other briefly, eyebrows furrowed, before saying in unison, "Tomorrow."

Chapter Two
The Stories of the Devil House

My dad was going to start his job at the Weston Public Library, or, at least, he would if he could get to his car on time to drive me to school. Weston's library was conveniently located next door to the Weston Preparatory School, which meant that all class library visits, all study hall times, and any computer necessities would lead my classmates straight to my father.

The problem there was not that my dad was embarrassing. It was just that he could ramble on about different wars, plants, people, or whatever other random thing he was learning about most recently.

My dad could talk to anyone, even a stranger, about every detail of each book in the library for hours. That was his life's passion! But, seeing as this would be my first time getting to 'socialize' with my Weston peers, I'd prefer not to be referred to as 'the girl with the wacky librarian dad.' I just wanted them to know me as Summer.

I leaned across the car from the passenger seat and honked the horn several times. "Hurry up, Dad!" I yelled, leaning back to my side and out the window.

My dad came stumbling out of the house, flustered as he tied his tie around his collar and attempted to hang on to his ragged old briefcase with the same hand.

He opened the car door, slid inside, and started the ignition with shaking hands. He drove off, tires squealing against the pavement as our beater went roaring around the corner of the forest, past the only actual neighborhood of the town.

I twisted in my seat and looped his tie around so that it was correctly placed against his shirt. "You okay, Dad?" I asked.

"Oh, of course," he said, but the beads of sweat beading on his forehead told me differently.

"Nervous for work?" I asked more gently. He nodded, glancing over at me as I returned to sit flat in my seat. "Nervous for school?" I nodded, reaching down to make sure I had everything I needed in my backpack that my parents had made me keep from the past school year.

As I tugged the zipper closed, I was reminded of Florida. I remembered my friends, my teachers, and everything normal that had been sucked away from me so fast. I felt my eyes begin to water.

"Summer, don't cry, sweet girl," my dad coaxed, "it's always hard starting in a new place, but I promise, they're going to love you, and you'll love them. You just have to be patient, and be yourself. Just give it a chance, okay?" I nodded, blinking the tears away and forcing a smile.

We pulled up in front of the school, and my dad parked in the spot directly between the two buildings. "Perks of being a librarian." He smiled, pointing at the 'Reserved' sign attached to the parking spot.

I grinned back, genuinely this time. I leaned across the console and gave him a tight hug. He patted my back and said, "Have a good day, Summer." I nodded and opened the car door, grabbing my backpack and hurrying around the side of the car to the front door.

I walked in and was immediately greeted by a little old lady at a makeshift front desk. The table beneath the blue and white plaid tablecloth was leaning severely on one of the legs as if it'd fall over any minute.

"Hello, dear! You must be the new student from Florida!" The woman smiled at me. She had a wheezy voice and seemed to emit warmth—that reminded me of my parents.

"Yes, ma'am. My name is Summer York. I need to pick up my schedule for the year. Is this where I get it?" The woman shuffled through some papers and handed one to me with my name highlighted atop it.

"Here you are, dear. And if you have any problems today, just tell your teacher you need to come to see Mrs. Marks at the front desk. That's me." She winked, waving me through the door to the school behind her.

"Thank you!" I called over my shoulder. *Okay,* I thought to myself, *that's one friend.* I pushed through the door to the hallway of the school, shuddering at the possibility of Mrs. Marks being my only acquaintance for the day.

I walked further into the depths of the school, noting how small the building itself was, and how the halls were crowded with students from multiple grade levels. Every one of my peers that I walked past turned to stare at me. "That's her," I heard a girl whisper to her friend, "the girl at the Devil House."

Devil House? I turned to face that girl, confused. She jumped in fright and spun away with her friend, hurrying in the opposite direction. I sighed, slumping my shoulders and hoping to turn invisible as I went to find my first class.

Whoever decided to give me a history class first period had found their way onto my hate list. English, math, science, or any other subject were courses that I'd learned to love because of my parents. History was not one that I found quite as enjoyable.

Mr. Rapp, a pinched face man with a balding head and a starkly perfect posture stood at the blackboard and pointed me to the back of the room, where an open chair sat next to a boy with a friendly looking face.

I was grateful; at least, to be seated at the rearmost part of the room to prevent being stared at all class. But, as I took my seat and faced forward, I realized that the students entering the class and already sitting were still staring unabashedly, despite having to crane their necks. I looked down at my desk, letting my hair fall around my face. *If I can't see them, perhaps they can't see me,* I thought, tapping into a childish philosophy.

A tap on my shoulder yanked me out of my misery. I glanced next to me at my desk neighbor, who was looking at me with a wide, welcoming smile. "Hi, I'm Bobby Hayes. You must be the newest Weston resident, right?" He held out his large hand to shake mine, which looked petite in comparison.

"Nice to meet you, Bobby," I said, trying to relax for the first time that day, "and yes, I just moved here. My name is Summer York."

No one had looked at me in a genuinely friendly way since I'd walked past Mrs. Marks a few minutes before, and this boy didn't seem concerned at all that I was from the "Devil House," whatever that meant. Bobby gave me hope for this seemingly judgmental town.

"How are you liking Weston so far?" he asked, curiosity in his tone, not suspicion. I smiled in my fake way at first and was about to tell him that I thought it was great. But I saw him raise his eyebrow. "You don't have to sugarcoat it to me. I can probably guess your response."

I laughed lightly. "Well, you caught me. I guess I've gotten used to lying about it for my parents."

He smiled all-knowingly. "People pleaser?"

I shrugged. "I guess so, but only when it comes to the two of them. For me, it's like repayment for them adopting me." I hadn't meant to say that part, but talking to Bobby felt strangely comfortable.

Bobby raised his eyebrows again, more in surprise than suspicion. "You're adopted? Excuse me for snooping, but what happened to your biological parents?" This conversation had quickly changed the topic, but I wasn't skeptical of telling Bobby the truth.

He didn't seem afraid to ask the questions that needed to be asked in a trusting friendship, but I hadn't exactly had to answer those questions before, especially not in the first five minutes of meeting someone.

"Um—sorry, I haven't talked about this in a long time." I chortled nervously.

"You don't have to if you don't want to! I tend to be very blunt when I'm curious about something."

I shook my head, insistent. "No, it's okay. I'll tell you.

"My adoptive parents told me that my birth mother was quite young when she gave me up, and she told the two of them that my father had died not long after I'd been born. My parents never found out if she was in any sort of financial trouble, or experiencing a mental state where she just couldn't have that connection to my birth father.

"Regardless of what her problem was, she had simply decided when I was a couple of months old that she didn't want me anymore."

His face fell. "Wow, Summer, I'm so sorry."

I shrugged, trying not to bring down the mood. "I'm okay with it now because my true parents have always been here for me. I don't let it bother me, at least not as much as I did when I was younger.

"My mother moved on; I moved on with the life I was meant to have, and she'll never be my parent in the way my adoptive mom and dad are."

Bobby nodded, smiling. "I'm glad you're happy with how all of it turned out, Summer. It's nice to meet you too."

I opened my mouth to respond to Bobby how nice it was to have made a friend so soon when Mr. Rapp gave a wheezy 'Ahem' and the class fell silent. I looked forward to find Mr. Rapp staring at me with his beady eyes peeking over his crooked nose.

"Students, welcome to homeroom. I trust you all had an educational and beneficial summer. I hope you didn't waste away every bit of your brain mass on unproductive social activities." He didn't appear to be joking at this comment. "I assume most of you have heard that we are welcoming a new student to Weston and Weston Prep this year, and we are lucky enough to have her in our class. Miss York, would you stand please?"

Stand? Why did I have to stand?

I pushed my squeaky chair back as dozens of heads whipped to face me. I looked Mr. Rapp in the eyes, attempting to be confident in the presence of the frightening man. And then, he smiled at me. I didn't expect this. "Tell us a little about yourself, Miss York."

Perfect, I thought to myself sarcastically.

"Um, my name is Summer York. I moved here from Seaside, Florida about a week ago. I've since taken up the hobby of cleaning my house." I smiled at my joke, but Bobby and Mr. Rapp were the only two to chuckle at it. I smiled tightly and said, "Um, that's about it." I cringed internally as I sat back down.

"She didn't mention that she's living in the Devil House," a girl a couple of desks up whispered intently, cat-like green eyes screwed up in a tight and irritated fashion.

"I don't know, Jen, maybe she has no idea," a timid-looking girl with glasses said skeptically from the seat next to her.

Jen shook her head. "Daisy, there's no way! In any case, anyone who lives in Devil House will be a lost cause." She huffed, obviously not caring that I was about five feet away from her conversation. At least I knew one thing for sure—I wasn't the only one in my town that thought my house was strange.

After he began class, Mr. Rapp seemed considerably warmer. Bobby even whispered to me that his reputation had rumored him to be the best teacher in the school. I could hear my dad's voice in the back of my mind, telling me not to judge a book by its' cover, or its' introduction!

Even though the class was history-based, I enjoyed myself. Mr. Rapp discussed the curriculum, and what we'd need to prepare ourselves for; I found myself genuinely excited. When the bell rang, though, there was something more important I wanted to learn about. "So, Summer, what's your next class?" Bobby asked me as we packed our bags and left the room.

"Science with Mrs. Carter," I said quickly, wanting to cut to the chase. "Hey, Bobby, what does 'Devil house' mean?" He glanced at me out of the corner of his eye, shoulders lifting a bit under his backpack straps.

"I don't know what you're talking about," he replied nonchalantly, attempting to walk a little faster. "Bobby, please tell me. You have to know! It seems like everyone in this school knows except for me—and I live there!"

He sighed, looking at me with a pitiful expression. "Okay, but I'll tell you at lunch. I don't have time to tell you now. Mrs. Carter's class is right down there," he said as he pointed to the end of the hall.

"Okay, bye, Bobby. I'll see you at lunch."

"See you, Summer," he said, high-fiving me as he turned and walked away.

Mrs. Carter was also a nice teacher, or, at least, she was very friendly when I introduced myself to her. She told me to sit in the back, just as Mr. Rapp had. This time, though, I wasn't seated next to Bobby or anyone that seemed as friendly as him. I wasn't seated next to anybody at all. Luckily for me, though, Mrs. Carter didn't make me stand up as Mr. Rapp did. She just pointed me out to my peers, who had already been staring at me like I was a ghost before we began our lesson.

Science passed fairly quickly, and I had one last class until lunch, which was math. My classmates in math may have been awkward and way smarter than me, but at least they weren't blatantly judgmental like the other kids I'd come across so far. They allowed me to pass the class period in comfortable and welcomed silence.

After math was lunch, which meant that I'd already made it through half of my day. I went to the cafeteria, looking around at all the circular tables that were occupied already, and not seeing Bobby.

Abandoning my hopes of hearing the Devil House tale and having a friend to join for lunch, I decided to sit alone in the back corner of the room. I pulled my lunch box from my backpack and examined the apple that my mom had packed for me. Of course, it was rotten, just like the majority of my day had been so far. I had accepted that I'd be eating alone when I heard from behind me, "Hey, stranger!" I whirled my head around and saw Bobby take a seat next to me.

"Hey, Bobby!" I smiled. "Do you sit at this table?" He laughed and looked around.

"Yep! I have every year! I'm glad you found it already! Hey, isn't it neat that the entire school is so small, everyone goes to this lunch period?"

"Oh, it's something." I laughed sarcastically, gazing around the room at the many grade levels that could be identified throughout.

Bobby, seeing my pitiful lunch, insisted I leave my stuff at the table and follow him for a moment. He led me to the lunch line, where the 'mystery meat sandwich' of the day was so disgusting looking, that I just settled for a salad with a few leaves of lettuce and hardly any dressing. I also made a mental note to pack myself a lunch better than the one I had that day in the future.

I followed Bobby back to that corner table, which now had a few of his friends that he introduced me to, and each of them seemed very nice and open. There was Haley, a quiet girl who had been in my science class. The first words she'd spoken to me had been apologetic for the way people stared at me obnoxiously in there before Mrs. Carter got control of them—needless to say, I liked Haley already.

Next, there was Annie, as well as her twin, Will, and Will's girlfriend, Maysie. I recognized them all from the hallway, and they didn't bring up the mockery I'd faced in regards to my Devil House relation either. I got more comfortable as time passed in the lunch hour, eager to be welcomed to a friend group with ease.

I spent that first lunch mostly in silence, trying to gain further knowledge of everyone's personalities. For instance, Maysie had a knack for making people laugh, and Annie always seemed to have a story to tell from her day when the previous conversation came to an end; Will consistently had some backhand retort to these stories.

Haley was very outgoing after a moment of getting used to me being around the group and seemed to be the most amicable of the group, as well. She also seemed to be very clingy to Bobby, which interested me because Bobby didn't seem to pay nearly as much attention to her. I wondered if there was some romantic history between my two new friends.

At the thought of history, I was reminded of Bobby's promise from this morning to tell me the story of Devil House. I looked at my watch; we only had twelve minutes until we left lunch, but he'd have to tell me fast because I couldn't wait for another second!

"Bobby," I interjected into their conversation, "remember what you said you'd tell me this morning?" I gave him a piercing look to remind him. His eyebrows lifted in concern, and he looked around the table at his friends.

"What is it, Bobby? What does she want to know?" Haley asked, leaning over closer to him.

Bobby kept his eyes on me this time, though, as he said to his friends, "She wants to hear the story of Devil House."

The group gasped audibly. I looked at them and rolled my eyes. "Oh please, guys! I'm sure I couldn't be that bothered by some cheesy horror story! I'll be fine!"

"It's not that, Summer," Maysie said solemnly, "but we don't want you to feel embarrassed by it or upset about it. It's got a really bad reputation in the town. Are you sure you want to know?" I nodded vigorously.

"Yes, I do! I need to know what it is that everyone has been making such a big deal about all day. And, just for the record, I've been in that house for a while now, and I've never noticed anything devilish about it!"

Will frowned, but merely shrugged at Bobby. "She's going to find out someday, man. It's up to you."

Bobby nodded, looked back at me, and said, "Okay, I'll tell you, but sorry if it upsets you."

I shook my head calmly. "Just tell me." He nodded and began reciting a story that seemed ingrained in his memory.

"Mr. Charles Ray McDevell was the owner of the largest house in Weston, back in the early 1900s. He was very rich, but he lived alone in that giant mansion. I don't know if you've noticed the other houses on your street or not?" I nodded curtly, wide-eyed.

"Okay, good. So, McDevell moved into the house that he'd requested to be built on this location, hoping to be the head of the cul-de-sac in front of him—"

"Behind him," I corrected. "The cul-de-sac is behind the house."

He smiled, as did the rest of the table, knowingly. "It hasn't always been that way." My heart raced as I sat there, realizing this could explain the strange lawn and fence. This story may very well have been what I'd been searching for in all my time in Weston!

Bobby continued, "When McDevell moved in, he expected the neighbors to come flocking by to greet him. He was from a town where southern hospitality was very important; he assumed Weston would be the same. About the normal townspeople, this guess was correct, but about his street, he'd thought wrong.

His neighbors, four unmarried women, and their young children stayed isolated, moving through shadows and socializing only at night. He was so confused by their behavior that he attempted to ignore them, focusing on the rest of the neighborhood more than what was close to him. That was a mistake."

"Hold on," I interrupted, "you're telling me this like it's a scary story you've told a hundred times. Is this the *truth*?"

Bobby nodded energetically, and Maysie added, "Honey, I swear, this is the whole, entire, and honest truth. Can he keep going? He's almost at the good part!" I shrugged skeptically, and Bobby grinned, almost wickedly, as he continued his eerie tale.

"So, Mr. McDevell was working as the city banker, and he was highly respected and very powerful after only a couple weeks of living in that house. He had a large influence over many in that town. The majority of the men in Weston were willing to do him a favor so that he'd give them some leverage if they were ever in a state of bankruptcy.

One night in the winter, Mr. McDevell came home late from work, later than normal. He had gotten out of his car, gone inside, and begun to heat some soup one of the housewives of the town had brought by for him."

"That's an oddly specific detail." I chuckled, and Haley and Annie shushed me dramatically.

"I'm almost there, Summer, just keep listening! McDevell heard an odd noise from the front yard, and he peeked out the window to see if his neighbors were finally making the trip down the block to welcome him.

"He was horrified to see four women with fire between them, dancing and throwing sparks around, speaking in a different language! Mr. McDevell was afraid, so he ran from his house, out the back door, and through the edge of the forest.

"His final destination was the town hall, and, when he got there, he took it upon himself to ring the city's bell. He gathered all the men and all the women with pitchforks and axes and the like. When everyone was waiting around town hall to see how to help the most popular man in Weston, he shared his story.

"He explained in a panic that he'd seen the women worshipping the devil, mere minutes away from where they stood! He insisted that the strength of the Christian neighborhood must be used for God. Now, he didn't know if they were worshipping the devil or not, but he did know that he needed the town's help to stop the act, and this was the best way to persuade them.

"So they went, screaming Bible verses through the cold, winter air, trekking through the snow and trees, past the outskirts of the neighborhood. The mob went through what once was the backyard of Mr. McDevell's property, crushing the gate as they went.

"Out the crowd emerged, onto the cul-de-sac. The women were already standing there, no mysterious fire, each in normal clothes and with normal-looking faces. The crowd paused for a moment, feeling a smidge of temporary guilt for making assumptions about these women.

"They stood there in a face-off, the women and the townspeople, neither willing to budge. Mr. McDevell, though, was insistent to the people of the mob that these women were evil. Skeptical as the town was when McDevell let out a sort of battle cry and charged at the women, the mass of people followed him, out of fear that the banker would punish them financially if they did not do so.

"They only got a bit past Mr. McDevell's property when they realized they couldn't get to the women. It was as if there was a force blocking the women off from their attackers. 'Deviltry!' Mr. McDevell screamed, 'This is an unjust act against the Lord!'"

"What did the women say?" I asked, sitting on the edge of my seat, tension in my shoulders.

"They stood there, looked at one another, and, in unison, let out a shrieking laugh that sent the entire town retreating, except for McDevell. He stood there staring in disbelief as he attempted to collect himself. And this part got a little lost in the story-telling through the years, but what I do know is that the women spoke in total synchronization, voices as monotone and demonic as one could only imagine in nightmares. They stood there defiantly, threatening McDevell into retreat.

"The very next day, McDevell hired a work crew to build up a fence in the front of his house, and tear down the fence in front. Or, at the very least, finish the job the townspeople had done to it. He only gave the crew half an hour to do it, claiming he needed to be shielded as quickly as possible.

"In the weeks after the event, Charles McDevell hardly left his house. All of the housewives of the neighborhood pitied him, bringing him baskets of food and drinks to comfort him. Even the local pastor tried to pay him visits and speak blessings over the house.

"The town's efforts were generous, of course, but for McDevell, it wasn't enough. Soon, he packed his bags into his car and left without another word to anyone in town. Something terrified him out of that house that he just couldn't bear to take any longer.

"Months after its' abandonment, the house went up for sale, but it sat there for decades without being bought. Rumors came and went that Mr. McDevell had died in a town on the opposite side of the country, and at that point, the city of Weston's council took over the selling of the house. Still, not a soul in town displayed a willingness to buy it from the council. Weston as a whole feared the place.

"Those city council members ended up surrendering the property rights to a man in town, Fred Morrison, who claimed that he, as a realtor from the area, would do best at selling it. He hoped ghost hunters or thrill-seekers from across the country might pay to see something like it.

"After many years, there was a light that came on in the attic of the house. No one had been seen entering or exiting the place, so the town was convinced by then that it *was* the devil's abode.

"As the light continued to stay on, the town grew antsy, feeling the need to destroy the house once and for all. Whenever people would try to approach the house to tear it down, there would be that same block as there had been in front of the women. No one could get in except for the town's realtor, who still swore someone would buy the house.

"Mr. Morrison died, after dedicating a large chunk of his life to selling the house. His son, Freddy, took over selling the house for Weston. Freddy grew older, more years passed, and people forgot about the house and the families on the other side of it.

"Yes, those women were rumored to have children living there with them. They were their own solitary community. Someone claimed to see two of those kids sitting on the roof of the McDevell house a few years after McDevell himself had fled the town.

"Devil House remained untouched since the time Freddy took over, or at least, it did until your parents came along.

"When the townspeople saw them look at the house with Freddy, they waited anxiously on their porches for the original realtor's son to walk back into town. He had a jubilant smile, an almost crazed look in his eyes.

"My little brother was out playing in the neighborhood when he was walking, and as soon as he saw the old man, he ran up to him and asked, 'What happened with Devil House, Mr. Freddy?'

"Morrison looked down at him, picked him up, and twirled round and round with him, both of them laughing.

'I sold it; I finally sold it!' The town looked on with concern, for someone new would be moving into the house. No one knew when they'd arrive, or what type of folks they'd be, but the town knew one thing for sure; Devil House was back in business.

"So, there you have it," Bobby said, "the story of Devil House, I mean, your house."

I sat there, shocked for a second, and then a thought came to my mind. "Bobby, whatever happened to the people that lived on the street behind the house?"

"Nothing"—he smiled mischievously—"the story tells us that they're still there to this day!"

I rolled my eyes. "Okay, now I know you've just been messing with me!"

Bobby shook his head. "No, honestly, Summer! The kids from the women go to this school!"

I rolled my eyes. "Okay, Bobby. I can't imagine those people are the same ones from a century ago, but if you're so convinced, then who are they?" I asked pointedly.

"Oh, there's only one that he cares about!" Annie laughed, reaching over and smacking him on the shoulder. I never heard who that 'one' was, though, because Bobby just rolled his eyes as the bell rang, signaling lunch was over. As we stood to leave, I laughed and said, "I can't imagine anyone even living down the street from me, seeing as I have been there for a substantial amount of time now and never seen any of them there!" My group shrugged and nodded as if this thought process made sense, but I heard Annie whisper to Haley on the way out that she hoped I'd have to meet them eventually, for entertainment's sake!

My other classes were pretty good during the second half of the day. I didn't have as much luck finding a friend in the two classes following lunch. Psychology and my office assistant position with Mrs. Marks were interesting, but I didn't feel nearly as comfortable as I had with Bobby or his friends.

English came at the end of the day and in there, unfortunately, were the two judgmental girls from this morning, Jen and Daisy. Both of them clutched at their cross necklaces and shuddered when I walked past them to my seat.

I was so irritated by their strange behavior and the impact that Devil House's reputation was having on me, that I didn't even notice when I sat down right next to someone.

When I finally sensed her presence, I glanced up, looking out of the corner of my eye to gauge whether she was welcoming of me or not. Much to my relief, she was smiling right at me.

"Hello," she said, "you must be my new neighbor! I'm Charlotte Skies." I grinned back, suddenly realizing that my neighbors might not be so bad if they were like this girl, despite the mystery her whole street had inflicted on my conscience in the past few weeks.

Aside from her welcoming spirit, Charlotte Skies had to have been the most beautiful person I'd ever seen, and I wondered if this was the neighbor of mine that Annie claimed Bobby took interest in. She had voluminous blonde hair that waved and flowed down past her shoulders, framing her face flawlessly.

She had tan skin that looked more intensely bright than mine, giving off the appearance that she'd been beachside for years instead of near the mountains for the duration of her life. She radiated light and warmth, and I hoped she'd genuinely want to befriend me.

"Yes, I'm your new neighbor. My name is Summer York. It's nice to finally meet someone else from the street!"

I hoped that saying this would strike some sort of a nerve, or bring about an explanation as to why everyone had been so shut-in, but Charlotte just upturned her lips at their corners a bit, nodded, and said, "Oh, yes, we're all very busy! We don't get out of the house much, except for school!

"Speaking of which, how do you like it so far? Isn't Weston Prep the best place ever?" She laughed, rolling her eyes at what an abysmal idea this was.

I shook my head with gusto, laughing along with her. "Honestly, I haven't noticed much of anything other than people staring all day!"

"Hey," Charlotte said seriously, patting my arm with her tiny, warm hand, "I'm sorry. I know it must be hard moving to a new place. But, just think, you're only going to be stuck here for a couple more years, and then you can move back home for college! I, on the other hand…" She trailed off, looking down at her nails in an exasperated fashion, but then she shook her head, smiling again.

"So, did you find a group to sit with at lunch?" I matched her grin, thankful for her contagious positive energy.

"Yeah, I'm sitting with Bobby Hayes, Haley Fallbrook, Annie and Will Bradbury, and Maysie Thompson." Charlotte nodded, recognizing the names.

"I know them!" She looked around, before leaning closer and whispering, "That Bobby sure is a cutie, isn't he?" I giggled, wondering if Bobby would be eager to hear her say that.

"I didn't notice at lunch; do you sit with your—I mean, our—other neighbors?"

She nodded. "Yep, all of us on Lightenborough Drive tend to stick to ourselves!" She sighed, eyes flicking back down at her hands as if trying to hide any traces of the defeated attitude that I could sense from her.

I had a strange but certain feeling that Charlotte Skies was not the type that was okay with being a lone wolf. She seemed to want more than just her neighbors as her friends. She acted toward and spoke of her situation as if she felt trapped, and I more than sympathized with that feeling, especially since moving to Weston—perhaps it was a trademark of the town.

When the class period began, our English teacher, Ms. Germaine, had a brief discussion with us about the year's reading list, and everything that would be required of us. She even assigned a project that would be a large percentage of this semester's grade.

Ms. Germaine told us the task list of the project would include reading *Dracula* by Bram Stoker, and, with a partner, completing a poster board summary outside of school, as well as a full-on essay about thematic ideas portrayed throughout.

Given that my dad was a librarian, I couldn't find much to complain about in regards to the pleasure of this first project. I'd read the novel years ago when my dad told me it was the most thrilling book he'd ever had the joy of reading.

Charlotte and I chose to be partners without ever consulting any further options, and I offered that she could come to my house to start it that very night. I figured I'd better offer because I could not expect that I'd get an invitation into the hidden depths of what I now knew to be Lightenborough Drive.

Within our fifty-minute class period, I learned that Charlotte was a very focused, dedicated student, and a respectful person overall. She answered and questioned Ms. Germaine when necessary, and she didn't talk during instruction as Daisy and Jen did—I was growing to dislike the two of them more and more; she also made friendly conversation with me whenever there was an opportunity.

At the end of the class, and the end of the school day, Charlotte walked out with me. "So, anyway, I have some plans at home, but I can come over in a couple of hours."

"Okay," I responded cheerfully, "do you need a ride home? My dad's driving me."

Charlotte shook her head. "No, thank you, though. I always walk with our other neighbors."

She grinned. "Speaking of, there's someone I want you to meet." She waved her hand down the hall, and suddenly, I saw him.

He locked his gaze with mine, and time seemed to stop. I stared into the depths of his dark eyes, admiring his prominent jawline and face shape. His dark hair hung low over his forehead, and he was, in short, extremely attractive. He looked at me in a puzzled yet irritated way, apparently inspecting my features as well. He looked down quickly, and I snapped out of my trance, clearing my throat and looking back to Charlotte as she repeatedly said my name.

"Yes?" She giggled. "Uh, Summer, this is Demitri. He lives on Lightenborough Drive, too." I looked at this mysterious stranger again and extended my hand.

"Nice to meet you, Demitri. I'm Summer." He took my hand in his, shaking it firmly and nodding briefly, then looking to Charlotte.

"Are you ready to go?" She grinned as if his attitude wasn't strange at all, and motioned for me to follow them out of the front door.

"You know, Summer, if you want to walk home with us, you can! I know you said your dad was driving you, but…"

"No," Demitri interjected. Charlotte flashed an embarrassed glare his way. And he returned her expression with one of equal intensity. I felt my own face flame, feeling extremely rejected from my new neighbors already. *Why would Demitri so quickly feel the need to shut me out? I was the new girl, and I could certainly use some friends.*

I tried to shake off these bitter feelings on account of the fact that I felt unusually drawn to him. As he pushed through the front door of the school, I wished desperately that I could walk with him and follow him and learn more about him, but without even saying goodbye, he took the corner and started down the sidewalk of the main road.

"Sorry about him," Charlotte said casually, rolling her eyes. "He's just not used to new people. He'll come around though. See you soon!" Just as quickly, she was gone, heading over to join him at the edge of the schoolyard.

"So, how was the rest of your first day?" I jumped slightly as Bobby tapped my shoulder.

I exhaled, "Hey, Bobby. It was pretty good. I got to meet one of my neighbors. She was really nice. Do you know her? Her name is Charlotte."

Bobby nodded, smiling and saying with a tone of awe in his voice, "She's the most beautiful girl in the entire town. That's not all there is to her though." He smiled coyly as he looked at her retreating figure. "She's the nicest one, and she has the best reputation out of the lot of them."

"Oh!" Will laughed, slinging his arm around Bobby's shoulder jokingly, Haley walking up beside him. "I know who you two must be talking about. Bobby's been in love with Charlotte Skies since she started going to school here freshman year. I'm sure many other guys here feel the same, no matter how sketchy she is!" Will roared with laughter, all of it pointed at Bobby, having known this secret for years.

Bobby shrugged shyly, muttering, "Yeah, yeah, knock it off, Will." I looked at Bobby with pity before looking across the schoolyard to see Charlotte again—I wondered if she knew that she held his heart in her hands.

I glanced back to Bobby, who admired her with a pained expression. "You should tell her how you feel! She looks nice enough; she may even like you back!" I said, nudging him.

He laughed with Will this time. "There's no point when she would just turn me down!"

I shook my head. "Bobby, don't say that! You're handsome and friendly and funny. You don't give yourself enough credit!"

"Well, thanks, Summer. I don't know, though, I'm still terrified to talk to her."

"She's got a point though, Bobby. After all this time, shouldn't you just make a move or move on? I'm sure there are lots of other girls here who would love to go out with you!" Haley said, and after careful inspection of the sincerity in her eyes, I could tell that it wasn't just any girl she knew of who'd want to go out with him.

"Maybe so, Hales, maybe so. Anyways, Summer, was Charlotte the only one you met?" I shook my head, tight-lipped, and said, "No, I met Demitri, too."

"Ooh, Demitri North," Annie said, walking up with Haley to stand beside me.

"Isn't he so hot?" She giggled as she read into my expression.

I was taken aback. "Uh—yeah—he's pretty cute! I don't know if he's my type, though. He seemed like a real jerk when I talked to him."

"Oh please, honey. Jerk or not, he's every girl's type. No offense, Will," Maysie said.

"None taken," Will replied, taking her hand in his. "Hell, I'd date the guy, no questions asked!" This brought about another round of laughter from my little group as we stood outside the school.

Annie continued then, "There's no shame in it, Summer; everyone at this school knows that Demitri North is the most attractive guy in this town, and all three counties neighboring ours. He is pure eye candy!"

I glanced back at him, standing off to the side with Charlotte. He was staring at his shoes; his eyebrows furrowed, an annoyed look on his face. They appeared to be arguing about something. "He doesn't seem like he's too sociable, though."

"Yeah, we've all tried to talk to him, but the guy has his walls way up, I guess." Bobby shrugged. "Probably better to just stay away from that whole group unless they come to you. It'll be interesting to see what happens now that you're living on the same street as them."

"Speaking of," Haley said quietly, "there they are – all four of them, together." Two other girls walked up to Demitri and Charlotte, and without greeting, they turned in unison and began strolling down the sidewalk. Charlotte and Demitri had seemed to fall silent upon their arrival.

Apparently, I wasn't the only one to notice this because Bobby said, "The two talking are Analise Marsh and Lydia Snow. They're cousins; their fathers were brothers. No one knows for sure, though, because no one has ever seen a man on that street. Most people get the two of them confused with one another because they never leave each other's side; they even have the same schedule! I guess it's just a relative thing."

"I don't know," Will said in his low voice, "I certainly don't try to stick to Annie's side all the time!" Bobby burst into laughter; Annie playfully smacking the top of Will's head.

I looked back to those two cousins as they moved further and further away, Analise and Lydia. They had the same facial structure and eye shape. Analise had skin the color of creamy coffee with kinky, black, shoulder-length hair, while Lydia had skin so opaque and translucent, she seemed to glow. She had hair so blonde, it appeared white like her skin, and it streamed in a straight line down her back.

Both girls looked as if they were gossiping about something that they didn't want the other two to hear about. They had identical, menacing-looking smiles on their faces as they snickered with one another. It gave me chills to see their malicious looks.

At the last second, before they disappeared into the woods, I noticed Demitri turn around. I felt that he was turning to look at me, and wondered if he had felt the same odd spark between us. I was pulled back to reality as I heard the horn of my dad's car from in front of the library. "Summer, come on, dear!" I cringed as a couple of people giggled and muttered things about my dad being the librarian.

"I'll see you all tomorrow," I said, smiling at my friends quickly and rushing to the car. I realized after a moment that I didn't mind people associating me with my dad being a librarian – it'd be better than them associating me with Devil House!

I talked to my dad on the drive about how my day went, and he told me about learning the ropes of the library, which, in his opinion, was a little slice of Heaven. He claimed it had more books than what he ever dreamed of having in the bookstore back in Rosemary Beach.

I was glad that my dad had a good day at work. Reflecting on it that afternoon as he drove us to the house, I concluded that my day had been fairly good as well. Of course, it had come with a few odd occurrences throughout, but I felt grateful for the day I had overall.

Dad parked the car in front of our house and I walked in, finding myself immediately surprised. The original light fixture that hung from the ceiling just past the entryway of the house looked completely different; the chandelier structure was abstract and had different colored glass fragments hanging from it, creating a magical ambiance on the inside of the house. It was a captivating design, and the glistening light now seemed to spread through the whole first floor of the house.

I went up the stairs that were no longer cluttered by boxes, and then down the hall to my mom's loft. She was in there, painting directly on the walls in all kinds of colors. She mostly painted the leaves of trees and the mountains so that to the untrained eye, there could be some question as to which side of the room was a real window, and which was a painted scenic design on a wall.

She turned to me with a bright, beaming smile as I opened the door. "Well, hey, sweet girl! How was your day?"

"It was good, Mom! I made some friends in each class, and I also found a group to sit with at lunch!"

"That's awesome, Summer. I'm so happy for you! I missed you, though. I'm so glad you're home."

She gave me a tight hug before I backed away, remembering what I'd walked in to find just moments before. "Mom, when did you change the chandelier?"

She smiled. "It's a little project with glass effects I've been playing around with for the past few days, but your father sent one of his assistants to stop by and hang it up today. I feel like it sort of completes the look of the place, don't you think?"

I nodded vigorously. "Yes! I love your painting in here, too! It makes me wonder if it was you who painted my bedroom." I grinned at her, and she still looked confused.

"I've never been able to get up there, so there's your answer to that question!" I just shrugged at her, still unable to piece together what had happened in there. Then I remembered the plans I'd made for myself a few hours before.

"Oh! Mom, our neighbor, Charlotte Skies, is coming over tonight to start an English project with me; is that okay?" I asked with a hopeful look on my face.

She radiated happiness. "Yes, it's high time we met one of our neighbors! I'd love to have her join us for dinner if she wishes!"

I clapped my hands together. "That'd be great! I can go down the street and ask her to stay longer." I bid my mom a goodbye for now, and went down the stairs, out the back patio door – which, as I now knew all too well, was previously the front.

I walked to the makeshift fence and placed my hand on one of the poorly hung "DANGER" signs, pushing it aside to reveal a gap in the fence just large enough for me to squirm through.

I paused for a moment as I stared down the street. It seemed so much larger here now that I was up close and personal with it. I no longer had a balcony's distance between the endless road and myself. As I stood there, staring out at it, I felt so small. There was a bit of wind that rustled the trees, and for a moment, I feared that daring to venture back here would be a very, very bad idea.

Then, I stopped myself from having these foolish thoughts, remembering how kind and open Charlotte had been this morning, and how eager I'd felt only a couple of moments before about inviting her to dinner. I nodded as if assuring myself, gathered up some courage, and took the first step to the other side.

Chapter Three
The Boy from Lightenborough Drive

I began walking away from the comfort of my house and immediately realized that I'd made a mistake in coming here – I was definitely out of my league. I realized as I looked around Lightenborough Drive that I didn't even know which house was Charlotte's.

I looked to my left at the brick house nearest me, and the yellow wooden house closest to the woods. I looked across the street from those to the dank wooden house neighboring my own, and another brick house across from the yellow one that was completely covered by a mossy tree. If I were basing a house off personality, I'd sense Charlotte was in the brightest of the three, the yellow house in the left corner, but I was hesitant to go knock on the door of one of my other strange neighbors.

So, there I stood, in the middle of the cul-de-sac, surrounded by all four of the houses that were cloaked by massive trees of the forest. The wind seemed to pick up eerily, and I turned to each house slowly, contemplating them. I settled with the fact that I'd just have to try all of them, but as to which I'd approach first, I had no idea. On my third scan of the houses, my eyes skimmed their way to the right side of the street, and I gasped suddenly at what I saw.

Demitri North was standing on the porch of the extremely run-down cabin, the one next to mine on the right. His elbows rested on the porch's half-wall, looking at me with a curious and smug expression. "Lost?" he asked me, smiling in a wickedly teasing sort of way. *So attractive...* my brain was screaming, but I wasn't able to form a response to him. Demitri began to step off of the porch, walking down the stairs and not taking his eyes off me once – not even blinking. He had a strange swagger in his stride, and the muscles in his arms seemed to flex and ripple as he shoved his hands into his pockets.

Snap out of it! I told myself, taking a deep breath, and finally saying, "Um, yes. I'm looking for Charlotte's house." Demitri looked over at my house, taking in the cleaner appearance of it that was visible from where we stood thanks to all the newly non-boarded windows.

Demitri was so close to me that I could smell him now; he smelled like the forest. Each time I inhaled, I caught a trace of pine trees and winter and warmth. He took another step nearer, looking down into my eyes. His were dark and piercing, with a bit of a haunting quality to them. "And why would you be looking for Charlotte's house, may I ask?"

I didn't fully process what he said. He was standing so close to me, if he had leaned down, he would've been able to kiss me.

With a shake of my head, I stopped this laughable thought. This was the same guy who'd glared at me during lunch for no reason at all. He seemed moody and irritating, and not someone that I wanted to mess with. I took a step back, trying to break his hold on me, but he followed suit, matching my step away with another step closer.

"Why are you looking for her house?" he asked again, emphasizing every word. His voice was so warm and sultry; it seemed easy to just fall into a trap of listening to him talk all day. At the same time, I sensed a threat lying there, as if my reason for wanting to see Charlotte needed to be good enough for me to stay out of trouble with him.

But, instead of backing off from his intimidation attempt a second time, I drew up the nerve to respond. "I'm doing an English project with her, and I needed to ask what time she's coming over."

He nodded, as if my answer was satisfactory, but then he said abruptly, "She's not here."

My mouth hung agape for a second, unsure of how to respond. "I don't know when she's wanting to work on the project, then." I finally replied, crossing my arms to emphasize our distance.

He smirked again, shaking his head slightly. "She probably won't. Charlie isn't necessarily—what's the word—*reliable* when it comes to homework or any type of school activity."

I stepped back now, feeling disappointed that the one neighbor I thought I'd connected with, and whom I'd assumed to be a good student as well, had bailed on me already. I simply nodded at Demitri with slight defeat in my posture and then began to walk back to the fence between my house and the street.

I heard Demitri muttering to himself as I slumped away. He groaned in frustration and then said, "Wait, wait,

wait!" I heard his feet clapping against the gravel as he jogged to catch up with me. I turned around, eyeing him cautiously.

"I can help you on this project if you need me to," Demitri said grudgingly.

I cocked my head to the side a bit. "And why would you do that? You don't like me."

Demitri put his hands in a surrendering fashion, saying, "I don't dislike you! I just don't particularly know or trust you."

I chuckled at this one, responding, "Right back at you!"

I sighed now, looking him hard in the eyes. He seemed to be genuine, so without further hesitation, I said, "All right, let's go."

We walked in silence to my house; he moved the warning sign aside and waved me in first. "I should take this fence down, don't you think?" I asked, looking at him with a smile. He shrugged, that hardness coming back over his eyes. "Maybe it's better if it stays up." I looked away with embarrassment, thinking I'd completely misread his attempts at friendliness.

It seemed like there were layers upon layers of walls surrounding Demitri's soul. We were standing so close, but in reality, we were so far apart. It was maddening, trying to figure out which side of himself that he showed me was the real side; was he truly funny and friendly, the type who volunteered to help with homework? Or was he closed off and barred from the world, trying to put up fences literally and figuratively between him and me?

We walked inside the house; I heard my dad stacking books in his office, and my mom humming in her loft, so I decided we'd just go on up to my room and let them be.

"It's kind of weird, but my room is in the attic, and we have to go outside to get in…"

"I know," he interrupted, "I've seen your light on at night sometimes." He winced.

"That sounded less weird in my head, I swear." I giggled, shaking my head at him and holding the third-floor balcony door open, leading him up the rattling stairs I'd grown so used to. There was yet another odd comment from Demitri to send my mind reeling – I just couldn't seem to read him.

I ducked into the window, and he followed with ease. He looked around, not seeming surprised by the unique paintings or odd amounts of potted plants around the room, as I'd expected, but with a calm sort of demeanor.

"Well"—I filled the silence—"this is my room. Most of it was like this when I got here."

He nodded in approval. "I like it; I think I've been somewhere similar to it before. It feels like home in a way."

I looked around, impressed that the design of it hadn't brought about a snarky remark from him, "Well, thanks! Do you want to get started now?"

It turned out Demitri had read *Dracula* for fun over the summer, and he knew it practically by heart. We were able to start on our poster quickly, copying over the information and writing down a thorough analysis. He laughed at my attempted drawing of fangs with blood on them, and I was in awe over his masterful creation of a cloaked man scaling down the walls of a castle.

"Demitri, you are such an artist!" I exclaimed when he raised his head from his elaborate sketch. He studied it for a moment, a pleasant look on his face.

Then, looking at the symbols on the walls, he softly said, "Art is timeless. It's constantly changing and evolving, but there's also nothing so solidly in its' place in the world. It is an escape through which I can create whatever world I want to create."

I felt myself admiring the walls with him as he spoke, entranced by things I hadn't noticed before. Aside from the swirls I'd seen on the first day, I was now making out shapes from the green designs. I saw a tree with a tire swing attached, and it seemed to be moving; it was painted so fluidly. I saw birds painted flying over ocean waves at the bottom of the wall, and I felt free just looking at them. I also saw what I thought could be more writing in that strange vision-evoking language, and reminded myself to look at that later.

I looked to Demitri to find him staring at me with awe etched onto his face. "Why are you crying?" he whispered.

I raised a hand to my cheek and felt a tear there. "I-I guess I just never noticed how beautiful it is in here. It's very moving." I gestured to the walls.

He nodded, smiling a little. "Yes, who is your painter? Whomever he or she is, they're very talented."

I shrugged. "As I said, it's been like this the whole time I've been here."

He responded, "Hm," and continued to gaze at the walls.

"Well, I guess I'd better be going," he said abruptly, looking out the window and noticing the sun setting behind the trees.

I nodded. "Yeah, that's fine. Thank you for helping me, Demitri."

He muttered a quick, "You're welcome," standing from the floor and walking to the window. I began putting my art supplies away, turning my back to him. I didn't hear the window move, but I didn't question it for a brief moment. Not, at least, until I heard nearly silent footsteps moving across my carpet once more.

I could hear breathing behind me, soft but tense, and the smell of the forest came rushing back to me again. I slowly turned my head to the side, seeing the outline of his black shirt and jeans from my peripheral vision. "Did you need something?" I practically whispered. He said nothing, but he reached forward and grabbed my wrist with a firm hand, turning me slowly to face him, pulling me closer.

Then before I even comprehended what was happening, he was kissing me, and I was kissing him back. Everything had a sort of dreamlike quality to it; his hands in my hair, his warm lips, and the passion trapped within the kiss. It was as if we knew we shouldn't be doing it, but our lips and bodies together proved how little we cared.

Still kissing me, he put his hands on my waist and walked forwards, pushing me so that I stepped backward until I was against the wall. I lowered a trembling hand from behind Demitri's neck, placing it against the wall to steady myself, and instantly, the kiss, Demitri, and even my room, were gone. I felt a nightmarish vision come to life around me, though I could sense it was all inside my head.

"Lorena, please listen to me," a steady voice of a woman pleaded.

"And how can I do that, Fallon? How can I listen to you, when I have just exiled four others for this same crime?" a sterner voice said.

I squinted my eyes and saw the hazy outlines of two pacing women swim into focus. They were in the middle of a huge ballroom type of place. The woman called Lorena was standing in front of a large chair that sat at the top of a set of steps like a queen would. The other woman, Fallon, was positioned at the bottom of the steps.

Holding my hands up to my face, I could see that I was there, too, in the room. I didn't have the same quality as they did, though; it was like I was solid and everything around me, though visible, was blurred as if a part of an alternate reality.

Fallon, by the time I'd looked around the room, had seemed to put together her thoughts. "Ren, I love him. I love him with all my heart. I know it doesn't make any sort of sense for us, and I know that we were warned against this as pixies, but I've grown now, and I make my own choices; I choose Peter."

I wondered what in the world she could've possibly meant by pixies, but I let it go. This was not real; it couldn't have been. I was trapped in some mysterious sort of a dream.

As I watched Fallon make this declaration of love, I saw that she had a determined posture about her. I walked closer and determined that she seemed recognizable somehow. I didn't know if it was her warm auburn hair, the hazy outline of her face, or her strong and comforting voice, but she seemed so familiar to me.

I looked to Lorena now, and she looked tenser than ever. She looked down at Fallon, sighed, and walked briskly down the steps, fingers laced together in front of her. She strolled right up to Fallon and placed a hand on her shoulder.

"Fal, you've been my best friend for years, and I'll always love you."

Fallon smiled. "And you'll always be my best friend, Ren!" She leaned forward and embraced Lorena. Lorena patted her back, but then grasped something from behind Fallon's hair and gave it a hard yank. Fallon gasped.

Two brilliant blue wings burst from where Lorena had tugged at Fallon's back. I sucked in a frantic breath, trying to move to piece together if what I was seeing were two real wings attached to Fallon's back. My mouth was agape as I studied them, their vivid blue color reflecting off of the white marble floor.

Golden sparks seemed to fly from Lorena's hands, and instantly Fallon was on her knees, sobbing. "No, please, Lorena! You're making a mistake; they will not harm us!" But, Lorena wouldn't listen to her so-called friend's cries, fashioning a glowing dagger out of midair, and slowly stalking around Fallon, like a predator behind her back.

"Fallon, I'm sorry to have to do this, but you leave me no choice. You must serve as an example to those who could further taint the blood of the faire folk." Lorena grasped one of the wings on Fallon's back and, using her knife, with a look of malice in her eyes, she sheared the wing completely off.

Fallon screamed, and it was terrible. The wing dissolved in midair, and Fallon's weight fell forward, onto her hands. I shuddered, trying to turn away, but finding myself forced to observe this horrendous scene. There was another slash of the dagger and another blood-curdling scream from Fallon. Her wings had both seemed to disintegrate, and where they once were, a golden stream of blood was dripping from Fallon's back. Lorena snapped her fingers, and whatever spell had been pinning Fallon to that spot released her. She fell further now, to her elbows; face down on the cold floor that was now drenched with her gold blood.

Soft sobs shook Fallon's limp body, and from the side of the vision, two grand doors were opened and a young man about the age of the two women ran inside. "Fallon!" He cried out to her, stopping in horror as he saw what had been done to her.

He looked up at Lorena and glared. "You!" He pointed to her, and, with all power in his stance, raised his hands so that his palms aimed at Lorena. A white sort of smoke began billowing around him, and he screwed up his face at the effort.

"Oh, please, Peter." Lorena laughed, twirling her fingers and sending golden sparks his way, completely diffusing his curse upon her. Peter groaned in pain, stumbled a moment, and was suddenly on his knees, bound by glowing golden shackles.

The next second, he was levitating above more glistening air that Lorena moved, and she set him down next to Fallon's still bloody body. Her golden blood now appeared to be changing to a muddy red color as it continued to flow from the wound.

The shackles opened and reclosed so that Peter and Fallon were chained together, and he fought the spell of Lorena hard to try to rub Fallon's arm and soothe her. "Fallon, Fallon, do you hear me? Are you okay?" He said in a panicked voice. Fallon slowly sat up to look at him, laying her head on his shoulder and murmuring in the assurance that she was.

"Fal, I'm so sorry to have to do this, but exile wouldn't have been enough in this situation. Both of you—" Lorena sighed, in a mock disappointed tone—"will be executed." She smiled gleefully then. "And this will cease to be a problem any longer!" I could tell just by the way she spoke that Lorena wasn't kind at all, and I began to feel more and more heartbroken for Fallon and Peter, though I had no clue as to why these two strangely magical people—or, I assumed they were people—couldn't be together.

Fallon and Peter looked into each other's eyes and kissed deeply before grasping each other's hands and looking at Lorena. Fallon spoke, smirking despite her obvious pain; "You're too late for that, Ren. I have a feeling this will be a problem for you for many years to come." Peter chuckled as Lorena paused in her pacing, slowly turning back to face the two of them.

She tried to compose herself quickly, smiling back with toxic sweetness at Fallon and asking, "And why would that be Fal?" Peter responded this time, a smug look crossing his face; "Because, Lorena, we may die today, but our blood will live on forever." Lorena gasped marching forward to Fallon, taking hold of her and making her stand separate from Peter, who cried out in protest.

Lorena threw Fallon hard against the nearest wall, shaking her violently against it despite her shrieks at the wounds on her back being practically pummeled. "Don't tell me you did this, Fallon. Not after all those years of us promising each other we wouldn't. Don't tell me you would have a child, an abomination of nature's laws as well as our own, with a warlock?"

So, that's what Peter was, a warlock. I'd never have known, for he looked completely normal. Fallon suddenly grasped Lorena's arms with her own blood-soaked hands, pushing her back hard. "Yes, I did. A beautiful baby girl named Blair, hidden where you will never find her." She huffed at her in defiant anger, limping back to Peter and helping him to stand too.

"Ren, it's been too many years of refusing to let people love whom they're meant to. You had your heart broken once by the rule; you can be the one to lift it!"

"*No!*" *Lorena let out a strangled cry, turning back to face the two with blazing eyes.*

"The rule is in place for a reason, not by my desire, but for the good of the kingdom that I rule. I will not let my friend defy me. I am the Grand Enchantress, and I have more power than you. Though you are jealous of that, Fallon, I am not going to let you take it away." Fallon made to retort back, likely about how she couldn't care less about power, but the words never left her lips.

Lorena snapped her fingers, and from a door at the ceiling, eight guards in black uniforms fluttered down, wings closing when they touched the ground. Fear was visible in Fallon and Peter now, and they whispered to one another as if trying to plan their escape though they were both so weak.

"Guards, take them away and execute them both within the hour. Let their story be known throughout the kingdom; I am done playing games." Lorena walked back to her throne without giving Fallon and Peter a second glance. Her dress trailed behind her with a disturbing grace, the train of it tainted from Fallon's blood.

Fallon and Peter struggled, trying to stumble toward a nearby exit, but there was no use. The guards swarmed them, separating them and taking hold of their arms, flying the two up and to the door in the ceiling they'd just emerged from.

"Oh, and Fallon, Peter?" The guards paused, turning the prisoners to look down at Lorena, who smiled devilishly up at them. "I will find her... Blair. I will use her to show them what happens to creatures that disobey

me if it's the last thing I ever do." Peter shouted a slew of curses at her as Fallon let out a choked sob, and they were taken into the door, which slammed shut, allowing silence to fill the room.

As for Lorena, she sat on her throne, breathing deeply but shakily, and then, all of a sudden, she began hysterically crying. She put her head in her hands for a moment, her body shaking with despair, before composing herself. It was as if she forced out her sadness and regret within thirty seconds, then continuing to sit stoically as the Grand Enchantress. A light grew around her, spreading out and touching each corner of the room, and suddenly, the vision was gone.

I woke up in my bed, staring at the stars painted onto the ceiling. I was extraordinarily dizzy, and it felt as if my brain was banging against my skull. I sat up slowly, looking around my room.

Demitri was gone. There was no note, no sign of him leaving, or anything else. I didn't even see the project we'd done together. I looked up and jumped back against my headboard with a start.

Charlotte Skies was standing on my balcony, smiling and waving at me. I quickly stood and walked to open the window. "Sorry, you scared me!" I exclaimed, motioning for her to come in. She laughed. "Yeah, I know, I've stood here yelling your name and knocking on the window for the past five minutes!

"Your mom let me in the back door, and she told me you'd be up here most likely. Do you still want to do the project?" I nodded, looking out the window to the ghostly street, where I had been a few hours before with Demitri. I wondered where he'd gone.

At the thought of that, I exclaimed, "Oh! I already did the project. Demitri came over and helped me with it. I know it's here somewhere…" I trailed off, searching all around for where the beautiful project was.

"Uh, what do you mean Demitri helped you with it? You certainly can't mean Demitri North, right?" She was looking at me with utter dismay.

I nodded slowly. "Yeah, he was here. I guess I fell asleep on my bed and he left, but he was definitely—"

"Honey, he went a town over right after school. He couldn't have possibly been here," Charlotte interrupted. I didn't know what to say, I felt so humiliated.

How had I imagined the project, the talk of the paintings, the kiss, everything?

"Oh," I said with a grimace, "I guess it was just a really weird dream, then."

Charlotte giggled, "It's okay, Summer, I don't blame you! He is quite dreamy!"

"Are you two dating?" I asked suddenly, getting out the poster board from where it had been before Demitri and I had started working on it, or at least before I thought we'd started working on it. Charlotte began getting out different things from her bag, too, writing on the poster in swirly font and leaving me to draw the artwork, attempting to draw how Demitri had in my dream.

Charlotte responded, "No, we aren't dating. Demitri and I have been best friends for as long as I can remember. We have a lot in common, at least, more so than our other neighbors." She mimed throwing up as she hinted at Analise and Lydia, and I laughed, remembering their unpleasant dispositions and feeling no pity.

For a few minutes, we worked in silence, giving me time to reminisce on my day. I was at a new school with new friends, and unfortunately, a few peers who didn't like me. That was something I could get over, though.

What was abnormal about my day was that I had met a boy that I'd shared strange chemistry and an exhilarating kiss, and then, I had come to find out that it was all a farce. To top off all of the madness, I had passed out again when I'd touched the wall, the vision I'd experienced during my blackout was more vivid than the last.

The visions were so confusing; first and foremost because they involved fairies and warlocks. The last had even mentioned the existence of a 'grand faire enchantress,' Lorena, who, if she was real, must've been a true menace to those she ruled.

Rehashing of all this in my mind brought me around to question whether all this was true, or if it was just a daydream that had a freaky coincidence to the other one that I'd had when I was near the wall. Were fairies, magic, and mythical creatures real? Was this world more than what I'd always thought it to be?

And if I did decide to believe that fairies and warlocks and whatever else existed, then I had to wrestle with the fact that Lorena existed, and was spreading malice through the world. Her cruelty against those such as Fallon and Peter, who were now likely long dead, was nothing short of heartless.

My own heart hurt for them, whether they were real or a figment of my imagination. I knew what I needed to do to determine if there was something more to my visions. I had to dive deeper into the mysterious transcriptions on the wall, and I swore to myself that I would as soon as Charlotte left. Luckily for me, that didn't seem to be too far away, based on the quick progress of the project.

When Charlotte climbed through the window and I told her goodnight, I watched for a moment as she traipsed through the backyard, moving the same teetering sign I'd moved earlier to get out. I then quickly closed the window and shut the curtains, scurrying back to the largest wall I'd been at earlier.

I scanned from the top of the wall to the bottom, picking out a few words here and there, and then feeling a sensation of dizziness wash over me. I stopped, stumbling back and catching my breath. *I need to take it slow with this,* I thought to myself. I looked over to my desk and decided that the chair in front of it may be my best option to tackle this mysterious language without fainting every time.

I grabbed the chair from my desk and rolled it across the carpet to that spot in front of the wall, relaxing into it before starting at the top of the wall again. I squinted hard, trying to pick apart the symbols to discover this language that then translated itself in a way that came so naturally to me. I had to accept it at that moment; there was some strange sort of enchanted quality to this wall. With a shaky breath, I began slowly reading the symbols that transformed into the words, *"The History of the Faire Folk and the Corruption Within*:

Before humankind existed, and after God created the heavens and the earth, a single tree burst forth from the ground, filled with not just life from the earth, but also angelic magic bestowed unto it. From this magic came the first of the faire folk; an entire race was born. These beings would grow from pure pixies to fantastical fairies, each blessed with specific powers relating to the region of the Earth in which they would be sent to live, or the talent they were to be assigned to perform. It was clear that this species was set on a course of helping maintain a balance between humans and nature.

God sent the heavens' magic down to the earth soon after the creation of humans, in the form of guardian angels that protected each human from sin. However, hellfire also crept its way into Earth, and demons presented themselves.

From possessing humans to influencing sin and evil, these demons brought forth nothing but trouble for humankind, and for the faire folk as well. Demons attempted to mate with the humans, and from that combination, another powerful race, the warlock, was born. Blessed and burdened with immense amounts of power, the warlock was a creature thought of as so foul by the faire court that it was forbidden to come into contact with them, except for emergency magical situations only.

There was, however, one bloodline of warlocks that were considered to be the purest of any sort of creature. Decades after the demons of hell introduced the mere idea of mating with mortals, a guardian angel fell in love with his human.

Soon after, the human and angel produced a child, a warlock of light who wasn't tainted by the darkness of demonic blood. When the Lord discovered the angel's act of misconduct, though, the angel sought to hide the child with other dark warlocks to protect it. This effectively led to the entire line of descent of the light warlocks being lost, but the stories of it remained.

This legend of this warlock bloodline became so famous throughout history that it was clear that someday when the line was to be rediscovered, the family of light warlocks would be deemed the rulers of the entire warlock species, and they would become known as the Ware Elite.

Centuries passed, and the races of the faire folk and warlocks became so isolated that the traces of demons or angels were only a slim part of the makeup of warlocks and no part of fairies. That is, until near the 1500s.

In crossing from the area that is now Russia, a fairy of the snow, Katia, met a young warlock by the name of Damian Freedman. Damian was no warlock of the light nature, and therefore, he was not bound by the angel's blood to live life performing good deeds. Perhaps it was his disregard for the laws of nature and magical species' that led Damian to ask Katia if he could court her.

Thus, the two fell in love, but they never told a soul of their relationship; for this love was forbidden by the grand faire court's enchantress, and also by the king of the warlocks, who was ruling until the day the warlock of light was rediscovered.

Years turned into decades, and Katia and Damian were no longer the only warlocks and fairies to break the rules in the name of love. The next was a fairy of the sky, Anastrella, one of the first in charge of aligning the stars and the moon in ways that developed human understanding of the cosmos.

The visions she created were famous. She, along with her fellow sky fairies, dazzled humanity with the constellations and galaxies they could view with their telescopes. Occasionally, a human was lucky enough to see a sky fairy in action: a shooting star. The legend is that Anastrella looked for years and years for a sky fairy with whom she could find love, but she could not find one whose soul fit with hers.

Anastrella, instead, found a warlock by the name of Quinton Toll. Quinton was a warlock with great power, and he lived near Anastrella in the forests of the north. He had watched for years how she painted the night sky to life again and again. He fell in love with the mere idea of her, and revered her quietly, for he believed a fairy would never love a creature with such dirty blood as him.

However, he was wrong. Anastrella saw him admiring her one night and approached him to ask why. She claimed that his proclamations of awe toward her, as well as his kind demeanor, brought her back to visit him in the nights following. And so there was another quiet, forbidden relationship unfolding.

The next pair of lovers was made up of Vivyanna of the Marsh and Trace Gideon, a fairy and warlock both living near what would become Louisiana. Vivyanna was once a happy, kind fairy, whose work was to look over the swamps of Louisiana and the creatures within them.

Around 1715, warlock Trace Gideon moved into the swamp area, seeking isolation from other warlocks in the lands. Instead of the lonely life he'd planned on, he found "Vivy", who caught his attention right away with her ferocity and willingness to handle wild creatures. Trace fell in love with her, but she didn't make it particularly easy for him to win her heart. He tried for decades to prove himself to her and her heart was only won with, of all things, his first successful attempt to wrestle with an alligator. The two kept their romance a secret, hidden deep within the bog lands of the South, far from the Grand Faire Enchantress.

The most recent fairy-warlock relationship began with a warlock named Oliver North. Oliver was not a warlock of the old bloodlines, as the previous three had been. He was a direct descendent of a demon, Mordent, and a woman, Priscilla North. Oliver was born around 1800 in what is now London. With so much cloud cover around, it was clear to the curious and adventurous Oliver that there were dark fairies in the region, and his assumptions were correct.

He began to search for these fairies and found exactly who he was looking for. Genesis of the dark was in charge of London's shadows. It was a rare thing for a fairy to have power that brought darkness to the world and not light, but someone had to do it, and Genesis, one of the oldest fairies in existence, was one of the fairies charged with this duty.

She was a stickler for the rules, having created a few of them herself. When it came to the rule prohibiting fairy contact with warlocks, she made an exception. Oliver had tried to find Genesis for a few years before she finally revealed her presence in the area. When she did, she soon realized that letting down her walls and joining into a relationship with Oliver was one of the best decisions she could ever make. They fell in love, and in the early 20th century, a miracle occurred; Genesis became pregnant.

Of course, this had never been heard of before, and all the previous relationships mentioned had been together for centuries, wanting to safely have children, but fearing the risk for the pregnant fairy if it were to occur. They had all managed to contact one another over the years, so this was a bit of information that was quickly spread between them. Once they knew that Genesis had successfully gotten pregnant, and had a baby boy with Oliver, Katia and Damian, Anastrella and Quinton, and Vivyanna and Trace all quickly attempted to have kids, so ready to have a family after centuries of wishing for something they thought to be impossible.

These children, once born, were of the fairy nature in build, skilled in warlock spell mastery, and with the power scale of a warlock and fairy combined. Each of the fairies and warlocks became families after so many years, and just when happiness seemed prevalent in all of these families, things took a turn for the worse.

The Grand Faire Enchantress of so many years decided to retire, allowing her granddaughter, Lorena, to take over rule. Lorena had been a kind young pixie in her youth, and she had resented the rule of her grandmother.

Her grandmother was primarily in charge of raising Lorena as a pixie, and she made it infinitely clear to her protégé that any sort of relations with warlocks was not to be tolerated. To imprint such a belief in Lorena, her grandmother committed an evil act, a test of Lorena's will.

As a young fairy, Lorena was introduced to a young warlock, a son of a hierarchical figure in the warlock rule. This warlock tempted Lorena, and acted as her friend for a long time, so long that Lorena began to fall for him. Ignoring her responsibilities as the next Grand Faire Enchantress, Lorena declared her love, and the warlock did not return it.

It turned out that he had only been a pawn in the Enchantress' wicked plan to hold Lorena accountable, and he was returned to the warlock guard with a promotion and a hefty sum from Lorena's grandmother, who'd hired him from the beginning.

The warlock's role in Lorena's heartbreak was a mere business agreement between the warlocks and fairies, and the former was granted immense quantities of treasure for their contribution before going their separate ways from fairies once more. As for Lorena's grandmother, she was then certain that Lorena had learned her lesson and was ready to rule the faire folk.

Lorena, however, was heartbroken. She felt betrayed, surrounded by hate on all sides, and she still loved the warlock despite learning that the entire relationship had been a lie. After years of trying to recover from this terrible blow, Lorena took her place as the Grand Faire Enchantress, close to the year 1900.

Lorena's first nomination to the Faire Grand Court was her best friend, Fallon of the Sea. Fallon and Lorena were both brought up near the ocean, sent to protect the balance between creatures of the sea and the humans that were so drawn to it. However, Lorena never felt the connection to the sea that Fallon did. This wouldn't have been a problem for her, though, since it was always her destiny to rule.

For years, Lorena tried to keep up with Fallon's magical successes in their home, and now, it was Fallon's turn to follow Lorena's lead on the faire court. Fallon was loyal and celebrated the rule that Lorena was finally charged with. But, as good of a friend and faire court member, as she was, Fallon had a secret.

Fallon was in love with a warlock named Peter Kane. Despite the law, and despite the hurt that Fallon had helped Lorena cope with at the hands of a warlock, Fallon had been in love with Peter for many years.

The same year Lorena had become Grand Enchantress, the fairy world began to hear rumors of the four fairy women in loving relationships with warlocks, and how they had children of their own. How their secret had been found out was still beyond each couple, for the couples only intermingled with each other, and stayed isolated aside from that.

Whatever had occurred to release this information though didn't matter after a while, because Lorena knew, and once she was fully aware of the situation, she would not let them live in peace. They hid their children away, trying to separate themselves temporarily so Lorena wouldn't bother the young pixies.

They were right to do so because soon into the search, Lorena found them: Katia and Damian, Anastrella and Quinton, Vivyanna and Trace, and Genesis and Oliver. She ordered her guards to have them brought to the Faire Palace, hidden near the tree from which fairy life had originated."

The words began to shift on the wall, and I closed my eyes, shaking violently as another vision overtook me. I grasped the chair arms for support and allowed the next illusion to overcome my senses as if it was another page in a book.

I was back in the castle, this time staring at the backs of eight people, all of whom looked like mere teenagers, cuffed and on their knees before Lorena in her throne. This time, Lorena had several chairs on either side of her: the Faire Grand Court. In the seat immediately to her right sat Fallon.

Fallon looked young and beautiful, her long, brown hair brushed back into elegant golden clips, and she wore a dress that flowed down like blue waves. She sat up straight and proper in her royal seat, but one glance at her face told me she was so unhappy. Lines creased her forehead with worry, and her fingers clutched the arm of the chair with tension as she watched the scene unfold before her.

Lorena stood from her chair and walked forward, just to the end of the steps. "Now, what to do about you all."

She looked each one of them in the eye before the man closest to the end shouted up, "You can't do this. We are warlocks, and we can't possibly be under your jurisdiction."

Lorena glanced at him, smirking and nodding. "You are right, Trace. Absolutely. Well, if any of you gentlemen would like to leave your faire lady's side and exit this place forever, go ahead." She snapped her fingers and a door opened at the back of the room.

She fanned her hand again and the cuffs faded from the wrist of each warlock. "Oliver," a dark-haired woman with shadows beneath her eyes whispered next to him, "you wouldn't leave me, would you? You wouldn't leave me and Demitri?"

I gasped, stepping forward. The more I'd seen from this mysterious wall, the more I'd begun to believe, piecing the puzzle of mystery and coincidence together as I became more informed. From the Devil house story I'd heard this morning to this, it seemed to somehow fit that my new neighbors were somehow tied to this mad world I'd been learning about today. When I thought about Demitri North, in all his allure and peculiarity, it didn't shock me in the least that he could be the son of this warlock, Oliver North, and the fairy next to him, who must've been Genesis.

As I shook my head, trying to focus solely on this vision, I became horrified as I watched Oliver stand, and without haste, walk out the door. Following him quickly, despite the protests of the mothers of their children, and their lovers for so many years were all of the warlocks.

Trace practically ran out, and Damian and Quinton followed only after promising their wives that they would find them and free them as soon as they had a chance. My heart ached for the fairies as slow tears slid down each of their cheeks, and they realized they were alone.

Lorena chuckled. "Well, that was easy! Don't you see, girls, this is why warlocks can't be trusted; they are evil!" Fallon stood sharply from her seat, looking as if she wanted to say something, but instead, she cast a look of pity on the four fairies and flew out the door in the ceiling. Lorena glanced up at her briefly before shaking her head and looking back to the fairies on the ground. I wondered if Lorena knew at that moment that there was something hidden in Fallon's life, a relationship that Lorena would have never expected.

"You have disobeyed the laws of the fairies for centuries. I don't care that you've loyally protected the Earth, or done your jobs well. This is an act of high treason. Let everyone learn from what happens here today. There will be executions next, mark my words," Lorena said to no one in particular. I felt assured that message was meant for Fallon, though, and that thought made me feel sick to my stomach, knowing the doom that awaited both Fallon and Peter.

A blonde fairy next to Genesis, with ratty hair and tear-covered cheeks, let out a shuddering sob. "No, no, not you four, Anastrella. Anyone who commits the same crime after you, don't you get it?"

Lorena turned, muttering to herself in a frustrated tone. She looked back up with a smile, motioning to a fairy on the end of the row of chairs. "Jade, write this down." She cleared her throat, straightened up, and her voice rang out clearly, "As of today, the grand faire enchantress has exiled Genesis, Katia, Anastrella, Vivyanna, and all offspring of the four aforementioned faire folk until the end of time. Guards, remove them from my sight, I can't bear to look at traitors longer than I have to."

The vision faded away until I was looking at the deep green of the wall once more. I quickly moved some boxes away from the floor to reveal the last passage on this section of the wall. This passage rang loud and clear in my mind as if it was being narrated from the same deep and soothing voice I'd heard when the wall spoke to me on that first day in Weston. The only difference was that this time, I felt like I'd heard that boy's voice, not too long before...

"Genesis and her son, Demitri, Anastrella and her daughter, Charlotte, Katia and her daughter, Lydia, and Vivyanna and her daughter, Analise moved together to a remote location, deep within the forest, under the shelter of the mountains, where they live to this day."

That settled my assumption, then. The children my age weren't the same as me, or normal human children. I trembled a bit from the shock, but after all I'd read and discovered thus far, I felt this was not the worst news that I could've received. Lorena living around the corner from me would've been a prospect much worse than this.

This area they moved to was previously uninhabited by fairies because it was so hidden by the forest and lacked sufficient human life for the fairies to work with.

That being said, Lorena has not since bothered the exiled fairies, for they have not left their town or come into contact with any other magical creatures, spare Fallon, who did reach out to them almost eighty years after their exile sentence, in 1983.

She found out where they were hiding after much effort of searching and contacting fairies that were once considered relatives to them. As soon as she heard even a whisper of a possibility of their whereabouts, Fallon rushed to them.

When Fallon came to the exiled fairies, she took a particular interest in their children. These children, who had deemed themselves to be called warefae, surprised her because they looked so much like a regular fairy, but had immensely larger sums of power.

Fairies could typically perform charms based on nature, with a particular emphasis on individual areas of excellence. For example, water fairies could use fire magic but would have stronger charms produced of water magic. Regardless of the type of charm, the fairy enchantments were typically beneficial to humans.

Warlocks were more power-hungry beings, with no influence over nature, but instead, spells that tapped into pure magical energy. Warlock spells specialized in bringing success to their kind, or harm to those who went against them.

The warefae children had the organic light of fairies in their souls, though resentment for the faire folk in general. This grudge was because all they had known was an exile from fairies like Lorena.

The darkness of warlocks was not prevalent in warefae, aside from their unusually feisty and hot-tempered attitudes when angered. They disliked warlocks as much, if not more than, fairies due to their belief that since their fathers had abandoned them and their mothers, all warlocks must be disloyal, unkind beasts.

Fallon pitied these children when she met them and tried to comfort them in her brief visit with proclamations that someday, one of the warefae would mend the bond between the two species, leading this clan of warefae and their fairy mothers out of exile.

Why Fallon was being so kind and curious toward the warefae was unknown to them, but they could assume only one explanation. Fallon was pregnant at the time, very much so, and her motherly instincts certainly must have been kicking in. Fallon flew boldly into the street on which they'd been hidden for so long and, after putting ideas of freedom and strength into the warfae's heads, begged for the mothers to take her daughter in when she was born.

"They've found Peter and I's hiding place," she said once all the fairies had gathered around her.

"I fear for what will happen to us all too soon. Please, will you help hide us, or our daughter?" The four women felt for Fallon, but they were not going to put their children in danger for the three that were now on the Grand Enchantress's hit list.

"We're sorry, Fallon, but we've been on our own for decades now, and your friend Lorena hasn't found us yet. We can't allow you to jeopardize our security or put us

back on her bad side. Even talking to you now is putting our lives in danger," Vivyanna told her.

Tears trickled down Fallon's cheeks as she nodded with understanding. "My heart aches for you, it does, but will you truly not take in my daughter and help her? She will be all alone, and have no idea who she is otherwise."

One of the children who had grown to be as kind and loving as her star fairy mother, Charlotte, interjected into the conversation:

"Mother, please, we need to help her! She would have done the same for us, I'm sure of it!" Anastrella looked up at Charlotte, wrinkles creasing near her eyes out of worry and tension for the situation.

"You see, Charlotte, that's part of the problem, though," Genesis said. She went on to explain how Fallon didn't help them, seeing as she left them to face Lorena's wrath and exile. She escaped without even watching the exile be placed upon them, though she was fully aware that she was deserving of the same punishment.

"I understand, but now, there is no chance that Peter and I would get an exile sentence. It will be death for us, and for Blair, if Lorena, whom I promise you is not my friend, finds us." Fallon tried reasoning with the fairy mothers, but it was no use. She looked past the fairies, to where the warefae were sitting silently, watching, and she said, "May the magic always protect you, and keep a lookout for your chance to stand up for what's right." With a droop to her wings and a hand placed lightly on her very pregnant belly, she flew away, never to be seen again.

The Enchantress found Fallon and Peter Kane's secret only a few months after Fallon's visit to Weston in that terrible year of 1983. Unfortunately, they were executed, as the Enchantress had promised.

The story goes that Fallon did give birth to the child whom they hid from the queen, a baby by the name of Blair. Blair has never been found, and since she doesn't know her secret, she will never know the truth about her powers, her parents, or the world of magic."

The light of the room came rushing around me, and I sat in my chair, shell-shocked at everything I'd just learned, still thinking to myself that Fallon looked oddly familiar. I looked at the clock on my desk; it was one in the morning. I quickly went to shut the light of my room off, and then another light caught my eye. I quietly snuck over to the window, squatting in front of it so only my eyes were visible from above the windowsill. I saw the door of Demitri's house was open, and he was sitting on the porch, accompanied by Charlotte.

I was infinitely confused. Charlotte had said before that Demitri had gone out of town right after school, and yet here he was, at one in the morning, sitting on his porch. I stared at them both, sitting side by side, wondering how it could be possible that these two weren't human. They seemed so normal, and crouching there by the window, I felt like couldn't wrap my mind around connecting the dots between what I'd seen in the wall and what seemed to be real life.

I saw them whispering with their heads close together, and my curiosity got the best of me. I shut off my light, snuck out of my window, and went all the way downstairs. I pushed open the kitchen door carefully and crept across the backyard, stopping and squatting down beside the fence, moving a sign barely an inch to the side. I tried not to make a sound, straining to hear what they were discussing.

"Dem, you were stupid today, going up there with her. I had to cover for you, and I still think she had her doubts. Summer's not going to be an easy one to have living by us, let me assure you." I gasped, shrinking down below the windowsill.

So I was right! Demitri had come to my house today. Going to the street, kissing him, and finding the message on the wall had all happened to me.

But then, why would he just leave? After that moment we'd shared, he left me and allowed Charlotte to make me feel stupid for even believing it had happened. Between the presence of their names in the writing on the wall and the odd behavior after school today, I felt more strongly that maybe the world of fairies and warlocks was not so far-fetched as it had seemed only a few weeks ago when I'd first heard the voice from the wall. Maybe it explained everything about the mystery of Weston.

"Charlotte, I think there's something—how do I put this—different about her. Something more than just human blood."

She cocked her head to the side, smiling a bit. "Are you sure this isn't just wishful thinking because you have a crush on her?"

She giggled, and Demitri very obviously rolled his eyes. "I can't have a crush on a girl I just met, Char…"

"But you sure can kiss one, huh?" Charlotte was hysterically laughing now. Demitri stood abruptly, hands balling into fists as he paced the patio.

"Dem, I was only kidding, relax! I'm sure there's nothing different about her except for the nerve to walk up to you! She's sweet; you should go for it! Start over, and pretend like the kiss never happened."

He sat back down, staring intently into Charlotte's eyes. "Charlie, listen. I think she can read the writing on the wall. I think she saw the visions I enchanted into the paintings earlier today, and that's why she passed out! And she couldn't possibly have read what I wrote unless she had fairy blood inside of her!"

I could see Charlotte's eyes grow wide. "That couldn't be possible. Maybe you just forgot that you wrote a part in English." She nodded, as if confident before her voice suddenly went up a complete octave and she exclaimed, "I thought you said it was written in Faire! Didn't you write it in Faire, Dem?"

"I did, Charlotte, stop freaking out and help me!" Demitri slouched in defeat and ran a hand through his hair. Charlotte took a huffy breath, looking over at him while leaning her back against one of the rickety posts.

"Okay, sorry. Maybe a long, long time ago, she had some random strand of fairy blood in her veins, but it probably didn't even carry over." As quickly as she said it though, she shook her head. "That's not possible; we would have been able to tell right when we met her."

I exhaled a breath of relief, glad that she'd thought that my being anything but human was out of the question. I was still struggling to accept the existence of magical creatures in general, and finding out that I was one as well would've likely sent me over the deep end.

Demitri remained silent for a moment, looking off past Charlotte, as if he didn't hear her possible explanation, before sitting up with a start. "Maybe Summer didn't see the visions. Maybe she just has—um—narcolepsy! It's possible for humans that have narcolepsy to pass out at random times, right?" He guffawed in a way I'd imagine a madman would. "Maybe it was all in my head anyway, right Charlie? Maybe none of it happened!" Charlotte looked at him with pity for a second before putting a hand lightly on his shoulder and standing to walk down the street to her house.

"We'll see, Demitri. We'll see."

Demitri was left alone on the porch, watching her as she vanished into the yellow house. He exhaled a great breath and looked right at my fence. I dropped the sign quickly, hoping he hadn't seen me watching them. I waited for a moment there in the dark, only the light of the night sky shining over me. I slowly rose from my crouched position, peeking my eyes through the fence once more to find that this time, Demitri was gone. However, the door to his house was still slightly swung open.

It dawned on me then that it had indeed been Demitri that had painted this room so beautifully. I walked back up into my room, admiring the way the stars and constellations shone on the ceiling. Looking at it again, I felt like I wasn't uncovering some mystery left here by whoever occupied the room before me; it felt like I was being shown the depths of a complex soul, who used this room as a place to escape confinements of a street he rejected so much.

I lay down on my bed, feeling that I would be seriously regretting my decision to stay up this late in the morning. I was also strangely at peace with all that I'd learned. Despite the chaos of the afternoon, and the absurd nature of the visions, the language I could mysteriously read on the wall, and the mere thought of the presence of fairies on Earth, I felt like the entirety of the day had filled in gaps of knowledge of the world as I'd seen it before.

With a sigh of relief at the prospect of sleep, I shut my eyes, and for the first time in the day, no vision filled my head. Nothing seemed to fill my mind at all. Nothing, that is, but the boy from Lightenborough Drive.

Chapter Four
Confrontation

The second day of school passed without nearly as much chaos as the first. I'd seemed to redeem myself in the eyes of many of my fellow juniors, due to their approval of my sarcastic humor. I'd become an acquaintance, on a first-name basis with many of the students very quickly.

The only ones in the school that hadn't seemed to accept my presence were Jen and her sort-of-follower, Daisy. They refused to talk to me or acknowledge my existence, but all in all, I had a good lunch group, and a solid foundation of friends now, so I wasn't complaining.

Aside from Jen and Daisy, the only one I felt any sort of rejection from was Demitri. He wasn't at school the day after we kissed—and I now did not doubt that my time with him was real, thanks to that conversation I'd eavesdropped on between him and Charlotte. In class, when I tried to ask Charlotte where he was, claiming casually that I noticed he wasn't at lunch, she didn't fumble and reveal his true whereabouts, as I'd hoped.

Charlotte did seem slightly tenser around me in general, though. It was as if the notion that I'd uncovered her secret made her uncomfortable. I wanted to bring it up to her, just to get it out in the open, but I feared that she wouldn't want to be friends with me if I revealed that information.

Demitri returned from his mysterious vacation—though I figured he was just hiding out at home—the next day. The first time I saw him, I was taken a bit by surprise. I looked up from a paper I was skimming over as I left my previous class to meet the dark eyes of the boy I had kissed just days before.

I was so shocked to see him that time that I'm pretty sure my mouth was slightly agape as I passed him in the hall, and despite my dramatic reaction, he did not attempt to acknowledge my existence. My face flamed with embarrassment as I walked past him, wondering why he was making such an effort to ignore me. Maybe, like me, he'd been caught up in the moment, so shocked to see me that first time that his face remained stony and averted. I hoped so, at least.

I was proven wrong after my next class; I passed him in the hall again, this time, attempting to flash him a brief smile. I was met with a stoic expression, just his eyes watching me. This made me so angry that the entire rest of my day was ruined.

I had gone to lunch still fuming from the encounter. Maysie's jokes couldn't make me laugh, and though Haley and Bobby kept pestering me to figure out what was wrong, a few of my unpleasant responses suggested to them that they should drop it. Will and Annie even made eyes at each other—I presumed it was some sort of twin telepathic connection—and hastily avoided conversation with me for the remainder of the lunch hour.

I passed by Demitri once more that day, on the way out to the library to meet my dad and go home; this time, I refused to look at him at all. I could feel the cold gaze of his eyes upon me, but this time, I refused to give him the satisfaction of my return of attention.

I had even remained silent in the car, until my dad asked playfully, "So, what's got you in a funk?" I looked at him, tried to smile a bit, and responded that nothing was wrong, and I was wonderful.

I didn't want my parents to know that I was dealing with an ill-mannered boy who was scheming to make me believe I'd imagined a kiss we'd shared. I didn't want them to clue into the whole realm of secrets I had weighed down on me now—they might not have believed me if I told them, but I couldn't have thought up that elaborate story in my wildest dreams.

Though I hadn't told my dad the truth about what was upsetting me, I felt a bit of the day's burden lift from my shoulders at the notion of being home, away from all my problems with Demitri, and the strange behavior of Charlotte. For the rest of the drive, I remained comfortable but irritated, just trying to forget about the day's confusion and the complete rudeness of Demitri.

When Dad and I got home after school, my mom had made a big fish dinner, to celebrate our first week being over halfway done. My parents chatted during the meal about how much they loved being here – my dad was having so many happy readers visit him at the library, and my mom mentioned a local art auction that she was thinking about entering.

It pleased me to see how well my parents were adjusting to their lives in Weston. My mom's art studio was filling up already with color. Just for me, she painted a small canvas to look like a beachfront view. It made me miss the feeling of the warm sun and the sound of the ocean.

Thinking of the beach gave me an idea to write to Al, as I'd been meaning to do for the past couple of weeks. After looking at my mom's recent artwork, I headed down to my dad's office of books, grabbing a pen and paper and sitting at his big, old-fashioned desk. Then, I began to write:

Dear Al,

Things have been interesting here in Weston. I started school, which has been fine. The house is weird though – almost haunting. I've heard some crazy rumors about this place and the people in it, specifically my neighbors. My classmates have told me stories about deviltry and satanists and the like, but if I'm being honest with myself, I think it's something more than that – something magical.

Speaking of which, do you happen to have any books about magic? Not like abracadabra magic, I mean like fairies and warlocks with powers type of magic! If not, that's fine – I'm just trying to find out what I can and not bother my parents with my paranoia.

Anyways, how are things with the bookstore? Keeping everything spiffy, like my dad would insist? I'm sure you're doing great, so don't worry! Miss you, and I'll write again soon.

Love,
Summer

I put the paper into a stamped envelope, and set it out for my dad to drop at the post office at some point. I was on the stairs, heading back up to my room when I heard a thumping echo of a knock at the door. Before I got up to the balcony door, I heard my dad greet the visitor. "Hello, young man. How are you on this fine evening?"

"I'm good, sir, how are you?"

I felt like I'd been punched in the gut upon hearing that voice. It was Demitri outside of my door, talking to my dad. I tried to think of an excuse that could help me out of whatever situation was coming my way. As I tried to walk quietly, further toward the stairs, I strained to hear the continued conversation between my dad and Demitri North. *Why was he here after his mysterious silence?*

Demitri's voice seemed to drop in volume as he explained his reasoning for being at my house, but I got a general idea of his motive as my dad exclaimed, "Well, I'm sure Summer is in her room! Let me go get her."

Quickly, I turned around and ran up the stairs and out the door to my room, tip-toeing all the way. "Summer!" my dad called, the stairs creaking as he walked up after me.

"No, no, no!" I whispered as I quickly ran out the patio door, finally ducking through my window.

"Sweetie?" Dad called as he stuck his head outside, "you have a visitor!"

I leaned against my wall, racking my brain for a way out of this until I finally just yelled back that I had homework to do. "Summer, this young man really seems to want to talk to you, dear."

I closed my eyes, and exhaled, frustrated. "No, thanks, Dad!"

"Summer, don't be so unfriendly! I'll tell him you'll be down in a moment." I put my face in my hands and groaned with irritation. *Leave it to Dad to be so hospitable.*

I ran to my bathroom and quickly ran my hands through my hair. My run up the stairs hadn't exactly done well for my appearance, but if I didn't get downstairs soon, my dad would likely send Demitri up to me. I looked at myself in the mirror for a moment before shaking my head and whispering, "You will not be intimidated," to myself.

I dashed downstairs and through the house, pausing once before coming into view of the door. My dad had gone into his office, so Demitri stood by the door rather awkwardly, hands stuffed into the pockets of his faded black jeans. He was looking around at the paintings Mom had hung in the hallway until his eyes suddenly flicked to me and stayed there. His gaze cut through the air like a knife, seemingly staring into my soul. I crossed my arms in front of myself and looked down a bit, walking almost bashfully toward him. I saw that my dad's glass office door was shut, but I didn't trust this rickety old house as an enforcer of privacy, so I motioned for Demitri to follow me out the front door. He nodded and allowed me to exit first, closing the door behind himself with a mighty thud.

I turned toward him then, waiting for him to explain his reason for being here, but he seemed at a loss for words. Head tilted slightly, he looked into my eyes with a more curious look than I'd seen before. Seeing this slight vulnerability in his typically fierce demeanor, I jumped at the chance to confront him. "What do you want, Demitri? You've made it pretty clear these past couple of days that you don't want anything to do with me."

He scoffed and rolled his eyes then; his normal attitude had returned quickly. "You have no clue what you're talking about, Summer. You don't know me."

"And I'm not particularly interested in that either. I don't need one more reason for the people here to be wary of me."

He seemed genuinely taken aback at this. "What do you mean, people are wary of you?"

"Oh, please." I laughed, sitting down on the front step. Demitri following my lead. "Don't tell me you haven't heard all the Devil house stories." He smirked a bit and nodded. "Yes, but I didn't pay attention. The things they say about us are worse – it's always been that way. You just have to let it roll right off you."

I nodded. "I do. They haven't bothered me since the first day. I've been more bothered by the way Charlotte has acted. Honestly, the way you've treated me hasn't sat right with me either." He sighed, picking at a rip on the knee of his jeans, silent for a few moments while I stared at his troubled expression.

"Do you want to get dinner with me?" he asked suddenly, dark eyes on mine.

"Oh," I exclaimed with surprise, "I, uh, already ate…"

"That's okay," he said quickly, standing. "Maybe some other time." He began walking down the grass, striding around the corner to his side of the street.

I watched him for a moment; my heart beating fast as I was instantly filled with regret. In a spur-of-the-moment decision, I stood and raced across the yard, yelling, "Wait!" I reached him and grabbed his hand, quickly letting go as he spun around like he'd touched a plague victim. "I'll go with you," I said. My head was pounding with worry and regret that I'd just reached out for him like that. He just nodded, though, as I told him I needed to tell my parents that I was going out.

After I ran into my dad's office to give him the news, I walked back out the door and met Demitri at the edge of the driveway. "Do you have a car?" I asked him, disappointed slightly as he shook his head.

"Well," I said, looking at the clear sunset-filled sky, "at least the weather's nice." He chuckled, smiling down at me as we fell into step down the gravel road, two lone figures between the trees on our way into town.

We stayed silent for most of the journey to the restaurant, but when our hands brushed every once in a while, I felt a jolt go up and down my arm, almost as if the electricity between us was truly palpable. "Have you tried Hal's yet?" he asked as the buildings in town came into view.

"No," I said, knowing from driving by it every day this week that he was referring to Hal's Diner. It was named after my new friend, Haley, and run by her parents.

"I like that place, and it has very good milkshakes if you don't want to have a second dinner." I agreed that the diner was a nice choice, and the rest of the walk was peaceful as we passed the city hall, and one of the churches. The church bells tolled signaling it was now seven, and the sun was still setting behind the sleepy town. As we reached Hal's, Demitri opened the door for me; we stepped into the bustle and spritely music of the restaurant.

A blonde woman with cropped hair walked energetically around the small room, picking up empty plates and smiling at the customers. "Hello, kids!" she exclaimed as she saw us enter, "go ahead and take any empty table, and I'll bring some menus in a moment." I smiled and thanked her, turning to Demitri to see if he had any preference on our table. He nodded toward one in the corner; his hand hovering at the small of my back, sending shivers up my spine as I let him lead me to the booth.

We sat down across from each other, and the small woman came by with menus and two complimentary bottles of old-fashioned Coca-Cola. After glancing over the menu, we ordered – a chocolate shake for me and a cheeseburger for Demitri. Our food came out from the kitchen quickly, and we both sat there silently eating.

After a few moments, my curiosity got the best of me, and I began to monologue my thoughts aloud, much to Demitri's entertainment. "You couldn't have possibly come to my house just to take me to dinner, especially after you've been so stand-offish with me all day today at school. There must be something you want to talk about, and it's been worrying me ever since you showed up at my door. It's not just that bothering me—I know that something happened on Monday after school. I know you were in my room, and that you worked on that project with me, and that we—uh—kissed…" I paused because, at this point, Demitri was laughing at me as he chewed on his bite of burger.

I kicked his shin under the table, giggling back but saying, "I'm serious! I heard you and Charlotte talking about it on the street that night."

His smile fell at that point, a more frustrated expression clouding his face as he muttered, "I don't know what you're talking about."

I laughed sarcastically. "I know I'm not imagining this. I know what I saw!" I crossed my arms, leaning back to emphasize my point. "I know that something happened on Monday after school." He chewed his food slowly now, and I could almost see the wheels turning in his mind as he searched for an excuse.

"Do you have a boyfriend back home?" he asked after a moment of his pondering.

I scoffed, rolling my eyes. "Way to change the subject, Demitri."

"No, I'm serious—" he laughed—"I'm just trying to get to know you better." I nodded then, recognizing that he didn't deny my statement.

After he stared at me a moment, I sighed and shook my head before admitting, "No, I never got around to that."

"Really? Why is that?" He stopped eating now, focusing solely on me as I shrugged and tried to look anywhere but directly into his eyes.

"I don't know, I think I was always just waiting for something. My dad owned a bookstore," I explained, "so growing up, I read all sorts of stories about love and iconic literary relationships. I've gone through my entire life wanting something like that—something with passion, something that would change my whole life."

"So, what? Did you never find it?"

"Not yet, but I think I will"—I smiled—"I just have very high standards, that's all."

He laughed. "Yeah, you want some guy to just step right out of a book!"

"No, it's not that! I want my own version of a romance. Besides, is it wrong to expect love to come with some sort of—um—how do I phrase this?"

"Magic?" Demitri offered, smirking. I knew then that we were both thinking of the events of Monday, even if we weren't directly addressing the topic. "Exactly."

After we finished our little meal and paid the friendly hostess, we left Hal's to find darkness aside from the faint streetlights dotting the town. Demitri extended his elbow politely, and I linked my arm through his as we walked home.

"We should be friends," I said, "and not just behind the backs of everyone at school and everyone on the street." I looked up to his face to see his reaction, which seemed almost pained.

"Look, Summer. I'm sorry about how I've acted toward you lately, but I don't know how else to make our friendship work. We're from two completely different worlds, and trying to force everyone to see us in a certain way wouldn't be good for either of us."

"But, Demitri, you said it yourself! Maybe we're not as different as we seem…"

"Whatever you heard the other night, or whatever you thought you heard, you need to just forget about it. There's a line that shouldn't be crossed here, Summer." I sighed with frustration, yielding my argument and looking straight ahead, falling back into step as we silently inched closer and closer to Lightenborough Drive.

Demitri walked me to my door and we separated our arms from one another, pausing to look at one another in the house's dim exterior lighting. "Well, this was nice," he said, mouth turning up at the corners. I nodded, tucking a strand of hair behind my ear as the wind blew gently. I didn't know what to say to him. One second, it seemed like there was a tangible friendship between us. The next moment, Demitri North was distant and cold toward me. I was trying to keep my distance and not allow the sudden shifts in his behavior to bother me.

As I looked down to fiddle with the key, Demitri bent down and kissed me warmly on the cheek, letting his lips linger there for a few moments before stepping back and turning into the dark of the night, disappearing into the black as he turned to go to his own house.

I smiled to myself, letting my hand skim my cheek before shaking myself back to reality and unlocking the door. I walked in a daydream state to my mom's loft, hoping I'd stop blushing by the time I got there.

"Hey, sunshine," Mom said as I opened the door, smiling at me as she got more paint from a bottle on a shelf. "How was your time with your friend?"

"It was… good," I said casually, not wanting to reveal anything to her about the range of emotions I'd experienced just from the walk home. I regretted not bringing up any of the mysteries I kept replaying in my mind, but I certainly wasn't going to let my mom in on any of that.

My mom walked over to give me a loving hug before returning to her easel and changing to a new conversation. "So, remember at dinner how I was talking about enrolling in the art auction at town hall this weekend?" My mom smiled at me with complete glee as I moved to sit on the cozy chair near the window.

"Yeah, Mom, that's awesome," I said, "which painting were you wanting to auction off?"

My mom had a smug look on her face and she said, "Well, it's a new one. I don't think you've seen it yet." My mom stopped me from looking around the room to get a glimpse of her newest painting, instead, telling me to stay put and close my eyes.

I heard her stand as nimbly as she could, open the room's closet door and rummage through the propped-up stack of paintings. "Mom, I'm getting impatient!" I laughed as she hummed to herself. She clicked her tongue and said, "I've just about… found it! Okay, eyes closed! Give me a moment." I heard her padding back across the carpet before finally stopping in front of me and giving me the go-ahead to open my eyes.

My heartbeat seemed to temporarily falter out of shock. It was a painting of me. Of course, my mom had painted me before, but I didn't ever think of those canvases as anything more than documentation of me at a certain age.

This painting, though, showed me in a whole new light. There wasn't anything specific that made me seem so oddly beautiful; it was just as if my entire self—my face, my hair, my eyes, and all the rest of me—were glowing. I told my mom that it was amazing and I was honored to be the subject of, what I believed to be her best work.

Once the feeling of awe had passed, though, a sense of dread came over me. I was embarrassed at the thought of my face possibly hanging on someone's wall. I'd rather it just be a family item, but at the suggestion of this, my mother frowned, saying that I should be flattered and optimistic that someone may pay good money for this.

When my mom saw my concern, she claimed that this wasn't even an exact painting of me, and it was meant more to represent the "female spirit." All I could do was smile, nod, and sulk to my room for the night. *Oh well,* I thought to myself, cringing at the thought of the painting being up for auction. I hoped no one from my school would attend, or—God forbid—have that painting end up in their house.

The stars had appeared in full force by the time I made my trek up to my room, and I was already debating which part of the wall I should read before I would go to sleep. Part of me wished I had discussed the wall with Demitri at the diner, but I felt that whatever friendship was forming needed to be built on trust before I began confronting him about his contribution to the art in the room.

I ducked my head and hoisted myself through the window, shutting it behind me and turning on the low lamplight. The sight before me completely took my breath away. A sense of horror washed over me as I saw a coat of dark green paint covering up the beautiful paintings and words etched onto the walls.

"No, no, no!" I cried out, turning to the nearest wall and practically clawing at it, but finding the paint to be completely dry. The only things left from my once-magical room were the constellations on the ceiling. I noticed a tear slip down my cheek—I felt so defeated.

Am I losing my mind? I wondered. I could've sworn that the swirls on the wall were there that very morning. In my heart, I truly believed the visions, the strange encounter with Demitri, and my sudden discovery of a completely hidden world had occurred. Demitri didn't exactly confirm all of this when I mentioned it in Hal's Diner, but he certainly hadn't denied it! I sat on the edge of my bed, wondering if the events of this evening had even happened. *Maybe this move has finally driven me insane. Have all of the mysteries been in my head?* I thought of my letter to Al, wishing suddenly that I hadn't have been so honest about the magic that I thought to be true when in all likelihood, it wasn't.

No, I decided stubbornly at that moment. I needed to trust my instincts, and I couldn't just let this go. I knew that no matter how enigmatic it all seemed, there was something unfathomable hidden within the history of this street, and I was going to find out what. I shut my light off and paced my room, beginning to contemplate what I was going to do the next day.

I decided that after school, I was going to go down the street to Charlotte's house, and I was going to tell her that I had a fairly confident idea of what was going on there. I was going to confront her about her secret and get some answers, whether she wanted to give them to me or not. If Demitri wanted to throw a wall up between us during any sort of honest conversation, I'd have to take advantage of Charlotte's naturally friendly demeanor. I needed answers, and after seeing the sudden change to my room, I was more determined than ever to get them.

Thursday afternoon, my mom and dad decided it was perfect weather to go for an evening picnic and hike in the mountains. To get out of this, and get some snooping done on the street, I assured them that while I wanted nothing more than to go on the hike, but, seeing as I had a lot of homework, I intended on doing a bunch of school tasks and going to sleep early.

The next afternoon, I watched as my parents began their leisurely drive down the block, turning down the side street that led directly out to the mountain. When they were out of my view, I raced back up to my room to get dressed and form a plan.

It was, in fact, a nice day outside, so I settled for a tank top and some old ripped jeans. I braided my hair down my back and as I looked in my mirror, I felt that I looked like someone who meant business.

I went to the window, peering onto the street that was beginning to illuminate as the sun slunk up and over the roof of my house. The street had a twinkling quality to it from the sun; the way the light hit the treetops created an enchanted quality.

I noticed something aside from the beauty of Lightenborough Drive, though. There was movement visible in each of the windows, now that I was watching them in direct light. My plan was already unfolding, as step one was to ensure that everyone who lived on the street was home.

The next step in my plan was to walk down to Charlotte's house, and, if I was let in to speak with her, I'd then expose to her that I'd caught onto the secret of her, Demitri, and the rest of the street, and I wanted her to prove my assumptions correct.

I felt reckless and daring as I headed down the stairs, boldly marching across the back lawn and pushing aside the warning sign hung to the fence. I strode down the street, eyes set on the yellow house at the end of it, not sparing a glance at any house aside from it.

When I got to the house, I climbed up the porch steps with assurance and tapped my knuckles against the peeling white paint on the door. I counted about ten seconds before knocking again, beginning to feel some doubt in the sanity of my plan now.

What am I going to say? Why did I not think this through more? Anxious feelings began to course through my veins about my true preparedness for this task, but before my doubts could fully convince me to retreat, the door opened quickly.

A girl was there, a young woman. She seemed only a year or two older than me. I recognized her from my vision as Anastrella, but this Anastrella was more beautiful and brighter than the tired, weakened woman I remembered from the grand chamber of the castle where she'd been exiled.

She wore a bright blue top with white capri pants, and her vivid blonde hair was twisted atop her head. The lines that had once creased her face had no mark on her now, and I felt taken aback by the observation that time did not affect her whatsoever. *Well, this certainly proves she's immortal,* I thought to myself, trying to maintain my composure.

Her eyes seemed to widen with shock upon seeing me at the door, but she quickly smoothed her surprise into a kind smile. "Well, hello there. Are you lost?" I smiled back, realizing they must have not had any visitors down this street, what with the Devil House accusations and all.

"No, I live at that house at the end of the street." I pointed to Devil House and at this, she nodded and smiled with a bit more tension.

"Ah, I see. Are you a friend of Charlotte's?"

I smiled and told her that I was, following with, "Are you her sister?" I wanted to throw her off-guard, and see if she'd tell me the truth or not, but after a thought seemed to pass through her mind, she nodded vigorously, assuring me that she was Charlotte's sister. She then told me that her name was, in fact, Anastrella. *Well, at least she told me the truth about one thing.*

Anastrella invited me in, an offer I had not expected, and said that Charlotte was just making some breakfast for lunch for the two of them. I followed her into the house, letting out a gasp at what I saw; the inside of the house did not reflect the lack of care put into the outside.

The living room came directly off the entryway, and it was filled with bright blue couches, a glass coffee table, and a white ceiling fan. This room was connected to the kitchen, which smelled of sweet waffles and had very nice appliances. Charlotte stood by the stove, wearing the soft pink sundress she'd worn to school. She turned with a surprised gasp, and nearly dropped the spatula she was using to fry up some bacon next to the waffle maker.

Charlotte had a natural glow to her, even without makeup on, and her skin seemed to glisten with the sunlight coming in from the window behind her table.

"So, you found me, huh?" She laughed, turning from me to the food again.

"Yeah, I did! My parents went up to the mountains for a hike and picnic, so I figured I'd check out the rest of the street!"

She murmured a drawn-out and sarcastic "Oh, lovely!" Her statement was dripping in so much sweetness, that it seemed very forced, but she resumed her hospitality by offering me a waffle, which I simply couldn't refuse, even if she was hinting that she was not pleased with my visit.

I sat down at the table with Charlotte and Anastrella, answering questions about my childhood in Florida and my parents, not giving away too much detail so as not to accidentally let anything slip about my true motivation for being there.

The conversation was pleasant, and the breakfast was extraordinarily tasty, but as soon as we were done with the food, I made sure to ask Charlotte if I could talk to her about some 'school stuff.'

"Uh, yeah," she responded before turning to Anastrella, "we'll be on the back porch, um, sis." She smiled briefly at her 'sister' and led me out the back door, sitting down on the white porch swing.

"So, what's up? Are you okay?" She looked genuinely concerned as she studied my face, and I smiled, realizing this was the Charlotte Skies I knew. The tension with Demitri had gotten her caught up in a brief spell of awkwardness with me, and it comforted me to see that when it came down to it, she still cared about me.

I took a deep breath, wondering if she'd dare to maintain our friendship once I revealed my new knowledge. I stuttered a bit before realizing that I should start with a casual conversation in an attempt to catch her by surprise by turning the job of revealing the secret to her.

"Well," I started, "I've just had some concern with my parents adjusting to the town. When you and your mom moved here, did you feel like that?"

She smiled and responded, "My mom and I have lived here a very long time, and it's always been just us, and…" She trailed off, eyes opening wide as she noted the smile unfolding on my face. She'd admitted that Anastrella was her mom, and there was no backing out of that now.

I got her.

Still, she tried to cover her tracks. "Um, did I say mom? I meant sister. Yep, I can say some crazy things sometimes." She laughed shakily but I gave her a stern look.

"Charlotte, don't play dumb. I know your secret. I know about the fairies and the warlocks. I know about the exile and the warefae." I scoffed, "I'm not saying I'm believing it easily, but I'm acknowledging its existence."

Charlotte sat back with a great exhale, shutting her eyes tightly. We sat there in silence like that for a good two to three minutes, just listening to the wind rustle the trees in Charlotte's yard. Finally, Charlotte opened one eye, peering into my face.

"Well, crap. I was hoping I'd imagined that." I smiled at her with pity. As hard as it was for me to figure out how to approach her with this, being caught completely out of the blue by these accusations could not have been easy. "I'm sorry, Charlotte, but I had to tell you what I've seen and heard. I had to know if it was true or not."

Charlotte nodded slowly, narrowing her eyebrows and asking in the most serious tone I'd ever heard her use, "You swear that you won't tell a soul? Swear on your own life?" I nodded urgently.

Even if I were tempted to tell anyone about this, no one would believe me, and the rumors of Devil House only being home to freaks would be validated. Plus, I cared about Charlotte, and I didn't want her or anyone else here to have to suffer because of my random discovery.

Charlotte sighed with relief at my promise before finally acknowledging that if it was the writing on the wall I learned from then yes, it was true. I whooped with joy, so happy to have my sanity confirmed, sparking a twinkling laugh from Charlotte. "But wait, is all of it true? All of the visions and the writing?"

Charlotte nodded. "Yep, every word!"

I frowned then, realizing, "So you all are really in exile? That's terrible!"

Charlotte shrugged. "It's what I've always known. I've been here since I was young—as long as I can remember."

"Wait," I said suddenly, tensing up a bit, "you say you've been here since you were young?"

She nodded slowly, biting her lip as if she could read my question off of my face. "I was born in 1890. Demitri was born in 1886, and Analise and Lydia were both born in 1887." I felt my breathing go shallow, before I regained my composure, realizing I'd already expected this based on the wall and the knowledge of Anastrella's immortality.

"Okay. That's okay," I said, nodding.

She looked at me cautiously. "Are you sure? You're not going to freak out on me?" I nodded, patting her hand on the swing next to me. I thought of our previous conversation, and my heart tightened once more.

"What about the exile, though? Nothing can be done about this?" I whispered.

Charlotte shook her head at me, a sad-looking crossing her eyes. We sat there in silence for a moment, before she took a deep breath and said, "Well, I know Demitri will be interested to hear about this. Come on…"

She made to grab my wrist and pull me up, but I quickly pulled away with an insistent, "No, Charlotte, not him!" I had planned to confront him before, but by that point, I no longer wanted to speak to him.

Charlotte raised an eyebrow at me and said, "Oh come on, Summer. Don't be a baby!"

"Charlotte, I heard him tell you about the kiss. It means nothing to him. And that's embarrassing enough already—I mean, who kisses someone they don't even know?"

She rolled her eyes. "I promise, Summer, his reaction proves he's only trying to save face because he's embarrassed too. And you know the solution to this, don't you?" I shook my head slowly, confused. She smirked and said, "Act like it meant nothing to you either." She turned from me then to walk in the house saying in a singsong voice, "I'll be in here when you're ready!"

I sat in silence for a moment more, mentally preparing myself for what I was about to get myself into, before realizing that Charlotte was right. I didn't need to feel any shame over what happened; *he kissed me!* It wasn't the other way around.

I felt a newfound determination at that moment, just as I had felt before making up my mind that I was going to speak with Charlotte and confirm what I'd learned a little while before. Besides, maybe Charlotte was right; maybe

Demitri's moodiness was a cover for how much he did care. Regardless of his opinion or attitude, I stood from the swing and walked with the purpose to confront another of the warefae with my knowledge.

When I walked in through the backdoor, Charlotte was standing with her elbows on the kitchen counter, pointing to me to go into the living room, where Anastrella was sitting on the couch, hands folded in her lap, looking directly at me.

Uh oh. I guessed that Charlotte had told Anastrella that I had discovered their secret. That meant I had been the first outsider in eighteen years to know, and the first human, too. I had been scared of Demitri finding out that I knew, but the thought of the mothers knowing after they'd protected their children for nearly a century frightened the hell out of me.

"Summer, please join me, dear." Anastrella motioned for me to sit next to her on the couch. And after muttering a *yes ma'am* and glancing at Charlotte, who seemed completely unconcerned as she gave me an encouraging thumbs-up, sat down on the couch.

She stared at me much like Charlotte did, the same blue eyes that seemed to see right into my soul. I felt like she was so much older than I was now, from her mannerisms to the way she sat so still.

After a moment of peering into my face, Anastrella said simply, "So, I hear that you have heard a couple of stories about this place that you wanted to ask me about?" I looked over my shoulder glaringly at Charlotte who chuckled silently with an apologetic look. Looking back at

Anastrella, I figured that this might be a good time to ask some of the questions that had been nagging at me since I'd begun to learn all of this on my first night in Weston.

"Um, yes," I began slowly, "so you're Anastrella of the Skies? A star fairy?"

She smiled softly now and nodded. "I am. I used to be able to do much more with the constellations and such. Now, if I influence the night at all, it's only ever parts of the sky that are prominent in this area."

Her face fell when she talked about this part, and her melancholy thoughts exposed me to the same face from that fateful day with Lorena I'd seen in the vision. I thought for a moment with wonder that this same woman was one that the town was utterly afraid of, and believed to be as cruel as the devil.

"I'm sorry," I whispered, placing a hand on hers to comfort her, "I'm sorry about the stupid rules, and Lorena, and the exile, and Quinton, and…" I allowed my voice to trail off, feeling like there was so much left to mourn for in her situation, but not quite finding the words to say it.

Anastrella squeezed my hand back. "You know, in all my years, I don't think I've ever met a human as kind as you. I think I should tell you though, I've made my peace with it all after all these years."

"But it's not fair!" I interrupted, "I mean, what about Quinton? What about any of the warlocks? Have they ever come back to you all?" Anastrella shook her head slowly, whispering, "I haven't seen Quinton since the day we were exiled."

She sat there for a moment, before shaking her head as if to clear it and saying, "But, I'd like to think he's still out there, waiting for me to be free." She smiled softly. "Is there anything else you'd like to know right now, Summer?"

I thought about the vast openness to the question, before saying at last, "I'd like to know about why the town thinks my house is Devil House."

After a brief pause, Anastrella and Charlotte both turned to each other and laughed.

"What's so funny?" I asked, thinking how far from comical my treatment had been on the first day of school because of this story.

"We're sorry, Summer," Charlotte said, moving to sit on the other chair in the living room, "It's just that this story has been a hot topic of the town for a lot of years." I nodded, urging them to go on, and Anastrella began the retelling of the story, the true side of the story.

"Charles McDevell was a selfish man, and he wanted all of us to flock to him as soon as he moved into the house he built. This was only a year or two after we'd been exiled and hid here. We all ignored him for a while, of course, but one night, he tried to sneak out into our council meeting." I nodded, eyes wide and eager.

"When he approached us, he felt this was the perfect opportunity to get us all to invest in the bank. As I said before, he wanted to take us in, almost as his own. We thought it was comical, and we wanted him to quickly leave us alone, but McDevell was embarrassed. He'd never been rejected by anyone in the town thus far.

"That's why he went into the town that night. He claimed we'd been witches as if trying to turn our town into Salem. The townspeople came skeptically at first, but when we realized they were there, we felt some fear upon seeing their pitchforks and torches.

"What we didn't know also," Anastrella said, looking pointedly at Charlotte now, whose shoulders shook with silent laughter, "was that our children were behind us, hidden in the trees."

"I'm sorry!" Charlotte exclaimed, laughing out loud now.

I looked between the two, confusion filling me up, before Anastrella quickly shushed her daughter, a smile playing on her face. "The warefae were younger at the time, and still in training. Something they had learned already, though, was how to perform a warlock shield spell.

From where they flew above us, they cast the spell, invisible to all except us, who could see the shimmer of magic. When McDevell ran at us, he rebounded backward, off the force field. The townspeople panicked, and a mass exodus from the street commenced.

When McDevell was left there alone, one of the warefae—"

"Demitri," Charlotte cut in, looking to me with a wink, "he's always the most hot-tempered of us all." Anastrella waved at her daughter to let her finish the tale again, and when she continued, she said, "Well, Demitri, then. He cast a line of dark magic, sending it to McDevell making him retreat into his home. We reprimanded him for that, of course, but he was in his moody-teenager phase at the time; he didn't exactly want to listen to us." She smiled fondly, shrugging off the motherly affection and focusing.

"For weeks after, we couldn't go to the market in town without getting spat upon or yelled at, so we stopped going during the day, and began sneaking in at night, always paying for what we took, of course. McDevell was terrified of us. He had the fence built, and when he couldn't get any sort of apology or explanation from us, he left the town altogether."

"Wow." I breathed, thinking of how different the truth was from what I'd heard. "What about after he left? Why could no one come in the house but the realtor?"

She chuckled, shaking her head. "That certainly wasn't the case. Anyone could get in the house, but no one wanted to. Besides, once Demitri started living there in the early '40s, the story came back into harsh light, and people began to believe we were still here."

The thought of Demitri living in my room made my heart beat a bit faster, but I knew I had to respond somehow without giving away my reaction to that bit of information. "Well…you were still here," I said bluntly after quite a moment's silence, bringing about laughter from the other two.

"Wait, I still have one question," I said, trying to bring them back to the story once more. "Why is it called Devil House? Even if he thought you were witches, that doesn't have anything to do with the Devil."

Charlotte answered this one eagerly, "It's a play on words. McDevell's house became Devell's house, and as time went on, that just became Devil House." I nodded, it all seemed so clear now.

Before I could thank Anastrella for telling me the story, Charlotte cut in. "Mom, we're going to go see Demitri now. I think he'd be so interested to know that this little detective has found us out," she said, smiling sweetly at me. I blushed and laughed awkwardly, looking at Anastrella's beaming face.

"Go on, now, you two. But be careful. I fear that if the other three fairies found out that a human has learned our secret, their reactions would be quite a bit more exaggerated than mine."

With Anastrella's warning in mind, Charlotte and I dashed out of the house, Charlotte practically mocking my stress, and me whispering with relief about Anastrella's kind nature.

I followed Charlotte back down the street toward Demitri's house, and she waltzed up the steps to the cracked open door. I made to follow her, but as I lifted my foot to climb the porch steps, she turned quickly and threw navy blue sparks from her fingertips. I felt a tingle go through my ankle, and I looked down to see that Charlotte's sparks held my foot, frozen in midair.

I looked up at her with confusion and a bit of shock, but she simply shook her head and motioned for me to walk back by the fence. She moved her hand again and my foot was free to step back, away from the porch stairs, and I quickly moved to stand by my fence.

I watched as Charlotte pushed the door open quietly; tip-toeing into the house and barely whispering Demitri's name. She disappeared inside for a moment, and the next second she was walking back outside with Demitri in her tracks.

"What's this about, Charlotte?" he asked quietly, almost closing the door behind him. Charlotte nodded over at me and said, "You were right; she knows about us." Demitri stopped walking, catching my eyes briefly. I kept my eyes cold, not revealing anything, and crossing my arms, still bitter that he'd said we shouldn't be friends.

"Okay, you two, enough with this. Move on." Charlotte rolled her eyes, walking past me and ducking under the warning sign in the fence. I turned quickly and followed her, letting the sign fall behind me, leaving Demitri chuckling coldly as he moved it behind me.

"You remember how to get to my room, right? It's right up the stairs and out the door..."

"Oh, honey, you know about us now. There's no reason for that." She laughed, looking up at the window, bending her knees slightly, and letting her wings unfurl to help her glide through the air, landing softly on the balcony.

I felt my mouth fall open as I admired her wings; the beautiful wisps curving from her shoulders were almost in a butterfly shape, but more elongated and elegant. Her wings were navy blue, like the sparks that she used to stop the air around my ankle from letting me move, and on these wings, there were golden patches that looked like twinkling stars that Anastrella would paint through a night sky.

There was something else, though, I noticed as I squinted up at her wings on my balcony. There were parts, almost slashes, of gray through her wings. It tarnished the beauty that was there, but it also added some mystery to their dazzling effect.

I was caught off guard amid my admiration of Charlotte's wings by a pair of firm hands grasping my upper arms. "Hey!" I exclaimed in protest, trying to turn my head to be met by the shushing of Demitri.

"Calm down," he muttered against my hair, "this is just the fastest way to get you up there."

I let out a shriek as I found myself suddenly floating off of the ground. Panicked, I kicked my legs in a bicycle fashion, accidentally jamming my heel into Demitri's shin, causing him to yell out a curse word that would make one forget that he was part fairy.

Charlotte laughed at me as Demitri raised me to her, and she exclaimed, "Don't be scared, Summer, he's not going to drop you." We flew over the railing and my feet firmly landed on the balcony. Demitri released my arms, chuckling as he backed up, and I turned to face them stiffly, my arms straight with tension and practically stuck to my sides.

I let out a drawn-out exhale, trying to relax, looking now at Demitri's wings, which were more jagged on the edges than Charlotte's. Demitri's wings were black, and I remembered now that this must be because his mother, Genesis, was a shadow fairy. His wings also had gray slashes within them and a hint of silver that was so slight; one could have mistaken it for a reflection of light off of them.

"Are you done gawking?" Charlotte giggled, and I nodded, muttering a quick apology as the two rolled their shoulders backward, which caused their wings to curl in upon themselves and rest back in what I assumed to be an area deep to their shoulder blades.

Charlotte ducked through the window, and Demitri made to follow her but I caught his arm first. "Hey, sorry I kicked you. I just got a little freaked out."

He smiled at me for the first time since a week ago and said, "Don't worry about it, kid." I smiled back, noting silently that a couple of months ago, I would find the concept of being *flown up to my balcony* to be completely insane.

"So," I began, sitting on the edge of my bed with Charlotte, as Demitri opted for the desk chair, "you both know that I know everything, so I guess I have no hesitation in asking what happened to my walls?"

I looked pointedly at Demitri with this one, and I assumed my accusing look is what evicted a sheepish one from him. "Yeah, sorry about that. I guess I thought I'd rather be safe than sorry, and stop you from learning anything else about us. We're still not supposed to be talking to you about this." He looked deliberately at Charlotte as he said that part, and she waved her hand lazily away as if to say that it was no big deal.

"Ahem." I caught his attention again. "I'd like my room back to how it was when I got here." I narrowed my eyes until he let out a defeated sigh and consented to fix it.

Demitri closed his eyes and muttered what seemed to be a sort of enchantment. He waved his hand, and the all-green paint on the wall faded away, revealing the beautiful scrolled writing, swirls, and symbols painted. I felt myself grinning ear to ear, and both Charlotte and Demitri's eyes were on me as I gazed my way around my room, feeling my sense of comfort had been returned.

"Wait, how is it you found out about us? Everything on this wall is written in Faire, which is only supposed to be understood by those of fairy descent." Demitri leaned forward in the chair, staring at me intently. I was at a loss for words, remembering the conversation I'd overheard between the two of them.

Charlotte coaxed, "You were adopted, right? You could have fairy blood somewhere in your family."

I nodded. "I mean, it could be possible. But I think I'm a human. I don't have wings or anything, like you guys do. I've tried to find my birth mother before but I've never…" my voice trailed off, and the two warefae flashed concerned looks at each other. I didn't want their pity, but I did begin to feel rising insecurity at my lack of certainty about my past.

"Never mind that, Demitri. It doesn't matter how she found out. She did, and now, here we are," Charlotte said as she flashed a quick smile my way. "If she's part fairy it's probably a part hidden very deep within. Anyway, you must have a lot of questions. Anything you want to ask us?"

I felt as overwhelmed as I had when Anastrella asked me this, not even knowing where to start. Thinking back to moments before, when I stared up at the balcony, I blurted out suddenly, "Your wings. Tell me about your wings."

"Well," Charlotte began, "a fairy's wings represent the purpose that they're given at birth. Typically, it's that of their parents, but every once in a while, the Faire Tree releases a burst of magic, and another type of fairy will be born, beginning a new family line.

"My mother's wings are navy and gold, like mine. Demitri's mom, Genesis, has black wings because she's a dark fairy, and she passed those onto him. Of course, all of our wings—the warefae I mean—are a bit gray, because the blood of a warlock tarnishes the pure fairy blood."

I processed this for a moment and then asked about the wings of our other neighbors, Lydia and Analise. Upon hearing their names, Charlotte and Demitri exchanged an almost comedic glance between themselves. I had to clear my throat to regain their attention, at which time, Demitri finally said, "You may remember that Lydia's mom, Katia, is a snow fairy, and Analise's mom, Vivyanna, is a marsh fairy." I nodded, and he continued, "Well, they have white wings and copper wings, respectively."

"Are you all friends with one another?" I asked, trying to read Demitri's stony gaze.

Charlotte interjected this time, "That is an interesting question."

"We do not necessarily agree with the two of them," Demitri said bluntly.

"But how can that be?" I wondered aloud, "You four have only had each other for a long time."

The two of them sighed now, clearly not wanting to attempt to make me understand their situation before they began. "Fine," I said sulkily, "clearly there's some childhood drama I'm missing out on that neither of you wants to share!"

Charlotte let out a snort and lounged back on my bed. "Absolutely! You're a genius, Summer!" She winked at me, flicking her blonde hair over her shoulder.

Then, Demitri leaned back in my desk chair, saying, "All right, what else do you want to know?"

I pondered everything I'd learned, using the temporary silence to think back to the part of the fairy story written on the wall that had tugged at my heartstrings the most. "Fallon and Peter – what happened to them?" I looked to Charlotte this time, and there was sadness clouding over her eyes, but she kept her silence.

Demitri looked unfeelingly off at the spot on the wall where I'd seen the vision of their deaths. He then turned to look back at me with a point-blank stare. "Fallon came to see us, as you've likely already seen, almost eighteen years ago. She was very kind, and very in love with Peter. She was concerned about her child but was pleased to know that, like Lydia, Analise, Charlotte, and I, the child would grow to an adult state, and then live an immortal life. She knew what she was getting herself into, and I think we all tried to make peace with the notion that she and Peter both died without regrets."

"Maybe she died without regrets, but she could've been spared if she had just been given a chance to live here. Charlotte, you even suggested you all could take the child."

"Yes, Summer, I did, but you have to understand why our mothers had to send her away. At that point, Fallon was being followed, and if we had hidden her here, we would have all been killed for trying to help her. She was a fairy marked for death." I nodded slowly, trying to wrap my mind around it still, but not finding the words. I couldn't comprehend how sending away a pregnant and scared mother, no matter the circumstances, could be excusable.

With a heavy exhale and a greatly strained effort, I tried to change the conversation up a bit, searching for something more comical or light to discuss. The room was in definite need of a tension reliever, and thankfully, the two warefae picked up on that, following my lead into a more relaxed atmosphere.

A little while later, I brought them down to the kitchen to make us an easy frozen pizza for dinner, listening to them talk about what it'd been like to grow up together here. They had a very playfully compassionate relationship, and I felt clear that there was no romance between the two of them.

As the two chatted alone, I spotted a sealed envelope on the edge of the kitchen table. It was addressed to me by Al. I hurriedly moved into the other room and opened it.

Dear Summer,

I haven't gotten a letter from you yet, and it's been two weeks since you left, so I just wanted to check on you. Your dad called me to check in and said you were starting school tomorrow. How are you?

I've been to Weston before, almost eighteen years ago, and I think it's a very nice town. Specifically, on your street, I think there are some kind people there. (Don't ask me how I know them – that story is too long to retell through a letter!)

The store is doing well. You can come to visit and help out anytime you want! I hope to hear from you soon.

Love,
Al

My heartbeat was fast as I read this letter. Al had been here – and close to her accident too. This accident had left her with large scars on her shoulders, and a need to stay hidden. She thought these people were nice, but she couldn't explain to me how she knew them. One thought echoed through my mind – *could Al be a nickname for Fallon?* I raced to my dad's office to grab a paper and began to write.

Al,
I'm receiving your letter before you get my first one, and I hope this letter finds you well.

I have a question – is your real name Fallon? If so, I have heard some stories about you. I don't think I should say what over writing, just in case you don't know, but just as a hint – if you knew someone named Lorena growing up, I'm sorry. If that doesn't make any sense to you, then just ignore that! I miss you and would love to come to visit soon.

Love,
Summer

I sealed the envelope, setting it on my dad's desk, walking slowly back to the kitchen – almost in a daze. "Summer, where've you been? The pizza's ready and you – Summer, what's wrong?" Charlotte asked, rushing over and putting her hand on my arm. Demitri turned in his chair, staring at me with concern.

"I think I know Fallon."

"What?" the pair said in unison. I sat down at the table next to Demitri, and Charlotte brought me over a piece of pizza – I didn't even feel like I could eat it.

"How do you know, Summer?" Demitri said, slowly and calmly.

"I think I've grown up with her since I was a baby. My parents took her in after they adopted me, and she had been in an accident that had left her with two giant scars on her back, up by her shoulders. Demitri and Charlotte eyed each other at this remark – they must've known this would happen when a fairy loses its wings.

"She always told me to call her Al, and my mom told me when I was younger that her real name was something else, but she'd changed it to hide from whoever attacked her – I always assumed it was an ex-boyfriend or someone like that. Al could be a nickname for Fallon."

The two nodded, seeming on the edge of their seats at what information would be enough proof to make them believe for sure. "She wrote me a letter and said that she knew you guys – all of you on this street. She said she visited Weston around the time before she came to Florida. Who else do you know that's ever been here and communicated with everyone on the street?"

"Absolutely no one," Charlotte said right away, "Fallon would be the only one." We sat there in silence as I processed how close I had been to a fairy for my whole life and had not realized it. And if it was true, poor Al—Fallon—for going through all the suffering and loss that she'd gone through. I took a deep breath. "I just wrote a letter to send to her; I'm going to ask her directly for the truth. I need to get an answer, and I want to find out what happened to Peter and her daughter, too, if it is her."

Demitri gave me an odd look at that comment but seemed to shake his head and get whatever thought he had out of his mind. He placed his hand on mine gently, earning a smug and eager look from Charlotte. I looked into his dark eyes, full of sympathy, and he said, "You'll figure it out, Summer. It'll be okay." I smiled softly at him, and we all had some dinner and tried to get back to normal conversation.

The most interesting topic that we revisited was a continuation of the chat in my room. After a bit of encouragement from me, the two began to gossip in a completely unfiltered way about their least favorite neighbors. Even though they had been raised in such proximity, and sat together at lunch every day at school, Charlotte and Demitri had always considered Lydia and Analise to be their adversaries, in a sort of childlike way.

The two had been so silent about the rift between the pairs in my room, but once they had some food in front of them, they seemed to have no boundaries to this topic of discussion. After hearing of the two girls' petty and jealous natures, and their years' worth of attempts at convincing Demitri to marry one of them, I began to develop my sort of defensive resentment toward them.

All too quickly, the sun began to set on our street. We were back upstairs by then, sitting in my room and just talking, at peace with the knowledge that I was a keeper of their secret, and they were keepers of one of my own, as well. They were willing to spend as much time with me as I needed, answering my questions and listening to my curiosities.

Charlotte stood from my bed around nine, to go star painting with Anastrella. I stood too and found myself wrapped in her warm arms. "I'm so glad I don't have to hide from you too," she whispered, before waltzing her way to the window, winking once, and ducking out. I watched through the curtain as she spread her wings and glided through the air, back to her yellow house.

I couldn't help but note the silence in my room, as Demitri and I found ourselves alone. I heard the creak of the chair as he stood and walked toward the window, and I looked away as he made to leave. I heard a hesitant intake of breath as he half-whispered, "For the record, I think the fence should come down, too." I turned then, grinning softly at him, and for a second time that day, he returned the gesture. He slung his other leg through the window, took a few steps, and jumped straight over the balcony.

I drew in a sharp gasp, rushing to the window and half diving through it to stand on the balcony, finding him chuckling on the ground below me, wings closing leisurely. He turned then and strolled back to his house, walking up to his porch steps, turning to raise a hand to me in a gesture of parting. I waved at him, and, shuddering as if he dreaded to do so, he pushed his way into the dark house, not bothering to shut the door behind him.

Chapter Five
The Line Between Friendship and Foolishness

The next day was Friday – I'd made it through the week. It hadn't even been twenty-four hours since I'd spent the evening with Charlotte and Demitri, so I figured I should try to go talk to them during lunch, before Lydia and Analise got to the table, of course. "Hey, guys!" I'd exclaimed brightly as I slid into the seat next to Charlotte.

Her eyes widened with surprise at the sight of me. "Summer, what are you doing?" I was kind of surprised at her reaction. I'd assumed that after all the time we'd spent together the evening before, and all the truth that had been shared between us, sitting down at that table for a moment wouldn't be a problem.

Defensively, I began to say, "I wasn't going to stay here the whole time; I just came to say hi…"

"Summer, it's nothing against you, but you don't want people to know you've been with us outside of school. Look around you," Demitri whispered. I peered over his shoulder and looked out at the whole cafeteria.

He was right. People were glaring over at me, whispering through their wicked smiles and pointing with accusatory fingers. I felt so small at that moment, and I realized that Charlotte, Demitri, and even the other two warefae weren't only exiled from their rightful places of living. They were also facing a different type of exile right here—within the school. It made my heart ache for them, but I didn't have time to dwell on that at the moment.

"Summer, go back to your table with your friends." Charlotte urged.

"Well, you're my friends too!" I stammered, and she smiled sadly at me.

"We are, but you don't want everyone here to know that, honey." I nodded, getting ready to stand when I noticed Demitri's eyes flick above my head, then feeling a long-nailed hand grip my shoulder.

"I'm sorry, are you lost?" a harsh voice growled. I looked up slowly to see Lydia's cold, unnaturally light blue eyes piercing mine. Her white-blonde hair menacingly framed her face.

I stood quickly, moving aside. "Sorry, I was just talking to Charlotte about—um—" I looked at Charlotte, trying to get a hint from her eyes about what to say.

"She was talking to me about our English project!" Charlotte blurted. Analise giggled next to Lydia at my scared silence, and both girls took their normal seats, failing to pay me any more attention.

I looked back to Demitri to try to meet his eyes, but they were downturned as he picked at his sandwich. I exhaled with a huff and spun on my heel to go back to my table, ignoring the vicious stares of my drama-loving classmates.

I tried to play it cool as I took my seat next to Bobby, but my friends were experiencing the same sort of shock as the rest of the cafeteria's occupants. I quickly realized this when Annie exclaimed, "Well, look who made it out of there alive, ladies and gents!" I laughed along with the group, looking back over my shoulder briefly to see Charlotte's eyes were narrowed, and she appeared to be speaking to Lydia through gritted teeth.

I turned back to my table, still hurt from getting sent away from my friends, despite my sympathy for their situation. I said oversensitive, "What's the big deal, guys? I was just talking to Charlotte about that English book project we have due this week."

"That's great, Summer, but no one goes to their table. I don't think I've ever seen anyone walk over to that part of the cafeteria, to be honest with you." Maysie said in a hushed tone of awe.

"It's just very bold of you is all we're saying," Haley added, "plus, you've got Jen all over your case now. Look." She motioned over my shoulder, and I shifted to see Jen beckoning friends over, pointing at me and making dramatic hand gestures. *Oh, please. After everything I'd seen in the past week, a girl like her couldn't scare me.* I rolled my eyes at the mere thought of it.

I urged my friends to let it go, insisting that I hadn't had anything to say to Demitri, Analise, or Lydia during my trip across the cafeteria, but the group still eyed me with skepticism despite my attempts to diffuse the tension. I even caught Annie whisper something to Will, which was then not-so-subtly passed around the table to everyone but me. The remainder of the lunch hour passed at a painfully slow pace, and I barely even noticed when Bobby invited me to tag along to the first football game of the season the next night. I murmured my agreement, distracted and looking over to Demitri, snapping back into the conversation when the group cheered that I'd get into the Weston spirit. "Go Wolves!" Haley exclaimed mockingly, nudging my shoulder.

I laughed lightly – in a forced way. I didn't want to go to a football game, but for my sanity, I needed to keep enough of an image to maintain this friend group and not be alone at lunch. I clearly wouldn't be able to resort to sitting at the table with Lydia and Analise, even if Charlotte and Demitri enjoyed my company. When the bell rang to dismiss us to the next class, I hurried from the cafeteria, ready to be done with this day.

I walked into English class hearing a sudden and confrontational, "You!" I looked over in surprise, and then dread, to see both Jen and Daisy leaning against their desks, arms crossed.

I was not in the mood to deal with this after the lunch hour I'd just been through, so I asked with mock sweetness, "Can I help you, ladies?"

"Yeah," Daisy started, backing off at a harsh look from Jen, who cut her off and blurted out, "Admit it, you worship the devil, don't you?"

I laughed at her bluntness. "Definitely not. Just because I live in a house with some stupid legend attached doesn't mean it's real. Trust me, the house is not haunted." I thought of the magic words on my wall and smiled innocently, trying to diffuse any of their suspicions.

Jen stuttered for a moment, clearly having expected me to admit to being a satanist. "Uh, well, what about your neighbors? I saw you go talk to them," she suddenly argued. A crowd of classmates now gathered to listen, confirming that though they'd gotten to know me through the previous week, they still doubted, and they still clung to this elementary gossip.

I looked around, glancing over the heads of the crowd to Charlotte at the back of the room. She gave me a little wink as if to nudge me toward the right thing to say, which I still didn't quite know. Jen cleared her throat, staring at me with interrogating eyes, and I took a deep breath before responding:

"Look, Jen, I'm sure you've heard the story of Devil House. There is a fence blocking my house from my neighbors, so I haven't gone back there. I don't even know any of them aside from Charlotte, whom I don't even know that well! I only went to talk to Charlotte at lunch today because we are working on the project for this class together."

All eyes shot back to Charlotte, who nodded sweetly and said brightly, "That's true!" I was glad she hadn't taken anything I said too seriously, expecting she was all too used to this treatment from her peers – well, peers in the sense that she at least looked eighteen years old, and not one hundred and ten, as she was.

Jen looked back at me slowly, and then asked suspiciously, "Well, why haven't you been to church on Sunday?" I let out a relieved breath at this question because this had an answer that I didn't have to lie about.

"Well, my dad works on Sundays at the library, which is open every day of the week but Saturday. Aside from that, my mother is Catholic and doesn't want to go to a Baptist church, so she just reads her bible every day, most of the time with me," I paused, watching Jen digest this information. "She paints a lot of religious art, I promise," I added on as an awkward side note. Jen looked me in the eyes and then, standing up straight; she took two steps toward me, Daisy following her lead timidly.

I braced for Jen to spit some more insults at me, but instead, she stuck her hand out for me to shake. "Welcome to Weston, Summer York." Jen smiled tightly, turning to sit down. I nodded back at her almost appreciatively, quickly getting to my seat as the bell rang, and our teacher entered.

"Wow, look at you go, girl!" Charlotte whispered to me, low-fiving me below the table. I grinned sheepishly at her, but it faded quickly as I made to apologize for having to lie about her, and the whole street. She waved her hand dismissively, pushing my shoulder playfully as if to tell me not to worry about it. I nodded hesitantly, looking to the front of the class as the lecture began.

It was strange to think that after only a week, the Devil House scandal that I'd seemed to be wrapped in had now become an invalid topic at the school. By no means was this a bad thing, but it was strange to think that only five days into my classes, I had hardly a reason to stress!

The only true problem I found myself having was that I had to pretend to not be friends with Charlotte and Demitri at school to sustain this amicable status with classmates such as Jen and Daisy. I hoped that as time went on, I could work to help my classmates see that branching out a bit more to my neighbors wouldn't be scary.

I went home after school, and, after talking a bit with my parents about their hike from the night before, I went through fence and marched my way over to Charlotte's house.

Anastrella answered the door, this time looking around outside as if surveying for anyone watching us. When she'd confirmed my isolation out on the street, she let me in and directed me toward the back patio, where Charlotte was sitting on the porch swing, shooting little navy sparks from her fingertips to make glistening designs that hung in midair in front of her. I pushed open the patio door, silently taking a seat next to her and admiring her magical proficiency.

Demitri came over a little after I'd arrived, and it was then, when both of them were there, that I decided to speak with them about the lunch fiasco. "Okay, what happened out there today?" I asked, looking between the two of them.

"Summer, look. We've lived here our whole lives, but we've only been able to go to school in this town for the past two years. As you can probably guess, if you don't age after getting to eighteen, you can't exactly enroll in kindergarten and go all the way through," Demitri said.

"What's your point?" I asked, "how does that have to do with me not being able to talk to you at lunch?"

"Summer, he's saying that the stories of Devil House, the evil women, whatever they like to call it now, are stories that all these kids have grown up believing, and now, unless you want to face the wrath of Jen and her sidekicks, you have to avoid us during lunch hour so that you aren't associated with any of that offensive gossip." I sighed reluctantly. I didn't like this explanation, but it made sense.

"You know, Charlotte, when your mom told me the real Devil House story, there was one piece of it that I couldn't quite understand."

"What's that, Summer?" she asked, kicking off from the ground so the swing rocked back and forth a bit.

I looked to Demitri now, locking my gaze onto his dark eyes and asking Charlotte, "Why was it that the light was always on in my room after all those years?" Part of me already knew this answer, but I wanted to hear the explanation for myself. I wanted to know that they trusted me with more than the basic knowledge of fairies and warlocks.

The two looked at one another silently, before Charlotte said cautiously, "Well, I'm sure you remember my mom said that for quite a few years, Demitri—"

He cleared his throat, cutting her off and shaking his head. "What is it? Stop keeping secrets from me, guys!" I was getting irritated with them now. I stared at him, and he stared back, the same hardened look in his eyes as he'd had the first time I'd met him.

Finally, he exhaled with defeat and said, "Okay, fine, I'll tell you. But don't get freaked out…" he trailed off for a second, and when I nodded vigorously, he started again. "A couple of years after we'd moved here, I was already exhausted with the exile. Despite what my mother had told me over and over, I believed my father must have wanted to look for me. That's why I'm the only one to take on my father's last name. I still believe he's out there waiting for me."

He let out a shaky breath, looking down at the ground. I saw that Charlotte was glancing at him with pitying eyes. "So, I felt rebellious, and I told my mom I was going to leave. I would've left permanently too, except once I got to London, where my father was rumored to be, I realized that the fairy world wasn't the same as it had been in our mothers' time.

"Lorena had made it cold, dark, and not full of true magic, as it should be. I came back almost as soon as I left after Charlotte came to find me and bring me back." She nodded at him solemnly when he turned to her in a way that appeared to me as gratefulness.

"I felt like there was a rift between my mother and me, even though I had returned. So, I spent most of my time back on the street—um—in your room." I learned this from Anastrella, so it was no shock to me, but as Demitri was unaware of this knowledge of mine; his face blushed a deep scarlet color. He looked sheepishly at me, and then hurriedly explained, "As soon as your parents bought the house, I moved out. But I love that room. It's the one place I could go, especially when things were bad between my mom and me, and be truly free."

I nodded, almost guilty now that I'd even brought up the sensitive subject. "I understand; I know what it's like to feel trapped. There's nothing to be embarrassed about.

Trust me—" I laughed now—"I would never have stayed in that room if you hadn't have painted it to be as beautiful as it is! It would scare me otherwise!" He smiled at me softly, nodding and looking away. We all sat there like that for a moment, in reflective silence.

A little while later, I told them I had to leave, to do my homework, have dinner, and such. Demitri offered to walk me home, and I accepted, telling myself to not get too excited. This was nothing more than a friendly walk home.

We bid Anastrella and Charlotte good night, and Demitri held the door open for me as we made our way out. I looked over at him as we walked slowly, side-by-side down the street. His hair hung over his forehead, shifting subtly as the wind whisked its' way around us. His hands were jammed tensely into his jeans' pockets, and he seemed on edge.

Despite how many efforts I'd been making to avoid any conversation about the sudden and irrational kiss we'd shared only a week before, I still thought of that moment every time I looked at him. Staring at him, even then, everything dark and seemingly dangerous about him brought me back to those feelings of carelessness and rebelliousness that I'd felt in my room on that first day of school. I wondered if he felt it too.

"So," I said, trying to break the ice. He looked up at me, chuckling gruffly and replying with a smug, "So." *Wow.* Someone was not in the mood for conversation. I thought back to no more than fifteen minutes before when he'd seemed so open in Charlotte's backyard to discuss some of his actual emotions. Boldly, I decided to jump to that topic again.

"What you were talking about earlier, with the staying in my room for a while…"

"Oh, yeah, sorry about that. I hope that doesn't make you feel uncomfortable that I lived there…"

"No, not at all!" I said, feeling the tension rise as we both tumbled over each other's sentences.

"I was just going to say that I'm glad it helped. And thank you, for setting it up for me so nicely." He nodded at me curtly, looking away and allowing us to fall into silence once more. We were passing his house now, and seeing as I felt frantic to find something else to talk about, I chose to question the explanation behind the constantly ajar door.

"Why is it that you always leave the door to your house opened? Is it because you lived in my room?" I asked hurriedly, searching his face for a reaction as he looked to the door, and then straight ahead at my house.

"Um, I guess so. I think when I first left on a quest for my father; my mom took it personally as if she was not parenting well enough. She was torn up about it, so she always left the door open, just hoping and waiting for me to come home. When I came back, I was in my—I mean your—room so often that she never shut it again, just in case I wanted to come home to sleep for the night. Now, it's just been a habit for so many years, that it bugs her to see it closed. She likes the air to come in from the door, too. It makes her feel free like I wanted to be all those years ago."

I nodded, eager to continue diving into the depths of his soul, but our journey had come to its' end already; we'd stopped right in front of my fence. Even though he began to turn to leave me, I reached for his wrist to stop him, more of my curiosities rushing forth from my lips.

"What is your mom like? Personality-wise, I mean." Demitri looked down at my hand, and I hastily let go. Shaking his head, as if focusing himself on the question, he looked up to me. There was a hesitant look in his eyes at this one as if he knew what to say but couldn't quite find the words to say it with.

"My mother is a stern woman. She was always traditional and tightly wound. Ever since my father left her, though, she's become progressively more bitter and cold. For a shadow fairy, that's always sort of dangerous because naturally dark powers can change to a sense of evil very quickly.

"That's why it's difficult for me sometimes, being—how to put this—happy. I am the combination of a dark shadow fairy and a demon-blooded warlock. Sort of the worst of both realms." He laughed without humor, looking up to the now blackening sky.

I felt so much sadness for this boy who had so much depth to his heart. I wished he didn't have to have that darkness weighing down on him, but it made sense to me, why he was the way that he was.

I realized I had been staring intently at him when I noticed his eyes were completely locked on mine. "Will you go to the homecoming dance with me?" he asked suddenly. My eyes widened with slight shock as he continued, "I know we might be judged for it, and Charlotte's nervous about all of the negative attention, but I think we'd have a lot of fun together, and I don't really want to risk you being asked by someone else." I hadn't even thought about the dance other than when my friends had mentioned that it'd be early next month.

"Um, sure," I said, hands messing with my hair nervously, not entirely confident in what to say.

"Oh, okay," he said with a hint of a smile, as if surprised that I'd said yes at all. It seemed as if he made to step toward me, but then he stepped back instead. He smiled ever so slightly before winking at me with one of those brown eyes, so dark; they seemed to be a charcoal color.

He whispered, "Goodnight, Summer," and turned over his shoulder to stroll back to his obscured house.

"Goodnight," I called after him, smiling to myself as I lifted the warning sign to get into my yard. *Were we friends? Were we more than friends?* I wasn't sure, and for the time being, I didn't believe Demitri North was either. It made us stand quite awkwardly over the line between friendship and foolishness, and while that scared me a bit, I felt like the risk might just be worth taking here.

I tried to wipe my mind of Demitri that night as I ate dinner with my parents, but I had so many questions, for and about him, running through my mind. I tuned out my parents' conversations and failed to stop thinking of him, or homecoming, or Charlotte, or anything to do with the supernatural reality.

It was odd to me that I could be doing something so mundane as eating dinner with my family, while just down the street, fairies and warefae were going about their lives. I felt like I needed to tell my parents to make them see what was happening, but they would never believe me. I just held out hope that Al would respond to my letter soon enough.

Chapter Six
Something More

September arrived fast; I was thriving in classes, and I'd been to a couple of football games before finally admitting to my friends that I was more into art than sports. This confession was much to the dismay of Will, who was on the team. I'd remained, mostly, in the confines of Lightenborough Drive, and spent time on the street with Demitri and Charlotte. I was still awaiting a response from Al, but my mind had been occupied by something else – the homecoming dance, just under twenty-four hours away. I wasn't planning on going originally, but Demitri's invitation had changed my mind.

After almost a month, I had managed to change the school-wide opinions that he and Charlotte were all that bad – the turn-around had started with Jen and Daisy being more open-minded toward me, and in turn, my closest neighbors. Charlotte and Demitri had even started sitting with my friends at lunch, much to the obvious irritation of Lydia and Analise. My friends, for the most part, liked our new seating arrangement – especially Bobby, who exuded happiness at the chance to sit next to Charlotte.

"Okay, guys," Haley said at lunch that day, "my parents are going to close the diner early tomorrow night, so we'll have it all to ourselves before we go to the dance."

"That's so kind of them!" Charlotte beamed, earning a slight look of mistrust from Haley – I theorized that her skepticism was due to jealousy, and an unreciprocated desire for a relationship with Bobby.

When Charlotte spoke, Bobby watched her with admiration and child-like wonder, as if he'd never seen anyone more beautiful. He was right, of course – Charlotte did have an unmatched glow about her. Still, Bobby seemed to gaze at Charlotte more than any other guy in the school.

"So," Charlotte said now, "who is taking who to homecoming?"

"Well," Bobby stuttered for a second, "Will is taking Maysie since they're dating. Demitri is taking Summer, as I'm sure you've heard"

"And who are you taking, Mr. Hayes?" Charlotte smiled sweetly.

Bobby looked sheepish. "I hadn't asked anyone yet. Are you going with anybody?"

She shook her head. "I'm free as a bird! Unless someone were to ask me today."

"Well, do you want to go with me?" Bobby asked hesitantly. Haley picked at her salad tensely, watching this scene play out with pure horror in her expression.

"Absolutely! I'll be wearing blue, so you should get a tie to match, don't you think?" She put her hand on his on the table, smiling eagerly – I thought Bobby would pass out!

"Are you excited for tomorrow?" Demitri said quietly in my ear. I looked back, smiling, and nodded. "Nervous for the groups to be going together?" he continued.

"Not really," I said quietly, observing the table. Annie and Haley were pretty much going together as friends, even though Haley wanted to go with Bobby. Will had Maysie, Charlotte had Bobby, and now, I'd be with Demitri. "I think everyone's been getting along great." *Just like I'd hoped.*

Driving home from school that day, I realized how much I started to feel like I was fitting in there, in Weston. Each day was the same. I'd get up and go to school with my dad, meander through my day, and hang out with Demitri and Charlotte after school. Demitri always walked me home, but things were different now, I thought. We were closer than ever to being something more. It wasn't tension, exactly – we viewed that first kiss as a thing of the past; what I felt was a desire to tell him that I was practically enamored with him, after knowing him for just a month.

Every night, I had dinner and spent the evenings with my parents, who were very happy there in the town. My mom had sold a lot of her paintings at an auction for such a substantial sum that she said she was planning on using the money for her and my dad's anniversary trip, later in September.

At that point, I didn't even mind that it was a painting of my face—along with several others, of course—that produced the money for their little getaway. I wasn't embarrassed to have someone from the town see my face;

the 'new girl' feeling that had once been lingering had long since worn off, and I couldn't be happier.

After dinner with my parents that night, I ducked through the fence and, right on schedule, Demitri emerged from his front door with a grin to join me. We fell in to step side by side, as we always did, en route to Charlotte's house. Our hands hung by our sides; the backs of our knuckles brushed lightly every once in a while, making my stomach feel full of butterflies. Charlotte met us at the door before we had a chance to knock and we went out back to sit around the porch table, where in the past two weeks, we'd built up quite an impressive collection of board and card games.

We chatted about the happenings of the day, spirits ramping up occasionally when one of us would make a competitive move in a game. Once, after taking my turn, I sat back and looked at each of these two warefae, who had become my closest friends in the weeks since school started. I felt so grateful for the way my life had played out since moving to Weston. I was at peace and truly believed that things had fallen into their rightful place at last. For a single moment, everything had been perfect.

Suddenly, Demitri sat up sharply, blurting out, "Charlotte, the council!" Charlotte let out a quick gasp and hurriedly stood from her cushioned chair between Demitri and me. She frantically shot her arm down to me, grabbing my hand and pulling me up and toward the door, checking her watch on her wrist as she went. Demitri was hot on our tails as we dashed through the kitchen and past the living room. I didn't even get a chance to say goodbye to Anastrella.

"What, Charlotte, what's wrong?" I cried frantically as she pushed me out the door and into the light of the setting sun.

"You've got to go! You've got to go! Quick, Dem, just fly her home." Charlotte ran a shaky hand through her hair and shut the door in my face.

"What was that about..." I began to ask Demitri to find myself swept off my feet, suddenly in a cradle.

"Demitri! Put me down!" I felt his feet kick off the ground, and his wings sweep from his shoulder blades. He shushed me and flew us straight up, above the line of sight of the windows of any house on the street. I huffed, crossing my arms in stubbornness, hoping to send him a silent message of irritation. "This is not okay," I muttered, and I could hear that Demitri-like wicked chuckle under his breath. Demitri flew me over my fence and straight up to my balcony, letting me down gently.

"Do me a favor," he whispered, hand lingering on my shoulder slightly, "stay in tonight, and stay away from the window." With that mysterious bit of advice, he jumped from the balcony and flew himself directly over to his porch. He looked back at me with his typical wave, and I waved back before walking down the stairs and into the house.

I was not going to be hiding indoors tonight. I was going to find out what was happening, whether Demitri and Charlotte wanted me to or not.

"Hey, honey, how were your friends doing?" my mom asked as I walked into the pristine and bright kitchen.

"Good," I said quickly, grabbing water from the fridge and turning to head back up the stairs.

"Summer, what's the rush, dear?" my dad asked, looking at me leaving so hurriedly with a skeptical look in his eyes.

I paused, slowing down a bit, and said, "Nothing, Dad! I just…" I trailed off, trying to think of a good excuse, and I settled on, "I have a lot of homework to finish before tomorrow."

"Really? They gave you homework on homecoming weekend?"

I nodded at my mom, who rolled her eyes and said, "I remember when your dad and I were in school, we hardly had homework during the entire first month of school!" My dad agreed, telling her that from a librarian's view, things were way different these days. I laughed, keeping up this casual flow of conversation for a few more minutes before bidding them goodnight about an hour after the sun had gone down all the way.

I went back up to my room and showered. Afterward, I put on some comfy pajamas and peered carefully out the window.

Stars were beginning to shine overhead, and darkness swam through the skies. I wondered if Anastrella and Charlotte had anything to do with the twinkling lights over the street that hung miles and miles above.

I went to my desk, braiding my hair behind my back and checking the clock that sat atop it. It was eight. I wondered when the 'council' that Demitri and Charlotte panicked about would be occurring.

Returning to my window, I looked out on the street from my balcony to find nothing but silence and the rustling of trees. I sighed in disappointment, moving to sit on my bed and scan a stack of books I had sitting on my bedside table, choosing one to read.

I sat anxiously, barely paying any mind to the words on the pages. I kept looking to the window for some sort of a sign, wondering what my warefae friends had been trying to keep me from. It was this thought, maybe, that made me ultra-aware of the soft sounds of doors closing in the direction of the street. My heart rate quickened as I worried this was what I'd been waiting for; *it's just in my head,* I thought, trying to squeeze my eyes shut, and plugging my ears – suddenly hoping nothing was going on.

The noise increased; the sound of doors was now replaced by a muffled pair of voices in the middle of the street. I finally turned off my light, crawled across the floor, and snuck to the window, where I allowed my eyes to only surpass the rim. I saw no light illuminating my backyard, which meant my parents had thankfully shut the kitchen light off. I assumed they were already in their bedroom under my mother's loft, which faced the opposite way from the street.

I cautiously raised myself a bit more to see what was happening. They were gathering down there – the fairies and the warefae. The mothers were in the center and the children stood more casually outside of the group. They formed a pair of circles – one within the other.

I noted that, like Anastrella, all of the fairies looked better than when I'd seen them previously in the vision from the wall. Vivyanna had muscles that were well defined and intimidating, but along with her fighter's build, she had her hair in beautiful braids that went all the way down her back. She wore a green top with gold embellishments, khaki pants and, strangely enough, no shoes.

I noted then that none of the fairies wore shoes, and none of them had their wings out either, which I thought to be odd. It was as if they were having a late-night neighborhood chat, nothing more.

Anastrella had her blonde hair in elegant curls, as did Charlotte, and she wore a ground-length navy dress. Katia almost glowed in the moonlight; her bright white hair and opaque skin were almost identical shades as what the snow would look like in the winter. She did look beautiful, though, which I now assumed to be a normal fairy trait. She wore a blue tank top and white jeans.

Genesis was very interesting to me. She was the only one that looked close to how she did on the day of the trial and exile. Her dark hair had been cropped to her shoulders, and her eyes appeared sunken in as if she was so tired that she didn't even have energy in her skin. It was strange – she looked—from the surface—like any other seventeen-year-old, but also like she had aged for multiple centuries at the same time.

Her skin, upon further inspection, had a sort of a grayish-white quality to it, reflecting the shadows from within her, I assumed. She was in a black dress that covered both arms completely, and went all the way to the ground, billowing around her so that she appeared similar to a Grim Reaper. She looked haughty compared to the rest, and she raised a hand, bringing a stop to the whispers that had been emitting from the group.

She spoke then, in a slow, proper voice. "The monthly council of the year 2000, on the eighth of this month, is one we've prepared for over the past month since our discussions. We, the council of the faire and warefae, are meeting today to discuss the plans for protecting our homes, as we did when we were first banished here, nearly a century ago. Fairies of the council, speak now with your courses of action."

So, I tried to work out in my mind, *the four fairies started a council that the warefae must've joined when they got older, and Genesis was in charge.* I listened as Vivyanna stepped to the center of the circle.

"As the rains come this month, Analise and I will use the marshland powers to convert the mud and water into a surrounding ground-level barrier, traces of magic lying within. This will block any other fairies from entering our coveted area. I will need assistance from the warefae in regards to strengthening the magic enough, and possibly the addition of a warlock spell to help as well." She stepped back, bowing herself out, and was met by the complete silence of the group.

Katia stepped forward next, saying swiftly, with hints of a Russian accent, "The ice will come in a couple of months. Until everything in the forest is frozen, all that Lydia and I can do is sweep the perimeter of the forest, just in case." Katia's way of concluding her announcement mimicked Vivyanna's way of leaving the circle; she gave a curt a bow, met by complete silence. It was odd to me, but now I assumed it was a part of the custom of the council meeting.

Anastrella's turn was next, and she smiled whilst talking, which comforted me because I saw the Anastrella I was used to, despite the fancy gathering.

"I've been working with Katia some to get some early cloud cover. I'm concerned because some sky fairies from neighboring towns are getting suspicious – they don't know if there's a clan over here or not, so they likely think I'm a rogue. I've noticed more of the faire palace's soldiers coming in to check on things, so it's getting harder to do my job. Lorena warned us about not being seen, but to do my job requires me to be seen."

"What is the problem then, Anastrella?" Genesis asked sharply, and Anastrella met her stone-cold gaze with an equally powerful glare.

"The problem, Genesis, is that this is the first year in the new century. The honoring of the stars and moon is more important this year than it's been in my time on the Earth thus far.

"The sky fairies are going to be more active this year than ever before, completely rearranging the sky in these last months of this year to celebrate their work over the past century. Setting up my sky-level protections and visuals for the humans is going to have to occur in a tight window of time, and being seen and hunted by the fairies because I'm not a publicly known sky fairy is my greatest concern at the moment."

"We'll get it done safely, Mom. We always do." Charlotte whispered encouragingly, and Anastrella smiled back at her. Genesis sighed and nodded, and Anastrella bowed herself out in silence.

"Finally, my shadows come back with the leaves of the trees, but they are also here when the leaves start to fall. I will begin as soon as possible to bring the cover of darkness on our lands to ensure that we aren't spotted from above or tracked by the Enchanted Guards.

Demitri will be helping me to spread this shade around, and, of course, we'll talk again on the eighth day of the tenth month, to give updates on the next month's duties and previous problems." She paused, looking around for any questions, but finding none.

"Warefae, do you have any problems with the duties set before you?" None of the children spoke or moved in fact. I supposed they didn't have a leader of their subgroup, like how Genesis led the fairies.

"Okay, with that, I suppose we should cast the group enchantment, and then the meeting can be… adjourned…" her voice trailed off, and I realized she was staring right at me.

"Demitri, get that girl from the window." I sucked in a breath, and he looked to his mother, shaking his head slowly in protest. I slid down the wall, hiding as I had tried to do that night I'd listened in on Charlotte and Demitri talking.

"Now!" I heard Genesis yell, piercing the silence of the night. I sat shaking a bit and I heard Demitri land softly on the balcony.

"I don't want to come down there," I whispered, knowing he was squatting down by the window to talk to me.

"That's why I told you to stay in here and not be seen," he said through gritted teeth.

I looked up at him, and he must've noted the fear in my eyes because his harsh look quickly softened and he reached out his hand. "It's going to be okay. I'll protect you." I took a deep breath, trying to find the bravery within myself that I'd accessed so many times since moving here.

I stood, took his hand, and ducked out of the window. This time, I allowed him to scoop me up. Draping a hand around his shoulders and keeping my eyes on his face, he flew us to the center of the street, where the women stood in a circle. I avoided their eyes as much as I possibly could, my teeth chattering and the gravel digging into the soles of my feet awkwardly.

Demitri stepped away from me, not reaching for my hand this time as he moved to complete the outer circle of the warefae. Genesis walked up to me, clearly lacking an understanding of the concept of personal space. "Do you know what we are?" She whispered coldly. I nodded ever so slightly, and she shot a glare suddenly at Charlotte. "It was she who told you, wasn't it?"

She was so accusing that it made me suddenly angry with her for her judgmental demeanor, not afraid of her. I wasn't the only one either, because Anastrella suddenly stepped forward, saying, "Genesis, you go too far. You may have problems with me, but you will not try to convict my daughter of any crime without genuine evidence."

Genesis stepped back, nodding in acknowledgment, but not apologizing for her accusation. She turned back to me, walking forward and grabbing my wrist tightly in one of her bony hands. "You, human child, should not know about us. You have no right." I whimpered slightly and she threw my arm down with such force that I fell, scraping my palm on the uneven ground.

Demitri was by me then, kindly helping me up despite the disgusted inhalation of his mother. "Demitri, you wouldn't dare tell a human of our existence, would you?" Her eyes narrowed at him.

He sighed, still holding my hand as I stood shakily next to him. "Mother, she found out on her own. She read paintings I've made in the room next door. She moved in this past August, and she's known since then."

"How?" Vivyanna asked abruptly, moving to look at me.

"How did she read it?"

"We don't know," Charlotte interjected.

"Demitri only painted in Faire, I've checked myself. We haven't been able to understand how the visions can be seen by the human mind."

"There is a simple solution then, isn't there?" Katia interjected. "She isn't human." Lydia and Analise gasped, glancing at each other with wide eyes before they looked back to me, horrorstruck.

"Yes, we guessed that she must have a small part of faire blood somewhere in her family history. The issue is she was adopted, so she doesn't know who her parents are," Anastrella said calmly.

"Anastrella, you knew about this? And you never thought to summon the council for a reckoning on how to handle this?"

"No, Genesis, I didn't want to tell you for this exact reason. What harm is it really that Summer knows? She doesn't need her memory erased, or to be harmed by guardian fairies that would only come get her and us if we summoned them here."

Genesis still glared at her, and I watched this standoff until Vivyanna came close to me, reaching up to touch my cheek, looking deep into my eyes. I took a couple of steps back, letting go of Demitri's hand, but Vivyanna merely looked at me. "What is it, Vivy?" Katia asked, following near her to peer into my face.

"I don't think we have to look too far into her family tree to find her fairy blood."

"What are you saying?" Genesis asked, now turning with Anastrella to see what the fuss was about. Vivyanna turned over her shoulder, grabbing my hand and pulling me in front of her so she was behind me, and the other three fairy women were in front of me.

Vivyanna traced her hand along the outline of my hair and said, "Look at her closely. Look at her eyes, her hair, the freckles dotting her skin. Who do we know that she mirrors almost exactly?"

The fairies stood in silence for a moment, observing me meticulously until Anastrella gasped, whispering, "Fallon." I stepped back quickly, accidentally stomping on Vivyanna's foot, but, luckily, she didn't seem phased as she joined the other three. I could see the warefae behind the fairies, standing on their tiptoes and looking over their mothers' shoulders, as if I were some exhibit in a museum.

My mind was racing a hundred miles an hour. *I had wondered if it was true if Fallon could be my mom. If Fallon was Al, whom I'd known for so long, was she not only a fairy but my mother as well? It would make sense – thinking back to the visions now, I could recognize Al's hair, her voice, her blurred face. She'd been there for my whole life and I hadn't even known.*

I felt the street become shaky around me, and my knees went weak suddenly. Charlotte was there this time, wrapping an arm around my waist to support me. "Mom, we need to call it a night, she's probably in shock." I couldn't find words to acknowledge her statement. I tried to focus on my breathing, but it was too unsteady.

The entire world around me seemed to be falling apart. I saw Anastrella nod, and whisper to Genesis that they should give me some time to process this information, and grudgingly, Genesis agreed. What happened next was all foggy to me, but I remembered seeing the fairies and warefae rise in the air, casting sparks from their hands and speaking enchantments, and seeing a sort of glittering blanket fall across the street.

Charlotte flew me to my room, setting me down gently on my bed and covering me with my blanket. She whispered calming and encouraging words, telling me not to worry. *That was easy for her to say.*

My head was swimming with a hundred different thoughts. There was a lingering fear from the fairies discovering my knowledge of their magic and that of their children. That meant I was more of a threat to them now, and Genesis in particular seemed skeptical and untrusting toward me.

That was a problem for another moment, though, because at this time, the only thing I could think of was the shock of recognition in the eyes of the fairies as they saw Fallon's face in mine. In one sense, it would explain how I could get past the barriers, understand the writing in Faire, and not be completely opposed to the ideas of magic and fairies and warlocks; it was already in my blood.

In another sense, though, I was so normal. I didn't have wings or sparks that flew from my hands, and I'd never cast a spell or manipulated the elements. I felt like laughing aloud at the mere possibility of me fluttering around with a magic wand or something. *It couldn't be. It must just be a coincidence.* I tried to reason with myself as I struggled to fall asleep that night. But still, despite all of my reasons to think that I couldn't be Fallon's daughter, and I couldn't be anything but human, a tiny voice in my mind persistently asked myself, *or am I?*

Chapter Seven
Homecoming

Friday was the most painfully stressful day I'd ever experienced. I woke up on Saturday and my head was still throbbing from my lack of sleep the night before when I'd gone to bed with incredible tension after my terrifying experience with the fairies and warefae. I peeked out of my window to see the empty street. I ensured it was completely still and lifeless before I bounded downstairs to have breakfast.

"Happy homecoming day!" my mother called from where she waited at the kitchen table; my dad smiling as he made us fluffy pancakes. I ran across the room to the table and flung my arms around her. She laughed, smoothing my hair down and saying, "Isn't someone excited!" as I clutched her even tighter.

"Yeah, super excited to see you!" I muttered against her shoulder. I wanted to talk to her about everything, but I didn't want to put her through the stress.

I sat down across from her, and my dad came over with the food and a small envelope. "What's that, Dad?" I asked as I stacked my plate with pancakes.

"Sweetheart, I picked this up from the post office this morning, when I went into town for some grocery shopping. It's addressed to you, from Al!" I lit up, snatching it out of his hand and tearing the envelope open, pulling out its' contents.

My parents eyed each other and then looked to me with toothy grins spreading on their faces at what we saw – a roundtrip ticket to Florida, set for tomorrow.

"I guess Al wants to see you, Honey," my dad said, patting my shoulder as he sat down.

"That'll be a nice treat," my mom said, studying the ticket, "It'll be a long day though. Your first flight is at eight in the morning – David, you can drive her to the airport." She laughed.

"You'll fly back at eight in the morning on Monday, but that works good, because it's Labor Day and you don't have school anyways! That'll be fun! It's a short trip, but I'm sure you'll love being home."

I grinned, thinking to myself that my claim must be true. I was almost completely sure that Al was Fallon – she didn't send a letter in response, but I figured that was because she had too much to say. The thought struck me then – she might want to talk to me about being my mother. I didn't know if I truly believed that part was connected yet, but what I couldn't process more was that by tomorrow, I'd already have my answers.

After breakfast, I went upstairs to start packing and getting everything ready for the homecoming dance that night. I pulled my duffel bag from the closet and packed a swimsuit, just in case, and a comfy outfit for the flight home. The trip was too short to pack more than that.

Next, I set out my dress and makeup for the dance, and decided to shower off before I started getting ready –

it was early still, but I'd rather take my time and be ready to meet up with my friends this afternoon. When I'd hastily stepped in and pulled the curtain across the bathtub, I paid attention to the way the water ran down my back.

I reached my hand over my shoulder and felt around my shoulder blade. Nothing. No wings or feathers or anything that could make me fly. I smiled to myself, the whole encounter with the fairies seeming like a foolish memory—maybe even a dream. I was going home, and I was going to see Al—that's all that mattered.

After I'd toweled off and gotten dressed, I twisted my sopping hair onto my head and hurried to put on some comfy clothes until I got ready for the dance. As I opened the drawer by my closet, I had a strange sensation that I wasn't alone, and this feeling was confirmed when my lamp flicked on behind me without me touching it.

I turned slowly to see Demitri lounging in my desk chair, looking at me with curiosity, and a bit of fire lingering behind his eyes. "Good morning," he said quite plainly.

I crossed my arms. "Good morning, can you turn around?"

He nodded his head, spinning the chair and looking now to the bag packed next to my nightstand. "Where are you going?"

"Nowhere," I said, before sighing and admitting, "I'm going back to Florida."

"Why?" I hurriedly pulled on my clothes and dried my hair with the towel, walking to sit on my bed. He turned around as he heard me get on the bed. "I'm visiting Al."

"Oh, that was quick."

"Yeah, she sent a roundtrip ticket for me. It's for tomorrow." He nodded.

There was so much tension between us; it was strange. Our normal flow of easygoing conversation and warm friendship was absent. Last night clearly had been tough on both of us.

"You know, just because you can fly up here doesn't mean you can come in my room whenever you want. It's not yours anymore." I said, smiling playfully.

He smiled tightly, nodding once, and standing to walk to the window. A strange feeling came over me then, like my heart was being tugged at.

"Wait," I said as he unlatched the window. He turned to me, and there was stillness in the air like there had been the day we'd kissed. I didn't feel that electricity necessarily, but I felt a need for him to stay. "Come here," I whispered, patting the space on the bed next to me. He hesitated, looking at me with a bit of worry in his expression, before he came over and merely sat atop the covers, kicking off his shoes to the floor and crossing his arms.

He refused to look at me, keeping his eyes on the ceiling as he leaned back against the headboard. I didn't care; I just wanted to talk to him once more before he left. I leaned back as he was, crossing my arms as well to mimic his gesture of distance between us.

We sat in silence for several minutes. I was under the sheets and he was on top of them, but despite our proximity, I felt a rift between us. He must've noticed too because when he spoke, it was not a casual conversation about homecoming, or Florida, or anything else, but the question I'd been dreading.

"Summer, what do you think about everything that happened last night? You seem to be uncomfortable about it, and I understand if you don't want to talk about it, but, Summer." He gently touched my chin with his finger, turning my face so mine was mere inches from his. "You're my best friend. Please, talk to me." He urged.

I took a deep breath, sinking further back into my pillow, but admitting to myself that I may have made this situation worse by trying to deal with it alone this morning. "Okay," I whispered, "okay, I'll talk."

He smiled softly, nodding as an encouragement for me to continue.

I started talking, and it felt like a dam on my heart was crumbling away, and all the feelings I'd been suppressing since the night before flowed out in a rush. I told Demitri about my fear that I was a warefae, and that the way I'd lived my entire life so far had been a lie.

I went on about how I was so ready to go home, and part of me wanted to escape Weston, but another part of me worried that the whole time I'd be in Florida with Al, I'd just be stressed about whether or not magic was in my veins – and most importantly, if she was my birth mom.

"And I think the part that's getting to me the most," I said after about fifteen minutes of sharing my innermost thoughts with Demitri, "is that I don't know what's going to happen to me if it is true.

"Am I going to have to leave my parents? What about my friends at school? What will they think if I just disappear?" I felt myself getting hysterical now, and tears began to stream down my face as I finally acknowledged what had been contributing most to my stress, and that was the dread that everything I knew and loved about my life would have to change.

Demitri sat up more now looking alarmed at the sudden downturn of my attitude. He placed his arm over my shoulder, rubbing my arm soothingly. "Summer, it's gonna be okay. You're not going to have to leave your parents, and nothing bad is going to happen! We don't even know if it's true or not, and please, don't worry about that until you get a chance to talk to Al! Enjoy the dance tonight, and then enjoy your time back home, and this will all work itself out after a while."

I sighed, resting my head on his shoulder and closing my eyes. "Thank you, Demitri. Thank you for listening to me." I pulled the blanket a bit higher up my shoulders, yawning and settling down next to him.

"You're welcome, Summer." He squeezed my shoulder once before lifting his arm over my head and crossing his arms on his chest once more.

I was exhausted from my lack of rest already, and I simply couldn't resist as I felt myself drifting into sleep peacefully, relieved to have gotten every worry off of my chest. "Are you awake, Summer?" I heard Demitri whisper against my hair. Or at least, I thought he did. By that point, what was real and what was a dream were unbeknownst to me.

I was flying. I was flying over the ocean, and it was so real that I could smell the sea salt spray on my face and feel the breeze in my hair. I looked down and saw silvery fish swimming near the surface below me. I reached my hand out and somehow, sparks flew from my fingertips, lifting the water into a wave that followed me a bit before white capping and crashing back down into the sea.

I continued onto calmer waters and saw my reflection glistening back up at me. I had wings. They were bright blue and white, and they fluttered gently, glistening in the sunlight. I gasped, giggling as I reached my hand behind my back, skimming one of them where it attached to my shoulder blade. It was silky smooth, and I felt it tingling where my hand touched it.

I was so at peace, and I wasn't even worried that I had wings attached to my body, which I had feared so much when awake. That was the weird thing, too; even though I knew I was asleep, it felt so real. It was incredible, and I never wanted it to end. I stopped flying though, pausing to listen to the sound of the waves.

I looked around, though, because I thought I heard distant cannons or something of the sort. There was a 'da dum, da dum, da dum' sound in the distance; feeling like it was closing in now. I felt a bit panicked as I tried to find the source of it, but I realized that maybe this sound wasn't in the dream. Maybe, it was a heartbeat.

I could feel myself waking up though I desperately didn't want to. I sighed, clinging tighter to my pillow.

Wait, I realized, *this is not my pillow...* I barely fluttered my lashes open; just enough to make out that what I was laying on was not my pillow, but the warm chest of Demitri North.

Holy crap! I couldn't believe what was happening right now. I felt his soft breathing rustling my hair slightly, and I could hear the da dum, da dum, of his heartbeat below my ear. I wondered what time it was, not daring to move so as not to wake him. I squinted, trying to distinguish if he was above or below the blankets, and he was still atop them. *What a gentleman,* I thought, rolling my eyes.

I was lying on my side; my hands clutched to my chest, and my legs next to where his were, separated by the safety of the sheets. Looking down at the bed, using the light streaming into my room as a guide. I saw that his arm was still hung around me, but due to the way I was laying on him now, his hand had slid onto my hip. *Ugh, this was not the plan!* I'd wanted him to stay and talk to me a bit, not take a nap on top of him as if we were dating. As much as I might have wanted that, it hadn't happened yet! I looked back at his hand and wondered if he wanted what I did as well.

I looked up at his face and saw so much innocence there. His eyes were closed, and his mouth was parted a bit. Lines of worry and stress that so often plagued his forehead had gone. I wondered what he was dreaming about. I speculated that in his dreams, he was flying, or swimming, or running, or free. I wondered, in the smallest, most faint part of my mind, if he dreamt of me.

I laid there like that, fully awake and aware, for a few more minutes until I felt myself drifting off to sleep again.

This time, I didn't dream at all. It was so peaceful and quiet like I was awake and asleep at the same time. I listened to the rhythmic beating of Demitri's heart, and it soothed me like a lullaby.

All too soon, I felt a slight pressure on my head, like I was being lifted, before feeling the cold softness of my pillow beneath me. I subconsciously reached out for the body that had warmed mine, only finding a hand that had reached out to meet my own.

I could feel the hand's thumb pad tracing circles on my hand gently before slowly dropping it to the bed and pulling the sheets up over my arms. I felt a pair of warm lips press softly to my forehead. Then, as quick as they came, they were gone. I wanted to wake up to tell him goodbye, but I couldn't force myself into my awakened state, no matter how determinedly I tried.

A while later, I woke again. I felt despair washing over me in the silence of the room, now empty and consuming instead of welcoming. I wanted him to come back; I needed him to.

I rolled out of bed, seeing that it was 1.30 now. Sitting at my desk chair, in front of the small mirror, I began putting on makeup and twisting my now dry hair into an elegant braid that I'd pin-up before I left for pictures.

I was meeting up with the group at Hal's around three. We were going to take pictures for an hour and a half or so, and then Haley's parents were going to cook us a nice meal. The dance was in the school gym at six, and I was excited—I'd never been to dance like this before.

I went downstairs a bit later to eat lunch with my mom, who helped me finish up my makeup while my dad went to work at the library for a bit. When he got back a bit later, he offered for me to take his car to drive Demitri and Charlotte with me to the dance—I'd gotten my license in Florida but never really used it since I didn't have my car. It'd be nice to have the car to myself tonight.

Finally, I went upstairs and changed into my dress. It was silver and had sparkles all around it, and tapered off at my knees. I looked at myself in my mirror as I put on my heels, thinking that I felt beautiful—like I had when I saw myself in my mom's painting.

I went out onto the balcony, seeing Demitri and Charlotte walking together through the fence. "Come in through the patio door," I called down to them as I went through the house. I met them in the kitchen, as they were greeted by my parents. Demitri smiled at me softly, and I felt us both acknowledge the peace we'd felt in bed together earlier today with that glance. He looked handsome, wearing a black suit and almost metallic tie. His black hair looked even darker as it framed his face. Charlotte looked flawless in her cobalt blue dress; her hair in voluminous curls.

"All right, kids," my mom said, turning on her digital camera carefully, "let me grab a picture of you before you head out!" We stood by the patio window, the ugly fence as our background. Charlotte and I got a picture together, and then the three of us, and then Demitri and I.

As I moved to get the keys from my dad, he whispered, "You look beautiful, Summer," earning an appreciative grin from me.

We went to Hal's, driving through the town that was slowly buzzing to life. It was palpable that everyone was preparing for the dance. The restaurant had a "Closed" sign up on the door, but when we walked in, we heard fun music and saw our group taking pictures by some cute balloons that had been hung as a backdrop on the wall. We knew the fun was just beginning!

"Hi, you three!" Haley's mother said, bustling around, taking drinks to people. "Come on in, and take some pictures!" The group saw us and we went over to greet them.

"You guys look great!" Bobby said as he walked over, hugging me and shaking Demitri's hand. "Wow, Charlotte," he said, eyes looking at her in adoration.

"Right back at you, Bobby," she smiled, nervously pulling at her hair. Demitri and I eyed each other as we saw this adorable pair's interaction.

We all took pictures for about an hour—Haley's poor mom must've been so tired of getting the group to stand still by the end of it. She took photos of just the girls, just the boys, everyone individually, couples, and on and on until she finally exclaimed, "Okay, enough! Come to the table to eat some dinner!" We all laughed in pity at her frustration, sitting at the table where Haley's dad placed burgers and fries at every seat.

Everyone was eating very carefully—except Will, who was ridiculed as he got ketchup on his nice suit.

"Will!" Maysie exclaimed trying to blot a napkin over it, "we can't take any good pictures at the dance now!"

"What's the problem?" he said through a mouthful of food, "your dress is red, so I'm trying to match!" Maysie just rolled her eyes, and Annie went on a tangent about his stupidity.

Haley sat quietly for most of the meal. She looked pretty and seemed to go along with being Annie's "date" like a champ, but I could tell that she wanted more of the attention that Bobby was directing toward Charlotte. I couldn't feel too guilty though—Bobby was my first friend here, and Charlotte was one of my closest. To see them end up together would be very exciting!

Soon enough, we were headed to the school. I saw twinkling lights atop the trees, illuminating the path into the gymnasium. Other small groups of kids walked in as well, and the chaperones—a bunch of parents that lived in town—stood around the outskirts of the gym, talking and watching as kids slowly made their way to the dance floor.

The first song was slow—Demitri took my hand as my group fell into step with the rest of the school. "Would you please dance with me, Summer?" he asked, beaming as I put my arm on his shoulder.

"Of course, Demitri." I smiled shyly back. We danced the rest of the night away with our friends—during slow songs, it felt as if everything melted away, and my head on his shoulder was the only connection in the whole empty world. During faster songs, I giggled and jumped around with my group, and for these, Demitri stood by, seeming content to simply watch for the most part. From what

Charlotte had told me, I knew this was the first school dance either she or Demitri had gone to. They both seemed to be enjoying themselves tremendously.

At one point, I walked over to the table to get some water, hearing Demitri whisper my name. I turned, and he said quietly, "Will you go for a walk with me?" I nodded, taking his hand and waving to Charlotte to meet me outside when she was ready to leave Bobby.

Once we were out of the school and the noise had died down, I was struck by the nighttime beauty of the town. The soft lights still glowed along the path of the main road. Hal's Diner's sign was dimmed, but the building still emitted comfort, just by sitting there. Crickets chirped in a unified chorus, and the stars danced as we had inside—I silently applauded Anastrella for that.

I sat on the porch swing outside of the library with Demitri—my hand still in his. It had grown comfortable there. "Summer, I must tell you," Demitri said, "you are not at all what I expected you to be."

I laughed. "Why, because I may not be human? Trust me, I'm not what I expected either!" In my mind, I feared what would come of the trip to Florida I was taking the next day. The hours of the day of the dance had passed so quickly, it felt like I was hurtling through to my destiny to realize the truth.

"That's not what I mean," Demitri said nervously. "When I saw you first, I thought you were beautiful, but I had no idea of your character. You're strong and brave, incredibly kind, and fearless. You take on every challenge that comes your way with grace, and it seems to me that you accept your fate better than anyone—you adjust and overcome better than anyone I've seen in my lifetime." I blushed, flattered.

"Thank you, Demitri. You're a lot better than I thought you'd be when I first met you, too." I squeezed his hand lightly. "You don't give yourself enough credit."

He looked down at our fingers laced together. "Summer, I'd like to have a relationship with you. Not just as friends—as, um."

"You want to be my boyfriend?" I asked with surprise.

He looked at me with wide eyes. "Yeah, that's it. If that's okay with you, that is."

I didn't respond for a moment. This boy was sweet, thoughtful, and had such a genuine demeanor. He knew a lot of things about me—things that I hadn't even known before—and still, he never judged me for it. Aside from that, he was remarkably attractive. I knew without a doubt that I wanted to be with him.

I threw my arms around him and squealed with excitement. "Yes! Yes! Yes!" He laughed with relief, hugging me back.

"I'd love to be your girlfriend," I exclaimed, looking up at him now. He brushed my hair back from my face, and, much more gently than the first time, he kissed me. We stayed there like that, kissing under the stars of Weston, until Charlotte cleared her throat, laughing as we slid away from each other with embarrassment.

"Finally!" she exclaimed, high-fiving Demitri as we walked to my dad's car and drove home.

That night, I went to bed with a smile on my face. I'd had a lot of fun with my friends, and Demitri and I were officially in a relationship. The impending threat of what I may find out in Florida was not on my mind at all as I lay there, dreaming of Demitri spinning me around the dance floor, and kissing me under the night skies of this small town.

Chapter Eight
Free Fall

Saturday had felt like the best day of the year. It was as if my birthday, Christmas, and the first day of summer had all rolled into one Demitri-filled day. Sunday was different—I woke up early and my dad dropped me off at the airport. For the entire flight, I was filled with dread. I wanted to go back already—back home to Lightenborough Drive. I missed the house that I'd once feared as being devilish, and I missed the room with the paintings that I'd once considered to be bad omens. I missed Demitri and wished I could've spent this day with him. I felt lonely without him, Charlotte, my school friends, or my parents to keep me company on the early morning flight.

At the airport in Florida, I grabbed my suitcase and suddenly knew she was there, waiting for me. It was as if I could sense her presence. I walked toward the parking garage and saw her, despite the vast amount of people. She wore jeans and an old "Rosemary Beach Books" t-shirt, and her hair looked a little longer than it had when I'd seen her about a month before. She grinned and waved me over excitedly. I tried to force a smile back, and my heart beat faster and faster the closer I got to her.

She embraced me tightly, rubbing my back as she did so. I tried to calm down—I'd known Al for as long as I could remember. I was comfortable with her. I couldn't let whatever she'd tell me ruin the relationship that I'd formed with her over the past seventeen years.

The car ride to the library was a quiet one, but enjoyable at the same time. We rolled all of the windows down in Al's old SUV, smelling the sea salt in the air the closer we got to Rosemary Beach. I missed it—it felt nice to be back.

Al parked behind the bookstore, and we went through the storage room and immediately up the stairs inside to the loft where she lived. She helped me put down my luggage and then went to sit in the chair by the large window that looked over the bookstore. I sat down across from her, remembering how much I loved sitting up there as a little girl—watching the people shopping and trying to guess which books they'd end up with. "So," she said suddenly, breaking the silence. I felt my heart rate speed up again as I looked into her piercing blue eyes. "How much do you know?" she asked directly.

I breathed deeply. "You're Fallon?" I felt like I knew that much, but also as if I should ask, to confirm my suspicions. She nodded, and I exhaled heavily. "So that means you're a fairy, right? It's true?"

To this, she looked vaguely down at the store, "No, I'm not. Not anymore, at least."

She turned slightly in her chair so I could see the large scars showing above the collar of her shirt. "When I lost my wings, I lost my magic. Any fairy without wings ages normally and becomes human." I stared in awe, remembering how glorious her wings looked in the vision on the wall.

"What happened to Peter?" I asked next. Her eyes seemed misty as she looked back at me.

"He was killed," she said plainly, "but he helped me escape. I don't think Lorena ever knew that I made it out alive, nor did anyone else."

I nodded. "The fairies in Weston thought you were dead."

She laughed emptily at that. "Sometimes I've wished I was. I've been trapped here, unable to fly, use my magic, or be with Peter." She smiled at me a bit. "But, I've had you." I smiled back, remembering all that we'd gone through together.

She leaned forward in her chair, reaching out for my hand. "Summer," she said a bit shakily, "you're my daughter. I'm your mother, and Peter is your father." I felt myself draw in a nervous breath, looking down at my hand in hers, and suddenly smiling. I jumped forward and hugged her, allowing myself to feel small as she embraced me and we cried together—the truth was finally out, and the pressure was lifted off of us both.

When I leaned back, I asked suddenly, "Why did you not want me? Why did you give me away?"

"It was because of Lorena," she said, with malice in her tone. "As soon as you were born, Lorena was on our trail. I had tried to find us shelter before, with the Weston fairies, but they refused, as I'd expected. Peter tried to reason with the warlocks, but they were no help either.

Eventually, we had to flee our home and we ended up here, in Florida.

"We met Clara and David when I was seeking shelter in the bookstore from those fairies one night. We tried to explain our situation while leaving as much out as I could—I told them I was threatened and had to leave you for your safety. They said they'd take you in, and I could come back for you whenever I wanted.

"After Lorena had Peter killed, I came back. I'd realized that no permanent fairies were living in this area, so I was safe from Lorena if she ever were to find out that I was alive. As for you, I didn't want you to have a life of running, and as a new human, only seventeen years old with no education or means to get a job and provide in this world, I had no choice but to watch you grow up from a bit of a distance. Clara and David were wonderful, though. They let me be close to you and take part in every major event in your life.

"After a while, Clara and David found out about our secret of what we are. They took it rather well and agreed that eventually, you should be around others of your kind, to learn and not to be afraid. That's why you had to move now. You're old enough to learn about who you are and the others can show you what you need to know."

"Wait," I interjected, my head spinning, "Mom and Dad know about magic?" She nodded. "And," I continued, "I'm—I'm not...?" I struggled to get the words out.

Fallon nodded again. "Yes, Summer. You're warefae, not a human."

I breathed shakily. "I can't be. I don't have wings; I can't do spells. I don't have sparks that fly from my hands!"

"That's why I wanted you to go there, to Weston. There, they can teach you how to unlock your magic and use it for good."

"Why couldn't you come with us?"

"I'm not a fairy anymore, darling. I belong in this world. You belong in that world." I hugged her again, thinking of her selflessness through the years, and how much she and Peter had endured for me.

That afternoon, we spent hours at the beach. We sat in silence, mother and daughter, soaking up the sun. It was so enjoyable and relaxing, and it gave me time to think as well.

While we were there, enjoying being oceanside, we were also talking about everything we could—how things were in the Faire Palace, what Peter was like and how they met, and about me. I was Summer, but now I was Blair as well. It was confusing knowing that I had this power that was sitting dormant, just waiting for me to unlock it.

"Fallon," I said, now growing accustomed to this being Al's real name, "what do I have to do to start using my magic?"

She smiled as if reflecting on her own memory of this process, saying, "You have to free fall. You put your trust in yourself and your abilities, and then you'll get your wings." She laughed at my wide-eyed and disbelieving expression, and I joined in, thinking of how abysmal it sounded to free fall and just hope some wings would appear.

"Do you think Lorena can be stopped?" I asked next, dreading having to live a life in hiding.

She looked off into the distance for a moment before taking a deep breath and saying, "I hope so. I do."

I saw so much more of myself in her now—in her face, her hair, her freckles. It was nice to feel like we belonged together. As I stared at her sea-blue eyes, I leaned back on my towel and asked her, "What does it mean to be a fairy of the sea?" She smiled, looking out over the vast ocean like it was an old friend.

"My powers are rooted in the ocean. The sparks I use—could use, I mean—were essentially bits of water fused with electricity in the air. That's the way it is with each fairy. They can tap into what makes them strongest."

She paused, checking to make sure I was following what she was saying. "The responsibilities given to each fairy are assigned by the Faire Tree, which gives life to fairies. My responsibility, and your responsibility as well, is to take care of the ocean and try to maintain peace between humans and the sea. It's a fun job, as the ocean itself is naturally inclined to make peace with humans. When shadow fairies, or dark fairies, come in with storms or clouds, it becomes a bit harder to protect the humans, but it's manageable"—she looked out to the water again—"and worth it."

Fallon had so much wisdom to share with me. As I sat there, basking in the sun with her, I was aware that we had so much to catch up on. Though we'd been around each other for my whole life, there'd been a wall between us, between the way things were and the way things had seemed.

Fallon talked with me about Demitri and how our relationship had grown from friendship to romance over the past month. She helped me calm my fears about having a boyfriend—something Clara would likely be bad at. She talked with me about other things, as she had when I'd considered her to be an older sister, and in those moments, I decided that though things had changed between us, our relationship was stronger than it had ever been.

For the remainder of my stay, we hung around the bookstore, got a nice dinner, and just enjoyed our time together, still relishing in the feeling of being completely honest with one another. I wondered, thinking of that, how I would go about talking with my parents about their knowledge of me being a warefae.

The next day came all too soon. Fallon woke me up gently, helped me pack my things, and drove me to the airport. I felt tears on my cheeks as she waved goodbye when she dropped me off, and I tried to shake them away.

"I'll see you again soon," she had promised, "you can come to stay over holiday break if you're not busy with Demitri!" She had laughed at her comment, but I smiled, knowing I was going home and he'd be there.

I waited anxiously at the airport, on the flight, and in my dad's car on the drive back. I couldn't wait to see him, and everyone else there, for that matter.

When I got home, I talked to my parents about the trip. At first, I only spoke about the beach and the feeling of being back in Florida, but then, I knew I had to take the conversation to the level I'd spoken with Fallon.

"Mom? Dad? Fallon told me everything. I know that you know what I am." The pair eyed each other, not with fear, but with a sense of relief.

My mom looked back at me. "We didn't feel that it was our place to tell you, Summer. Fallon agreed with us."

"We thought it was something you should learn on your own," my dad chimed in. I nodded, feeling that the way I learned about the world of magic and fairies and warlocks was the best way I could, to accept what my future would be.

We talked for a while more about how homecoming went since I hadn't had time to speak to them after the dance, and I told them that I officially was in a relationship—my mom seemed to celebrate that news more so than my dad. After eating dinner together and telling them goodnight, I went up to my room.

I dashed upstairs, up and up, and finally, out the door to the balcony. I peered out to the street. The sun had set already. It wasn't even that late, but the street appeared as if night had fallen onto it.

I went all the way up the stairs, pushing open my window and heaving my bag into my room. Before I ducked inside, though, I turned around, squinting out from my railing to see Demitri not sitting on his porch this time, but sitting on his roof. He was looking up at the stars and the moon and the clouds.

"Demitri!" I called across the way. I saw him sit up and lift his hand in a welcoming gesture. I waved him over, and I noticed him hesitate a bit. My leaving had come at an inconvenient time—had he changed his mind about being with me? After a hesitation, though, he did stand up, unleash his magnificent darkened wings, and begin the slow and graceful flight to me.

"Hey, how are you?" He smiled, seeming excited, but holding back politely.

"I'm good, Demitri. Really good." In the darkness, I wondered if he could see the sparkle in my eye. He nodded in response to me, hovering there directly in front of me, only the railing of my balcony between us.

"So how was…" What he was going to say next, I had no idea. I had been waiting all day for this, and I couldn't wait any longer. I reached my hands out, clutching his shirt and pulling him toward me, kissing him like my life depended on it.

Demitri seemed shocked at first, jolting a bit and almost pulling away from me, but when he realized that I wasn't letting go of his shirt, he flew himself closer to me, taking my face in his hands and kissing me back with all the passion he had been building up over the past months.

Everything that had been acclimating between us, from our frantic first kiss to our tender friendship and the trust that had built since had led to this—our new relationship. Now, I was home and ready to give it the time that it needed to grow.

When we finally broke apart, we rested our foreheads against each other, just breathing. I kept my eyes closed, savoring the moment. "I have to admit, I wasn't expecting that," Demitri whispered, and I opened my eyes to see the smile shining through his. I laughed lightly, placing a dainty kiss on his lips once more before waving him into my room. He landed on my balcony and retracted his wings before stepping in behind me.

I turned my lamp on and began unpacking my bag and throwing my clothes and swimsuit into the hamper in my closet. Demitri sat down in my desk chair, watching me, still in shock at the fact that I'd so adamantly kissed him.

"So," I said, wanting to get straight to the point, "I have some news."

"About Al?"

My heart panged as I saw her face in my mind. "Yes. Al is Fallon, and she's also my mother." There was a moment of silence as the realization of that new truth washed over him. It still felt surprising to me, and I'd known for over a day now.

"I can't believe she was alone for all that time," he said, a look of guilt clouding his face.

I shook my head. "It's not your fault. Fallon's strong. Besides, she had my parents. They took care of her, and me, which made all the difference in the world." I held out my hand, and he took it and squeezed it lightly. "What'd I miss while I was gone?" I asked.

"It wasn't a very eventful day. The only thing exciting that's happened is that this morning, Lydia and Analise got in a huge fight"—he laughed at the memory—"and the two of them almost blew up the street, they were throwing so much magic at each other!"

"Oh, my gosh! What were they fighting about?" I asked. He laughed again, clearly entertained upon the reliving of this story, and murmured something about Lydia making it snow in Analise's room when I finally walked out to sit across from him on the bed. "Well, regardless of who tried to blow up who, I'm glad I'm back. I missed the beach and Fallon, but it was much easier letting go this time." He stood and moved next to me, wrapping his arms around my shoulders and squeezing me close.

He whispered against my hair, "I'm glad you're back, too."

He left that night after we'd talked a bit more about my trip and what had gone on there. Before he left, he kissed me goodnight, and I watched as he flew back to his house. I shut my window and got into bed, feeling the familiar coziness of being under those blankets.

I admired the way the painted constellations shone on my ceiling and noticed for the first time that being on the top floor of the house made me feel like I was nestled on a cloud. I felt relief, and I slept the most soundly I ever had.

The next morning, I got up and dressed for school, noticing immediately that I was smiling without trying to. *A fresh start,* I thought to myself, both with my new boyfriend, and my new knowledge of being one of the warefae.

At school, I kept my eye on the clock, just waiting for classes to be done. As soon as it was, I immediately dashed outside and down the street to Charlotte and Anastrella's house. I told my parents that I'd be gone for the evening, which they accepted, knowing I'd want to see my friends. What they didn't know was that I would hopefully have done some life-altering things by the time I got home that night.

I knocked on the door and was greeted eagerly by Anastrella, who let me in and ushered me to Charlotte's room. I'd never been in there, seeing as we typically spent our time on the back patio. I opened the door to see that despite the house's small size, Charlotte's room was somehow huge. The ceilings were extremely high and vaulted, and I saw Charlotte now, fluttering around near the roof, making little fireworks with sparks spew from her fingertips.

"Hey, Charlotte," I called softly, my voice echoing through the vast room. She looked down, quickly diving to land elegantly in front of me. This was my first chance to talk to her since I'd gone to Florida.

We chatted for a bit about what had happened to us over the past week, and then, I finally broke the news to her that Fallon was alive and my mother, and that I, too, was warefae.

She looked taken aback but nodded, and so I soldiered on with this topic. "I want to get all of you together, even Analise and Lydia, and figure out how to go about this."

She nodded again, talking to herself about planning and getting the council together, but I cut her off. "No, Charlotte. I mean I want to go today. Right now, actually." A smile spread across her face upon seeing how determined I was to implement myself into the group.

We said goodbye to Anastrella, then bounded down the street to Demitri's house, where Charlotte walked up the porch steps silently and brought him outside. His eyes lit up when he saw me, and he walked over and gave me a tight hug. Charlotte squealed, and we broke apart suddenly, thinking something was wrong. "Yeah, that won't get old any time soon!" We laughed with relief—Charlotte was as excited as we were about our relationship.

After we got Demitri, we didn't bother telling him the plan yet. Charlotte went across the street to knock on the door and ask for Analise, and Demitri instinctively went next door to request Lydia's presence. I, in the meantime, was alone, standing there on the street.

I couldn't help but notice the harsh difference between the tree-covered street that was almost enchanted in appearance, and the ugly fence that looked like prison bars around my house. I stood there staring at it, my hands on my hips, contemplating if my parents would be mad at me for what I was about to do. I decided they would think I was enhancing the artistic ambiance of the place and commenced my work.

I reached up and put my hands firmly around the jagged top of the poorly placed fence, and, pulling hard, broke an entire plank of wood down from the rest of them. I continued down the fence line, breaking and pulling on the barrier between my house and the rest of Lightenborough Drive. I tore the warning signs down and yanked jagged scraps of wood off their weakly nailed supports.

I made a huge pile of the broken pieces as I made my way to the end of the fence and with a final heave, pulled the last piece of wood off and threw it to the ground, brushing my hands off and admiring my work.

I turned around then to see all four of the warefae staring at me, Demitri and Charlotte nodding with approval, and Analise and Lydia looking fairly skeptical. I tried for a smile, feeling awkward with everyone watching me, and I walked forward to join the group. Then, I grinned eagerly, looking to each of them, Analise and Lydia in particular. When they didn't return the gesture, I felt my nervousness bubble up.

I breathed deeply, hoping I could gain their support on my next endeavor, though they looked at me with extreme hesitation. "So, I've been thinking, as I'm sure you all have at one point or another, about what happened on the night of the council."

I was greeted by more silence, except Demitri was frowning in a puzzled way, not in frustration. He cocked his head, with a look of curiosity in his eyes, wondering where I was going with this conversation. Charlotte alone was still grinning and nodding, urging me to go on.

"Well, I know now. I talked with my birth mother, and I know that I'm like you all."

Analise scoffed at this. "Like us? You wouldn't even know where to start. So, you've read our history, cool. But, you have no idea what it's been like to grow up like this. You can't be one of us without that."

I felt taken aback by this, not having expected her defensive reaction to my upfront sharing of this new knowledge. To my surprise, Lydia, who had been so cruel to me at school before, said, "Cool it, Analise. If she has powers, she needs to learn how to use them. Plus, when was the last time we've seen another one of us?"

Analise chuckled almost sarcastically. "Not since the four of us were brought together." Lydia nodded as if to prove her point. I smiled with gratitude at her and she merely shrugged, looking down at her boots.

"Okay," Charlotte cut in, "so now, all we have to do is get her to access her powers. I know when we all were pixies; it was easy to start using our powers. Our mothers got us to use our wings at a very young age, and we've had the ability ever since. For Summer"—she paced back and forth in between the other three and I now, a laugh seeming to be consistently playing over her lips—"it'll be a more... interesting experience."

Demitri walked up beside me now, placing a hand on my shoulder softly. "Summer, are you sure this is what you want? This world, and magic in general, it's not always beautiful." He seemed so unsure, but I just nodded, and so he let go of me and stepped back behind Charlotte.

"Okay, now that whatever that was has been worked out, let's get started," Lydia said, looking to Analise now. "Analise, what is the most basic part of the magic of the warefae?"

She hesitated for a moment, looking curiously at Lydia, before saying, "Our wings, just like fairies."

Lydia nodded, looking to Charlotte, almost as if for confirmation, before saying, "And do any of you know the best way to make a fairy's wings emerge?"

"The free fall?" I asked hesitantly, remembering what Fallon had told me.

No one said anything, so Lydia flicked her white hair over her shoulder, looked me directly in the eyes with an all-knowing smirk, and echoed my words as she said, "The free fall."

Analise cackled at this, looking at me and saying, "There's no way she can handle it!"

At that same moment, Demitri exclaimed, "No, that's not happening." I rolled my eyes and looked to Charlotte, asking what exactly this would entail.

Charlotte sighed, saying, "Well, you get dropped from an extreme height. That's the basic principle. We were taught that wings of a fairy or warefae should instinctively begin working if the body is presented with a type of extreme danger that only wings can save someone from—falling."

"Okay, so what's the problem? We live close to the mountains! Someone flies me up there, I'll jump, and I'll get my wings."

"The problem," Demitri said, "is that this is incredibly unwise to do without the help of the fairies, and…"

"Oh, please, Dem, there are four of us, and we're not going to drop her! We don't need our mothers to help us with this," Charlotte cut in.

"Fine!" he exclaimed, clearly frustrated, "I'm not taking any part in this, though. I don't think this is a good idea." He walked over to his porch and sat on the steps like a pouty toddler.

Charlotte rolled her eyes and said, "Okay, you two. Are you game to help Summer and I?" They eyed each other briefly before nodding. Charlotte walked over to me and rolled her shoulders, allowing her deep blue wings to unfold. It was then that I became certain that I wanted wings of my own very badly, and I was willing to free fall to get them.

"All right, let's go." Charlotte walked up behind me and put her dainty hands beneath my arms. She pushed us off the ground, holding me securely, Analise and Lydia falling into the formation beside us. We flew over the vast forest, up and up into the chilly atmosphere and thin air pressure, until we were into the mountain range. The mountains were covered in snow and ice, and the outfit I'd been wearing from that morning was not nearly thick enough to warm me.

"You're shaking, Summer! Are you okay?" Charlotte yelled at me over the howling winds. I nodded, teeth chattering. We flew to the edge of a mountain that was flat at the edge, landing there in the snow.

"Charlotte, her lips are blue!" Analise exclaimed, peering at me with sudden concern.

"I know, Ana, I'm working on it."

She paced for a second, staring at me with my arms wrapped around myself before I could see her eyes light up. She moved my arms down by my side for a second, then swirled her hands around in a circular formation. It seemed like parts of the air were clumping together in front of me, like a miniature twister.

Charlotte snapped, and these particles seemed to weave themselves into a large coat. She waved her hands, and this mysterious material settled itself onto me. I could barely see it shimmering over my clothes, but I felt so much warmer. "Oh, thank you. That is much better!"

"If you are warefae, you'll become better adapted to extreme temperatures very soon," Lydia explained.

Suddenly, Demitri flew up the side of the cliff and landed in front of me. "I changed my mind," he said, "I want to help you to be like us, like you're supposed to be." He flashed me a grin, and I tried to return it, my cheeks fighting frostbite to form an unnatural-looking smile.

The other three seemed pleased that he was there, too, and we prepared for the free fall for a couple of minutes before Charlotte flew me straight out from where the mountain was. The other three dove down into the clouds, separating themselves in case something were to go wrong.

"Charlotte, I don't know if I'm ready," I yelled, looking down at the nothingness I suddenly saw below my feet. My stomach was practically doing backflips, and I felt like I'd be sick. "Summer, you are perfectly safe! If it doesn't work, they'll catch you and we'll just go back home! No worries, okay?" I breathed shallowly, closing my eyes and nodding vigorously. "Okay, I'm going to let go now, Summer." I felt every muscle in my body tense up as she counted, "One, two, three!"

I don't remember if I screamed, cried, or even breathed. Quite frankly, I have no recollection of how far I fell. I could only sense an oddly empty feeling. Time seemed to go by so slowly as if I'd keep going forever.

At long last, I felt a bit of a tingle. The sensation was not exactly from my shoulder blades, but from somewhere within, as if there was a stirring in my spinal cord. Someone grunted as our bodies slammed together, the air knocked out of both of us as I was caught in a sort of mid-air tackle. I opened my eyes to see Analise's braided hair flying behind her shoulder as her momentum carried us.

"You okay?" she shouted over the wind as she flew us back up toward the mountain. Honestly, I felt sick. My head was pounding. I just nodded, though, not wanting to seem dramatic to Analise because, in my mind, it was a miracle that she was even helping me now!

When we got back to the mountain, the other three were already waiting for us. Analise set me gently on the ground, and I coughed for a minute as I sat there, still trying to catch my breath. I stood up after a moment, looking between them and requesting to do the free fall again.

They all looked shocked, and Charlotte was the first to speak this time. "But, Summer, that could not have been easy on you! Besides, nothing happened anyways. You don't have wings. Let's go back."

"No!" I yelled over the now howling wind. "I know something happened when I fell. I felt something strange on my back. If I fall once more, I'll know for sure."

Charlotte skeptically walked behind me, prying my shirt away from my back a bit and peering down the top of my spine. She gasped, motioning for the others to join her. "What? What is it?" I asked frantically.

Analise was the first to answer, "It's the place where your wings should be! It's glowing! It seems to be a bright teal color. Or, is that turquoise?"

"It doesn't matter!" cried Lydia, "either way, you've got to go again, Summer!"

I agreed with her, walking to the edge of the mountaintop and holding my arms out for one of them to fly me out from the rocky slope. This time, I felt Demitri's firm grip on my waist. We lifted off and the girls descended quickly. This time, I felt less scared than before, but anxious about what would happen.

"You can do this," he insisted. "One, two, three." His fingers slid from my hips. I fell in a much more aware state this time around. It again felt as if time had slowed down, but, this time, in a way that allowed me to look around with my eyes wide open. I was falling, but this time, I was comfortable with the weight of the gravity pulling me down.

I felt a growing tingling in my shoulders, followed by an immense amount of pain. I saw that I had passed by Analise, and then Lydia, whom both yelled to Charlotte that I was falling a lot faster this time. I realized that wasn't by accident, though, as I saw her out of the corner of my eye, speeding toward me. My body was hurtling toward the ground at such lightning speeds because it was toying with fate, scaring the four of them so that just before I hit the ground, as I was about to, I could unfurl the wings that were ready to emerge. And, oh, did they feel wonderful.

It didn't even take a shoulder shrug, just a simple thought of *Open* for the wings to burst forth. It hurt to release them, but as I felt my feet stop inches above the ground, feeling the graceful flutter of my wings that spanned from my back, the pain felt like a distant memory.

"Oh. My. Gosh!" I yelled, emphasizing every word. I practiced moving my wings slowly, then quickly fluttering them, toying with them. I giggled deliriously; it was such a strange feeling. It was as if I was having a dream that had suddenly and mysteriously become reality. I flipped and dove through the air, up and down the street.

"No way!" I heard Charlotte yell, flying right up to me, grabbing my hands and spinning me around. "I knew you could do it! I just knew it!" Analise and Lydia flew down side by side, eyeing each other before each of them approached me to give me cautious hugs. "I've got to admit, Summer, I didn't think you had it in you. Congratulations."

"Thank you," I said sincerely. It was nice to feel like we were all on the same side.

I touched down on the ground by Charlotte then, Demitri landing beside us, and the other two girls heading back inside their houses. The sun was already setting. I hadn't even realized how fast the afternoon had gone by. All I knew for sure was that I had two wings attached to my back that shimmered at the edges. I reached behind me to run my fingertips along with one of them, and it felt silky smooth, but light as air at the same time. It was amazing. Every inch of my wings felt so sensitive. It was as if they picked up on everything happening around me.

"Okay, hotshot, now you've got to put them away before your parents see," Charlotte said, motioning to the fact that I'd taken down the entire fencing barrier between us earlier today. I laughed, shaking my head because my parents could know about my wings. I figured, regardless, I should try to think of words to bring them in. *Um, close? Stop? Go back?* Nothing was working. "Try moving your shoulders," Demitri suggested, but I shook my head and explained that's not what I did last time.

The two seemed puzzled as I tried to think of more words, and when I thought to *retract,* my wings seemed to fold in on themselves and tuck in behind my shoulder blades, resting comfortably in their own special pockets. As my wings hid, Charlotte exclaimed, "Wait! Bring them back out again!" I laughed, thinking *open*, and feeling the freedom of their expansion.

Demitri and Charlotte eyed each other suspiciously before Charlotte grasped my hand and lifted us both off the ground, flying toward her house. I had to purposefully think of flapping my wings to keep up with her, and when we landed in her backyard, I asked in a panicked voice, "Charlotte, what's wrong?"

"Just, stay here," she coaxed as she bounded into the house and returned almost immediately with Anastrella. She stopped in the doorway, jaw-dropping before she beamed and strode forward to hug me. "Oh, congratulations, Summer! This is magnificent!"

"Thank you, Anastrella! I think I'm still a bit in shock."

I laughed, but Charlotte cut off our cheerful conversation. "Mom! Look at her wings closely." Anastrella studied me for a moment, cocking her head and staring my wings up and down. She looked back to Charlotte with confusion. Demitri walked next to me, lining his wings up right next to mine. I looked back a bit to see that my wings were wider and shorter than his were, but his were more jagged around the edges than mine, which looked more delicate, and as blue as the ocean on a Caribbean spring day.

I noticed something else odd, though, and I figured Anastrella noticed at the same time I did, based on her sharp intake of breath. "What on Earth is that white light in her wings for?" Compared to Demitri and Charlotte's wings, and even Analise's and Lydia's, my wings seemed to glow in an extraordinarily bright way, without the smudges of how warlock's blood made them dull. There were even small spots within my wings that were so bright; they shone out a white light, not a gray glow like the rest of the warefae.

"Am I not part warlock?" I asked, trying to put together the pieces. "No, you must be. You have the same color wings and general features as Fallon, so I do not doubt that you are Blair, the daughter of her and Peter. She was never with anyone else, to my understanding."

I pondered that for a moment. It seemed that Blair was this new identity I was trying to take on, but at the same time, I was myself because of my parents, meaning Clara and David York. They'd instilled values in me as a young girl that I hadn't been able to get from Fallon and Peter, which wasn't their fault, of course. At least I now knew that my birth mother had contributed to some of the lessons I'd learned through life as well.

I shook myself out of my reflection, noticing Charlotte whispering different possibilities to Anastrella to explain my unique wings. Anastrella shook her head, turning to me. "I know you'll probably be hesitant about this, Summer, but I think we need to take our concerns to

Demitri's mother, Genesis. She knows more about the warefae and warlocks than us all, and she's spent the most years studying them," Anastrella suggested, despite my immediate rejection of this idea.

"Summer, what other choice do we have? We need to know what's different about you, especially before we begin training you to use your magic." I sighed, consenting, at last, to venture into the depths of Demitri's dark house.

When we walked up the steps to go into the house, the three preceding me into the doorway shrugged their shoulders and closed their wings, so I followed suit and thought to *retract*. The door creaked open eerily, and we all tread lightly into the entryway.

It was unlit, just as Demitri had told me so long ago. I felt like the darkness was choking me and as if I couldn't breathe if I wasn't returned to the light soon. "Genesis?" Anastrella called. Silence filled the house. Demitri walked further into a room in the back, I heard muffled voices, and then Genesis walked out quickly, Demitri close behind her. She flicked her hand up toward the ceiling, orange sparks cracking and suddenly illuminating the room. I blinked, adjusting to the sudden brightness of the place, to find Genesis very close to me, hands on her hips, staring into my eyes with a territorially threatening look.

"What is it that is wrong with your wings?" she asked finally. I was taken aback at how interested she seemed, and even her menacing demeanor seemed to fade away slightly. "I don't know what's wrong with them. There's a white light on them that looks different than the other warefae."

She nodded then, asking if she could see them. I nodded. *Open.* Genesis stepped back, scanning them meticulously. "Well," she said with an attitude of a physician, "it's odd first and foremost that you can control them without any sort of movement of your shoulders. That suggests an unnatural level of power. May I?" She reached her hand out to my wings and I nodded again.

Genesis walked behind me, delicately running her hand over my wings, humming to herself. Demitri walked up in front of me and whispered that she was trying to sense the magic in my wings. She walked back around me, and I felt nervous about what she'd say. She stopped directly next to Anastrella, pointing to my wings and explaining what she'd studied.

"The amount of magic in her wings surpasses the normal amounts of a fairy, but also the normal amounts of a warefae. Yet, I am certain based on her appearance, and the nature of her magic, that there are traces of Fallon's magic that course through her veins now." We all nodded, already knowing that much, but I felt lost as to how my magic could somehow be greater than the others, who seemed so powerful to me.

Genesis continued now, saying, "Her mother's element was focused around the ocean, and the preservation of the sea and all aspects of it. This explains the ocean-like color of her wings. As for the white beams of light that shine through the teal, I have a theory, but I feel like it's next to impossible…" She trailed off, looking puzzled as she met my eyes, before taking a hesitant breath and saying, "Come with me." She turned on her heel then and walked toward the back of the house.

I looked to Demitri, who nodded and motioned for me to move forward. I followed Genesis quickly, so as not to get lost. The other three trailed after us as well. I heard another noise as if a match was striking, and then light flew from Genesis' hand to the fixture on the ceiling. Looking around the room, there were maps and drawings of castles and constellations all along the wall. There were stacks and stacks of books on shelves and a huge desk in the middle of the room. Genesis moved to stand behind this now, motioning all of us to come closer, to the front of the desk.

Genesis rummaged in a pile of papers on the floor before pulling one up and laying it across the table. "This," she said in a hushed tone, "is a document representing an ancient warlock legend. It is called, as the ware-folk named it, *The Legend of the Light*." The four of us looked around at one another skeptically before shrugging and looking down at the document Genesis was referring to now.

She pointed to it, at the ancient markings and symbols that were different from the ones painted in my room, but I could still read them. As she had said, the words read 'The Legend of the Light.' There was an elaborate drawing below depicting an angel and a human, and a cord between them, linking to a sort of rune that I couldn't recognize. I thought briefly of the story I'd read of an angel and a human forming a different type of warlock on my wall in my room, and realized this must be the legend that painting referred to.

"The warlocks have believed since the beginning of time that one day, a demon and a human wouldn't be the only ones to contribute to the initiation of the warlock lineage." She pointed to the angel, and I looked up at her. "I read that in a painting Demitri put on my wall. So, it's true; there's a line of warlocks descended from angels?" Genesis nodded. "That is the legend in its most watered-down form.

Now, the importance here is that the warlocks always emphasized that once this line was brought into existence, the family associated with the angels and the lighter, more powerful magic would be honored. They would be practical royalty; they'd live in the Chief Warlock's Manor, in the mountains of Scotland, and have reign over the entire warlock population."

"But why?" Demitri interrupted. "Because, son, fairies aren't the only ones who look down upon the warlocks for their impure bloodline. They, themselves, have historically been very ashamed of their blood status, and they've taught their young that someday, when the Legend of the Light is fulfilled, they will be a hierarchical race, promoting the light bloodline most of all."

She pointed next to the runes drawn on the outside edge of the paper, which I could read, but chose not to prevent a spell of dizziness from washing over me. I wasn't used to reading in the warlock language at that point.

"The entire purpose of these scripts here is to signify that the warlock of light would have abnormally strong powers. They'd be strengthened by God's angels; knowing this made the warlocks ultra-aware of the fact that they'd have a being with heavenly strength, as well as capability of immense power, amongst their kind. It has been a possibility and hope that has been both revered and feared by generations of warlocks."

"But, Genesis, what does this have to do with Summer?" Charlotte asked, confused. Genesis held up her hand as if demanding her patience. She pointed, at last, to the cord and the mysterious symbol in the middle of the old paper.

"The key point about the entire legend is that the warlock of light was believed to be the connection between all creatures of magic in the world. All of the legends, every story, every species are thought to be under the ultimate control of the warlock of light." She pointed to the symbol, which looked like a mix between a star and an oddly shaped swirl. "This is the universal symbol for the preservation of magic, and this cord here represents the strengthening of these efforts, as well as connections and alliances the early warlocks believed to be possible between magical species."

"You mean... more than warlocks and fairies?" I asked skeptically, to which she nodded.

"Yes, of course. There are vampires and werewolves, wizards and witches, nymphs, sprites, goblins, trolls, mermaids, and all the rest. Anything you could've dreamed to be real in your wildest imaginations is likely not just a fantasy."

I took a deep breath, surprised at myself for struggling to absorb this information even though I, myself, was a warefae. *I had wings in my back, but I couldn't handle the thought of a creature with unnaturally pointy teeth!*

"Now, for how this relates to you. The white on Miss York's wings reflect a lack of tarnish that is brought about by the blood of a warlock, specifically a warlock with the blood of a demon somewhere in its' lineage. The fact that there's any deviation from her base color signifies that she isn't a complete fairy, which we knew already because Fallon was with Peter.

"That brings to mind the possibility that Peter, unknowingly, was the warlock of light, and now that he has passed on, you would be the direct inheritor of this lineage and this power."

I gasped, and I was not alone in this. Anastrella stepped closer to Genesis now, whispering hesitantly, "But what on Earth does this mean, Genesis? What must Summer be burdened with, so soon after learning any of this about her past and her powers?"

Genesis hesitated before saying calmly, "She shouldn't have to learn anything, not from us, at least. I am of the strong belief, now more than ever before, that you should leave, Ms. York. Leave Weston forever."

Chapter Nine
Where to Start

Genesis continued as if this was the most obvious solution. "Peter and Fallon made their mistakes, and it got Peter killed, and Fallon close to it. I will not risk the safety we've always provided for our children here by encouraging an alliance between the warefae, the fairies, and the warlock of light. That is a recipe for temptation for Lorena and her cronies to come after us.

"The knowledge of your existence would be enough to make Lorena want to hunt and kill you. I don't want to be caught in the crossfires of that whole situation, and on behalf of the fairy and warefae councils, I—"

"You have no say over the warefae council's decisions," Charlotte intruded harshly, years of resentment turning her cold as ice in response to Genesis' overprotectiveness.

Genesis glared at Charlotte, pointing her finger suddenly at her and opening her mouth to speak when Demitri cut in. "No, Mother! Summer isn't leaving! What happened to her mom is, in part, due to our fear of doing what we knew to be *right*. I will not allow us to make that mistake again!"

"What do you care, Demitri? You barely know the girl. You wouldn't even notice if she were gone, I promise you. We'd all be better off without her."

"That's not true! Mother, I am in love with her. If she leaves, I'm leaving with her." He looked at me then, and I felt myself blushing, but also beaming, as I looked at him. I didn't care if his mom didn't like me, or if she wanted me to leave Weston forever. I was going to stay right here because Demitri *loved me,* and I loved him so much in return that it made my heart feel like it'd just burst with joy.

I could sense Genesis staring between us, her tension and fury and anger rising until Anastrella put a hand on her shoulder, and she just sighed in defeat. "Fine," she whispered, facing obvious internal turmoil, "but she must be trained to use her powers the *right* way. If not, she could destroy us all."

She snapped her fingers and the light went out, and the rest of us took that as a sign to leave. As soon as we got outside of the door and walked down the porch steps, I turned around to Demitri behind me and wrapped my arms around him.

"Please, don't listen to her. You don't have to leave," he whispered into my ear. Having him stick up for me and go against his mother's will must have been tough for him, but the fact that he'd professed that he was in love with me in front of her and that he wanted me to stay with him, made me want to hug him even tighter.

Suddenly, I heard the familiar creak of my house's patio door slide open, and my dad called, "Summer! It's getting late, dear!" I backed up quickly, instructing my wings to close up as Anastrella motioned for me to hurry. "I'll see you all tomorrow!" I whispered, turning on my heel and running to my house.

"Hey, Dad! How was your night?"

"Good! I helped your mom clean the downstairs. We were wondering if you could get to the upstairs sometime tomorrow?" I nodded, following him into the kitchen and sitting at the table, where my mom was drinking a cup of warm tea.

"We saw that you've been busy this afternoon, young lady!" My mom eyed me with a smile playing behind her eyes.

"You saw me, huh?"

She laughed. "Well, of course, Summer! We're not completely blind, you know." I smiled, so glad that they accepted me, no matter how different I was from them. "Now, give us a twirl." I stood again, opened my wings, and slowly turned around.

"Oh, Summer," my dad whispered, in awe.

"They're glorious, darling," my mom cut in, "and we are so proud of you, and happy for you as well." I closed my wings and hugged them both, thanking them for their compliments and taking pride in my newfound magic.

"There's one more thing we noticed from today." My dad laughed, pointing at the giant heap of broken fence, illuminated by the light of the moon and stars.

"Oh," I started, looking sheepish, "oops!"

"Not to worry, Summer. We're not complaining; it looks much better this way, with all the open space. I was in my artist's loft while you were doing it, I suppose, so I was facing the opposite way of the house. Did you have any help or did you do this alone?"

I smiled proudly, boasting that I'd done it all alone, holding out my hands to show them the splinters. They eyed one another skeptically before my dad let out a nervous chuckle and said, "Sure, honey. We see *lots* of splinters!" Confused, I turned my palms over to look at them and gasped in shock.

"What's wrong, Summer?"

"My hands! They must've healed themselves!" It was like the splinters had been forced out on my skin's accord, and there were no marks to show any sort of perforation of my palm. I guessed it was my newfound magical blood that made me heal quickly.

My dad took my hand and studied it. "That's very interesting. I wonder if there's any research in the library that could give us some data on this situation. What do you think, Summer?" I shook my head, thinking of how protective the warefae and their mothers had been just by letting me into their little group—they were still hesitant to do so.

"Give me some time, Dad," I said, remembering the massive piles of books Genesis had in her office next door. "Maybe I can get closer to them and get you access to some of their historical documents and such." He nodded with appreciation, and my mom changed the conversational topic.

"Oh, Summer, before I forget, a boy named Bobby came by the house earlier today. Bobby Hayes, do you know him?"

"Yes, of course," I said, "what did he want?"

"Well, he said that at school today, he forgot to mention the surprise birthday party they're throwing for—what were their names, David?"

"Will and Annie, dear."

"Yes! The twins' birthdays are tomorrow, and so they're throwing them a surprise party at the courtyard across from the diner, tomorrow night."

I smiled. "Okay, I'll think about it. Is that all right with you guys?" They both nodded eagerly.

"You're enjoying your time here, honey! We don't want to stop you."

Soon after that, I went upstairs to shower and get ready for bed. As I pulled the sheets back, I heard a knock at my window. "Come in!" I called. "Hey!" Demitri said as he ducked in and pulled my desk chair to the side of the bed.

"Hey! How's your night been?" He shrugged. "It's been all right. Mother's breathing down my neck still about how dangerous and terrifying you are." He tickled me then, and I giggled at his persistent playfulness despite his stress.

"It's okay, though," he continued, taking my hand, "I think after all this time, I've finally found a reason to stand up for myself against my mother." I must've looked puzzled then, because he leaned forward and kissed my cheek, saying, "That reason is you."

I felt myself blush. After a moment's silence, I remembered my conversation with my parents. "Come to a party with me!" I insisted.

He laughed with surprise. "What, now?"

I rambled on, "No, I mean for tomorrow!

"Bobby invited me, and it's going to be at the park—it's a surprise party for Will and Annie's birthdays. I was thinking we should ask Charlotte, too. Bobby would love that! What do you think?"

He nodded, saying, "You know, it's strange. Until you came along, the town wasn't even willing to socialize with us. Now, we can go to Homecoming and a party within the same week." He looked sad for a moment. "It was hard being rejected for all those years."

I sighed with pity, and then squeezed his hand. "Hey, you can fly, right?"

"Well... of course!"

I continued, "And you can perform magical spells that alter the course of nature?" He scoffed, rolling his eyes. "I wouldn't go *that* far..."

"Then why on Earth would the opinion of some human teenagers mean anything to you? It doesn't matter!" He stared at me for a moment; eyes narrowed, before flashing a grin and kissing me.

"Goodnight, Summer," he said as he headed out the window.

"Goodnight, Demitri," I said, "I... I love you." I sounded nervous when I said it, but when Demitri turned around, I thought I saw a disbelieving tear in his eye.

"I love you, too."

In the first period, the next day, Bobby and I worked out all the details of the party. Haley would handle food, of course. Maysie was buying fireworks, and Bobby and I were supposed to go half and half on decorations. Charlotte worked her social magic during the day and convinced a lot of people from our class—even Jen and Daisy—to come along to celebrate the twins.

After school, I had dinner with my parents and then told them I had to get ready for the party early, to be there to set up with Bobby and the rest of my friends. I went to my closet and picked out a silver knee-length dress with long sleeves, as well as a pair of shiny black boots. I dressed and twisted my hair up into a fancy bun atop my head. I heard a quick buzzing of wings and moved to my window to see Charlotte hurtling toward me at full speed. I jumped out of the way just in time for her to fly straight through the open window.

"Summer! I have a huge problem; I have no idea what I'm going to wear!"

I laughed at her. "You realize we're leaving in twenty minutes, right?" She tore through my closet mercilessly before grabbing a dark blue velvet dress, holding it up to her figure, and changing her clothes right there in the middle of my room. "Charlotte!" I cried out, turning around and closing my eyes.

"Oh, please, Summer! I'm certainly not ashamed!" I laughed at her confidence.

"Hey, Charlotte, I almost forgot to ask," I began, thinking of something Bobby had asked me during class that day, "What do you think of Bobby Hayes?" She zipped up the dress and I turned around, seeing her looking thoughtfully off into space for a moment before smiling softly.

"Bobby Hayes has been the only boy that hasn't been completely enamored by my looks only, and hasn't gossiped about how frightening I must be throughout the entire time we've been going to school at Weston Prep." She looked sad now, staring down at her bare feet.

"Nothing could ever happen between us, though. He's a human, and I'm a warefae."

"Oh, stop it, Charlotte! Look at Demitri and me! I mean, I didn't find out I wasn't human until later, but there could be something magic about Bobby, too! You'd never know if you don't try!"

She shrugged, insisting that despite her sadness about not ever having a chance to be with a human, even a good one like Bobby, she wanted to go enjoy the party with us. "I'll be back in a bit. I just have to run home grab a pair of shoes."

"Okay, but hurry! I'll ready in a few minutes, and Demitri should be done soon, too."

About thirty minutes later, we all piled into my parents' car and I reversed out of my driveway, turning onto the main road that would lead us into town. "Tell me again"—Charlotte griped, shifting around in her seat and adjusting her seatbelt—"why do we have to show up in this—no offense—ultra lame car? We have wings for a reason, you know! Now you can just fly anywhere with us!"

"Yeah, Charlotte, and how exactly are we supposed to leave the party without means of transportation?"

"We say we're walking, and when we're out of sight; we take off!"

"I don't think so. People aren't going to believe we're walking home after midnight to the outskirts of town. There's no light past these roads that late, and that would freak people out even more!"

"All right, fine! I'm already in here anyway"—she snorted—"I just figured I'd complain while I'm strapped in this hunk of metal!" I rolled my eyes, laughing at her,

"Hey, don't hate on the car! If it's good enough for me, it's good enough for you!"

We drove past the school and the library a bit, turning to the community park, where I could see a lot of people from my school beginning to gather under the gazebo.

"All right, let's do this," I said, unbuckling and turning the car off.

"Oh, yeah," Charlotte said, smoothing down her borrowed dress as she stepped into the chilly night air, "Party time!"

I latched my fingers with Demitri's, and we fell into step with Charlotte, strutting our way to the crowd of people chatting and dancing to the soft set music. I went directly to Bobby, carrying some empty balloons and table decorations.

"Hey, Bobby!" I exclaimed excitedly.

"Hey, Summer. Thanks for bringing this stuff."

"No problem. I'm glad to help! I think Will and Annie are going to love this."

"Yeah," Charlotte joined in, "you set up a great party, Bobby."

He smiled. "Thanks, Charlotte. I'm glad you and Demitri could come too." Demitri nodded, taking my hand.

"So, let's address the elephant in the room," Maysie said, walking up arm in arm with Haylie.

"Are you two officially dating now?" I smiled at Demitri and nodded to the two girls, who jumped around with excitement and hugged me. I was glad that my friends were accepting us together—even if they weren't all warefae!

A bit later, after many more people had arrived, Will and Annie's parents drove into the parking lot. The pair stepped out simultaneously, and the whole crowd yelled. "Happy birthday!" They looked so happy to see everyone there, and Annie came over to hug all of us. A bit later, she pulled me aside, congratulating me on my new relationship. "I'm impressed you could pull that off, York," she said, elbowing me playfully.

Over the course of the night, we ended up mingling with more than just my friend group. I walked Demitri around to everyone, and the whole school loved him, just as I thought they would. Jen even shouted at me from across the field, "Hey, Summer!" and I waved at her and Daisy with a smile.

After we all had some cake and snacks from the diner and sang "Happy Birthday" to the twins, it started to get dark outside quickly. Maysie and Haley turned on some floodlights that had been set up on the outer edges of the park to illuminate the groups still lingering. Someone had started a little football game between a lot of the guys, and most of the girls sat on benches watching and laughing and talking.

"Summer," Demitri whispered as we stood with my friends again, watching Annie and Will were prepare for an epic twin arm-wrestling match at the table that had been cleared of snacks and sodas. I looked up at him. "What's wrong?"

"Where's Charlie?" I looked around the table, noticing that she wasn't anywhere to be seen.

Finally, I turned to the outskirts of the park where the party was, seeing Charlotte's blonde hair glistening from the reflection of the light shining on it. She was walking side by side with Bobby, and their hands hung close together. I saw her turn toward him, her body shaking with laughter, and her smile looking brighter than I'd ever seen it before.

I turned Demitri around so he could see where she was and felt him tense up next to me. I looked up, seeing worry lines creasing his forehead. "Uh oh, what's stressing you now?" I asked, trying to playfully shove his shoulder.

"Nothing," he replied stonily, turning back to see Annie complaining now about Will cheating in their arm-wrestle.

After a night of fun, fireworks competed with the bright stars to highlight the sky. Will and Annie cheered, and Will kissed Maysie with gratitude. Yes, the party had been Bobby's idea, but it was Maysie that had put the most time and effort into it.

Demitri had his arms around me, and even though the cold didn't affect me anymore, his embrace made me feel warm and comforted. As the fireworks continued, I took a curious peek back to where I had seen Charlotte and Bobby and was startled to see them locked in their own frenzied and half-crazed kiss. Demitri followed my gaze, and upon seeing them, he seemed to have the same uptight reaction he'd had when we saw them walking off together before.

I tried to tug on his arm gently, pulling him closer to me to face away from them. I wasn't sure why he was being so tense about Bobby and Charlotte, and whatever might be going on between them. Reluctantly, he turned away, seeming more quiet and distant in conversations for the rest of the night.

Around eleven, the party was over—we cleaned up the tables and all talked about how much we dreaded going to school the next day. When we finally left, Charlotte slid into the backseat of my car, exclaiming, "Wow! What a night!" as I drove back toward Lightenborough Drive.

I looked at her in my rearview mirror. "Well, it seems like someone enjoyed herself!"

She nodded vigorously with an ecstatic giggle, saying, "He is so sweet! He invited me to his house for dinner sometime next week!"

"That's great," I began to say, but Demitri cut me off with an irritated huff.

"What's your problem?" Charlotte asked looking at him sitting there with his arms crossed in the front seat.

He turned back to her, saying sarcastically, "Oh, nothing, Charlotte. Go ahead; hang out with the human! Break all the rules, why don't you?"

"Excuse me," her words cut through the icy air like daggers, "but you're not one to talk, Demitri. Besides, when you said you liked Summer, I told you to go for it!"

"That was different!" he cut in, his voice rising. "We knew something was different about Summer from the start. She wouldn't have been able to read the writings on her wall any other way."

"I don't care, Demitri, I don't! It's been almost two centuries! Finally, I meet a boy who is sweet and kind and wants to know me. Before Summer, no one wanted to know us at all! No one cared besides Bobby. He would've given me a chance before Summer made everyone like us."

"Charlotte, enough! What are you expecting to happen here, some sort of happily ever after? You think you're going to get to marry him and have kids, and, oh! Maybe he won't notice the fact that you're not aging! Charlotte, you can't possibly have expectations of a future with this guy, so what's the point?"

"The point," Charlotte said, tears flowing down her face, "is that I want one chance to be normal, Demitri. Just one! I'm so tired of this and having to follow all of these fake rules, and not being able to go anywhere but our stupid street! I'm over it!"

"You don't have a choice!" Demitri yelled, "This is the life we're stuck with! The rules we have are to prevent Lorena from finding and killing us."

"Well then, I quit! I don't care anymore," Charlotte screamed back at him, opening the car door as I sped down the dark street and flying away.

"Charlotte!" I cried, looking out the window and searching for her, seeing only a glint of starlight shining from her wings as she hurried away. Demitri unlocked my door next, leaning out the side and letting his wings unfurl as I rolled to a stop right there on the main road. There was no one around, and I wouldn't have cared if there had been.

"Where are you going?" He didn't answer me, still looking stonily after Charlotte. "Demitri North, I said where are you going?" He looked at me then, and I could see the pain he felt over hurting her, and my glare softened.

"I have to go after her," he whispered, reaching out a hand to cover mine, and then launching from the car, the door slamming shut behind him.

I sat there for a moment, still trying to process what had just happened. In Demitri's defense, Charlotte's sudden disregard for the natural order of life as a warefae was concerning. There wasn't too much that could ever go on between her and Bobby because it wouldn't be a lasting relationship, and she'd probably just get hurt.

But on the other hand, Charlotte undoubtedly deserved to be happy. She was so kind and genuine and had such a sweet soul. She would love Bobby as much as he'd love her if they were to be together, and it was such a shame that they could not be. At least, I didn't think they could be.

I put my head in my hands for a second, trying to focus, and then, deciding to address this whole thing in the morning, drove home in the darkness of the new day.

The next morning, I woke up early and made breakfast for my parents, trying to get on their good sides so that I could spend my afternoon out with Charlotte and Demitri. However, they didn't show up to be driven to school. At lunch, I sat next to Bobby, who whispered, "Where are the others?" I shrugged—I had no idea.

After school and dinner, I raced to their houses—Charlotte's first, and then, Demitri's, trying to find out where they had gone, and if they had spoken to anyone before they left. Anastrella hadn't seen Charlotte and offered to accompany me to talk to Genesis.

She had seemed worried, but Genesis seemed completely furious. "Where did you send him? I know he left with you last night; why is he gone!"

"I swear, I didn't tell him to go anywhere, Genesis." Her eyes narrowed at me, but underneath that, I saw the genuine concern she felt at the possibility that Demitri had left her again.

"I promise, he just went after Charlotte. It was Charlotte who was trying to leave, not Demitri. I know you're probably worried about him…"

"Oh, no, don't act like you know anything about me. You have no clue." I threw my hands up, part of me relieved that we could finally have this talk.

"Then please, Genesis, let me in! I'm warefae, I am not going anywhere, and, most importantly"—I looked at her earnestly now—"I love Demitri. I would never want him to leave, and that's why I came looking for him in the first place!"

She eyed me for a moment before holding open the door and jerking her head, motioning for me to come inside. I looked to Anastrella, who gave me an encouraging nod before going back to her house. I sighed in relief, entering as Genesis flicked the lights on and sat down at the kitchen table. I took the seat across from her.

She stared at me stonily for a second before taking a deep breath and saying, "My son has always resented me, I think, for not fighting harder for his father to come back."

I opened my mouth to assure her that this couldn't be true, but she held up her hand. "I don't want your pity. I have searched for his father for many years, but any of the warlocks that were involved in this… scandal… we got ourselves into have been in hiding for years." She paused for a moment, looking off into space. She seemed so sad and bitter as if her soul was in a terrible turmoil with itself.

I spoke then, voicing a curiosity I'd been too scared to ask Demitri, "Genesis, what is it like being a shadow fairy? What does the darkness do to you?" She looked at me with laughter hiding behind her eyes now, trying to figure out the right words to put to it, trying to describe her life.

"Being a shadow fairy—otherwise known as a dark fairy—comes with a natural persistence of gloomy thoughts. Negativity, depression, you name it. Dark fairies like to be in the dark because it's where our powers are strongest.

Dark fairies were also commonly leaders on the faire court because we have a grim yet realistic outlook on life, and how things could go wrong."

"Is that why you lead the council of the warefae and fairies?"

"Not necessarily; I lead the council because it was my idea to form it in the first place. Early on, I felt like we could get other members, and fight Lorena. But, alas, our children grew up, and only they joined, as a group of their own. As far as we know, there are no others like us, who have been exiled, aside from your mother." She paused, looking to me now. "I want to apologize for how that situation was handled back then. I believed Lorena was searching for Fallon, which she was, but we also could've done something to protect her. Demitri told me that she was still alive, but a human. I knew she lost her powers, but I had no idea she'd be alive." I nodded, appreciating her apology as she continued.

"Lorena is only about halfway done with her three centuries of allotted rule. Her treatment of the dark fairies has progressed to be much worse than it was when she started. She now considers them to have blood nearly as tainted as the demonic-blooded warlocks. Rumors have circulated in recent years that Lorena decreed that all dark fairies would be made slaves, servants, or soldiers for the Faire Palace." I shuddered at the thought of this, and Lorena's cruelty and power.

"And she's still going to be in power for another century and a half?" I gasped.

She nodded solemnly. "She won't age—fairies don't age, and are immortal unless their wings are cut off. Without our wings, we are mortal and human."

"That's what happened to my mother, isn't it?"

Genesis nodded. "Yes, your mother has no traces of magic left. She will age, and, eventually, can die as any human would."

"I saw her last weekend, in Florida." Genesis' eyes grew wide for a moment as if she still was shocked that she was alive.

"Demitri told me; how is she?"

"She's good. She is sad, of course, about losing Peter and I, but she's glad that I'm finally learning the truth about what I am."

Genesis nodded, then tilted her head a bit and asked, "Have you decided if you're going to learn to use your magic or not?"

Not having thought about it much before, I said, eagerly, "Yes, I want to."

Genesis stood then, motioning for me to follow her out to the back patio. I'd never been out here before, and it seemed like I had just walked into a deserted warzone. Scorch marks lined the fence, and great mounds of dirt lay on the outskirts of the yard. There were great divots in the grass, where it seemed like spells had blasted the earth apart. "This is where Demitri practices." Genesis motioned to the marks and the rubble. "I think this would be a good place for you to start as well."

"A… are you sure?" I stammered, looking at her with surprise. She nodded. "I think there may be more to you than I thought. I would like to help you." I nodded, my heart beating faster. "Okay, then. Let's get started."

Genesis explained that the best way for the warefae to access powers was to perform a balanced amount of warlock spells and fairy charms, at least at first. She insisted that even though it was mostly in her comfort zone, we should postpone the fairy charms and begin with a few ware spells.

She got a giant spell book out from a box under the patio, brushing some dust off the thick cover and snapping her fingers, making a wooden table appear. "What about that?" I exclaimed, completely impressed, "Is that a fairy thing or a warlock—er—enchantment?"

She laughed now. "It's fairy charms or warlock spells, Miss York.

"And yes, this is a 'fairy thing' because I am using the gifts of nature, such as the wood from the bark of trees."

"But it just appeared out of nowhere! There isn't a tree that you had to cut down!"

"But, don't you see, Miss York, that though there are no trees here in the yard to cut down, there is nature everywhere. All right, I guess since you've got me started on it, I'll teach you fairy charms first." She put the book down and walked over to me, her blouse billowing in the wind.

She stood directly in front of me, holding her hands out with her palms up. "Take my hands and close your eyes." I followed her directions, feeling her cold hands in mine. Her fingertips heated up all of a sudden, and I felt warmth shoot up my arms and into my chest.

"What is that?" I whispered. "This is how the magic works. Except normally, it starts so deep in your chest, it feels like it's coming from your lungs." I felt the heat moving up my arms now, and out of my fingertips as she let go of my hands with a startled motion. I opened my eyes, and she said, "And that is what it feels like when it moves through you." I nodded, feeling tingling reminiscent in my arms, and staring down at my hands.

"Okay, so how do I do that myself?" She breathed deeply now, turning around and moving the dark shadow that the house cast over the yard. She lifted her hands and the darkness moved around us in a magnificent swirling tornado-like motion, settling on the ground in a beautiful pattern of black stars and planets against the dirt.

"You have to use your power and take hold of it. Your strength will be the element of nature that you are best at moving. I would guess that its water seeing as that was your mother's ability. You can still be aided by other elements of nature, but not with as much proficiency as your element. That's what we'll start with first, then." "Okay, I'm ready," I said as I bounced on my toes enthusiastically.

"Okay"—she seemed to be suppressing a smile now—"try to slow down. Close your eyes, and feel the power of the water within you. Move the particles around in your soul, breathe with the ocean." I closed my eyes, thinking of the waves I saw this past weekend as if they were a heartbeat. I felt the warmth spread through my arms and suddenly, it was gone. "Ugh!" I exclaimed, opening my eyes.

"Try again," Genesis demanded.

Time after time, I tried, but still, nothing. No magic, no water, not even the tingling in my arms after a while. I sat on the porch, hopeless and exhausted. "This—isn't—working," I said between heaving breaths.

Genesis stood before me; eyes narrowed. "Now, correct me if I'm wrong, but the girl who marched up my doorstep earlier to tell me off for trying to push her away didn't seem like someone who'd give up. Isn't that right?" I looked at her, nodding slowly, feeling the courage building in myself as I remembered the reckless bravery I'd acted on earlier as I confronted Genesis.

"So, are you going to give up now, Summer?" I looked at her then, realizing this was the first time she'd said my name instead of calling me 'Miss York'. I stood from the patio, looking at her hopefully before closing my eyes and exhaling slowly.

I focused not just on waves, but also all kinds of water. I focused on raindrops, rivers, and waterfalls. I felt the spray of the sea, and coldness of a puddle at my feet, and the smooth fluidity with which it moved. I thought of all the water in the world, and imagined it under *my* control, but not just that. I imagined the water working with me, moving in a balanced way as if it was one with me.

Suddenly, the warmth hit me in my chest, like a painful electric shock that caused me to yelp in surprise. "Hold that feeling, Summer," I heard Genesis say, though I felt like she was worlds away now. "Let the power course through you." I gritted my teeth, feeling the water push through my veins at my command. My arms were trembling and shaking, but I felt that despite the abandonment of my senses, I was still in control.

I focused on my breathing, and as the magic moved to my hands, I pictured the power of the water flying out of my fingertips, turning into energy in the air, and like a flame from a match, I felt sparks spring to life from my hand. I opened my eyes to see brilliant blue little lights fluttering in the air in front of me. I didn't feel pain anymore; making these sparks felt as comfortable and familiar as if I'd been using this magic my whole life.

I laughed ecstatically. "Genesis, do you see this?"

She smiled, nodding eagerly. "That's it, Summer, you've got it! Try making something happen with water now." I dropped my hands, stopping the sparks and trying to decide what I wanted to do. I looked around at all the trees that formed a canopy behind the house, thinking that these trees must have water that I could take out of their roots. I wondered if I *could* do that.

I closed my eyes once more and tapped into my magic, feeling the elements of nature almost pulsing with my heartbeat. I felt heat rush through my veins, and opening my eyes, I raised my hands from my sides and into the air. "Whoa there, Summer! Don't kill the whole forest, please!" I laughed with shock, admiring what I'd just done. The trees were shriveling and turning brown as streams of water came up from the roots, suspended in mid-air.

With a grasping motion of my hands, I stopped the water in its path upward, pulling it back down with some invisible force into my palms, where the water transformed into pure power. I opened my arms with a burst, and slow, lulling raindrops propelled themselves forward, falling into the ground and giving the trees their color back.

Genesis placed a hand on my shoulder and said, "You're different than I thought you'd be."

"In what way?"

"You keep surprising me, and I have to say, I'm impressed with your grit." I smiled at her, and she in return, both of us glad that we'd overcome our differences.

For the remainder of the evening, I practiced harnessing the powers of nature with different fairy charms, and then Genesis got the giant spell booklet back out for me to begin using warlock abilities.

The first spell I performed was a simple shrinking spell on a log of firewood that Genesis had removed from the back porch. I was all set to perform the incantation, but when I said the ancient spell words in my mind, there was a flash and a bang, and the log was gone.

At least, we thought the log was gone until Genesis squatted down to the snow and picked up a little twig. "Perform the growth spell on the next page," Genesis said, and when I did, the same flash and loud noise occurred, and the log was back where it had been.

"Wow," Genesis said with wide eyes.

"What is it?"

"Well, my original assumption of you being related to a warlock of light is now more convincing than ever! You have an *insane* amount of power, and you've only been practicing magic for a couple of hours!"

"So, what does that mean? Is that going to be a problem?"

"No, no, Summer! You're incredibly gifted. You see, you possess powers that the fairy community had come to fear, but no one had ever fully been able to understand. Your father would have died before the warlock world would have even known about his lineage.

"You are the true, rightful leader of the warlocks, and your destiny awaits you, quite frankly. You can choose whatever path you want to, and you could go wherever you want to. Once you're trained in defending yourself and combating other mystical creatures, there are no limits on whom you could become."

My mind raced as I tried to process all that she told me, and I finally protested, "But, Genesis, I don't want to be a warlock ruler. I've seen what Lorena has done, and I don't want to end up like her!"

She pursed her lips, nodding, and then saying, "Follow me." As she walked quickly into the house. I followed her around the halls and finally, to a door in the back that was closed firmly.

She looked at me with her hand on the doorknob. "This is Demitri's room. I want you to go in there for a few minutes and just look around, take it all in. I think this will be pretty telling to you."

"Telling of what?" I asked, searching her eyes for some clue, but she merely patted my shoulder, opened the door to allow me in, and then walked down the hall and away.

When I walked in, I felt around on the wall next to me for a light switch, but seeing as there wasn't one, I focused very hard on the power of the sun, channeled that, and felt a light rush from my fingertips and into the star-like lights illuminating the ceiling, and the lamps spread around the room. I felt like I had to squint, it was so bright, but after a few moments of adjusting, I realized that this must be Demitri's safe haven in the house. It was the one place where he could try to bring some light into his dark world.

Looking around the room, I saw that his bed was made up neatly, without even a pillow out of place. He had a large window on the wall next to his bed, and when I opened the curtain, I saw the corner edge of Lydia's house and the vast greenness of the canopying forest outside his backyard.

It must've been like torture, having to stare out this window. He got to see the vast freedom of the forest and had probably stared out this window for hours of his life.

I walked around slowly to the gray desk that sat against the wall, across from his bed. Strewn across it were multiple piles of sketches and drawings. Some were of nature, others of outlines of fairies with their wings gloriously spread from their backs, and even more of them, surprisingly, were of me.

All different types of drawings, some of me smiling, and others of me just standing there, arms crossed, hair blowing in the wind, were in this pile. They each dated back to August when I'd first moved here. I felt overwhelmed emotionally looking at them, realizing that as beautiful as he'd made these pieces of art to be, he must've seen me as such.

I felt like I didn't want to intrude too much, so I replaced all of the papers I'd examined with awe, observing his room again now. The closet door positioned next to the bed was slightly ajar, and as I turned to leave the room, something glinting in the light caught my peripheral vision. I paused in my steps, turning and walking slowly up to the closet door, grasping one side and opening it all the way, floored at what I saw inside.

It was my mother's painting of me, hanging on one side of the closet, opposite of where his clothes were hung. My blue eyes and the mystical way I'd appeared had not changed at all since the day my mother had auctioned it off so successfully.

It was shocking to think that Demitri, all those months ago, had spent that kind of money on a painting of me. It made my heart leap with joy, knowing that it was safe here with him. I did wonder for a brief moment, though, why he never told me that he had it.

Feeling very fulfilled after seeing Demitri's little sanctuary, I took the light from the room with a whooshing feeling in my hands, closing the door and finding my way almost blindly to the living room once more.

"Did you see what I'd intended for you to see?" She asked, clearly referring to the painting of me.

"Yes," I said quietly, feeling passionate tears gathering in my eyes before I got a hold of myself and shoved them back down.

"Do you understand why I wanted you to see it?"

I whispered, 'no' this time, still trying to fit all the pieces together.

"You said you don't want to become like Lorena, but you forget that Lorena's soul is not only defined by her power as grand faire enchantress. She has been molded through the years by her isolation as well. Based on what you saw in my son's room, I think you should feel comforted at this point that you will never have to worry about feeling alone, isolated, power-hungry, and scared. You are loved, Summer. That is the difference between someone like you, and someone as cold and heartless as Lorena." I nodded slowly, understanding now the message that was to be gained from my walkthrough of his room.

Before she sent me home that evening, I paused at the door, turning back to her with a friendly look upon my face as I spoke. "You know, you're different than I thought you'd be." Genesis smiled, reflecting on our conversation from earlier on.

Her voice rang out brighter than I'd ever heard it, "In what way?"

"You keep surprising me, Genesis, and, I have to say, I am impressed with your kindness." With a smile and a pleasant goodbye, I walked down the patio steps, realizing that despite having a very productive day, Charlotte and Demitri were still missing, and that scared me terribly.

I looked to the darkening sky, which was full of clouds as if the atmosphere was stirring with anger. I paused in the middle of the street, thinking to myself that clouds are just lots of water, and raised my hands in concentration. Very quickly, the clouds began to spin around each other in the air, in a swirling fashion.

I brought my hands together though and then threw them apart, causing the clouds to turn to mist in the air at my command, revealing the beautiful, star-studded sky they had hidden behind them. I smiled then, realizing that as a half-fairy, this was sort of my job. I was bringing forth the beauty and balance of nature. It was magnificent what I could do, what all of us could do.

If only we weren't forced to stay on this street, hidden from the faire folk that so feared the existence of the warefae. They simply hadn't opened their minds and hearts up enough to accept that there could be coexistence, and even love, between warlocks and themselves.

They had placed themselves on a pedestal, thinking fairies were the most important mystical creatures. Lorena had enforced that belief with her rule. I felt concerned at the prospect of one hundred and fifty more long years of being trapped here before the next ruler could change the rules—and that wasn't even a guarantee.

I couldn't take it; I wouldn't take it! Instead of going home, I marched directly across the street, to Analise's house. I didn't know if she would take my idea on with a welcoming attitude, but I had to try. This was of utmost importance, and she and Lydia would have to work with me and hear me out in place of Charlotte and Demitri.

I knocked on the door of the brick house I knew to be Analise's, surprised to be greeted at the door by Lydia's mother. "Ah, daughter of Fallon," Katia said with her hand on her hip, "what are you doing here?"

"Oh, hello, Ms. Snow."

"Just Katia, please," she cut in.

"Sorry, hello, Katia," I said, frazzled now.

Her sharp blue eyes peered at me with impatience. "Analise and Lydia are at our house." She pointed to the end of the street. "Vivyanna and I are making dinner. You're welcome to stop by after it's done," she said, shutting the door in my face.

I took a sudden step back. I assumed that being an ice fairy, that was her attempt at friendliness. At least she hadn't acted how Genesis had toward me before we'd had our strange forging of a relationship today.

I walked diagonally from this house, then, to the other brick house of the street, Lydia's. It was so clean and perfect compared to the rest of the houses, and upon closer examination, I saw that the house was lined with beautiful icicles and tiny ice-sculpted snowflakes. It was like a winter wonderland dancing across the roof. I walked up the porch steps and knocked lightly against the glass door.

Analise opened it, and then an irritated look crossed her face. "Who is it?" Lydia asked, taking her place beside her in the doorway.

"Oh," she said, seeming equally disappointed, "what do you want?"

"Hey, guys," I said, trying to seem as sprightly as I could without revealing the awkwardness that I felt in their presence, "I was wondering if I could talk to you both for a second?"

"Oh, now you want to talk to us?" Analise said, marching forward out of the doorway. I backed up as she persistently came at me, almost growling like a ferocious animal. "What... what do you mean?" I stammered, "I never said I didn't want to talk to you guys."

Lydia followed behind her, saying with her steely tone, "Oh, no, of course not. You've just been implying it for the entire time you've been here. You never invite us to spend time with you, you don't trust us as much as you do Charlotte and Demitri, and you didn't offer to take us to the party last night." I felt guilt wash over me like a tsunami.

All this time, I'd thought that Charlotte and Demitri hadn't hung out with Analise and Lydia because they were bad people, but it made us just as rude for ignoring them all the time.

"Analise, Lydia, I'm so sorry…"

"Oh, save it!" Analise yelled the two of them on opposite sides of the street from me now. Analise closed her eyes and worked her face into a contorted sort of smirk before she launched copper sparks my way, sending a rush of murky, swamp water rushing to me.

This may have been her marsh power, but what she didn't know is that I wasn't a helpless human anymore. I threw my hands out in front of me, and water went straight up and away from me as if forming a shield. The murky brown rush of river crashed against it, curled over in mid-air, and hit Lydia straight on top of the head.

When the water had settled on the ground, Lydia screamed, her white hair now stained a sickly brown color, and her light blue top and sweatpants were sopping wet. "Oops, sorry!" I said, not having intended to splash the muck onto her. "Here, let me help you with that," I exclaimed in a panicked tone, sending a hose-like jet of water shooting from my hands, practically pummeling her with its violent spray.

The three of us stood there in shocked silence for a moment, my hands covering my mouth in complete humiliation. I then shakily brought them away from me again, motioning like I was pulling a rope with my hands; all of the water soaking Lydia vanished like tiny, crystalline raindrops into the atmosphere. Lydia still stood there with her mouth open, clearly disgusted at what had just been on her, her cheeks red from the heavy water droplets battering her moments before. Analise stood next to her, her eyes wide, and then suddenly, she let out a tension-relieved laugh.

She was doubled over, clutching her stomach as she snorted and giggled until Lydia and I joined in with her. Analise walked over and high-fived me, and Lydia shook her head, still in disbelief, motioning for me to join them in the house. Glad they had decided to move on from my epic misuse of my powers, I followed them through the glass door.

The inside of the house was even more spectacular than the outside. The walls were lined with great sheets of ice that seemed to twinkle in the light of the ice-designed chandelier. "Wow," I breathed, as I took my shoes off as the girls had, stepping lightly across the cold white tile that transformed into a bright carpet as we entered Lydia's room. It was slightly warmer in here I thought, likely because of all of the bright lights that shimmered from the ceiling and shone from the floor.

The girls each sat down on the fluffy pink rug in front of Lydia's pillow-covered bed as if they'd been doing this for years. I joined them eagerly, looking back and forth from one of them to the other.

"So," I said, not wanting to jump into my true purpose for visiting them just yet, "why is there always so much tension between you guys and the three of us?" They eyed each other carefully as if telepathically working out an answer, before Analise sighed, all humor gone from her eyes now.

"Well, it started when we were quite young. I think we were about twenty, right, Lydia?" Lydia nodded, keeping her eyes averted almost shamefully. Analise paused for a moment, screwing up her face again as she fought to remember those days almost two centuries prior.

"When Lydia and I began to mature, we realized that likely, the only chance of us ever having kids would be with…" She paused, looking up at me and bracing for something. "Well, Demitri would be our only chance of a relationship or children." I slouched back, thinking now I could draw up a pretty clear picture of what had happened.

I guessed that Lydia and Analise both got unbearably flirty and obnoxious, too much so for Demitri to bear. That's likely what turned him from the two girls in front of me, and Charlotte would have learned to resent them in Demitri's honor. Lydia retold the story almost exactly as I'd written it up in my mind, and it all made sense now.

"We're embarrassed by it, obviously," Analise said at last, "but after all this time, it seemed easier to just stick to ourselves." I nodded, seeing that there was true regret between them, soothing them with notions of forgiveness and moving on as far as both sides were concerned.

"I did come over here to talk about something more important, though." They shot one another a nervous glance again before looking at me and nodding slowly. I took a deep breath before assuring them that yes, I had thought this out quite thoroughly before even daring to run through the means of accomplishment in my mind.

They urged me on with frightened looks in their eyes, the possibilities of my actions endless in their minds because they knew so little about my powers or my desires for my position in the warefae realm of life. My wish seemed much simpler than spells or wings or the other complications of faire folk, though.

I closed my eyes tightly, not wanting to see their reactions as I said in a hurried flow of words, "I want to find Lorena and overthrow her, and the faire court, and the whole kingdom. I want to win us our freedom from exile and to end prejudice against the warefae from the fairy world once and for all."

I opened one eye, and then immediately wished I could shut it again upon seeing their reactions. Lydia's face appeared to be the same as when I'd doused her in water outside, and Analise was grimacing as if someone had just punched her hard in the stomach.

Worse than that, though, is that neither of the girls said anything. They didn't even try to use their weird telepathic method of communication that they seemed to have; both of their eyes were still on me like I was a strange circus exhibit that defied all logic and laws of nature.

"Guys?" I said finally, to be met by more silence. After several minutes of their blank-faced stares, I snapped my fingers in front of their faces, spraying light water droplets on them as someone would to a misbehaving dog. This was effective, though, because they both snapped out of the frozen states they were in, wiping their hands down their faces with shaking hands.

"I'm sorry, Summer," Lydia said finally, "but I think I must've heard you wrong. Did you say that you want to find *Lorena?* You want to find Lorena and *overthrow her?*"

"Yes!" I said energetically, still determined that it was, in fact, a good idea.

Analise blew out a dramatic breath, staring at me with wide eyes and saying, "Summer, it sounds great when you say it like that, but someone can't just go to the Faire Palace and ask Lorena if she wants to get rid of an exile sentence! She'd cut off our wings and kill us all!"

I shook my head. "Why couldn't we fight? We all have powers, powers that are stronger than fairies, even!"

"Okay, fine, but, assuming our mothers will refuse to go with us, there are only five of us. Four if you include the fact that you just started using your powers—"

"Today," I cut in, confident and unashamed of the fact that I was still learning.

"See," Lydia said, "we can't go off fighting for freedom like we're in some sort of a revolution. It's a cute notion though, Summer." She sat back on her hands, trying to act as if she were ignorant to what freedom meant to her, as was Analise. Despite how hard they tried, though, I could see the thought of what freedom meant toying in their minds; images of them *free* danced behind their eyes like a spark of possibility.

I sat in silence as I watched them work through this, resting my arms atop my knees with a sort of smug satisfaction. Before long, they were looking at one another with an exposed curiosity and clear desire to consider my plan. They looked at me, smiling almost ferociously after it was clear that they had silently decided they were totally and completely in agreement with me.

"Okay, Summer, how would you suggest we go about this?" Analise asked.

"Yes, Summer, before we even commit to it," Lydia said with a fake haughtiness, "we've got to know your *genius* plan." I laughed then, nodding and saying with all honesty that I didn't have the slightest of clues how we would go about this. Being so new to the warefae way of life, I didn't want to pretend that I knew the first thing about what the Faire Palace was like.

"Great, Summer, that's wonderful. I'm sure we could act as spies and sneak in underneath the Faire Tree," said Analise, laughing with Lydia as if the whole thing was fairly silly. "I'm serious, you two! We can figure something out!"

"Summer," Lydia said softly, "you have no plan. How can we follow you in this if you have no ideas?"

"Well," I said, "I may not have much of a plan, but I have an idea of where to should start."

Chapter Ten
A Crazy Idea

The next day, school was a disappointment again—Demitri and Charlotte were gone. I made the most of their absence by going on an after-school hike with my parents, walking behind them, and practicing little tricks with puddles as we walked. Once, I even stopped a small rain shower. I still felt down, though, without my two closest friends.

In their absence, I had made big plans. I had told Lydia and Analise to spread the news that I'd be calling a meeting with the present warefae and fairies. I wanted to get their opinions on the idea I'd presented to Lydia and Analise the night before. I hoped as the day went on that I'd see Charlotte and Demitri in the halls to debrief with them, but for now, my confidence would have to do.

That night, I was in my room getting ready when I saw Demitri enter through my window. I turned around with a smile and bounded across the room to greet him with a tight embrace. "Are you okay?" I whispered against his chest. He murmured that now he was, and I was so glad that he'd gotten back after two days. I stepped back, having so many questions for where he'd been since the party, but only being able to come up with, "Charlotte?"

"She's fine. She's home, and we worked everything out. I apologized, and so did she. She knows that life with Bobby or any other human isn't in the cards for her, so we stopped by his house on the way home and she told him that."

"Oh, no! Poor Charlotte," I said, pacing my room now, continuing, "Poor Bobby!"

Demitri nodded, sitting on my bed. "I know, but Charlotte explained that her life is different and she has things she's dealing with that she just can't tell him about."

"How did Bobby take it?" I asked nervously.

He looked at me with a look of admiration crossing his face at the memory. "He told her that he understood and that he only wants the best for her. He kissed her on the cheek and said that he hopes they can always be friends now." I felt tears well up in my eyes a little out of sadness for both of them. Charlotte and Bobby were two kind and deserving people, and the fact that they couldn't be together and they had to just accept their fates made my heart hurt for them.

"Hey," Demitri said, rubbing my back soothingly, "Charlie's going to be okay. She always is."

"It just doesn't seem fair," I protested, "that I get to be with you, and she can never even try to be with Bobby." He agreed solemnly, saying that rules were in place for a reason, which got me thinking about my quest from the previous night.

"Speaking of rules," I said vaguely, "we've got some to discuss at the meeting tonight." He looked taken back as I moved in front of my mirror to fix my hair and apply some mascara.

"Meeting? What kind of meeting?"

"Oh, tonight we're having a council meeting. I'm calling one, and Analise and Lydia thought it was a good idea, too."

He scoffed, "Since when do you hang out with Analise and Lydia?"

"Well, only since I've realized that you and Charlotte, specifically you, have been holding grudges against them for far too long." I narrowed my eyes at him with some mock sweetness to meet his gaze of disbelief.

"So that's what they told you, huh? Did they mention that they hounded me about dating one or both of them until I decided not to date anyone at all? Or did they tell you about how they tried to be fiercely competitive with Charlotte because they thought she was trying to steal me away from them, even though she never had a single romantic thought toward me? We distanced ourselves to avoid their jealousy and bitterness, and since they never made any efforts to socialize, we assumed that the tension and their numerous attempts to woo me wouldn't have ceased if we reached out." He shrugged. "It's just how it's always been."

I nodded, understanding, but still pointing out that they had changed. I implored him to give them a chance, and he reluctantly agreed. Midnight approached now, and I slipped into my closet, quickly changing into the light blue sundress that I knew would match my wings and give further proof to the others what the basis of my power was.

It was so interesting to me that since I'd begun to use my magic the day before, I no longer felt that cold chill that was coming in with autumn. I didn't feel pain when I bumped into things, which I hadn't done all day due to a newfound sense of grace that I assumed I should associate with the magic flowing through my veins.

I walked out of my closet, and Demitri's eyes scanned me with surprise. He looked at my face then, his gaze softening a bit as he whispered, "You look absolutely beautiful." If it hadn't been for me smiling and turning to allow my hair to fall over my face a bit, he would've seen me blush bright red.

He stood from my desk chair that essentially was his at this point, seeing as he sat in it more than I did, and he walked over to me and took my hands in his. He rested his forehead against mine and we stood there for a second, just like that. We listened together to the gentle howling of the winds outside and felt the night air drift easily through the window. I took a deep breath, thinking of what was about to happen, and said; "I need you to trust me down there in the meeting, okay?"

He stepped back, searching my eyes for any sort of explanation for this mysterious plea. When he realized I'd reveal nothing to him yet, his lips pursed with concern for a moment, but then he nodded in a solemn yet promising way. I squeezed his hands in gratitude before I turned to the window and walked out onto the balcony, commanding my wings to expand and feeling the comfort of their release and stretch. I felt Demitri's wing skim my own as he ducked out onto the balcony, and I shivered at the sensation of the contact.

The other council members, of the warefae and the fairies, were gathering below, and I felt a sudden surge of confidence as I saw all of these exiled women waiting in apprehensively to see what I had to say. Demitri took my hand in support, and we flew together down to the edge of the cul-de-sac, taking our place in the circle.

We all stood there in silence for a moment, and I could tell that this was, in part, because the ones who hadn't seen me since I'd learned of my powers were admiring my wings, likely wondering of the significance of the white patches of light on them, and piecing together the significance of my blue dress. After about a minute of their eyes on me in silence, I let go of Demitri's hand, ready to take this on alone.

"Thank you all for coming," I began, my voice surprisingly steadier than I thought it would be.

"What's all this about, dear?" Anastrella asked from across the circle, "Is something wrong?" I shook my head no at first, but then, after thinking about everything I'd been reflecting on for the past day, I nodded.

I sensed everyone in the circle growing tense, except for Analise and Lydia, of course, who stood there looking smug at their prior knowledge of this meeting. They also appeared to be a bit excited to see everyone's reactions.

"There is something wrong," I said confidently, looking to each of them, "and something has been wrong for a very, very long time. This exile is unacceptable, and it is not a way of life that can continue into eternity! There is nothing dangerous or threatening about us, and I'm sure my fellow warefae would second my opinion that we would be no danger to society." The others nodded in agreement, and so I continued. "As for you fairies, why is it that the Grand Enchantress should be in charge of whom anybody can love? Who gave Lorena the authority over *souls*?" Everyone looked taken aback now, throwing worried glances back and forth.

"I know it may sound crazy, what I'm about to suggest, but I think we should just give the idea a thought. I want us to all go to the Faire Palace and work to overthrow Lorena and win back freedom for us, and for all of the fairies that have been oppressed for over a century. She *must* be stopped, and I think deep down, you all know that." I paused, and everyone had vague looks of fear on their faces. "Well? What do you think?"

Genesis, whom I expected to support this idea after our conversation from yesterday, said hesitantly, "I understand where you're coming from, Summer. However, I feel that we would be drastically outnumbered if we stormed the palace. There are guards everywhere, and we don't have any way to boost our numbers."

"That's not true, though!" I argued, "think about it, Genesis; no fairies besides the four of you here have ever even seen a warefae, and that means none of Lorena's guards will know of the strength that lies in our magic. There are five of us with powers that surpass anything Lorena could have imagined. And, on top of our stronger fairy charms, we have a whole list of warlock spells that we could use!"

"Summer, you started learning those yesterday! I showed you a mere couple of spells!"

"Wait," Demitri cut in, "you two were *together* while I was gone?" I nodded, and Genesis did as well, shushing him in the process.

"Besides you being completely inexperienced, Summer, none of the warefae have ever even seen what these fairies are like. They can be vicious, and their cruelty would make any backyard fight we've had over the past century seem tame."

Some of the group laughed at this statement by Anastrella, but I looked at her intently and decided to reveal what I'd been holding as my statement of last hope.

"There's something else; I am not a normal warefae. I am a warefae descended of a warlock of light. That makes me the proper leader of all warlocks. I am confident that I, along with all of you, could take on Lorena and end this suffering and isolation once and for all. We should not live in fear."

I threw my hands up now, laughing without humor and saying in frustration, "I mean, do you want to spend forever on this street? There's a whole world passing us by out there!"

We all stood there in silence for a moment before finally, Demitri placed a hand on my shoulder. "I'll go with you, Summer." I smiled, placing my hand atop his in gratitude.

Charlotte stepped forward, the defeated look from the last time I had seen her no longer in her eyes. "I'm going, too. I am tired of being shut in on this street. I'm tired of never getting a chance to see what's out there." She looked to her mother, almost sadly, saying, "I'm grateful for the life you've given me, and the safety that you and all of the other fairies here have provided for us for all these years. But, Mom, it's time. I think you feel that too." Anastrella bit her lip, tears welling up in her eyes with overwhelming emotion.

"Well, obviously we're in," Analise said proudly, stepping forward with Lydia. "We worked through some of the details with Summer last night, and the girl knows what she's doing. She may be new, but she's got some wicked instincts." She winked at me supportively, and I nudged Demitri to show him the change that did seem to be occurring with the two of them.

"Okay, that's settled then," I said as I looked around the circle, "all of the warefae are in. Ladies, will you join us? Will you reclaim the freedom that is rightfully yours?" Another moment's silence passed before the circle was completed once more as every fairy stepped forward to take their place beside their children.

"Of course, we will fight beside you," Genesis said. Anastrella added, "We will *always* fight beside you."

The meeting adjourned on a hopeful note that night. We didn't know yet how we were going to go about our storming of the palace, but we knew for certain that we would be in for an almost painful amount of planning and training over the next few months.

The prospect of freedom, though, for the fairies and warefae who had been lacking that for so many years, seemed to light a different fire in their hearts and awaken a part of them that had been shut away for all this time. It was inspiring, and it made me hope that I could help them achieve that freedom in any way that I could.

When we went back to school, it felt like a completely different experience from the start of the year. Everyone was united together. Even Lydia and Analise had finally joined our group and fit in right away. There was no tension or conflict or anything negative between the warefae and the humans—there wasn't even a hint of jealousy from Haley toward Charlotte. She and Bobby hadn't had any issues since calling off their possible relationship, and our friends were closer with us than ever before. It was as if they knew what we were planning to do, and had joined in arms with us, ready to stand behind us.

This wasn't true, of course, because nobody knew what was happening within the mystery of Lightenborough Drive. The change was stemming from the kindness they'd seen from Demitri and Charlotte at Homecoming, and again at Will and Annie's party. Everyone had welcomed Lydia and Analise by association, and they charmed everyone. The openness and overall kindness my neighbors projected earned the respect of everyone, which eliminated stress in one part of my life, at least.

The closed-off attitude I'd found when I moved to Weston was no more. It certainly made it easier that I could make my friendship with Charlotte, Analise, and Lydia, and my relationship with Demitri, public.

School had been easy—almost too easy. It turned out that along with being temperature resistant, immune to all diseases, and having healing powers, I also gained heightened intelligence when I unlocked my powers as a warefae.

Being warefae was so natural for me. I had the magic and grace of fairies and the wisdom and skill of warlocks. Continuing the human life, I'd led the semester before seemed so mundane now. I finished homework in no time at all, and I aced all my tests without any study time put in.

Despite the lack of attention I placed on school now, I didn't have a free second to spare. As soon as I got home, had dinner with my parents, and told them I was going to do homework with Demitri and Charlotte, I reported to my training, along with the other warefae.

We couldn't do a lot of our work out in the street because that would risk the possibility of my parents seeing us, which I wasn't concerned about but the fairy mothers wanted to avoid as much as possible. Plus, we needed excess space to practice dueling with one another, so we moved our practices past the street, to a clearing deep within the forest.

I found myself there, almost two months later, in the dead of winter. We were in the middle of our fourth lesson of the night, Warlock Spells taught by Genesis. "So, the spell you must learn is this," Genesis said, as she began speaking a spell in ware that would form jets of green warlock magic that would shoot at whomever we would be attacking, completely disintegrating the poor creature before us. "Now you try it," she said, moving out of the way with the other fairies.

We all spoke at once, firing our green jets with ease, turning a couple of dead trees in front of us to ash. We then continued, repeating the spell by memory, no longer needing the words to perform the actions.

Muscle memory was a nice part of warlock spells. It certainly was a skill that made attacking much faster, and I found myself appreciating the ease of warlock magic so much more now. Once we knew the spells, the magic was so easy to perform, especially for me.

I could feel my warlock powers enhancing with each night I practiced, and the vast difference between my level of strength and the others' abilities made me feel proud but embarrassed. I was complimented frequently by the others, and it felt strange to be a standout of the group. When it came to all the other fairies' lessons in different types and uses of magic, I had superb skills, but my ocean-based water magic was what proved my abilities to be above and beyond the levels of the other warefae.

Our lessons felt very official, seeing as they were an hour each, and they had their different objectives and agendas. Anastrella began our night by teaching us the art of energy in nature. We learned how to tap into it, and how to find it anywhere. Every speck of dirt and every bit of the sky, we learned, held energy that fueled our magic, and it was so interesting to find our balance with the earth around us during her lessons.

Vivyanna taught us how to shield ourselves from others using our talents. With my magic, for example, I'd been playing around with a technique where an entire wall of water would come up in front of me. I could customize it to fend off whatever kind of attacking element was coming at me. Everyone else had the method that they were developing, and day after day, we were growing and strengthening our powers.

Katia, the fairy with the most stone-cold focus of them all, taught us about how to use our skills specifically to play the offensive role in a battle. "Attacking the attackers," she'd say, "is the best defense. The most important thing to take away from your lessons is that whoever has the most focus will win the battle, regardless of how trained you are in magic. If you're a fairy or a warefae, and you have focus, you are nearly indestructible." I was starting to take her words to heart—to do what we knew we had to do, we must all tap into our power to focus.

The other aspect of our training was duels, which we ended our nights with. In all of the duels that I watched, by far the most interesting was the one between Katia and Vivyanna. Katia flew around the sticky trapping mud that Vivy launched at her, all the while shooting tiny icicles at Vivy until her clothes were pinned to a tree, and she could no longer fire any of her magic upon Katia.

Katia had used her skills and attack method to prove defensive against Vivyanna's magic while gaining the upper hand as well. It was mesmerizing, and it was what I planned to use on this day, the day of my first duel with none other than Lydia.

Everyone moved to the edges of the clearing, speaking words of encouragement with a solemn, almost fearful tone. After Genesis' lesson had been completed, she had decided that it was my turn, at last, to learn to duel. The others had each taken a turn, and I knew it was only a matter of time before I was chosen to fight.

Lydia stood before me, her white-blonde hair pulled into a sleek and precise ponytail, and her face looking smug and menacing as she stared at me from across the way. We walked in circles around each other until she, at last, shrugged her shoulders and unfolded her wings. Without another motion, mine followed suit, and we hovered mere inches off the ground for several moments just like that, staring at each other without words.

I caught Demitri's eye behind Lydia's head, and cracked a small smile at him, in response to which his eyes opened wide in fear. Time seemed to slow as I saw the pick of ice hurtling at my head, to which I pulled up all the moisture from the snow on the ground in front of me and fed heat into it to create a boiling water wall, melting her ice weapon. She had tried to take advantage of my distraction, and as I backed up from the water wall mere inches from my face, I realized that had been all too close for comfort.

Lydia let out a growl of frustration, firing icy dagger after icy dagger at my water wall, only to watch it melt. I lowered my hands, watching the wall stay in midair upon my mind's command. After a few more minutes of this, Lydia stopped with a maddened scream, turning to Genesis and complaining, "It's not a duel if she cheats the whole time." Offended at the jab at my character, which was *not* that of a cheater, I threw my hands down, dispersing the water wall, and then motioned my arms in a zipping fashion.

Before Lydia even knew what was happening, I had her trapped in a circling wave pool of water. Her body flipped and spun in the air, and I tossed her over and over, watching her cough and splutter without pity. I didn't know what had come over me, but I'd never felt this sort of anger and strange satisfaction at my powers before.

I heard Analise whispering to Katia that I needed to stop, but Katia shushed her, saying Lydia had earned this for her offensive words. Lydia wasn't going to put up with this for long, though.

Within the wave, she'd begun to freeze the water around her. As she moved, she slowed, and I felt my arms shake as the water stopped moving. My feet hit the earth and I heaved over, breathing heavily with my hands on my knees. The effort of that floating wave pool was more than I'd ever exerted in my magic. The giant ice cube that Lydia was in began to crack a little at the edges, and then suddenly, very large divots formed in the middle. With a yell of fury from Lydia, the entire ice structure shattered, and each shard flew directly at me.

Unprepared, I squatted to the ground, retracted my wings, and threw my hands up over my face. I felt needle like-sensations of these tiny ice knives all over my arms, legs, and torso. I sat there for a second, shaking, feeling the warm blood run over my skin. I could see from the way my head was ducked toward my legs that the gold substance seemed to trickle from my pores and onto the snow below me. Silence echoed through the night, and I felt like I was in shock for a moment.

Then, I felt a chilly pat on my shoulder. I lowered my arms and looked up, blinking the blood from my forehead out of my eyes. Lydia stood there, mouth pressed into an apologetic line, her hand reached out toward me on the ground. I sighed in relief that the bitterness between us had ceased, and, standing up on my now healing legs, grabbed her hand for assistance. She wrapped her arm around my shoulder then and we walked over to the others approaching us.

"Are you okay, Summer?" Genesis asked. I nodded weakly, exhausted from the night's work. "This should be a lesson to us all that even when we think our enemies are down, that may not necessarily be so." She droned on for several minutes more about the progress we'd made that night, asking only the fairies to report again the next night, for refreshing on some more advanced fairy enchantments, and planning of what they'd be teaching over the upcoming holiday break.

We all flew out of the woods then, me at the front of the group, trying to get home as quickly as I could. I nearly catapulted through the window, running into my closet to change my clothes. I walked through the dark of my room, not even bothering to shut the window, getting under my blankets, burying my face in my pillow, and letting my tears run freely. I was sore all over. I was exhausted. I was overwhelmed. Part of me wondered if I was even meant to do this.

I felt a gentle hand rubbing my back, and a voice whispering soothingly that everything was going to be all right. I scooted over in my bed as Demitri sat down beside me, letting me cling to the front of his shirt and cry and cry. When I had finally calmed my sobs to silent tears trickling down my cheeks, he whispered, "Are you hurting still?" as he rubbed my arms, trying to feel for any remaining cuts there. I shook my head a little, feeling the pain grow more distant by the second. "What is it then?"

"I feel like I'm not good enough for this. I shouldn't have even thought this would be possible, and I think I'm putting you all in danger. I'm supposed to have all this power, but when it comes down to it, I think I'm only going to disappoint everyone."

"Summer, look at me," he said, touching my chin lightly. I looked into his dark eyes, and I saw the sincerity in them as he said, "You are the voice we all needed to hear about this. Everyone's been thinking it for years, but you are the only one brave enough to bring up the possibility of freedom.

You are the reason everyone can dream of change in our lives, and no one thinks you're not good enough, inexperienced, or anything else. You are the reason we're fighting, Summer. You're the reason *I'm* fighting." He kissed me on the forehead then, pulling me close once more and hugging me tightly. As I had those couple of months ago, I fell asleep by his side, dreaming of an open ocean, hearing his heartbeat in my dream world.

When I woke that next morning, he was gone, but only for a little while, I was certain. When I went into my closet to pick out my clothes, I checked what day it was on the calendar hanging inside the door. With a smile, I skimmed my closet before deciding on my red and green sweater with a cheesy Santa Claus decoration on it. It was December twenty-second, the last day of the fall semester.

When I went downstairs for breakfast, Dad was making cute snowman-shaped pancakes. "Good morning!" I said, kissing my mom on the cheek and sitting next to her at the table.

"Good morning, my love! Any big plans for the day?"

I laughed. "Nothing exciting, just school!"

"Ah, there is a bit of excitement there, of course, darling. There's nothing quite as nice as some luxurious cafeteria lunch food!" my dad joked.

After breakfast, I went out front to get in my dad's car, and I waited for a few minutes before everyone piled in. Since the library was closed for the holidays, I'd offered to drive them to school. Demitri hopped into the front seat with me, and the three girls slid into the back seat. "Merry almost Christmas, everybody!" I said as they shut the doors and buckled up.

"Summer, that's a very commercialized human holiday. We celebrate God, and the connection between God and our magic, but in regards to Santa Claus, we don't celebrate it much," Charlotte said, chuckling at my cheesy sweater and even cheesier Christmas-tree-shaped earrings.

"Well, I personally love Christmas. It's all about family, and good food, and presents, and Jesus, and holiday spirit!" I said, dancing around in my seat obnoxiously as I turned up the Christmas music crackling over the radio. I backed out of the driveway, turning down the main road to school.

Christmas time may not have meant very much to the warefae, but luckily for me, every human at school was just as into the holiday as I was. People passed out candy and got little presents for their friends. Teachers even joined in the festivities, many of them throwing parties and others bringing in cupcakes for the students.

At lunchtime, the Christmas fun turned slightly somber as Bobby presented Charlotte with a bouquet of poinsettia flowers. She squeezed his arm and gave him a little side hug from her seat next to his before they both sheepishly turned back to their food.

Charlotte had gone to Bobby's house after Will and Annie's party to explain that as much as she wanted to be with him, she couldn't. He had begged her to give him a reason that made sense, but she had said that she couldn't explain. He had been kind enough to let her go, but I could still see in his eyes that Charlotte Skies had the same hold on his heart that she had for as long as she'd been in school here. The only difference now was that after all this time; he had the same hold on her, no matter how much they tried to pass as being "just friends."

We all tried to enjoy the rest of the day, though, and classes flew by easily. The only thing that was throwing me off slightly was that Demitri hadn't reacted to the holiday at all. No mention of a present for me, or anything to celebrate with me. I blamed it on his lack of joyful nature, and so I took matters into my own hands as we walked to my car to meet up with the other warefae at the end of the day.

"Come over for dinner tonight," I demanded, squeezing his hand and looking up at his surprised face. "Summer, I—"

"I don't care for your excuses! It's almost Christmas and, I swear, we are going to celebrate! Besides, you have to meet my parents, and we have to tell them that we're dating." We had stopped walking and were staring each other down for a second, until he finally cracked a smirk and said, "Okay, okay, I'll do it."

"Yes!" I exclaimed, hugging him around the middle and practically skipping off to my car with him.

When I walked into my house a little after that, to be followed a few moments later by Dad returning from work, I brought both my parents into the living room to deliver my proposal for dinner. "So, Mom and Dad, you remember Demitri from next door, don't you?" They nodded, and my mom pointed out that they also remembered that he was my boyfriend now. I laughed sheepishly and said, "Well, I'd love for you both to let him come over for dinner to spend time with us. Besides, he needs some Christmas spirit. What do you say?"

My parents eyed each other cryptically for a moment before my mom turned to me with a twinkle in her eye, saying, "Well, I wondered how long it would take you to ask to bring him over for dinner!"

I took that as a "Yes," running over and hugging them both. My parents laughed at my enthusiasm and consented to let him come over for dinner in a couple of hours.

I busied myself around the house, almost frantic, decorating more and more until it was to be time for dinner. I cleaned the living room, dusted the chandelier, and even straightened the books in my father's office before adding more ornaments to the tree, more ribbon to the garland, and more pinecones to our table centerpiece. "Honey, is this necessary?" he asked when he walked in to get a copy of the library records off his desk as I straightened up in there.

"Yes, Dad, it is! When Demitri comes over later, if he walks in and sees our house in perfect order, he'll probably think you and mom are even more amazing than you already are!"

He eyed me over his glasses, a gleam in his eye. "Summer, dear, frankly I couldn't care less of what the boy thinks of me! What matters to me is that you adore him, and he adores you. Nothing else could make me happier than getting to see you find happiness in this lifetime."

I met his gaze then, smiling at the man who, technically speaking, was old enough to be my grandfather, but had taken me in with as much love and kindness as any daughter could've hoped for. I walked to him and hugged him tightly, thankful that I'd gotten so lucky as to call him my father.

"All right, darling," he said, patting my head and stepping back, wiping a single tear from his eye, "go on and get yourself ready, now. Mom will have dinner ready soon, and I expect the young man will be here shortly."

"Okay, Dad, I'll see you in a minute." I kissed his cheek and headed upstairs, stopping by the bathroom to brush my hair and apply a bit more lip-gloss.

I hadn't thought about how much time I had left with my parents until then. My dad seemed quite emotional talking about whom I'd be with forever, but what was still hard for me to comprehend was that I'd have *forever* to spend here. Living in the human world, yet also in the warefae world, overlapped where my parents were. Without them around, and once Fallon grew old and passed on, as well, I would no longer have a connection to my old life. *Would it bother them to see that I wouldn't be aging?*

I'd wanted so badly to live out who I *truly* was, but every once in a while since tapping into my warefae magic, all I wanted was to go back to being the little girl who would sit between my parents on the couch back in Florida, watching movies with them and being happy that I had a little family to call my own. I longed to return to dashing up and down the book store shelves with Fallon and going to the beach with her after work. I had never felt like my life belonged to me back then, but now, I missed those times immensely. *Why was it that everywhere I seemed to be in life, I wanted to be somewhere else?*

When the doorbell rang, rattling the old house, I dashed down the stairs to open the door. I tugged hard on the handle, and the ancient thing creaked open, revealing Demitri standing there, looking dark and heavenly against the white of the snow around the entryway. He held a bundle of red roses in his hand, and he eyed the green dress

I'd changed into with adulation. "You look beautiful, Summer. These are for you," he said, handing me the roses. I thanked him, motioning for him to come in. He walked past me, looking around in the hallway as I shut the door behind him and fastened the multiple locks up the side.

"Wow, this is a lot of decorations. That's impressive! Did your parents do this?" I smiled at the door, trying to hold back laughter at my supreme intuition, mumbling, "Yep!"

"Summer, dear." I turned from the door to see my parents standing at the end of the hall with their arms around each other. I hooked my arm through Demitri's and walked him down the hall. We stopped in front of my parents, and Demitri cleared his throat.

"Hello, Mr. and Mrs. York. My name is Demitri North. I go to school with Summer, and I live next door. I'm the one who escorted her to the homecoming dance. It's very nice to see you both again," he said, reaching forward and shaking both of their hands.

"It's nice to officially meet you, Demitri. It's good to see you again. Please, call us Clara and David," my mom said kindly.

"Let's head to the kitchen, you two," my dad said as he clapped Demitri playfully on the shoulder, "Clara almost has dinner ready."

My parents were very friendly at dinner, and Demitri seemed like a natural fit in our conversations. We had a fancy meal of steak, asparagus, and potatoes, crafted expertly by my parents. The atmosphere even felt romantic, with the sunset shining peacefully through the back window, making the snow sparkle.

When the meal was over, my mom brought out sugar cookies she'd made that day, and a bunch of different colored icings and sprinkles. My parents, Demitri, and I spent the better part of the evening decorating the 'cookies for Santa' and once it got dark, my parents told Demitri goodnight, and I pretended to walk him out the back door so he could go home.

He held my hand in the dark, our fingers laced together as we walked slowly through the snow. We stopped just at the edge of the yard, and he drew me in close to him, and we stood there for a moment, just hugging, soaking in each other's warmth.

"I love you," he whispered.

"I love you, too, so much," I said in return, feeling happiness ooze through my body like melted butter.

"I'll see you for training in a bit, okay?" I nodded, dreading letting him go, but knew that it was only for an hour or so.

I went upstairs feeling stir-crazy, wanting to go to lessons to see Demitri again. I smelled my flowers once again before setting them on my desk tenderly. I changed into more comfortable clothes and sat at my desk chair, looking at my flowers, literally drumming my fingers of boredom.

The seconds until nine o'clock seemed to drag by so slowly. At half past eight o'clock, I couldn't help but rise from my chair and fly from my window. I knew the fairies would be in the forest planning anyways, and I figured a little extra practice for me in the clearing couldn't hurt whatsoever.

When I flew over the street, the air seemed still, but in a peaceful way. It felt like the whole world was oblivious to the fact that in a few short months, we'd be going into battle. We had set the date of our little siege for spring break. It would be ideal because Genesis could tell my parents in a couple of weeks that she'd love for me to join her and Demitri on their vacation, and we wouldn't have to miss school and make the town suspicious. My parents wouldn't have to worry about me either.

The Faire Palace was hidden, so the fairies had told us, somewhere up in Canada. Or, it could've been near Canada. All I knew was that we were taking a "skiing vacation"—at least, that's what our cover would be.

In reality, we would be grouped, ready to fight Lorena, yet at the same time hoping that a peaceful conversation could be enough to convince her to change her way of ruling. It seemed like such a foreign concept to me, charging the Faire Palace, even though it was my idea.

I rerouted from the flying route to the forest then and moved straight up into the sky instead. I stopped there, hovering, looking around the darkness and then up at the stars. I could see star fairies far off in the distance, whooping and hollering and painting the sky. I smiled, knowing that someday soon, we'd have this luxury of freedom too. We wouldn't have to hide on this street, worried about Lorena's henchmen finding us and putting us in danger.

I could see it now, Demitri making the clouds and the shadows come to life over Weston. Charlotte would dot the sky with the light to contrast it. Lydia's work would come to life in the winter, and Analise would help the rivers keep running and safe for the life in them.

As for me, I wanted *everything*. I wanted to dance through rainfall and fill each lake. I wanted to venture out of Weston, to the ocean. Oh, it was the ocean that I wanted so desperately. Ever since I'd started using my powers, I felt the saltwater flow through my veins even more so than I had before. Being able to fly to the sea whenever my heart desired would feel like nothing less than complete rapture.

I twirled around in midair, giddy at the thought of such freedom, like the kind I got to experience in my dreams whenever I'd fallen asleep in Demitri's arms. Happiness, like the kind I got from spending time with my sweet friend Charlotte. I felt ready to take on Lorena and prove to her that we were no danger, and we weren't any kinds of monsters. I wanted to prove that we were strong, but we would use our strength for good.

I turned around to go back to the forest, ready for practice, when all of a sudden, I felt a painful thump across the back of my head, and I fell limp into a scratchy netting.

"Got her! You three keep looking! I'll hold her for a minute, and then we've got to get back to the Palace," a rough voice called out. I fought and struggled and clawed at his hands holding the net together through the holes in the rope. "Ouch! Stupid little demon!" the man yelled as I tore at his skin with my nails. I saw him bring his elbow up aggressively, a fiery glint in his glare. Before I could move out of the way, I felt a swift jab on my temple, and suddenly, the dark of the night swallowed up the world.

Chapter Eleven
The Palace

When I woke, I felt cold. That was odd to me, seeing as I hadn't been able to truly feel the bitter chill of winter since I'd acquired my powers. This was different, though. I felt cold internally, almost in my soul. I didn't understand how this could be possible except for the thought that lingered in my mind that this must be a very evil place that I'd found myself in.

I looked around, seeing bars like a prison. I knew then that this would make me a prisoner here. I felt my heartbeat pick up, so quickly that I could hear it. I tried to keep my breathing steady, looking around for a point of escape, finding nothing but the window behind me. I rushed over to it, stretching up onto my tiptoes and peeking out of it to see that I was in a very, very tall tower.

I saw some of the edges of a marble white castle peeking around the corner, and far off in the distance, there were mountains and sporadic trees. Everything, every single inch of the ground, was covered in snow, miles upon miles of it. This didn't seem like the type of snow from Weston, which had a magical winter-wonderland quality to it. This snow seemed to captivate everything, hushing out all the life from the land. I knew instinctively that I was in the Faire Palace.

I turned back to face the bars at the front of my little cell, walking closer to them and squinting as I saw a glimmer around them. As I got closer, I realized it was more than that. There was a silver haze surrounding it, moving like some sort of a floating substance. It swirled around each bar, dancing almost. Intrigued, I reached a hand toward it, allowing my pointer finger to barely skim it.

As soon as I touched the silver, I felt an almost electric zap shoot up my arm, and I was thrown back against the cinderblock wall. I heard a crack and winced as I slid down to the floor. I reached a hand back to my head and felt warmth there, and, when I pulled my hand around shakily to my face, I saw blood, but not the gold shimmering type I'd grown so used to. This blood was a grayish-white, almost pearly in appearance. I thought vaguely that this could be the warlock side of me showing as I examined my blood on the tips of my fingers.

I assumed that this wound wouldn't matter in a moment, and the pain would recede, but I realized that the bleed at the back of my skull wasn't the only thing wrong with me. I felt an indescribable emptiness, and when I reached back to feel for my wings, I noted a strange clip at the top edge of them, holding them together. Their texture wasn't the smooth, silky warmth that I'd felt before, but similar to that of a dead leaf with cracked, crumbly sides.

I couldn't use my fairy magic without my wings, and I couldn't fly either. So it was the warlock blood that I was bleeding at this moment, and I knew of no warlock spells

I could use to heal the gash on my head, which was making me dizzier by the second.

As for my wings, I could tell that the clips on them wouldn't come off without some sort of a key to unlock it, which I didn't have. I had to figure out some sort of way to escape. I presumed that I was on my own now, and none of my friends, my allies, were there to help me. I didn't know much about my present situation, spare the fact that I was a hostage in the Faire Palace, and I was likely in grave danger.

I paced my cell for a couple of hours, getting close to the enchanted bars every once in a while to try to peek into the hall of my cell, looking for guards. There was nothing there, and no one around at all near me. "Hello?" I called foolishly, wishing for one of my friends to walk around the corner to get me out.

Instead, I heard a door opening and the flutter of wings. The same voice of the one who'd taken me from Weston grunted, "What?"

"Who are you?" I responded. I heard a sigh and then the fairy flew over until he was in front of the bars in front of me. I was kind of shocked by how much he reminded me of Demitri. He had black wings and dark hair and skin. He had brownish-black eyes that had the same toughness Demitri had in his when we first met, and his lips pursed bitterly. His wings had no warlock mark.

"What'd you ask me?" he said lazily.

"I asked who you are," I said as I crossed my arms.

He smirked. "Are you serious? You don't want to know why you're here, or where you are, or anything else besides who *I* am?" I nodded, and he shook his head almost in disbelief.

"My name is Warren. And you are?" he asked sarcastically. I opened my mouth to tell him my real name but then decided that I probably shouldn't reveal who I was, to prevent any danger from coming to me.

"Um, Vera. I'm a river fairy."

"Huh. You don't look like a Vera to me." He chuckled, starting to turn to go back to the door he had come in from. "Wait! Are you a shadow fairy?" He paused, turning back to me and nodding with that same tight-lipped look, except this time, I could see some anger and sadness hiding behind his gaze.

"Is there something wrong with that?" I asked, cocking my head a bit.

"You don't know?" he said with irritation now. I thought back to the rumors of enslavement Genesis had mentioned once, I decided to portray cluelessness to find out the truth for myself.

When he believed that I had no idea what he was hinting at, he turned back to me and floated closer, muttering about me being a clueless rogue. He looked both ways as if to ensure there was no one around. "All dark fairies are enslaved. Lorena ordered it about fifty years ago. She claimed to the faire court that dark fairies were too dangerous and too close to the mindsets of demons to be allowed freedom in the fairy world.

"My father met my mother in enslavement, so I was born into this." Warren turned over his wrists, revealing a burn mark shaped like a wispy sort of tree on either one.

"It's the mark of the grand faire enchantress," he said, loathing filling his tone. "We're meant to be her guards now, and we scout fairies that break the rules or draw suspicion to put into prison as well."

"Oh, Warren, I'm so sorry. That's terrible." I thought of Demitri and Genesis, knowing that had they stayed in this world, Lorena would have made them into slaves too.

Warren turned his back on me again, saying, "It was foolish of you to fly above your dwelling. You haven't been registered with the palace—you're a rogue. No trace of your wing signature has been found in our record. Besides that, you should've known that fairies aren't allowed to break the cloudbank unless they're sky fairies. It risks our exposure.

"Is that what Lorena told you?" I shot back at him, making him halt once more.

He barely turned his face back to my general direction. "You've no idea what she's like. She's." He paused for a moment, as if searching for the right words. "She's got a soul like a devil." With that warning-like proclamation, he flew from the hall, letting the door slam behind him.

I sat there in shock for a moment, fearing that if Demitri and the others were to come for me, he and Genesis could be caught and enslaved as Warren was. *Don't come for me,* I pleaded as if he could hear me. *Stay home. Please, don't come to save me.* I'd have to figure out how to escape on my own, and fast. I just hoped that I'd get out of here in time to prevent the others from being harmed.

I could tell the time of day based on the light that seeped into the cell through the window. Mine was the only cell on my floor of the tower, so it was clear to me that my only contact, for the time being, would be Warren.

Warren was an interesting fairy with a complicated personality. He seemed to be in an eternal struggle with himself in regards to where he fits in in his world, and what his purpose was. Of course, this was all guesswork, because he didn't talk to me. He'd bring me my food three times a day, and dismissively and quickly fly out of my area to prevent himself from engaging in conversation, as we had the first day.

I steered clear of the bars at the front of the cell to prevent further damage to my skull, which after three days, had still not seemed to heal properly. I knew I needed my fairy magic for it to fully repair, but I didn't know how to remove the clips on my wings alone. That's when I came up with the idea of how I could save myself. "Hey, Warren. I was wondering if I could ask a favor of you," I said on the third morning of my stay. I couldn't imagine how panicked my parents, the fairies, and the warefae were at my lengthy absence.

Warren looked at me with his distant dark eyes of his and said, "It depends on what it is." I threw caution to the wind, figuring it couldn't get much worse than this anyways, and said, "Well, I want you to help me escape so I can kill Lorena and go home." He paused for a moment, eyes widening before he doubled over with laughter.

"You think you can defeat Lorena?" He howled with laughter, banging his fist against the cinder block behind him as he struggled to catch his breath.

I narrowed my eyes at him, saying, "I'm not kidding, Warren. Just let me out of here and I'll do it."

"Listen, small fry, you've got no magic, you're injured, you've got no strength. I'm not about to risk my neck for you when I don't even know you, and this is probably just a trick to tempt me to let you out. Nice try, though." He chuckled again as he turned to leave me.

I sat on the ground in frustration. I'd genuinely thought I'd be able to convince Warren to help me escape and stop Lorena. He seemed to hate her just as much as I did because of the servitude required of him. I'd even seen a flicker of pity in his eye at times that he'd deliver my meals to me.

In my moment of defeat, however, a possibility crossed my mind. It hit me when Warren mentioned my injury, and I remembered the shimmering white blood that oozed from my skull. I was a warefae, and "ware" was an equally, if not more, prominent part as the "fae" was. I looked at my hands, wondering if they'd be able to perform magic without the added strength of my wings. I was supposedly a descendent of the most powerful warlock family line, and that had to be something.

I thought of the few spells I had learned and remembered my first day with Genesis, learning about the fairy charms and warlock spells that would become the foundation of my magical education. I remembered the shrinking spell, looking around for something to try it on.

I saw the tray that my food had come on this morning, and I narrowed my eyes at it, reaching a hand forward, and casting the spell through my mind's eye.

My hand trembled as I felt heat rush through it, but nothing happened. I gritted my teeth, thought the spell again, and mustered up all the energy I could until suddenly, I felt a sense of release as the white light shone from my hands, wrapping around the tray and shrinking it smaller and smaller.

I'd figured out how to separate my warlock and fairy abilities, and realized this may be the very way I'd be saved. No one knew about my abilities here, and I could use them to my advantage. Looking around carefully, trying not to make a sound, I stood up and walked closer to the bars on the window, wrapping my hands around one and trying to remember the spell Genesis had taught us for freezing. If I could get it to be brittle enough, I could tear a bar away and use it to pry the wing clip off. The problem was that I hadn't paid much attention to this particular spell because the ice was something that came easily to fairies, as it was an element that could be manipulated through nature.

Now, without my fairy strength, I was left scouring my mind for the spell. "Aha!" I exclaimed as I thought it up, then closed my eyes and channeled the spell's power into my hands. I heard the bar creak as the ice began to coat it, when someone behind me gasped, "How is that possible?"

Warren stood there with wide, scared eyes. "Warren," I said, pulling myself away from the bars, "I can explain! Just listen to me!"

Warren shook his head, backing up from me slowly and saying, "I don't know, Vera, this is insane. Something is off about you, and I knew it from the start." He put his hands behind his head as if trying to catch his breath.

"Warren, listen, I'm just as confused about this as you are," I lied instinctively to him, but he still shook his head.

"Vera, you don't understand. Lorena gets back today, and she's told the head guards that you'll be one of the prisoners she interviews later on. I have to tell her what I saw, or else…" He paused, and I saw the fear in his eyes now. "she's going to kill my parents and me."

I sighed, thinking this over. "Warren, what do you mean, what you saw? I was just looking at how cold the bars are from the snow!" He cocked his head in confusion now and I winked at him, and then a look of understanding crossed his eyes. His lips turned up at the corners, and he just nodded, seeming a bit confused about what to do and saying, "All right, Vera, I'll come back for you soon."

"Thanks, Warren," I said genuinely, pacing my cell as he left.

Lorena was going to see me, and that wasn't going to change. I hoped that Warren would lie for me, but I didn't know for sure; regardless, I couldn't get out of the interrogation. I thought and thought about how I could best prepare for this, and then I realized that I couldn't possibly go into this meeting looking like myself. If Vivyanna, Anastrella, and the others thought I looked exactly like

Fallon, there was no way that Lorena, my birthmother's former best friend, wouldn't recognize me. She'd think of me as a sort of ghost from her past, and I didn't want her to realize that I was Blair, returned to the fairy world after my seventeen years in hiding.

As I paced my cold cell, I realized that I didn't have to go into this interrogation looking like myself. Before I'd been taken, Genesis had taught us of transformation spells. I had to speak what I wished to change, followed by the incantation, followed by what I wanted it to change into. I placed my hands on my head, thinking I could risk my hair first since it'd grow back.

"My hair," I said slowly, followed by the ware incantation, and after a moment's thought, I concluded the spell with, "Charlotte Skies' hair."

My brown locks grew about three inches and became more voluminous and curly than I'd ever seen them before. I looked down at my shoulder, touching the hair there with the tips of my fingers as the vibrant blonde color flowed down from my roots to the ends of my hair—Charlotte's hair on my head, that is.

My next most comparable feature to Fallon was my eyes. I closed my eyes and covered them as if I was a child playing peek-a-boo. "My eyes," I said, speaking the incantation again, "Lydia's eyes." I opened my eyes; feeling like a sort of film was clouding my vision. If all went how it was supposed to, Lydia's pale blue eyes would have covered my bright ocean-blue ones that matched my mother's.

I felt like I was safe to keep the rest of me looking as it normally did, hoping that these subtle changes would be enough to convince Lorena that my cover identity, Vera of the Rivers, was real.

When Warren came back almost an hour later, he was shocked again. "Vera," he hissed, "what happened to you?"

I smiled coyly, saying, "Warren, you're starting to worry me. I think you're seeing things that aren't real!" He shook his head in a tormented fashion before unlocking the cell door with a wave of his hand. He motioned me to walk forward, and so I did. As much as I wanted to take advantage of the open door and the option of escape, I didn't want to ruin any future chances of Warren helping me by losing his trust. So, I remained compliant as he formed cuffs of black sparks around my wrists, placed a hand on my shoulder, and escorted me from my cell.

My stomach dropped as we neared the door that wasn't a normal door at all, but a sort of trap door that opened from the floor and dropped straight down. Under normal circumstances, I'd be fine with this, but I didn't have my wings. I wouldn't have any control. My heart began to race, and Warren began to lower down through the trap door. "Um, Warren?"

His head popped back up through the door. "Yes, Vera?"

"Uh"—I laughed shakily—"I don't have my wings at the moment, so I don't know how I'm supposed to do this."

He rolled his eyes. "Don't be a baby. Just jump; I'll catch you."

He lowered himself back down through the trap door, and I walked up closer to it until my toes were on the edge of it. My legs shook slightly as I looked down at the vastness of the tower below. "Come on, Vera! We can't be late!" Warren called at me. I closed my eyes, feeling a sensation vaguely familiar to when I'd been dropped near the mountains in Weston when I first used my wings. Except for this time, there weren't four warefae there to catch me when I fell.

I stepped through the door into the nothingness below, closing my eyes and bracing for Warren to just abandon me, and watch me fall to my doom. I barely knew him, after all, and I figured he may be better off to be rid of me. But a few seconds after I dropped, when I thought I'd keep falling through eternity, I felt myself get swept up into a cradle. I opened my eyes to see Warren looking down as he lowered us more and more. "Thanks," I whispered, and he mumbled something inaudible in response.

The inside of the tower was just as flawless as the outside; the whole thing was white marble with gold embellishments everywhere I looked. There were fancy murals on walls that we passed so quickly; I turned my head just to try to put them together before it was too late to see them anymore.

The whole concept of "too late" toyed around in my mind for the next few minutes as we went down into the depths of the castle. *Was it too late for me to escape? Was it too late for me to be able to tell the people I loved that I loved them one last time?*

I felt my pulse quicken as Warren slowed, setting me down onto the ground. His face turned to stone, and I realized it must've been because of the other dark fairies flying around that first floor of the palace. We walked down the main hallway, and once we passed the part of the castle that the tower was in, the ceiling became lowered and shifted into beautiful mosaic glasswork. There were shapes of fairies that held so much life in them; they practically danced across the roof.

When I looked straight ahead once more, trying not to trip over my feet, I noticed a looming door, made of solid gold and embellished with little designs of the same tree burned onto Warren's wrist. We stopped right in front of the door. Warren raised his fist, and pounded on the center of the door three times, making a noise that sounded less like a knock and more like a booming drum.

The door slowly inched open in a fluid, haunting way, revealing the empty chamber that I'd seen in the visions from the paintings on the wall of my room. The grand stairway stood just as stoic and sturdy as it had been almost a century before, as well as nearly seventeen years before when my parents had been sentenced here.

There was a throne atop the stairs, without any chairs for the faire court surrounding it. Lorena sat on the throne, and I felt like I was living in an alternate reality as I saw her. As Warren and I walked forward, she stood proudly from her throne and began descending the stairs; her gold dress trailed behind her, and her shimmering wings unfurled gracefully. She was beautiful, undoubtedly so. But, there was cruelty I could see in her posture alone. She was tough, and I knew I'd have to be tough, too, if I wanted to survive this.

"Thank you, Warren. You have made me proud these past few months with all of the imprisonments you've made. I would like to meet with you after this to discuss your promotion."

"Yes, Enchantress." Warren bowed his head next to me.

Warren and I stopped walking in the center of the floor, from which position he backed up away from me. "Leave us," Lorena ordered, and he murmured his compliance before flying up to the door in the ceiling that had been there all those years ago, which was opened by what appeared to be another guard.

Lorena walked so close to me that I could smell a peach-like scent radiating from her, as if a sickly sweetness were there to cover up the bitter evil inside. She walked in a circle around me as if she were a lion and I were an antelope. I winced as I felt her cold, bony hands skim the edge of one of my crumbly wings. "Do you know," she said in her stern voice, "what it takes to kill a fairy?"

I closed my eyes, gaining my confidence and building my mental strength before barely turning my face toward her direction and saying, "Yes. Do you?"

She huffed at my snide remark, heels clicking against the marble floor as she walked to stand directly in front of me. "Of course I do, you insolent little…" She trailed off, smiling and lacing her fingers together in front of her stomach. "I'm sorry; I don't think we've been properly introduced. Tell me, dear, what is your name?"

"My name is Vera," I said very clearly and with an air of calm in my tone, "I am a river fairy."

"I see"—Lorena nodded—"and I am Lorena, the grand faire enchantress. I am, however, certain you've heard of *me*."

I nodded sarcastically. "Naturally, *Enchantress*." I said the word in a drawn out way, trying to emphasize the total absence of respect I had for her.

She glared at me, crossing her arms now like a petty teenage girl. "As I was saying before, traditionally, to kill a fairy, one would need to cut off a fairy's wings—the source of magic—before being able to fatally wound, or quickly kill a fairy. Once the immortal powers would wash away, the aging would begin, the blood would lose all traces of magic, etcetera.

"Now, though," she continued, "we've been developing products that would more quickly kill and drain magic from a fairy." She snapped her fingers, making golden sparks appear, and a little cabinet rose from the floor between us. I looked down at the vial of a shimmering red substance she pulled from the open cabinet door. "This," she said, holding the little tube between her finger and thumb, "is called halt serum. One drop of this, and a fairy can kiss its magic goodbye."

She paused for a moment before a single outburst of her laughter made me jump and she said, "Two drops and you could kiss your life goodbye as well!"

I shuddered at her pure wickedness, trying desperately to maintain my cool gaze toward her. Replacing the vial, she now removed a tool that looked like a Taser, but which Lorena explained was a Magical Current Interceptor, which would take the waves of magic pulsing through the bloodstream, and essentially makes them self-destruct to expose the fairy to the elements, danger, and eventual death.

"There are more things in the works," Lorena said with pride, "but as of now, we are moving ahead with the times in regards to our updates and more available methods of killing. Anyways, that was just an interesting bit of information. For now, I want to hear more about you."

Lorena snapped her fingers and at the base of the stairs, a smaller, but by no means less comfortable, chair rose from the ground. She turned from me, her shining, gold up-do of hair not moving an inch on her head as she waltzed her way to her mini-throne, dragging me behind her with some strange magical pull she was using over me.

As soon as Lorena had sat in her chair, she motioned her hand down, and my knees buckled, hitting the ground painfully. I still maintained a straight posture, though, holding as much pride and confidence in my shoulders as I could. "So, Vera, how did Warren come to bring you here from your home? And why is it that when he and the guards of his sector imprisoned you, they couldn't find anyone near you for miles?"

"Well," I said slowly, making sure to emphasize each word I spoke to make it sound like the truth, "I was trying to fly up a bit to see if clouds were coming in for a storm. You see, I'm a rogue river fairy, and I take my job very seriously. I, unfortunately, don't have a clan, though." She nodded, looking down at me over her unnaturally pointed nose. Her hair was pulled back from her face so tightly, that I figured she must feel pain in her skull from the styling of it.

Lorena sat up straighter in her seat, which I didn't think to be possible, and before she could open her mouth to speak again, I blurted out fearlessly, "I have a question for you." She raised her eyebrows, muttering under her breath about my disrespect and digging her nails into the arms of the chair with irritation.

Despite her reaction, I continued to speak, to assert myself in her presence. "I've heard rumors of a group of exiled fairies who have raised children they had with warlocks. Is this true?" I asked boldly, not sure where I was heading with my point.

Lorena's eyes flickered with fear for a second before she composed herself again, saying in a snapping tone, "Well, of course. We released the details of their treachery as a warning to all other fairies of what would happen if they committed the same crime."

"That didn't happen, though, am I correct?" She cocked her head slightly, saying, "What do you mean, young one?"

"I mean that you killed your own best friend because she committed the same crime. You didn't exile her. Did you also share that information with the fairy world?"

Lorena stood from her seat before I'd even finished my statement, flying at me and wrapping her hand around my throat. As I struggled to take a breath, she hissed at me, "I don't know what you think you heard about my so-called *best friend*, but she made her choices, and she deserved what she got. I warned that there would be death next, and I made the right choice by not sharing that it was she who met that fate." She threw me to the ground, turning her back on me and calling out, "Warren!" in a screeching voice.

He flew rapidly down from the ceiling, taking a knee in front of her and saying, "Yes, Enchantress?"

"Take this prisoner back to her cell." She turned to me with the same wicked smile she'd flashed at my parents just before they'd been taken for execution. "On second thought, take her to a cell in the North Tower."

"The North T-Tower?" Warren stammered, looking up at Lorena. "Are you sure, Enchantress? That tower hasn't been used in years—"

"Don't you question my decisions! Now, take her away!" Lorena shouted, her voice echoing throughout the chamber. Warren nodded solemnly before flitting over to me and hoisting me up from the ground. "Enjoy your stay, Miss Vera," Lorena called over her shoulder as we flew away, climbing up the steps to her place atop the fairy world.

Warren flew me back out of the huge doors we came in from, but instead of turning back to the tall tower I'd stayed in for the past couple of days, he flew me in the opposite direction, continuing down through the grand hallway beneath the mosaic ceiling. For some reason, I felt no fear, even though Lorena's sentence had seemed to spark some hesitation from Warren. I thought that his presence might be what was comforting me because if I closed my eyes and pretended enough, he could almost pass for Demitri in my head.

There was an archway at the end of the hall that we were approaching quickly. This was a part of the castle that seemed more central, for more halls and corridors were branching off this part, and I saw numerous fairies moving about. The majority of them were dark fairies, some in plainclothes that was carrying out duties of waiters or maids, others following around respectable looking fairies that must have been high-ranking members of the faire court. Finally, there were the guard fairies, like Warren, whom all wore a simple black shirt and gray pants. They were very militant, and the majority of them were male. Several of them escorted prisoners with clipped wings, and they all held menacing glowers on their faces.

As we passed beneath the huge archway, I looked up to see a phrase written overhead in Faire. "May the Purest be Preserved," I read aloud, looking up at Warren who kept his focus straight ahead.

"It's Lorena's motto that she took on several decades ago. It's supporting the promotion of fairies of light blood, the only ones Lorena believes to have a purpose on the Earth necessary enough to join the human world," Warren said through gritted teeth, nodding at a few of his fellow guards as they passed.

Disgusted with Lorena's rule, I hadn't even noticed that the archway had led us out into a beautiful courtyard. "Whoa," I breathed, looking around at the marvelous outside of the castle. There was snow lining the roof and pushed up to the outskirts of the courtyard to give a clear visual of the white marble flooring that was topped by the golden tree emblem in the center of the courtyard's ground.

"I know, it's pretty excessive isn't it," Warren said with years of built-up resentment in his tone, and I could sense him rolling his eyes behind me. "Wait until you see the tree."

I looked around the courtyard, but the fabled tree was nowhere to be seen. We kept our course on a straight-ahead path, Warren's hands firmly gripping my waist as he navigated the massive property. We flew into the furthest building, completely across the courtyard from the one I'd just come from. "See what I mean?" Warren said as we entered, and oh, how right he was.

The Faire Tree was breathtaking. It looked like something straight out of a fantasy painting. The entirety of the bark, from trunk to limbs, was solid gold. The leaves that swayed from the edges of it were as well, but their coloring was softer. The special thing about the leaves was the glittering, sparkly effect they had from every single angle the light hit them at. At the top of the tree, the branches curved in the same wispy way as they did in their marked form on Warren's wrists.

At that thought, I realized how sad and pitiful it was that Lorena had taken something so beautiful, pure, and full of magic, and turned it into something threatening that now loomed over populations of faire folk everywhere. Warren slowed a bit as we passed it, and I could see way up in the top of the tree, more dark fairies were tending to the branches, pruning them and ensuring everything was perfect. I looked down at the roots, which wove in and out of brownish-red colored dirt that made up the floor of this room. It was as if they were stretching, or perhaps clawing for something that was never quite in its' reach.

"How does it work?" I asked, unable to help myself from being so awestricken over this part of the fairy world that I'd considered being relatively insignificant when I'd first heard about it through Demitri's paintings. Warren stopped moving us forward for a moment, adjusting me in his arms so that he could point with one of his hands to the top edge of the tree, where all the branches seemed to point and gather.

"That right there is where the magic combines to create fairy life." His arm motioned down the curve of the tree now, all the way to the soil as he said, "The roots can sense what types of fairies are needed in the world, and what elements would be otherwise out of alignment. Then, the branches combine different aspects of magic within themselves, twisting and connecting and splitting off in all sorts of different ways. The result is a unique fusion of magic; the only other way this power can only be achieved is through the birth of a child descended from lines of fairies that were born of the tree. As old family lines pass on, new ones form through here."

"Pass on?" I asked, and Warren mumbled in affirmation, beginning to fly past the tree now, and into a dark and eerie hallway branching into one side of the large building. "I thought fairies were immortal; are they not?"

"They?" Warren chuckled, and I remembered I had to be very cautious, and hide the fact that I was a warefae.

"I meant we. Oops!" I laughed it off, and Warren explained, "Lorena has been encouraging the development of certain potions that would take the life of a fairy peacefully—I think they called the first one Stopper. She said that it was to be developed to relieve a fairy that had been around for too many years, to allow them to live out a quick human life before growing old in the human world and moving on to the next chapter. When it was released to the public several years ago, it was bought up very quickly.

"The second solution is called halt serum, I think. That one has had more controversy. It was advertised as being faster than Stopper, and longer-lasting, as well. The unfortunate part," Warren explained, "is that when the potion was first approved, it had some nasty side effects, and for many, made for a painful conversion process from fairy to human. It led to a lot of unintentional deaths. This potion was then voted on by Lorena, as well as a few of her faire court members that feared her retaliation if they shot down the idea, as a method of taking a fairy's magic to be used in prisons as an alternative option to cutting a fairy's wings only. It was too risky to keep in the public. However, Lorena still wanted it to be used—she argued that the wing-cutting process was too messy and irritating to listen to. It hasn't been determined which method is more painful, but I wouldn't think it'd matter at the moment. Being stripped of wings, magic, everything else that matters? I don't even know how someone could move on after that."

"Why would someone do that?" I asked skeptically, "Why would someone want to take away their magic?"

He shrugged then and said, "I guess that's the flip-side of immortality; we're going to get burnt out of it after a while."

"That's a pretty morbid thought, though! Why wouldn't we just enjoy the life we're given while we've got it?"

"Well, you can try to keep that mindset in here, but we'll see how much it changes after a couple of days."

"What do you m…" I began, pausing as my mouth dropped at what we were approaching. It was another tower with the entrance like an open door at the bottom.

When we flew in the entrance, each floor was circular with multiple cells on the borders of each floor, and space in the middle for guards to fly up and down. This tower was different from the other, though, in the fact that it was empty. "No one's done anything bad enough to get thrown in here in years. The entire fairy population heard stories about this North Tower, and when they did, crime went down significantly."

"Why am I in here? What I did wasn't bad," I said, feeling the fear grow in me as we flew up the dark tower.

There were no windows here and only one light, at the very top of the entire structure.

"Well, my only guess is that you pissed Lorena off enough to make her want you to be tortured."

"Tortured?" I cried out, struggling in his arms now as if escaping would do me some sort of good.

"Vera, stop! I'm not going to set the cell on the worst setting. Just the lightest."

"Oh, great," I said sarcastically, "just a little torture, not a whole lot! I'll be totally fine!"

Warren chuckled. "I'm going to miss your humor when I'm reassigned."

I felt like I stopped breathing for a moment. "You're—you're leaving me?" He muttered a somber affirmation as we stopped at one of the top floors of the tower. He waved a hand and the cobwebs and dust in the cell seemed to drift away.

He unlocked the door and set me down inside, fiddling with some sort of chair in the center of the room. "But, Warren, what if the next guard is more relentless than you are? What if they torture me?"

He snorted at this, and I assumed he must have been trying to distract me. "Oh, I can be mean, Vera. Remember my elbow-to-your-eye moment?"

I laughed at this a bit, feeling like that was so long ago. I'd been stuck here for days now, with no sign of rescue and no prospect of getting out. After a few moments, a pit of hopelessness began to form in my stomach, and my laughter turned to tears rolling down my cheeks.

Warren tensed up, not knowing how to handle this aside from patting my back lightly. "I'm never going to get out of here alive, am I?" I said, the stone-cold reality washing over me.

Warren breathed deeply for a moment, trying to work out a response before finally saying, "I'm being promoted now, Vera. I can try to convince Lorena to let you out so you can go home again."

I looked at him then, seeing the disappointment constantly lingering in his mind that he had no choice, and he was stuck here forever. Even if he could get me out, he was chained to this palace until Lorena believed his service was no longer required, which was likely to be no time soon. That thought gave me more perspective, helping me to stop crying and raise myself, above the defeat this cell would try to impose on me.

"All right, then, what is this chair for?" I asked, preparing myself for the worst.

"This is a dark chair, and it looks very harmless from a distance," Warren began, "but I should warn you. This thing was crafted by Lorena's most skilled dark fairies that specialize in fears and the general troubling of the soul."

"So what does that mean for me?" I asked, walking around the chair and finding nothing more to it than a black seatbelt piece of elastic hanging from one side.

"Well, once you sit down, I use this"—he pointed to the elastic—"to fasten you to the chair. Then, once the door is shut, you will see your worst nightmares come to life. There are terrible things in these visions, I've heard.

Many fairies have gone insane in here from being left in the machine for too long."

I looked at him with wide eyes, trying to brace myself for what I was going to see. I thought hard about what I'd feared in life, but nothing was coming to my mind. I guessed I'd find out soon enough.

I took a deep breath and sat into the chair, and Warren made the cuffs around my wrists vanish. I brushed my hair back from my face, sitting tall and hoping that if I acted brave, I would feel that way as well. He approached me, waving his hand at the elastic band that strapped itself across my lap with a clicking noise. I tried to shift then and failed to do so. The torture had begun.

"Okay, Vera, as soon as I leave this cell, the visions will commence. I'll come back as much as I can, but there is only so much I can do without Lorena noticing. I don't want to risk her knowing that I'm trying to be lenient on you." I nodded, understanding his desire to protect himself and his family.

"I have to go see Lorena about my promotion right now. My boss told me so when I went to the guards' chambers during your interrogation. I'll try to come back as quickly as I can." I nodded, trying not to look at him, but straight ahead at the dark walls. "Be brave, Vera," Warren said, shutting the door behind him and flying away with haste.

I looked around the room when he left, the eerie silence and the emptiness of the tower haunting me. I waited for someone to arrive with some sort of a projector to show me the horrid images Warren had described to me, but no one came.

For minutes, I sat in that chair, looking around the room, the ceiling, the bars, and everywhere else I could. There was no sign of life or movement at all. But then, I shifted in my seat to try to get more comfortable, and the elastic suddenly tightened across my legs. Panicked, I clawed at the band, trying desperately to get my hand under it and rip it from my legs, but it didn't budge at all. There was a dark stream of smoke that began wrapping around the legs of the chair, and I tried to hoist my feet from the ground, but the seat belt kept me from doing this too.

"Hello, Blair," I heard a familiar voice say. Very slowly, I looked up to the corner, where a woman stood, the edge of her dress billowing out from the darkness that hid her face. She took a single step forward, and then another, and one more until I realized that I was staring at *myself*. I had my brown hair, not blonde, and my bright blue eyes bore into my soul with a vicious sort of hunger.

"Or, should I call you Summer?" the other me asked next, continuing to walk toward me; her wings unfurling now in a dangerously elegant fashion. "I... I," I stammered, unsure of what to say.

"Or," my second self continued, squatting down in front of the chair so that we were level with one another, "should I call you Vera?" She cocked her head to the side, a wicked smile forming on her face before she began to cackle at me.

"You see, you don't know who you are. Aren't I right? You don't have an identity or a purpose, or." She paused, narrowing her eyes at me before delivering the final blow, "Anyone to love you."

"You're wrong," I said, trying to remain defiant though my heart was pounding and my mind was racing at this thought.

The other me stood up. "Oh, am I? Demitri and the others' love Summer, and so do your parents. Well, your fake parents anyways. Your real parents, were they around, would have loved Blair. Warren loves Vera."

"Warren doesn't love me. He hardly knows me!"

I exclaimed, but the other me just smirked, saying, "But don't you wonder? Demitri didn't even come for you. Warren, at least, is here for you."

"Yeah, because he's guarding my cell!"

I crossed my arms, shaking my head with irritation now, and then the other me said, "Fine, but don't forget, I'm always going to be with you, pointing out your flaws, making you wonder who you truly are because deep down, you don't know."

"And who are you?" I asked pointedly, leaning forward in the chair as the other me got right in my face.

"I'm the one you're afraid of." She paused, both of us breathing hard and in unison, staring one another down before she finally spoke again, telling me my fear. "What terrifies you most is this: having to accept one version of yourself for the *rest of your life*."

I drew in a sharp breath, my mind racing as I watched my face in front of me turn to ash, and then to dark smoke that rearranged itself on the ground, swirling around up and up as it made me cough and struggle to breathe. The names ran through my head as if they were being shouted, "Summer! Blair! Vera! Summer! Blair! Vera! Summer!"

When the smoke began to drift toward the ceiling, I could see the outline of a figure on the ground, growing more and more clear. I screamed, trying to look away but finding myself forced to look at the horrible sight lying at my feet. It was Demitri's cold, lifeless body. He had no wings, and his blood was red, not gold, as it dripped from his mouth, which hung open. His eyes stared at me without anything behind them, and they were so dark, they seemed devilish.

"Demitri?" I whispered, trying to coax him back. "Demitri!" I called again, chest heaving as my chair on the ground seemed to inch toward his body. "No, no, no!" I begged as if speaking to the room. "Stop, please!" I sobbed. I tried to close my eyes, but the room kept them held open. I couldn't even blink, and I certainly couldn't breathe.

This was it, my worst nightmare. It was worse than my own identity and worse than any other type of torture. I couldn't bear to think of a world that I was in without Demitri. I'd prefer a world in which Demitri didn't love me for who I was, more than one where I was forced to stare at his dead body.

"Demitri!" I called again, and the dark smoke began swirling around both of us again, like some sort of ubiquitous force within the room. Suddenly, my vision was clouded, and in my mind's eye, I could see only flashes of some type of picture.

I saw the corpses of my parents, Fallon, Charlotte, and everyone else I held dear. I saw my house on fire, massive storms on the beaches of Florida, and an entire world of negativity. It was so overwhelming; I didn't even know how to process it. I couldn't even recognize for the longest time that I was screaming, I just felt the hoarseness in my throat that told me it was so. Seeing as that was the only thing I could feel aside from how tightly I gripped the arms of the chair; I knew nothing else to do than hold on to those two things I could control.

The fear blinded me, and my soul was in shock, having never experienced such terror before. There was nothing I could do but sit and take the pain it caused my heart, and though I tried to find hope that the suffering would end soon, part of me wondered if my torture would ever cease.

I couldn't tell time at all, for there was no light from the windows, and all I could see were the images the room had imbedded into my mind. I couldn't feel hunger or exhaustion, and I couldn't hear anything except for the sound of rushing wind and my whimpering sobs.

Out of nowhere, the visions seemed to slow down, and I could begin to blink them away. With each closure of my eyes, the images broke up even more in my mind, and so I tried shutting my eyes tightly, and then, there was nothing. I tried to steady my breath and took pleasure in the calming emptiness that surrounded me. That little sense of freedom was so comforting, and it took me several moments to feel

Warren shaking me into consciousness. "Vera? Vera, open your eyes, please!"

I acquiesced his plea, peering around the room, my whole body trembling. Warren's eyes were full of concern as he gripped my shoulders. "Vera, are you okay?" I nodded sullenly, and then, wanting to prove my second self from the depths of the room wrong, I whispered, "Summer."

"What?" he asked as he leaned in closer, craning his head so that his ear was close to my lips.

"Summer," I whispered again, "my real name is Summer." I smiled softly, feeling glad to have admitted this, and, as Warren muttered under his breath and worked to undo the elastic across my lap, I touched my hair and just below my eyes, unashamedly changing them back to the way they naturally were with the warlock side of my magic.

"Why'd you never tell me?" Warren asked, jumping a bit as he noticed my changed appearance.

"Fear," I said matter-of-factly, "this room taught me that." Warren nodded in an understanding way, pushing the chair back to the wall of the room. I sunk, sitting on the floor and leaning my head back, letting the peace wash over me that I could just be with my thoughts at that moment. Warren stood at the wall across from me, resting against it with his arms crossed.

"You know, I couldn't see whatever it was you saw in there. No one can, that's the only beauty of it. It's just between you and your mind." I nodded at him, wondering how there could be any beauty in this torturous room at all, but not wanting to mention this because he was a naturally dark-minded fairy. "How did it go with Lorena?" I asked, trying to change the subject and think no longer about what I'd seen in this room.

Warren sighed. "It went okay, I guess. It was about as good as any meeting with Lorena could go." He shrugged, as if disappointed. "She said I got the promotion for sure, which is good for my family, but"—he looked at me skeptically—"it means I'm getting replaced, and very soon too."

I frowned. "So what do you think will happen if the next one is cruel?"

He looked at me for a moment, and I searched his face for some sort of emotion, but then he just shrugged again and said, "I'm sorry, Vera—I mean, Summer. There's nothing more I can do than this little bit of a break I can give you right now. What happens next is out of my control."

I wiped away any notion then that Warren felt any love for me—that was the chair trying to mess with me on a whole different level. Warren may have taken to liking me, yes. We may have even been friends. But, to love someone meant that one would be willing to risk everything, even their safety and comfort, to make sure that the one they loved was safe, happy, and protected. Warren played it safe when it came to me, and he wasn't going to be sacrificial or make any grand gestures.

But, I still appreciated his friendship and the small bit of comfort he'd helped me find in these terrible times in the prison of the Faire Palace, and all I could do to thank him would be to spend these last few minutes with him as my guard with an attitude of calm and graciousness.

"So what will you do, now that you'll be promoted?" He looked down at his shoes as he said dejectedly, "I'll be her guard. It's a tedious job that involves me being a soldier and her assistant all in one, but this is the one job in the castle that gives a way out for dark fairies eventually."

"Wow, Warren! That's great, isn't it? You'll be free after this!"

He shrugged. "Not really. My parents won't be free, so I'd just be free and guilty, which is almost worse."

I nodded, understanding what pressure to please one's parents felt like. "I get it Warren, it's important to you to make sure your parents are taken care of. But, hey," I said, and he looked me in the eyes then, "you've got to take care of yourself too, you know." He looked as if he was about to say something, but then he made a shushing noise. "Hey, don't tell me to shush!" I said jokingly, but by the frantic waving of his arms, I could sense something was wrong.

"Get in the chair! Quickly! My replacement is in the tower!" My heart skipped a beat as I hurried over to the chair and sat down, both Warren and I trying to fumble with the belt buckle. I could hear the fluttering of wings approaching now, and Warren cleared his throat, attempting to talk in a much deeper voice than his normal one was.

"So, as I was saying, prisoner filth, this is the last you'll be seeing of me, as the new guard is approaching now." Both of us turned to the door, and I struggled to keep myself composed and silent upon the arrival of the new guard. This fairy wasn't just any dark fairy; it was Demitri.

Chapter Twelve
The Rescuers

"Who are you, soldier?" Warren asked, standing and approaching the bars, but not opening the door quite yet. Demitri's gaze was cold and firm, definitely worse than when I saw him for the first time.

"I'm James. Didn't you hear that I'd be coming to take over?" he snarled.

"Yes," Warren said slowly, "but I was under the impression that you looked—er—somewhat different than you do."

"Well, clearly it's me," Demitri said in a tone dripping with attitude, "my name is on my uniform right here." He pointed at the gray embellishment of "James of the Dark" on his black uniform that was similar to Warren's.

Despite the shirt, and the name, Warren seemed a bit concerned about the legitimacy of 'James.' I expected he also felt strain upon leaving me with someone like him; the way Demitri was acting at this time made him seem like the type that would let someone go for far too long in the torture room, and not give any breaks for hours on end.

"Seriously, dude, don't you need to get down to Lorena? I hear you're her little puppet now." Demitri chuckled rudely. Warren looked down at his shoes briefly before squaring his shoulders and staring Demitri hard in the eye. "I don't know what your deal is, James, but I will promise you one thing. If I hear that you are abusing the prisoner by use of this cell, or any other medieval torture methods, I'll throw you in here so fast, you won't even have time to argue to Lorena and the faire court."

Demitri pretended to back off then, nodding almost respectfully before standing aside for the door to be opened and passed through by Warren. Before he left the cell and the tower, Warren turned to me and said, "Good luck, S…" He paused, not wanting to reveal my real name to anyone overhearing this conversation, and said instead, "I mean good luck, Vera."

I nodded at him from the chair, and as soon as the door closed, I overheard Warren handing Demitri keys and sharing some basic information about why I was imprisoned. Demitri played along, nodding and acting very serious about all of the side-notes Warren included with my case description. I felt the smoke begin to feel the room again, my breaths speeding up. I saw a blurry visual of Warren and Demitri both looking at me with concern before looking back at each other with faces void of emotion.

"Okay, sir, you'd better hurry to Lorena now. When I met with her before, she seemed very eager to get her new assistant." Warren nodded at Demitri curtly. With a sigh and a grimace, and one last pitying look at me, Warren turned and flew away.

I cried out a quick, "No!" as I saw a vision of Fallon's dead body on the floor in front of me. I caught a silhouette of Demitri grasping the cell's bars and fumbling with the key. I tried to close my eyes and noticed the smoke and horrible images begin to fade away.

"I hope you know that I'm not very merciful when it comes to prisoners," Demitri said quite loudly, winking at me as I opened my eyes and he walked to me through the open door of my cell. I felt joyful tears fill my eyes, and I laughed quietly. Demitri turned over his shoulder, listening to the fluttering wings of Warren fade further and further away.

When we couldn't hear the wings any longer, Demitri tore the belt from my lap and I stood quickly, throwing my arms around him in an embrace. I felt him shaking, as if in shock that I was here, and he was hugging me. He pulled away from the hug only to kiss me firmly on the lips, and then looked at my face intently. "How hurt are you?" he asked with concern.

I shrugged, trying to downplay it. "I have a pretty nasty scratch on the back of my head, but that's about it."

He spun me around, moving my hair aside with a gasp. "Summer! This is terrible!"

"How bad does it look?" I asked, thinking of the pounding that I'd felt in my head, which had only lulled to a dull thumping feeling quite recently.

"Well, it looks like you've got a cracked skull, to be blunt. Your blood has patched it up pretty decently, but the skull itself isn't showing any progress of healing."

"It's because of the clips," I said, and I felt Demitri begin to tamper with them.

"Ouch," I said as he tried to pull it apart and get it off my wings.

"Sorry." He cringed. "Oh, wait!" he whispered, getting out the set of keys that Warren had handed him and testing a few in the lock. "Aha!" Demitri said at last, and I heard a click and felt a weight drop from my wings. It felt like life was flooding back into them, and I felt relief in my head as my magic went to heal that area first.

"Oh, this is much better," I breathed, turning slightly to see the vibrant blue of my wings as they pulsed back to life. "Thank you."

"Summer, I'm so sorry," he said urgently, turning me back to face him and clutching my hands in his. I tried to protest his apology, but he cut me off, saying quickly, "None of us knew where to start looking for you. I had to go a town over to hear of a rumor that a water fairy had been captured, and even then, we had to plan a rescue quicker than we'd intended to be ready—"

"Demitri!" I exclaimed, cupping his cheek in my hand, "I promise, I'm all right. I'm just glad to see you. Where are the others?"

"They're sneaking in the tower now with an invisibility spell my mother found in that giant warlock book of hers. I just came in early once I confirmed the dark fairies' enslavement because I figured whomever your guard was needed to get away from you. Did he treat you very badly?"

I shook my head insistently. "Warren isn't bad. He and his family have been forced to do Lorena's bidding for a long time now. I think if all of this goes according to plan, we need to take care of them, too."

Demitri looked at me skeptically, saying, "I don't know, Summer. Sometimes dark fairies take pleasure in this type of thing"—he motioned to the cell around us—"speaking from my temptations and experiences."

I argued, "Warren is different. I think he doesn't know for sure how he feels about overpowering Lorena, but I know he certainly doesn't like her, and he's been a friend to me these past few days."

Demitri nodded. "Well, I'm grateful he was here, then."

"Me too," I agreed, thinking of how he'd made this imprisonment a bit easier on me than it might have been otherwise. Then, my eyes grew wide and I exclaimed with sudden realization, "My parents must be worried sick!"

Demitri waved his hand with an attitude of disregard. "They're under a convincing spell. They think you're away on a vacation with us. Actually," he paused, smiling a little, and said, "so does the entire town. That was Charlotte's work, of course; extravagance is a must with everything she does!"

I smiled, glad that there was some sense of normalcy for everyone.

"So what day is it?" I asked, and he sighed, shocking me that I'd been here five whole days already. I felt myself grow sad over missing Christmas Day with my parents for the first time in my life, but I didn't want to deal with that emotion at that moment. "Wow," I responded instead, "time flies when you're having fun, I guess!"

He chuckled. "I'm just glad this place didn't make you lose your sense of humor!" I forced a smile.

"Oh, it'd take a lot more than Lorena to do that!" a new voice said. I looked up, seeing Charlotte standing at the open door, smiling with her arms wide open. I rushed forward into her crushing hug. "I'm so glad you're okay, Summer," she whispered, and I squeezed her tighter.

One by one, they all flew up from the depths of the tower: Anastrella, Analise and Lydia, Vivyanna and Katia, and even Genesis. I hugged each of them with glee, thanking them for coming for me, and feeling happier than I had in days.

"Okay, Summer. This was a pretty extreme way to get us all here, but I think you've got us all convinced. Let's take Lorena down!" Analise said high-fiving Lydia and whooping in a war-cry sort of fashion.

"Whoa, whoa, slow down!" I said, laughing genuinely for the first time in days. "We have to make a plan." The girls eyed each other smugly, their attitudes telling me they had all the confidence in the world.

"I'm serious, you guys! I've been down there, in the grand chamber." I took a shaking breath now, looking at all of them as they stared at me with wide and intrigued eyes. "It's going to be dangerous. Lorena has an entire room full of guards at her disposal, right above her head. And on top of that, she's got so much control over this whole place, with the enslavement of dark fairies and her fearsome rule, that I'm pretty sure if we were all captured, we'd be put to death before the rumor of our attempted coup even got out to the fairy world."

"Why, Summer? What's she so defensive about?" Charlotte asked.

I shrugged grudgingly, saying, "I think she feels like if the news got out about how corrupt her dealings have been in the past with stuff like this, going against the faire court and killing whomever she wanted, she'd have a complete uprising of the faire folk on her hands." The group almost unanimously gasped, each glancing around the circle with a sort of panic.

"What about the faire court?" Anastrella asked, "what if we attacked Lorena while the faire court members were present so that we'd have witnesses in our favor?"

"That's a good idea, Ana! The only problem now is that we don't know when they meet next." Katia said, patting Anastrella's shoulder in praise.

I stood up straighter then, suddenly seeing clearly how we were going to get ourselves into the grand chamber and successfully confront Lorena. I smiled all-knowingly at the group then, and said with utmost assuredness, "I think I know how we can handle that."

It seemed like it had been no time at all between when I'd explained the plan when we'd sent Demitri off to uncover necessary information, and when the entire plot had begun to unfold. *Time truly does fly when having fun, or when planning an epic revolt against a corrupt fairy leader!* I thought with a smirk.

The first order of business, the part of the plan Demitri alone needed to attend to, would be for him to make his way through the castle and to the guards' living quarters, still pretending to be James, a young dark wizard that Demitri had cast a sleeping spell over and left to rest in one of the cells of the abandoned tower next to this one.

Once he found the living quarters, he was to pretend to need to speak with Lorena and ask one of the superior dark fairies when the next faire court meeting was, so as not to interrupt her. "And what is he supposed to do if the dark fairy asks him why he's wanting to meet with Lorena?" Genesis asked, a concerned look crossing her face, "Many dark fairies are naturals when it comes to detecting a liar in the act, you know."

"He doesn't have to lie, necessarily," Lydia suggested, "he could say he wants to talk to Lorena about an issue with a prisoner. It'd be short and to the point, and"—she motioned to the lack of any sort of surveillance around this particular cell—"judging by the state of your cell, Summer, I'd say there's a bit of a security issue here!" We all laughed, bouncing more ideas off one another and being open to what everyone had to say.

Once we'd sorted out the fine details, Demitri set off first, aiming to find another dark fairy heading back to the quarters, and tag along with them to gain entrance. One issue I'd thought up in regards to our little plan would be Warren. If he ran into Demitri, I felt certain that he'd try to come back and take over, to let me out of the torture chair for a while. If he did that, he'd find me not in the chair, and accompanied in a cell full of warefae and exiled fairies. At that point, he'd likely feel obligated to report me to Lorena to save his position and life.

We settled on the idea of some sort of distraction, and Analise volunteered herself for the task. She said that with a transformation of her shirt and jeans into some sort of a dress, she felt that she could look like some sort of esteemed faire court member. She decided she'd pretend to be a precious gemstones fairy, a type that was very rare and very special to the fairy world. Her coppery wings would seal the deal on this alter ego of hers', and after I described Warren to her, she seemed confident that she could find him and engage him in some sort of mock political discussion for a moment, ensuring that he wouldn't see Demitri during his outing.

So, after Demitri left, the other six of us worked on Analise's appearance until she looked regal and royal with an auburn colored long dress and delicate white flowers dotting her braided hair and surrounding her head like a crown. She had a wardrobe of some sort of Greek goddess, and she looked fearsome when the whole look was complete.

"Analise, you look so good!" Lydia exclaimed as we admired our teamwork on her before we all wished her good luck and watched as she flew out the cell door, down into the depths of the tower. Lydia stood by the edge of the cell door, clutching one of the bars in fear, clearly anxious at being separated from her best friend. The four mothers got a chance to discuss who all would likely still be a part of the faire court to determine how they may react to this situation. The division of tasks left Charlotte and me with the freedom to sit on the cold cell floor and chat about all kinds of things we'd missed during the past days apart.

"So, tell me about your friend, Warren," she said first, smirking as we'd sat down. I gave her a pointed look then, eyebrows narrowed and all, and she nodded with a laugh, saying, "I know, I know; you're in love with Demitri. But, seriously, he passed us when we were in the middle of flying up with our invisibility spells cast over us, and that fairy is not bad looking!"

"Well, I bet after all this is over, you can go talk to him and flirt a little! I'm sure he'd love that," I joked, nudging her shoulder.

Charlotte, however, wasn't laughing then. At the thought of flirting with someone else, even as a joke, a distant look crossed her face; I knew her mind and her heart were no longer with me, but with Bobby Hayes, back in Weston. I reached over and took her hand, squeezing it gently. "I'm sorry, Charlotte." She didn't respond but squeezed my hand back as if to tell me she'd be okay after a while.

"Who knows," I suggested, "maybe after all this is over, something will be allowed between you two, just like it probably will be with the fairies and the warlocks!" She shrugged, not even seeming to consider this possibility, lest she gets her hopes up under false pretenses. "I don't think so, Summer. It's kind of different for two magical beings to be in love, but someone from the human world and someone from our world just couldn't work out together.

"It's okay though," she insisted then, "I don't want you worrying about me, especially not while we've got more important things to do!"

"Oh, I can't think of anything more crucial to discuss!" I said with a very serious expression, standing with her and laughing together as we walked over to listen in on the fairies' conversation.

"Analise and Demitri should be back soon, right?" Vivyanna asked, looking concernedly over the edge of the cell floor. Genesis put a hand on her shoulder, assuring her that Analise would be able to handle herself out there, just as Demitri would.

It couldn't have been more than a minute later when we heard the flutter of wings approaching the cell. We all braced for whom it could be, preparing for the worst scenario and forming ourselves into a battle formation, just in case.

Analise shot straight up in front of the cell, screaming slightly and covering her face with her hands at the sight of all of us prepared to attack. This startled Lydia so much that she accidentally sent a puff of snow straight at Analise, and it hit her square in the stomach, making her double over, laughing but shooting a grin at Lydia that meant someday soon, payback would be so sweet!

"Well, what happened?" Katia asked, all of us staring impatiently at her. Analise looked flustered for a moment before tripping over her words a bit and getting out, "Um, yes, he's distracted."

"How so?" Genesis asked sort of skeptically, causing Analise to look visibly stressed. "He's going to run a "special errand" for me, Arianna of the Faire Court, keeper of precious gems."

She smiled then, a far-away look on her face, saying, "I think I was persuasive enough to keep him busy for quite a while. He certainly didn't suspect that I wasn't who I said I was." Charlotte and I eyed each other as we noticed the dreamy gaze that washed over her, realizing at the same moment that a fake name and an errand weren't Analise's only methods of distraction. Everyone congratulated her on her skillful deception, and after the fairies moved on to continue their discussion, the three of us warefae girls practically swarmed Analise.

"You kissed him, didn't you?" Charlotte exclaimed in an excited whisper. Analise's cheeks visibly blushed as she nodded sheepishly, a smile playing on her lips. "He's kind of irresistible. I'm glad *he* was your guard, Summer, and not some ugly guy!" She exclaimed with a tone of partial embarrassment, but mostly glee. Her comment earned a playful slap from me, and a snort of laughter from Charlotte.

Lydia seemed to be more skeptical of the excitement we had over Analise's surprising kiss. "Analise, be rational," she pleaded, "you don't want to be distracted before we go into all of this." At this point of the conversation, Analise just grasped Lydia's shoulder, gave her an all-knowing look, and finally convinced Lydia to relax and crack a smile. "It was one little kiss," she said as Lydia visibly calmed down, "I swear, if I see him in battle, it will be like it never happened; I'll fire marsh vines at him so fast, he won't even know what hit him!"

I could see that under the surface, Analise was only saying this to appease Lydia. I figured Charlotte could see this too, but neither of us was going to object to Analise's words. She and Lydia had an odd relationship, but they seemed to know exactly what one another needed to hear at all times.

Demitri came back no more than fifteen minutes later, looking slightly wide-eyed as if he'd just seen a ghost. "What's wrong, Demitri?" Genesis asked, approaching him with a look of concern that matched his. "One hour. The faire court meets in one hour."

We all looked around at one another then, fear building collectively as we realized that we wouldn't have as much time to prepare as we'd originally hoped for. I felt everyone's gaze settle on me, though, seeing as I was the initiator of this idea. "Okay, it's going to be fine," I said, "we've just got to walk right in there and act like we own the place."

I expected laughter to emerge upon my suggestion, as if that would never work. Instead, the entire group nodded almost in synchronization, a certain air of determination filling the room, filling us all.

"The guard said that when the faire court meetings are going on, Lorena leaves the grand chamber door unlocked, so that the guards can come and go without interrupting the meeting by knocking. There are fourteen faire court members, and from what I gathered, tensions are high between them and Lorena."

"Good," Vivyanna said, "that means they'll be easier to persuade, right?"

"I'm not so sure," I cut in, "since I've been here, I've found it clear that Lorena's rule is more based on fear than respect. The faire court members and the guards aren't thinking about themselves when complying with her demands so easily; they're worried about their families, their clans, and their own lives. No one is safe here."

"Well, that makes sense, Summer," Anastrella responded, "when a fairy becomes a grand faire enchantress or enchanter, they get an extra surge of power, all because of the Faire Tree. That's why the royal families no longer have the magic of their elements, and instead can shapeshift the golden magic that all fairies have as the basis of their bloodlines."

We discussed for a moment all the ways that this could pose a serious problem. The magic of the Faire Tree would make Lorena capable of dominating all of the fairy powers in the world. We decided in the end though, with a sense of false confidence weighing on us, that the shock of the existence and survival of the warefae, and our extraordinary powers, would improve our chances of beating her greatly.

"Besides," Demitri chimed in after our renewed assurance, "we have Summer, a descendent of a warlock of light! We don't even know the entire range of her powers yet!"

"Yes, but I don't either!" I countered, "I don't want to walk in, guns a blazing, if I don't even know what I'm supposed to be doing."

"Summer, look at me," Genesis said, and I turned to look into her soft, dark eyes, full of faith and genuine spirit. "You are ready, dear. We all followed you here to fight. Yes, I know we were here to rescue you, but you would've found a way out on your own, even if we hadn't have come for you. The true reason we're here is that we believe in what you want us to do, and we wholeheartedly trust your plan. We're all following you."

I smiled at her, and all the rest of them, feeling surrounded by love and support and finally believing that what I had around me was my fairy clan, my own magical family. "All right, then. I'll lead the way."

When the new hour had begun, and the faire court meeting would have commenced, we vacated the cell. We flew down the long tower, and I felt, at that moment, that we were invincible.

When we left the tower, passing the tree and venturing through the massive courtyards and hallways of the castle, we received several surprised stares from the on-looking servants and guards passing by. No one dared approach us, though; I expected we looked too intimidating. In our "war formation," I led the group, my wings and magic back to their full strength now, and my natural appearance not hidden by any warlock spells. I wanted to go in to see Lorena as my true self, not as a prisoner who pretended to be someone she wasn't. Flanking me on either side were Anastrella and Genesis, and behind them, Vivyanna and Katia. The warefae formed a line behind them, bringing up the back of the group with their strength that would surprise Lorena and, hopefully, would leave her vulnerable to our attack.

To the outside world, our group may have looked like a strange collection of older teenagers, flying mysteriously through a castle with looks of vengeance upon our faces. This would have been my thought process only months before.

To my clan, though, we were a group of fairies and warefae with age ranges from several centuries to mere years. There were fairy mothers, with hearts full of anger toward Lorena for relationships she ripped apart and exile sentences she'd implemented that hadn't been earned.

For the warefae, childhoods had been stolen, contact with fathers had been forbidden, and fear had been a constant whenever taking to the sky. As for me, I felt for all of them just as much as I felt for my parents and myself. We would put a stop to this, once and for all.

We approached the magnificent golden door, and without a moment's hesitation, I forced the air before me to move forth, allowing the door to creak open, and revealing the inside of the chamber.

There was an eerie silence filling the room as we flew in, our wings beating in unison as we drifted closer and closer to the stairs, atop which Lorena stood on a platform, surrounded by her faire court members.

My heart was beating practically up through my throat, but when I spoke, my voice did not quaver. "Hello, Lorena," I called out, and she merely turned her head to the side from where she stood in front of the faire court, addressing them with her back to us. She wore a similar golden dress to the one she'd had when I last saw her, but instead of considering her to be beautiful, the first thing the gold color that enveloped her reminded me of was greed.

"I am only to be addressed as Grand Faire Enchantress in these hallowed halls. Aside from that, I am in the middle of a faire court meeting. Leave the chamber at once, or I will summon the guards."

"Oh, I wouldn't do that if I were you, Ren," I said, remembering my mother's childhood nickname for the wicked enchantress. Upon hearing this, Lorena whirled around, speaking the name that had been haunting her for decades, "Fallon?"

"No, Lorena," I said as my group of attackers drew closer, "think again."

The faire court members remained in their seats behind Lorena, looking around nervously, not wanting to evoke an attack from us, but not wanting to reveal their fear to Lorena either.

Lorena studied me as I approached, saying with realization, "You! You're that prisoner, Vera! You've transformed yourself somehow."

"Wrong again! I pretended to be Vera, but that is not who I am. Wow, Ren, I'm surprised you haven't guessed it already." I held up a hand to my clan then, and we all stopped, just hovering there in midair.

It seemed that no one took a breath during those moments, when Lorena flew a tad lower, hovering over the stairs with curiosity tracing her face. She seemed to have the answer in her mind already, but a part of her didn't seem to believe it.

"You... you—"

"Go on, just say it," I said, smiling with mock sweetness. She narrowed her eyes at me, jerking back a bit and saying, "You're Fallon and the warlock's abomination, aren't you? You're the result of the defilement of nature's laws. You are a crossbreed of evil and good. You're that girl, Blair, are you not?"

I clapped very slowly and exaggeratedly, loving the way I was so clearly irritating her, "Bravo! Brava! Ten points to Lorena, everyone!" I said, waving my arms grandly around the room.

She glared at me, moving her hands slightly then, turning a small sort of golden fireball around between her fingertips, seeming poised to launch it at me any second. "Well, well, well; have you come to learn of how worthless your mother was before she died?"

"No, I already know how worthy she is—her and my father," I said, flying forward from my group a bit and Lorena doing the same. "I'm here for you." She and I were close enough to one another in the center of the cold marble room that I could hear her angry, heaving breaths; the rest of the chamber's occupants watched us in frightened silence.

"You see, Lorena, you've got the wrong idea about fairy and warlock relationships, and I'm here to tell you why." She cackled. "Oh, are you now? Well, this should be enlightening! A child has come here to tell me everything she knows about love, is that it?" She rolled her eyes dramatically.

"Lorena," I said softly, moving closer to her now, "Warlocks and fairies together are not bad. The warefae are not dangerous." I motioned to the clan. Lorena moved back from them, and me, as she noted our different wings. She glared at me. "You are too different. I will not tolerate the magic of the faire tree to be tainted by the blood of demons, like you all are. You are beasts," she hissed.

"That's where you're wrong, Lorena," I said, looking now to the faire court. "Grand Faire Enchantress Lorena has lied to all of you. She claims that the relations between fairies and warlocks are dangerous, and the children of the two magical species would be detrimental to both kinds of creatures. She knows this to be false, and yet, is this not what she told you as an explanation for her exile of the four fairies behind me?"

The fairy men and women sitting in the chairs above us looked around at one another, before nodding grudgingly, earning an evil stare from Lorena, who spun around then to see the fairies she had exiled so long ago. Vivyanna and Katia smirked, crossing their arms, as Anastrella waved daintily, and Genesis said eerily, "Hello again, Enchantress."

Lorena scoffed, turning to her faire court and saying, "This group is clearly out of the bounds of magical law! They knew the relations were not allowed, and they chose to defy it!"

"But, Lorena, you should know that love isn't exactly a force that can be stopped with a simple choice. It's a tie more powerful than magic, and there isn't anything you could've done on the exile day to stop the warlocks and fairies from loving one another for all of the years they've been apart.

"Lorena, please"—she looked me hard in the eyes to hear my request—"allow the fairy world to move on from the laws of centuries ago! Warlocks are not creatures of the dark! The children of fairies and warlocks aren't monsters either!"

"Children!" Lorena sneered, "I just can't believe it to be possible! Our species of light wouldn't dare carry on with genetic darkness."

"There you go making assumptions again, Lorena, and wrong ones, at that!" I said, shaking my head at her ignorance. "You, yourself, acknowledged that I must be the child of Peter and Fallon, did you not? So, you *have* to believe in our existence. If you didn't before, you must now, as we have you surrounded."

"This is madness. You are all unnatural creatures."

"No!" I yelled, turning to the faire court again, "we are the warefae! We are half warlocks and half fairies. Our fairy blood is dominant, so we get wings and can use our powers in charms, and, if we so choose, we are also able to learn warlock spells to use as well. We only want to help humans, not enforce the devil's work, or anything evil such as that. We came here in peace, to show you that we should be exiled no longer."

"Enough of this nonsense!" Lorena screamed, her voice echoing in the chamber. The faire court looked shocked, but they did seem to be nodding to one another as if agreeing that what I said made sense. "These warefae, or whatever they want to call themselves, were not given their magic by God. It was forced into bloodlines by demons of the Underearth! They cannot be trusted, lest their temptations for evil get the best of us all."

"We are not like this in the least!" I interrupted. "We have done our part in our small town for long enough to prove that we can live alongside humans, just like any other clan. Fairies, I am here today to ask your permission to relieve these fairies and warefae of the exile, and allow love and happiness to be driving forces in the fairy world once again!"

Lorena looked panicked as she stared at each of the faire court members, anger seeming to bubble over inside of her. "I'm warning you, I will take control and end you all, right here and right now!"

"Ladies and gentlemen, fairies of the court," I exclaimed, pointing to Lorena and feeling similar to a lawyer, "this is further proof that Lorena is exercising too much power! She has disregarded your views and opinions long enough, and she has snuffed out the rights of fairies to a point where she must be removed from power."

Lorena howled with frustration, beginning to circle me like a prowling lioness. "My faire court members, we must see reason. We cannot listen to this—this child! She cannot think clearly when there is demon blood in her brain."

I laughed at this, not wanting to reveal yet that I didn't have any demon blood within me, so as not to give up my advantage of power. I said instead, "Honestly, I think you all know deep down that you should listen to me. For years, you've probably thought the same things, after all, and just been unwilling to stand up for what you know to be right, which is defying Lorena's power!"

The group atop the stairs seemed to whisper amongst themselves, like a grand jury in a trial, but Lorena wouldn't have even the slightest hint of rebellion in her midst. "That's it!" She cried, "Guards! Guards, get in here!"

"Oh, you don't want to do that, Lorena. I told you already!" I said with a tone of pity as I heard the ceiling door begin to unlock, and the flutter of wings as the guards began to pour in from their quarters above.

"And why is that?" she asked smugly, her golden weaponry beginning to swirl larger and larger near her fingertips.

"Because, we may have come here in peace, but that doesn't mean we weren't prepared to fight." I paused for a second, eyeing the twenty or so dark fairies hovering by the ceiling and awaiting orders, hoping that our strategy for fighting would work in the end. Without further hesitation, I yelled, "Now!" and my clan burst forth into action.

Katia and Lydia immediately flew up to the top of the stairs, where some of the faire court members were attempting to rise from their seats, unsure if they should help defend Lorena. The two snow fairies worked from opposite sides, crafting a perfect block of ice across the entire row of chairs, freezing the lower halves and the wings of the faire court members within it. They could not move, which likely didn't bother many of them who were torn between fighting Lorena and running. Once the faire court members were stuck, Lydia and Katia flew back down to assist the others.

The rest of the clan had shot straight up to the ceiling, each fighting the guards in a paired-off fashion, mother and child together. Lorena yelled at the dark soldiers to trap us, and so they spread out, trying to harness each fighter in the grayish bands of smoke they launched from their hands.

Genesis and Demitri took on the bulk of the soldiers, Genesis using the same strength of power as the dark soldiers she was fighting, but with immensely larger amounts of skill and practice on her side. Demitri, meanwhile, seemed to shock them all by launching entire sheets of the black smoke at them, trapping the ones he fought in a sort of netting that numbed their powers.

Anastrella and Charlotte were quick to avoid the reaches of the dark fairies, shooting fiery hot bits of stardust at the guards, knocking some of them down to the ground temporarily, until their magic healed them and allowed them to fly once more.

Vivyanna and Analise shocked the dark soldiers with their mere existence. Marsh fairies weren't exactly commonplace up in Canada, where dark fairies had lived out their servitudes in the castle. The murky waters flying at them seemed to almost swallow them up, and they struggled against them fearfully. These soldiers seemed to be no match for the power of the warefae.

Lydia and Katia's ice shards were about as effective as Anastrella and Charlotte's shots of stardust were. The ice would knock the soldiers down for a few moments, but their magic allowed them to rebound quickly. I realized then that without some sort of a turn of events, we would be stuck like this for eternity, only harming one another at the surface, no one is ever truly able to win.

I, however, didn't have much time to dwell on this or see much of what the others did aside from the opening attacks of the battle, because as soon as Lorena had called her orders to her soldiers, she launched at me, arms outstretched and nails like claws in front of her.

She grasped hold of my shoulder, shoving me down to the ground, the gold magic in her hands burning me like hot lava. I slammed against the cold marble floor, grunting in pain as she tried to wrap her bony hands around my throat, burning and choking me simultaneously.

Unwilling to lay there idly and let her kill me, I forced my own hands up beneath her shoulders and fired a jet of water so strong upon her that she flew off of me and back into the air, crying out as she hit the ceiling.

Katia flew out from the center of the group, facing all of the dark soldiers. She let out a battle cry and launched a spray of ice shards at the guards so strong that it sent them all hurtling back to the edges of the room, their clothes, and wings pinned to the walls. She turned to smile at her daughter with pride, as a solid golden soldier of magical creation came forth from the wall, flying up behind her holding out its' palm.

Suddenly, a vial similar to the one Lorena had shown me—filled with halt serum—appeared. Lydia screamed for her mother to run, but she seemed to be unable to hear her, and too shocked to move. A needle formed at the end of the vial, and with a quick movement, the soldier grasped it in its' shining hand, stabbing Katia with the injection. "NO!" Vivyanna and Lydia yelled at the same time.

She let out a gasp as she fell to the ground. The other fairies exclaimed in shock and flew forward to her aid, but six more of these golden guards flew up from the floor, surrounding them and moving in slowly. I tried to move to help them, but I felt paralyzed. I glanced down and saw the golden cuffs were around my wrists once more. I looked up at the ceiling, realizing this attack and my trapped state were being initiated by Lorena—her hands had sparks flickering from them in the direction of the soldiers, and a thin stream keeping me still.

Katia let out a shaky breath, and her body began to flake away into golden specks. I gasped, feeling shocked and horrified; tears bested up in my eyes as I saw Lydia sobbing hysterically for her mom. Katia's body was gone—it was as if she had died and become part of the palace.

I noticed the golden soldiers close in further on the rest of my group, halt serum beginning to appear in each of their molten hands. "Summer, help!" Charlotte yelled. With a surge of determination, motivated to fight to save my clan, I clenched my fists and closed my eyes tight. I dug deep, thinking of Katia's bravery, and all of the sacrifices that had been made for the sake of the warefae. I thought of my parents, Fallon and Peter. I thought of the fear that Lorena kept over all of her subjects and all of the magical creatures whose lives she had taken.

I had a burst of determination, feeling my magic flow from my chest to my arms and down to my wrist. I heard a quick popping noise as the cuffs shattered. I flew immediately to Lorena, grabbing her by the throat and slamming her hard into the ceiling. I looked down and saw the magical soldiers begin to melt back into the ground.

I began to fly down to check on my friends, but Lorena was following me. I looked back to her instead, both of us taking heavy breaths as we flew around each other to the center of the room, each of us stalking our prey. There was a whooshing sound as my clan unanimously launched spells and magic at Lorena. She glanced down to throw a golden shield to deflect the attacks, and once she was distracted, I muttered a warlock spell to form the green jets Genesis had taught us. Lorena cried out, flying away quickly as the lightning-like line of sparks slammed into the marble wall behind her, forming a giant crack from the floor to the ceiling. "Guards, I need back up!" she ordered.

Everything happened so fast after that. The guards from the floor began working themselves free of their ice traps one by one. The guardians' quarter doors opened from the ceiling, and a swarm of the shadow fairies burst forth, their dark magic billowing around them. They flew so rapidly around the chamber that the smoke seemed to rush from the ceiling and swallow up the whole place. I heard shouts and screams from my clan, and terror began to rise in my heart.

I caught Lorena's eye as the clouding magic began to rise around us, and she smiled wickedly at me as the darkness took us in. I coughed and choked on the harsh smoke as it tormented my lungs and swirled around, and I felt two pairs of rough and calloused hands take my arms and force them behind my back. I tried to fire off spells and charms and any kind of magic I could, but nothing worked.

I felt myself being flown down to the ground, and my feet touched down, the two guards still holding me there. The smoke began to clear, and I saw Lorena in front of me. I looked side to side, seeing no one there but the two guards. I craned my head further, though, seeing my fairy and warefae allies on their knees behind me. Their wings were clipped and their hands were cuffed in front of them. I saw no fear in their eyes, even though they were devastated by Katia's loss, vulnerable, and surrounded by guards. I caught Demitri's gaze, and he nodded at me confidently, so I took a deep breath, and turned to face Lorena once more.

"You see, Blair, your time has run out. I would've done this long ago, if only I'd been able to find you. Here, today, you will die, and all your clan will die, and none of the faire folk will ever know of the trouble you've caused here today. It will just"—she smiled as if pleasantly imagining this scenario—"drift away like a bad dream."

I shook my head defiantly at her. "No, we will not drift away Lorena. No matter what happens, the faire court has seen the truth about you. The guards have known the truth about you for years, as well. Your time will end sooner than you think, I can promise you that."

Her face contorted in a frustrated scowl, but she seemed to compose herself in front of me and said, "We'll see about that." She stared then at the others, saying, "I thought I warned you girls of what would happen if you defied the laws. I thought what happened to Fallon and Peter would be enough to scare you into eternal hiding."

"We were, Lorena," Anastrella said, "but Summer—I mean, Blair—has taught us that to fear you would be to empower you. We came here to stand up for ourselves and our children, and, more than that, for the fairy world.

"You were hurt, Lorena," she said earnestly, "but that is not the fault of the warlocks. It is the fault of your prejudice and insecurities, and the fact that your grandmother tried to trick you into believing that warlocks did nothing but hurt. You overcompensate for the terror you evoke from fairies by trying to make fairies fear another species more. To preserve the state of purity you advertise so much, you block out any magic you've deemed impure or disgraceful. You've turned yourself into a monster, Lorena, and the warlocks had nothing to do with that. Your actions must stop after all of these years! Think of Peter, and Fallon, and now Katia. How many more lives must be lost before you realize your mistakes?"

Lorena threw her hands in the air, letting out a groan of frustration. "Enough with all of you! Warlocks are evil creatures, hell-bent on destroying our world. Relations with them were forbidden, and so you were exiled—"

"Yes, they were exiled in secret!" I shouted at her, looking past her to see the faire court members looking skeptically at one another from where they were stuck in the now melting ice block. "You told the faire court, sure, but when you gave the sentence, you exiled these women without the permission or consultation of the faire court, which is illegal!" Lorena scoffed, crossing her arms and flying straight forward until she was only inches from me.

"You listen here, you little brat," she whispered, "I am the grand faire enchantress. *I* am the grand faire enchantress. Soon enough, I will do away with the faire court, and they will be no problem to me. Tell your parents I say 'Hello,'" She glared at me once more before turning around and yelling, "Warren!"

I felt my heart skip a beat, and heard Analise gasp behind me. I looked up to the ceiling to see Warren fluttering down slowly to the ground, his dark eyes looking sadly at me. I saw his gaze shift behind me then, and his mouth hung agape a bit as he whispered, "Arianna?"

"Warren, I'm sorry," I heard her say back at him, regret weighing heavily in her tone, "my name is Analise. I came here with my clan to save Summer." He nodded at her, a look of understanding, and yet also bafflement, crossing his face as he glanced back to me.

I pled with him with my eyes, hoping he would see the message I was trying to share with him. *Please Warren, choose the right side. Choose our side.* These words echoed through my head over and over as he joined Lorena in the center of the room. "I believe you remember your little prisoner, Vera, do you not, Warren?" she asked, putting her hand on his shoulder firmly and digging her nails into his t-shirt. "The prisoner you helped to torture for her crimes, correct?" He seemed to stare through me as he simply nodded in response.

From midair, Lorena's hands began to shape-shift a blob of gold as she turned to face me, devilishly grinning as she fashioned a glistening dagger out of it. I could hear the clan trying to fight the guards off of her behind me as if to come to my aid, but they could do no good.

"Warren," Lorena whispered loudly so that her voice carried across the room and over to me, "I want you to take this dagger, and cut the wings off of *her*, the most evil being in this room. Do you understand me, Warren?" He gulped, his hand shaking as Lorena handed the dagger to him, but he nodded again, blinking quickly and taking shallow breaths. Lorena motioned for him to follow her as she flew forward slightly.

"Lorena, enough!" A member of the faire court shouted from her place atop the stairs, "This is an outrage! This girl and her clan have not committed any crime that warrants such a punishment! You've already killed one of them." Lorena threw up a hand and the talking immediately ceased, and the fairy seemed to become covered in gold so that she was an immobile statue. "In a few moments, you will no longer be a—um—whatever you are."

"Warefae," I said boldly, watching Warren, waiting for him to fly forwards to come to end my magic. "I am a warefae. And you may destroy my magic today, but you will never be able to erase the events that have taken place in this chamber."

Lorena merely shrugged off my threat, motioning for Warren to hurry up. "Cut her wings slowly, Warren. I want to see her suffer. Do this," she said, turning to him with an earnest gaze, "and I may just give you your freedom." His breath caught in his chest, as did mine. I knew it was over. Freedom was all Warren wanted out of this life, and I knew that our momentary comradery would by no means outweigh the prospect of a life without servitude.

I tried to catch his gaze, but he merely looked at the dagger in his hand. I braced myself for the pain, the same that my mother had experienced at the hands of Lorena herself. I tried to prepare mentally for what it would feel like to die. There would be no life with my parents, no fairies, no warefae, and no Demitri.

Life, as I'd known it to be now, would never be again. It seemed that when faced with the possibility of forever to live, I'd forgotten to truly enjoy the present, and not take any second of it for granted. That was my biggest regret.

Lorena turned to face me again, smirking and crossing her arms, and Warren's wings beat quickly as he began to fly forward. "Get to it, Warren, we haven't got..."

Her words were cut off and a sharp gasp escaped her lips. As soon as Warren had gotten close enough to Lorena, I saw the glint of the golden dagger move quickly behind her wings, and then in front of her throat. She seemed to linger in the air a moment, a look of shock, fury, and, hidden deep within her eyes, remorse, on her face, before falling to the ground in a heap of golden blood and wings.

Chapter Thirteen
The Sweet Bliss of Freedom

The silence in the room was deafening. I felt the guards' hold on me loosen in shock. The sight of Lorena on the floor before me was almost disgusting to look at, yet I couldn't take my eyes away from it. Everyone seemed to be holding their breaths as a collective unit, waiting for someone to acknowledge what had just happened.

Warren hovered over her, looking down at the dagger in his hand sheepishly, before dropping it beside the body as if it were burning him by being tainted with her evil blood. I looked around, and everyone was in shock. There were tear stains on the bloodied, but healing faces of my clan. Lydia looked shell shocked as if she would fall over as soon as the guards let her go. I jumped with shock as the faire court began to whoop and cheer, their ice block melting completely now and allowing them to rise. The fairy who'd opposed Lorena became freed from the gold Lorena had set upon her, and she then ordered the guards to release us.

They did so quickly and seemingly willingly, unclipping wings and removing handcuffs. "Whoa!" the guard next to me said as he let go of me, looking down at his wrists in a bewildered fashion. The other guard followed suit, exclaiming, "Warren, look!" and flying up to him. Warren turned the guard's arm over to study it, before examining his own with wide eyes. "What is it, young man?" A woman from the faire court called down, "Also, can someone please let us out of the ice!" Charlotte and her mother stopped their celebratory embracing momentarily to fly up the stairs and make the ice fade completely away.

The members of the faire court began to fly down the stairs to intermingle with us, thanking us for our heroism and willingness to stand up to Lorena. Others rushed to Warren to offer him money if he were to be their guards, and, after a long moment of trying to make an announcement, he yelled out, "Hey!" The whole room fell silent at once to hear what he had to say.

Warren held up his wrist, which was blank—the burn mark of the Faire Tree was missing. "With Lorena's death, the guards and servants in this castle are no longer bound to a single ruler. We have won our freedom, and we intend to take it"—he looked down then, and his cheeks reddened a bit, embarrassed at the magnitude of the proclamation he'd just made—"if that's okay with the court, of course."

The entirety of the faire court looked at each other around the room, nodding in unison before enthusiastically congratulating all the soldiers present. The dark fairies hollered and whooped so loudly, some embracing one another and others simply floating there, so overwhelmed with emotion that they'd taken to covering their faces with their hands.

I found Demitri among the crowd and wrapped my hands around his neck. We kissed there, both of our wings fluttering in unison as the sensation of flying took on another meaning altogether. "I'm so proud of you, Summer," he whispered into my ear a moment later hugging me tightly. I kissed him once on the cheek before closing my eyes, feeling the world around me fade away as I soaked in the sweet bliss of freedom.

When I'd coaxed myself into believing that this dream-like state was reality, I was able to open my eyes and find all the rest of our clan for a round of somber hugs and forced congratulations. I hugged every single one of those brave, brave women. Well, every one of them aside from Analise at first, for she and Warren were off to the side, hugging tightly, Analise apologizing furiously.

When they broke apart Analise went straight to Lydia, who was being comforted by Genesis and Vivyanna. Warren, meanwhile, looked around until his eyes found me in the crowd, and he immediately began to head over. "I'll give you two a moment," Charlotte said, turning around to go and hug Demitri.

"Well, you certainly surprised me," I said, giving Warren a one-armed hug when he joined me.

"I think I surprised myself a bit too," he said, looking overwhelmed, but still smiling.

"What made you do it?" I asked, pulling him aside so I could hear him over the chattering crowd, seeing Anastrella speaking with the talkative fairy that seemed to speak for the faire court and pointing to me out of the corner of my eye.

Warren sighed, rubbing a hand over his spiked hair. "I think at that moment, I saw you, and I saw Analise, and I saw all of my friends from the guard being forced to restrain all of you good warefae and fairies, and I got perspective on what was wrong about this world I've been trapped in for all these years"—he shrugged—"and I may have caught the end of your call-to-action speech, and, what can I say, I felt inspired." He put a hand on my arm, saying, "Summer, I wanted to thank you. You saved so many people's futures today because you were brave."

"But, Warren—"

"I know, I know, I delivered the final blow. That doesn't matter, though, because you encouraged me to do it."

I smiled at him, wiping touched tears from my eyes.

"So," I said, looking around the vast palace chamber, filling more and more with the newly freed guards and the celebratory fairies that'd heard the news. "What are you going to do now with all this freedom of yours?"

He turned his face up toward the ceiling and closed his eyes, a look of peace washing across his face before he said, "I don't know, and it's the best feeling in the world."

Minutes later, when Lorena's body had been removed from the premises, the mood lightened even more. The faire court members had begun to form a line at the top of the stairs, each of them smiling, like little kids ready to share a secret. There was a massive group of fairies and warefae collecting at the bottom of the stairs, preparing to hear their announcement.

The woman who was at the center of the faire court once more raised her hand to silence us. "Let us all know celebration on this day of ultimate freedom. First of all, we'd like to honor the brave sacrifice of Katia, without whom we would likely all be under the rule of darkness still." She said this pointedly at Lydia, who nodded back, a single tear running down her cheek, but a stony look of acceptance coming across her face regardless of her pain. "To the fairies, this is what we've waited for, our long-overdue release from the prison of Lorena's rule. As the leader of the faire court, it is my honor and privilege to welcome into official recognition the warefae species, who henceforth have the utmost respect of the world's fairies." She paused, and the whole room echoed with applausefor us – I felt my face turn red as they stared at us.

She continued, "The faire court's members would also like to recognize that on this day, we are overturning the laws stating that all fairies of dark nature are bound to an eternity of servitude to the Faire Palace, as well as the law that no fairies and warlock relations will be permitted.

Fairies have the right to decide for themselves what to do with their freedom, and to whom their hearts will belong. Any fairies previously exiled by Lorena for breaking her so-called law are under a sentence of exile no longer!"

This statement brought about overly excited celebrations from the guards, and the fairy mothers, all of whom hugged their children at the prospect of their freedom and the possibility of seeing the loves of their lives again.

The woman waved her hands in the air to calm everyone down, a toothy grin spread across her face despite her attempt to be authoritative. "The final matter of discussion today is the successor of Lorena. The faire court has discussed who will take over Lorena's position, and we have selected Blair, otherwise known as Summer, of the Sea. If you accept, Summer, we would be honored to have you serve as an honorable, respectful, fair, and just leader of the faire folk." I had been standing next to Demitri at the time, holding his hand and trying to take mental pictures of this moment in my mind to keep there forever.

When the head of the faire court had called out my name, though, in front of all of those urgent eyes of fairies and warefae who watched me, it was all I could do to stop myself from passing out. "Oh, my gosh." I breathed, looking up at Demitri who squeezed my hand a bit tighter. "Demitri, what do I do?"

He stared at me for a second before tucking a strand of my hair behind my ear, saying, "You go up there and say what comes to your heart." It seemed so simple when he put it that way, but I felt like my whole world, my life as I knew it, all hung in the way I responded to this.

I let go of his hand, flying slowly up the stairs to touch down beside the leader of the court. I looked down to the floor of the chamber, where the numbers of the crowd must have grown to above a thousand. Everyone in the palace on the day of Lorena's killing had made their way there to see if it was true and if their freedom had been fought for at last.

"I... I," I tried to start saying something, feeling utterly overwhelmed by the amount of pressure weighing on me, then looking to Demitri, and feeling a sudden clarity settle over me. I took a deep breath, looking then to the fairy next to me, her kind eyes almost knowing my answer before I'd said it.

"I'm honored at the nomination, ma'am, I truly am. I think that at this time, I am too young to be able to take on the full weight of the position." The woman patted my shoulder, nodding in understanding, and I looked back to the crowd, my eyes landing on one fairy that gave me a wonderful idea. "I do, however, have a suggestion on who the successor should be instead."

The fairy nodded next to me. "We would love to consider it. You, after all, are our revered hero now, Summer. Your opinion will hold great weight in the fairy world for a lot of years to come."

I smiled at her, saying, "The fairy to take the grand faire enchantress position shouldn't be filled with just anybody."

I paced the top of the stairs a bit, looking to the crowd now. "You want a leader who is absolutely nothing like Lorena. This fairy would be a leader opposite of what the fairy world has seen in the past several centuries. She is kind, she gives people chances, and she wants the best for the collective. She is well educated in the ways of the magical and human world, but not so much so that she sees the world as beneath her. She is loving and sees all magic as something beautiful, and not something to be feared."

"Well, by all means, dear, tell us who she is so we can decide if it would be a good fit for the faire court." I smiled down, catching the eye of the fairy that had helped me to uncover the truth about myself, and who'd welcomed me in even when she didn't know that I had the magical powers that I did. "If it were a perfect world, I'd recommend Anastrella of the Skies."

Anastrella clapped her hand over her mouth, and Charlotte clutched her arm, a surprised smile on her face. The court gathered behind me for a second, and I could hear them murmuring their consent and agreement. The head of the faire court then beckoned her up the stairs, and Anastrella flew up to join us.

"Anastrella, the faire court has decided that if you can prove yourself as a leader right here and right now, we will grant you the ultimate power of the grand faire enchantress." Anastrella didn't even have to take a breath before she answered. She just smiled and said, "If I were to be given this honor, I wouldn't even consider this to be my power, but our power, because for the first time in so many years, I would value the opinion of the faire court more than my own." That seemed to be all she needed to say because the faire court as a collective began clapping, and the entire room joined in their applause, especially the enthusiastic core of the warefae and fairy mothers up front.

"Fairies and warefae," the leader said, walking in front of Anastrella and fashioning a crown out of midair, lined with jewels and gemstones, gold and elegance. I knew at once she was a gemstone fairy, and I was amazed by her craft. She continued, placing the crown on Anastrella's blonde hair, "I, Jade, leader of the faire court, as well as every faire court member standing behind me, do so decree that on this special day, Anastrella of the Skies is to become Grand Faire Enchantress Anastrella, leader of the faire folk and protector of the magic of the Faire Tree. Welcome to the royal world, Anastrella."

As the leader, Jade stepped away from her, Anastrella closed her eyes and was suddenly lifted a couple of inches off the ground, being wrapped in what looked like silver silk, materializing in midair. Fairies below cheered as the shining light surged around her, setting her back down then and beginning to settle around her.

Anastrella was revealed as the silver silk fell in form of a beautiful floor-length dress. Her golden hair seemed to sparkle like the crown on her head, and she was beaming radiantly as she stood there, the new enchantress, now with a silver and gold shimmering wings instead of her navy ones. She was the rightful ruler, and I was so glad that my heart had told me so.

Anastrella stepped forward, making a small speech about how she would make it a priority to do right by the fairies, and how nothing in the fairy world would ever be as it had been in the past. To conclude her speech, she lowered her head, studying her hands a bit as she turned them over and over until finally, she raised her arms above her head, gold sparks bursting forth from her fingertips, like stars glistening throughout the chamber.

With a release of her arms, the sparks fell like dust from the sun, showering everyone watching from below. All at once, the crowd cheered and waved their arms wildly in celebration. Anastrella exuded the beauty of magic, and the future of the faire folk already seemed a bit brighter.

When the ceremony was over, she walked over to me on the stage and put a gentle hand on my shoulder. "Thank you," she whispered, winking at me before flying down to hug an enthusiastic Charlotte. Watching the two of them there, letting their happiness seep into my own heart, I felt that for the first time since I'd been at the palace, I could truly exhale.

After awhile, the guards and servants had left, practically fleeing the castle in ecstasy, heading off to form clans of their own. A sufficient number of them remained to become paid workers, as they'd deserved to be all along.

A pleasant silence had begun to fall over the chamber, and as Anastrella bid good night to the faire court, releasing those fairies to go and celebrate with their families, for the time being, I made my way down to my clan.

Everyone stood in a small clump, talking and embracing, each of them with relief on their faces. Charlotte and Demitri stood together, Charlotte's arm hooked in his elbow. Genesis stood next to Demitri, and on the other side of her, Vivyanna tried to force a smile, but her thoughts seemed elsewhere, probably on her close friend Katia.

On the other side of Charlotte, Lydia and Analise stood together, leaning into one another's arm. Poor Lydia seemed calmer just by being near Analise, and she also seemed ignorant of the fact that next to Analise, Warren was there, his hand lightly skimming hers. Hopeful and bashful expressions were shared between them when they locked eyes.

"Hey, there she is!" Charlotte exclaimed, motioning for me to fly between her and Demitri. "Our little hero," she said, and Demitri kissed me on the forehead. "So, why'd you give up the position, Summer?" Genesis asked, "It's the opportunity of a lifetime!" I shrugged, smiling up at Anastrella, who was approaching us after bidding Jade and the rest of the faire court a final goodbye. "I think the enchantress I recommended is going to do better than I ever could!"

The parts of the group with their backs to Anastrella turned and lightly applauded her, exclaiming their congratulations, still in disbelief. "Thanks, you guys, I really am flattered. This is all happening so fast," she said, looking down at her dress and letting a few more of those gorgeous golden sparks loose from her fingertips.

Charlotte laughed as she came to a stop next to her, taking her mother's hand in her own and asking, "So, you are a royal now, huh?" Anastrella smiled softly, putting her hand on Charlotte's cheek as if she saw something else behind her question. "Charlie, nothing is going to change between us." Charlotte turned away from the group a bit, but not before I saw a single tear drift down her cheek.

After glancing around at one another awkwardly for a moment, the rest of us flew a little ways away. I looked back to see Charlotte's shoulders shaking, her face hidden as she hugged her mom tightly. I looked up at Demitri beside me, my stomach suddenly feeling like a gaping hole.

"What have I done?" I asked shakily. "I've ruined everything. Charlotte's going to hate me now; I've taken her mom from her—"

"Charlotte is not going to hate you," he said, placing his hands on my shoulders and looking deep into my eyes with his soft brown stare. "Charlie and her mom have always had a very special relationship, but Anastrella is right, this isn't going to change that. This is an honor for her, and Anastrella is going to do so many amazing things for all faire folk. You were right to recommend her."

"But what if Charlotte moves here?" I asked, drawing in a sudden breath and asking, "What if you all decide to move here?"

"Summer! Don't worry! We aren't going anywhere for a long time! Besides, we still have a year left of school, and we don't want to burn all our bridges in Weston while we have such a good thing going there." I nodded, trying to foresee our entire futures before that was even possible.

"You're right, I just need to calm down." Demitri nodded, wrapping his arm around me as we went on with our group.

Charlotte and Anastrella joined us moments later, and Charlotte was laughing at something her mom said, though she was wiping her eyes as well. I caught her eye and sent a meaningful look her way, but she winked at me as if to tell me all would be okay.

"So, here's the plan," Anastrella said looking around at us all, "I am going to stay here during several days of the week, and then for the other part, I will return home to be with you all in Weston. I'm not saying this won't be a difficult adjustment at first because it will be strange, but the result of this will be much better than before. You are all welcome anytime to come to stay in the castle! We are taking on this adventure together; it won't be me alone." She smiled at each of us, looking around the circle. "We'll be okay."

She gave a pointed look to Lydia and said, "All we need to do is keep each other close, and remember that Katia will be in our hearts always. We wouldn't be here without her, and we need to remind ourselves of that and remember to live for her." Lydia smiled softly, nodding and wiping her tears. A few moments later, we were bidding Anastrella a bittersweet goodbye.

Charlotte was the last to hug her, and I saw no tears fall from her eyes this time. "Bye, Mom. I love you."

"I love you too, Charlie. And, hey," Anastrella said, smoothing down Charlotte's hair with her hand, "I'm still going to see you on Tuesday, okay!" Charlotte nodded, turning from her and holding onto her hand as long as she could before flying away to join us.

"Okay," she said with a blanket of enthusiasm covering her sadness, "let's go home." I held onto her hand as we flew out of the chamber, through the empty hallway, and out through the enormous wooden door.

"Wait," Charlotte whispered, pulling on my hand as we flew out the door and through the garden. I turned back to see Analise and Warren hovering by the door. Charlotte pulled us a little closer so that we were within range of hearing their conversation.

"Warren, you could come with me! I'm sure my mom wouldn't mind!" Warren smiled tightly, looking down at his hands in hers. "Analise, I would love to, but we've only just met. I think before I join your clan, I want to experience a little freedom with my parents first."

Analise nodded knowingly, a sad slouch visible in her shoulders. "But," he said, "I would love to court you, and visit you as much as your mother will allow me." Her eyes lit up, and she threw her arms around his neck.

When they pulled apart, Analise flew toward us, and Warren waved to Charlotte, Demitri, and me before turning to fly back to his parents in the castle. I wasn't sad to see him turn away; I had a feeling we'd be seeing Warren more for quite a long time.

My clan and I flew back to Weston, crossing the Canadian border and seeing mountains and rivers, snow and forests through the whole journey. Genesis and Vivyanna led the way, and the rest of us followed in a lazy sort of glide. We stayed far above the clouds once we got closer to cities and people that could see us during the day.

It was now the morning of December twenty-eighth, and I was very eager to see my parents again. We'd been flying for about three hours of dawn, and the sun was now rising on our horizon as we flew the final miles over our sleepy town. We began to descend until our street came into view, and we very quickly dove down so as not to be seen by a passerby.

When we landed in the cul-de-sac, we all stood there in silence for a minute, taking in this glorious moment of peace before we had to start our lives back up again.

"Well," Genesis said at last, "I would love it if we could all get together for dinner on New Year's Day."

The statement seemed so normal, especially after we'd all just escaped a death sentence together—all of us, but Katia. Staring around at the group, I could tell that we were all traumatized by seeing her body destroyed by Lorena. I hoped that her soul could rest, knowing we'd avenged her and that her daughter would be able to live in freedom because of her sacrifice.

Before I walked away, each of us shared a hug. The simplicity of that action reminded us all that what we fought for would mean freedom, and peace for a long time to come. We'd live without fear, and we'd be able to fly anywhere we wanted to whenever we wanted to. We could befriend fairies of other clans, and hopefully redefine and better fairy-warlock relations. We could dream that big, with Anastrella as our guide, but for now, we planned on dinner and went our separate ways.

When I got to the back door, I wondered how my parents would have been affected by the spell that had been cast on them. I hoped they wouldn't find my sudden arrival suspicious, and that they wouldn't worry about what I'd been up to. At least I'd made it home. If something had gone wrong with me, they may have lived in a world where I'd just drifted out of their memory. Shaking off that nasty thought, I pulled open the creaky back door, walking in and smelling the freshly brewed coffee in the kitchen.

"Hello?" I called out, looking around and admiring the way the rising sun that shone through the front door lit up the chandelier in the next room, its' colorful lights bouncing off the walls in their magical way.

My dad walked in the room almost a second later, his face lighting up as soon as he saw me. He crossed the room quickly and wrapped me in a hug; I buried my face in his chest, breathing in the feeling of home. He let go, stepping back to look at me sternly.

"You know, Summer, just because you're getting older doesn't mean you're allowed to take a vacation without telling us!" I looked sheepishly at my feet, trying to string together a random apology without giving anything away. He lifted my chin with his hand and winked at me, making me step back with surprise, searching his face. I saw a twinkle in his eye that made me wonder if he knew where I'd been.

Mom came down the stairs next, paint on her shirt and smeared a bit on her cheek. She stopped and smiled when she saw me, saying she had a feeling the house was complete again. She joined Dad and me, and the three of us stood there in silence a minute, just hugging and enjoying the feeling of reunion between us.

"So," she said, leading me to sit at the kitchen table while my dad fixed up some pancakes and bacon for breakfast, "how was this so-called trip?" I narrowed my eyes at them then, looking back and forth at their shared all-knowing smiles.

"What all do you know?" I asked without hesitation then, feeling like there was nothing to hide from them if Anastrella was in charge. Besides, I knew they wouldn't have anyone to talk to about this secret aside from me.

My mom reached across the table to grab my hand, though, saying, "Darling, some things are better left unsaid. You just have to trust that all of the pieces fit together like a puzzle, do you understand?" I nodded slowly, trying to not get overwhelmed by the sudden realization that my parents may have known all along—what I'd been trying to do, and what I'd won for us.

"But when did you—I mean how did you find out?" I stuttered as my dad sat next to me, setting down the heaping plate of food in front of us, and allowing us to dish up our portions. "Honey, we've known since we saw you start your training. We often take an evening hike when you've been 'at Charlotte's house', and we've seen you learn. Of course, we knew about Lorena from Fallon, and when we heard you mention that, we realized that you were going to do what you were destined to do."

They smiled at one another. "As soon as we saw you, we knew you were perfect, and you were meant to be our next little adventure. We vowed when we adopted you from Fallon to support you in all of your magical discoveries and endeavors." Tears welled up in my mom's eyes as she said, "You brought magic into our lives, in more ways than one."

I clutched both of their hands and looked between them in disbelief saying, "Thank you for this, for bringing me here."

"It's where you belong," Dad said.

And Mom corrected. "It's where *we* belong, and where we'll stay for a lot of years to come. Now," she said, letting go of my hand and wiping her eyes, "we should *not* let this breakfast get cold!"

No more than a minute later, Demitri and Charlotte knocked on the back door, and my dad motioned for them to come in. "Good morning, kids!" Mom said, and she patted the chair next to her for Charlotte, while Dad slid over to make room for Demitri.

"Good morning, Mr. and Mrs. York!" Charlotte said.

And both of my parents laughed as my dad said, "Oh, please, dear, call us Clara and David! You'll make us feel like we're old!"

"That's right, Charlotte, David and I are immortal at heart, like you all!" She winked at Charlotte, and Charlotte grinned as she turned to me, surprise in her eyes. I just shrugged, knowing I'd have to fill her in on just how much my parents knew later on. She giggled as I dug into my breakfast with one hand, holding Demitri's hand beneath the table with my other.

Looking around the room at the people—and warefae—I loved most in this world; I realized that nothing could make this moment more perfect. I was where I belonged; I was home. I had a long time until I had to worry about days without my parents or days when life would be any more complicated than it was right now.

Until that moment came, though, I decided right then and there that I would enjoy every second of forever that I got. I would cherish every single moment of my fairy tale.

Epilogue

It was summer when I finally decided to make another trip to Florida, and even then, leaving Weston had taken much more convincing from my parents and my clan than the first time around. They argued that I should update Fallon and be back by the ocean.

"You'll be glad you're doing this, Summer," Mom had said as she packed me a small bag of money and snacks in a backpack for my flight.

"You'll only be gone for a couple of days!" Demitri had said when I told him goodbye, but still, I'd felt fear about how it would go—telling Fallon everything.

I had flown over the ocean most of the time, seeing as it calmed me down better than anything and anyone in the world, especially now that I was so far from it all of the time.

I saw that town approaching now, getting closer and closer as I fluttered toward it from the sea. I flew over Seaside and then past it, looking down to see my beautiful old house practically smiling up at me. I wanted to stop, then, take a detour as a possible last chance at escape from what I was about to do, but I heard my parents in my mind, their urgency ringing loud and clear.

As soon as school was over that year, and I'd bid my friends goodbye on the last day, I'd gone home to find my parents urging me to go back to Florida and tell Fallon everything that had happened.

"Honey, Fallon's always been there for you. This is what she's been waiting for since before you were born. You haven't responded to her letters since you saw her last."

"Well, I have been sort of busy!"

"Summer! There is no excuse. You have to tell her what happened in December."

So, there I was, lowering myself to the street in front of the bookstore, folding my wings in as I walked slowly up to the door. I pushed it open, the bell on the door ringing. I heard footsteps walking around one of the shelves, and my heart was beating wildly in my chest.

When I saw her around the corner, though, and her blue eyes met mine, all the fear went away. "Summer?" she asked, a little bit of hope on her face as she walked toward me.

"Hi," I said shakily. She walked right up to me, enveloping me in a hug. "It's been a long time since I've heard from you. I've been worried," she whispered.

"Well," I said, smiling at her now, feeling joyous tears spring to my eyes, "I came to tell you that you're free. We killed Lorena and took control of the faire court. You don't have to hide anymore."

She blinked a few times, her mouth agape before she stumbled to sit in the nearest chair. "I never thought this day would come." She laughed in incredulity, placing her head in her hands and crying softly. I squatted down beside her, putting my hand atop hers' and just being there for her as this information sunk in.

A few minutes later, she stood, asking me if I wanted to join her for tea in her loft. I nodded enthusiastically, waiting for her to turn the sign on the door from "Open" to "Closed".

That night, we sat up in Fallon's loft, talking the whole time. She told me more details than last time—she spoke of how in love she and Peter were, and how he'd sacrificed himself at the last second, making a portal for her to escape through, allowing her to return and send me somewhere safe before she'd try to blend into society.

I told her then all about how I'd urged the clan to get trained and take on Lorena, and how I'd been taken, rescued, and led the fight to stop her. She seemed so proud of all I'd done, and the warefae woman that I'd become.

I finished by telling her how things had been since then. We had gone home to continue school and Grand Faire Enchantress Anastrella coming back twice a week to spend time with us. She had made so many changes in the fairy world already, and her legislation on freedom of the dark fairies, the legality of relations between fairies of different natures, and between fairies and warlocks, had been celebrated around the world.

I told her about the friends I'd made in school, and how much Bobby had changed the course of my high school days by letting the others from the clan and me into their friend group. I reflected on how much the warefae had come together as friends through the past year, and how Warren had joined our group smoothly, with only

Lydia a bit hesitant in regards to our open inclusion of him. He joined Anastrella in her visits to Weston.

"Well, you have been a busy girl since you left here last, haven't you?" Fallon said, sipping her tea next to me on the couch behind the window overlooking the book store. It was early the next morning at that point, and I felt so glad that I'd decided to come to visit now. I nodded, knowing that no statement could've been truer than that one.

We talked through the hours of the sunrise, and the sun soon began to shine through the street-side windows of the store. "Fallon?" I asked after we'd been silent for a few moments.

"Hm?" she responded, looking up from the coffee she'd just brewed.

"Do you think about how life would be if things would've been different with Lorena? You, Peter, and I should've been a proper family." She smiled at me softly then, but no sadness or regret seemed to trouble her expression.

"Summer, of course I wish that Peter and I could have been the ones to raise you. But, I have gotten to watch you grow up to become a beautiful young lady. I've seen you struggle with friends and doubts, and I've seen you learn to accept who you truly are. Clara and David were always very aware of how much I *loved* seeing you here at the bookstore, and that alone gave me a sense of motherhood, as I saw you run in and out of here through the years. I couldn't have hoped for a better chance to see you grow up given our circumstances."

She paused, looking up, as if to Heaven itself. "Peter will wait for me, I am certain. Our love will not have been destroyed by the years we've spent apart. And, Summer, when you think about it," she said, touching her heart, "I think you'll realize with time that we will always be a family, and we will always be together in here." I nodded, reaching out and grasping her hand briefly.

"Fallon, there's something else," I said, concern shrouding my face now. She nodded at me to go on, and I said shakily, "Did you know that Peter was the warlock of light? Do you believe that legend?" She seemed to search for the words for a moment before saying, "I believe there was something special about Peter, but he was a very peaceful warlock. He used his powers only for good unless we were in danger, but that may have been a sign of his immense amounts of power that he didn't want to tap into.

"However, if there was some ultimate source of strength within him, I think it remained untapped through his years." I nodded, figuring this may be a path I try to follow someday, but not at this moment. I just wanted to soak up every minute I'd have left with my mom for the time being.

"So, tell me more about Demitri," she'd urged, and I willingly dove into how our relationship had been since I left here last. We'd grown together so much as a couple, through our struggles and our triumphs together.

"I couldn't have done this without him," I shared with her. "I think I'm going to be with him forever." Just thinking about him brought a smile to my face, and Fallon was glad that I'd found someone so good for me.

When the sun had fully risen over the sea, I knew it was time for me to part ways with my birth mother for now. "I have to get back," I said, and she nodded, walking me to the door.

"You know," she whispered, pausing for a moment, "you could stay here with me. We could have that life you talked about, now that we don't have to hide anymore." She bit her lip, almost knowing already what my answer would be. I shook my head softly, but she smiled at me understandingly. "I figured that's what you'd say."

I cut in urgently, "It's nothing against you, of course. I'll be back here all the time to see you! It's just." I paused, a smile growing on my face as I thought of the house I used to consider devilish, and the fairies and warefae I'd once feared in my mind's eye. "I have to go *home*."

Weston hadn't become my home since I'd moved, but I now knew that home didn't have to be a definite location. My home was the place where fairies and warefae met up on my cul-de-sac, where my mom was painting and my dad was reading in his study. My home was a place where I felt the freedom of my wings beating behind me, and the wind blowing in my hair. My home was just that because of the people and magical beings that made it all that it was.

As I hugged Fallon and flew away, out over the open ocean, the sun kissing my cheeks as I went, I realized that my life was like a dream I'd had not so long ago. I flew close to the surface, my hands skimming the water and a few dolphins jumping up playfully beside me as I coasted through the waves.

There was infinite potential for what my life would become. As I closed my eyes and listened hard, I could even hear a heartbeat echoing in the distance, calling me home.

Acknowledgements

There are so many people involved in my writing journey, and I think the best place to start is my family. Thank you all for your love and support throughout the years I've been working on this book. Thank you for calming me down when I was nervous or frustrated. I couldn't have gotten to this point without all of you!

Thank you to my mom for being the first set of eyes on 'Fairy Tale' and for believing in me and my writing abilities for so many years.

Thank you to my dad for constant support and for always encouraging me to keep writing and trying my best at everything I do.

Thank you to Mason for being the best brother ever and for always pushing me to work hard. I know you love to read, and I hope you love reading this as much as you love any of your classic books!

Thank you to Brett for letting me bounce so many ideas off of you for this world I was creating. You were there with me during so many late night writing sessions and you have given me so much support. I couldn't have done this without you. I love you more.

Thank you to Allie for being my best friend and for always listening to me rant about books and book ideas. Every character that acts as Summer's friend in this book has a little piece of you in them, and yet none of them come close to how great you are!

Thank you to my teachers who have helped me to reach this point in my writing career. To Mrs. Carrillo for believing in me first, to Mrs. Toliver for helping me tap into another level of my writing abilities, and to Mrs. Ross, who helped me learn the art of refining my work—thank you to each one of you, and the many more who made such an impact on my life!

Thank you to everyone at Pegasus Publishers for this incredible opportunity. Thank you to Elaine Wadsworth for taking a chance on me. Thank you to Lesley Perry and my entire production team for all of the work you put in to make my book what it is now. Thank you to everyone at Pegasus who worked behind the scenes. Though I may not know all of your names, I will always be appreciative of what you've done for me and my story!

Finally, thank you to the readers for giving your time to my book. I sincerely hope that you enjoyed it and that it will help someone to realize that there is magic in accepting yourself, loving yourself, and knowing who you truly are!